INSIDE GLORIA

RJ Boucher

Publisher: RJ Boucher
(October 14, 2014)
Printed by CreateSpace,
an Amazon company.
ISBN-13: 978-0692313657 (Custom Universal)
ISBN-10: 0692313656

———

Publisher: RJ Boucher
(December 31, 2013)
Available through Amazon Digital Services, Inc.
Kindle EBook, ASIN: B00BVR3IFK

———

———

Cover designed by author

———

Inside Gloria is a work of fiction whose plot
characters are the product of the author's
imagination. While most of its story
coincides with actual events in history,
modification of either a few select facts
or a characterization of conditions
based on them was employed but
only in instances where it was deemed
necessary for conforming to the plot.
Such depictions were exercised with
discretion and aren't intended
to represent actual fact

September 1985

<< CHAPTER 1 >>

BY 1985 THE UNITED STATES nuclear arsenal consisted of 23,000 warheads and the Soviet Union 40,000, hundreds of times more than necessary to leave the other in ruin within an hour's notice, the remaining world little better off.

Situated 400 miles west of the African continent lay the small volcanic island of Sao Vicente, one of several others belonging the chain of the Cape Verde Islands. On the Costa family's final descent onto the small serene slice of land, both eight-year-old Heather and her younger brother of five years, David, were becoming evermore animated in viewing the endless ocean give way to the increasing details of the approaching landscape below. A Labor Day weekend departure from Kennedy, hours of never-ending ocean, and three lengthy layovers on different continents left the two normally well-behaved siblings beside themselves. Their present display of manic energy was at best masking an underlying exhaustion destined to soon take its toll.

Heather's enthusiasm could be heard echoed in her play-by-play descriptions of Mindelo, a port city bordered by an array of rugged appearing, low-lying volcanic mountains and their neighboring foothills of similar terrain. As only an aerial view could render, a vast network of wakes decreasing in numbers stretching to the fringes of an unobstructed open Atlantic Ocean bore witness to the vibrant maritime community of Porto Grande below. Situated in Mindelo's harbor, the small port was plainly visible through the unblemished clarity of a pristine Atlantic air mass. Awestruck, Heather grabbed her mother by the shoulder.

"Mummy, look at all the boats below!"

Mesmerized by the same array of rich scenery and focused out the same window, her mother, Linda, simply continued smiling in contentment. She affectionately kissed her daughter atop her head.

"I see it, honey. It's all so beautiful," her tranquil state mostly spawned from the relief of a long and grueling trip's conclusion.

While her full-blooded Portuguese and American-born husband, Dave, could deepen his tan by the mere effects of secondary light— so it may have seemed to her that is—at five-foot six or four inches shorter than him, Linda with dirty blond hair and blue eyes could also tan, but doing so usually required an entire season to achieve the same results that he could in a single day. It in turn caused their two blond-haired, blue-eyed children to become the subject of an ongoing friendly scandal where from time to time the couple would make sport about how Dave's darker characteristics reflecting his more dominant genes were inconsistent with any justification to the recessive features of their two children.

More fuel contributing to the controversy was both the timing and circumstances behind their daughter's birth. It resulted from their days of reckless behavior engaged in after college—often, in group efforts. During such episodes where an open display of sexual activity would frequently crossed the boundaries of couple's exclusivity with each other, there were often times afterwards when neither of the two could remember what had actually taken place during such events. Despite a blood test having cleared the minds of the duo, Dave would sometimes find humor in suggesting the probability that such seemingly sketchy results were likely the product of tampering. With each succeeding recall Linda became less amused; she wasn't the first time he mentioned it either.

With their plane drawing to its final decent on a remote runway, Linda secretly slipped her hand between the two seats before her.

There she grabbed her husband's side in an affectionate squeeze, him reciprocating in turn by cradling her hand into his.

Acknowledging they could soon relax and unwind, their subdued joy reflected no less appreciated than that of their two children displaying erratic behavior. The date at hand was August 31, 1985 and emotions were running especially deep for the duel. It was also three days prior to their nine-year wedding anniversary, and a good friend from year's back, Jim Woodson, was awaiting their arrival below. He was joined by his wife of five years, Pamela, whom they were yet to meet.

It had been over a decade since the Costas, Jim, and his girlfriend at the time, Nancy, were ever together in any casual setting. The breakup of the latter two eventually sent their old friend into seclusion to the point where Dave lost complete contact with him.

Jim was stationed with the Navy at the New London-Groton Sub Base in Connecticut from 1975 to 1977. Meanwhile Dave and Linda, a young couple in love, were savoring their last two years of college. Because studying was so effortless on the part of the quick learning, inseparable sweethearts, of which the two eventually graduating from Northeastern University in the late spring of 1976, a windfall of extra free time allotted by the need for less studying furnished them both the luxury of being able to stroll about Boston's Commonwealth Avenue's boulevard on most giving evenings. They'd do so in an effort of seeking out whatever frat house parties of acquaintances that might be taking place at the time; Boston being a collegiate town seldom left them disappointed in their endeavors.

As Dave was among acquaintances in a frat house common area casually drinking in the fall of 1975, peers of his pondering yet another failed attempt by Boston to win the World Series were also present with him. Being that a New York fan, he stood quietly basking in the collective grief of the others until his merry meditation of sadistic euphoria was cut short in sensing the phantom prickling of someone blatantly staring him down out of the line of vision.

Picking up on his uneasiness, Linda panned to a young man, someone alien to the crowd. What initially caught her attention was both the calm demeanor of the stranger and his short clean-cut hair, nonconforming with the general seventies collegian style of the time. Having pegged him as a military man, she was struck by the stranger's handsome appearance in spite a noticeable struggle with acne.

Out of reflex of being stared at, Dave turned to the young man, prompting a schoolmate to voice their concerns. Having done so in a protective manner, there being threatened that the stranger's presence somehow posed as an unwelcomed incursion to their group, the soft-spoken newcomer soon averted what seemed to be a heavy air of looming aggression.

"Dave, is that you?"

He reacted, slowly approaching and squaring off to the outsider.

"Your voice sounds real familiar."

"You don't know who I am, do you? And don't look at my hair either," he grinned, adding, "—or should I say the lack of it."

It was a somewhat awkward moment for Dave in not being able to recognize the stranger. He understood that his failure to do so was exposing the insignificance the young man likely represented in his past.

"Sorry, you've got to give me more, man," he tittered.

The young clean-cut stranger shook his head in jesting disgust. "Fairfield [Connecticut] High—remember? What the hell, bro!"

"Holy shit, Jim the asshole!"

The tension in the room rose momentarily, Jim the meanwhile grinning in submission.

"Okay granted, but you know the Navy broke me of that shit." Shaking his head, he continued. "Damn the bad luck and shit—a blanket party can make a chump change his attitude real quick. That shit messed me up for weeks which in turn set me back in boot camp as well."

Dave turned to Linda. "This is the guy that use to try provoking me into fights throughout my senior year. He started that probing shit the year before," grinning, he added, "that prick."

"Honey, you let him get away with that shit with your black belt?"

Dave shot Linda a look of disapproval for her exposing such a revelation.

"Man the bad luck and shit—are you telling me that the whole time I was messing with you, you could have Kung Fu'ed my sorry ass?" Jim paused. "Kind of wish you had back then—might have spared me a blanket party. Thanks for nothing, bro."

Amused by the easygoing disposition of his former adversary, Dave labored in containing a grin. The two eventually became best friends. In addition to being simpatico, it was the common thread of their dysfunctional yet mutual past that ended up congealing their newly formed bond. It in turn allowed the two to be able to cling onto some nostalgic hold to the memory of both their beloved hometown and youth.

In the following fall post Dave and Linda's graduation, Jim's assignment into submarine duty changed everything. The two inseparable couples were no longer so. Dave nevertheless still kept in touch with his friend until the forth leg of their group, Nancy, broke it off with him.

A decade later, the feel of the Costa's plane touching down on the only landing strip of Sao Vicente was therefore the sweetest sensation they had been able to relish since their last home cooked meal in Narragansett, Rhode Island.

In descending a metal, pull up stairway onto a tarmac, an unblemished pureness of fresh Atlantic air welcomed an exhausted family. Both Dave and Linda became especially enlivened with emotions the moment they laid eyes on Jim and his wife, Pamela. Still a safe distance away allowing for private dialogue, Linda uttered as if practicing ventriloquism. "Holy shit, Dave—she's stunning. How the hell did he manage that?"

Her remark was based on their friend's prior inability of being able to approach attractive women due to nerves. While his ex-girlfriend, Nancy, was attractive, it was Linda's setting of the two of them up that softened the blow of first contact for him.

While a tenancy of expressing her visual approval of women with Dave was sometimes done just to tease him, he was also mindful that such remarks masked as joking, subliminally echoed more than that of just any general observations. In addition, their marriage once endured a period of stifling tribulation subsequent to David's birth, and the Costa's latest round of playfulness was at last stemming from the shadows of those more abysmal days. The two were therefore able to both appreciate and savor the simplicity of healthier times, as a result leaving them both feeling even more revitalized than ever before in their lives.

Aware of Jim's likely jadedness at the hands of Nancy learned hearsay through mutual acquaintances, Dave and Linda's only concern about Pamela was thinly based on stereotype. It was founded based on people's sometimes-clouded judgment of when confronted by attractive opposites, often defying reasonable logic. In viewing her, they could see the likelihood of any man, especially one with the makeup of their old friend, where he could easily become overly smitten by such extraordinary looks as hers. Based on his experience with Nancy, the two were concerned about how their old friend could possibly still be left prone to whatever malevolent undercurrents might be laid hidden beneath someone like Pamela.

Although still slightly quirky by nature, Jim was that of matured individual displaced from his earlier more pugnacious days of before. Such deducing therefore wasn't without merit on the Costa's part. Their notions were based on some sketchy hearsay supporting a claim about how his ex-girlfriend, Nancy, ended their relationship without giving any notice that she had actually done so. As a whole, both Dave and Linda were still in the dark about that period of his past. Meanwhile presently witnessing firsthand their old friend thriving in a niche that he and Pamela had carved out on Sao Vicente was making their present reunion ever so much more anticipated.

Linda's cheers of greetings broke the silence of the breezy tropical air, whose soft whisper just prior lingered in the quiet of the plane's engines cutting out. Hugs were traded, including a bro-hug exchanged between the two old friends.

"Good to see you pal, it's been a while."

Upon completion of their exchange, Jim continued half-jokingly. "Not to undermine my glad to see you guys, but we simply don't get to see many familiar faces from back home in this neck of the woods." With a gesture projecting outward, he added, "what little woods we have, that is."

"Jimbo, do I detect a smidgen of homesickness in your voice?"

As if mimicking a maestro's bow, his old friend cradled Pamela against his side to face the others while extending his free arm outward. "Folks, this is my home, and this…" squeezing Pamela ever tighter, "is my beautiful wife, Pamela. So to answer your question, buddy—hell no!"

As an active journalist, Dave's many associations with attractive opposites did afford him some level of resistance to whatever possible drunken effects of theirs. Such ability still fell short of granting him any immunity to a melting stare of Pamela's. Caught in its grips, he belted that of a deafening cough in response before then diverting his attention over to his children. Following a disingenuous apology, he was then able to regain enough composure to exchange in a kiss and hug with her.

While it may have been excusable for any average man to stumble ever so slightly in the presence of a beautiful woman, especially one as captivating as Pamela, for Dave, the mere idea of deviating even slightly away from his usual cool demeanor for any reason was something he viewed synonymous with utter failure. Keen to this, Jim always kept his radar tuned for any instance where he might be able to relish such a rare moment of witnessing any hint of weakness on his friend's part. A decade elapse, Dave's reaction to Pamela still didn't go unnoticed by him. Nor did it by Linda, who felt less incline to keep quiet about it.

"Honey, got something caught in your throat?"

Opting not to respond, Dave labored in refraining from grinning. He knew he was busted.

Then whatever preliminary notion the Costa parents may have pinned on Pamela was laid to rest. Upon making eye contact with an initially bashful Heather and David, the two holding hands, she approached them.

"Oh my God, your kids are so adorable!"

In reaction, both parents found themselves privately immersed in the embarrassment of guilt. They did so for having stereotyped what appeared to be a genuine person—that versus the man-destroyer they had concocted her to play out in their corrupted imaginations.

Glancing upward to both Dave and Linda, the two standing side by side, a squatted Pamela took their two children by their hands and returned to her previous standing position of before.

"Can I keep them for a few days?"

Jim grinned. "In case you haven't noticed, Pamela loves kids. Good luck getting them back."

Following further pleasantries, the group of six eventually

squeezed into the Woodson's old beat-up Volvo before then heading to the port town of Mindelo. Once there, Jim gave his version of a grand tour en route to his house included paying visit to a couple of his leased slips located on Porto Grande's marina. The two moorings were the focal point of most the Woodson's word-of-mouth entrepreneurial enterprises, and by the standards of the island's economics, the couple did well for themselves. Jim and the dockmaster being drinking buddies didn't hurt their cause either. Such an opportune association managed to endow him with preferential treatment often perching him and Pamela atop the food chain in keeping abreast the latest business opportunities come available.

In negotiating some of Mindelo's narrow cobblestone streets, Jim concluded in speaking about Sao Vicente. "I know you guys must be exhausted to say the least, but I'll sum up Verde's history by saying that ten years ago they basically became their own entity. The people here may not have much money, but they're rich in heart—such a hospitable people too." Paused for a moment in reflection, he added, "Man I love the folks here."

In entering the Woodson's small stone driveway located on the outskirts of Mindelo, both an exhausted Dave and Linda couldn't help but appreciate their friend's home, one that reflected a degree of Colonial Portuguese architecture. Upon engaging the lever of his emergency break, Jim turned to the Costas, who were all crowded together like sardines in the backseat, the kids asleep.

"Oh yeah, before I forget—if you only do one thing for the rest of your life, you need to come back here for the Tobago Carnival before Ash Wednesday. It's our version of Mardi Gras, and believe me when I tell you this—it's a wild time, man."

A mischievous giggle then sprang from Pamela, of which its nature could be neither mistaken nor ignored. Slightly embarrassed and covering her mouth in a feeble attempt of covering her tracks, an elicited exchange of raised eyebrows traded between Dave and Linda didn't go unnoticed. Still facing them, Jim got a charge from their reactions, there adoring his wife's knack of being able to unintentionally coax different reactions out of people with her unrepressed free-spiritedness. Her uncanny ability of being able to generate such brow-raising countenance not only entertained him in their occurrences, but he actually thrived on it. No less was his appreciation when it served him well in courted other couples for his and Pamela's somewhat alternate type of social affairs.

Settling into the more simplistic comforts of their friend's home, the Costas took the remainder of the day to unwind. Later on that evening, Dave found himself giving into the reality that the possibility of catching any remnant of a sleep was waning into dawn. Familiar with Linda's uncanny ability of being able to keep in tune with him, even in a deep sleep, he gently rolled out of bed to avoid disturbing her. Even in guessing the events of the previous two days likely took their toll on her, he was still concerned about waking her. No less deliberation was therefore taken in his efforts than someone sneaking past a captor in quest of their freedom.

Heading outside to a serene oasis await, a world away from both the competitive challenges and complexities of back home, Dave hoped doing so might liberate him from the collective effects of life's previous unrelenting day-to-day grind. Its influence would stand to be evident by a racing heart sounding prominently in the still of Sao Vicente's tranquil darkness—its rapid cadence a reminder of reconsidering a lifestyle. It was hoped walking outside to where the stars were bright, the air was clean, and ones place in the world could be that of total anonymity, that doing so might melt away whatever anxieties of which could still be lurking beneath. Dave guessed a short stint of meditation in such an optimal setting and chased afterwards by a full night sound sleep might initiate the unraveling of whatever stresses that might still be consuming him.

Before any level of decompression could be realized early that Sunday morning, Jim was able to spot the escape of his friend through the narrow opening of his office door, it slightly ajar.

"Where do you think you're going, bro?"

Caught aback, Dave stopped, turned, and upon invitation entered his friend's office. There he made himself comfortable.

In spite of its disorganized appearance, Jim's office still excelled with an impressive array of electronic equipment. Adding to its ambiance, a collage of photos consumed his walls including some capturing stunning shots of Sao Vicente's pristine beaches. Also included were ones capturing revealing shots of Pamela in the buff accommodating the shooter with flirtatious poses.

While portraying an air of playfulness in them versus that of any obscenity, even conveying a hint of innocence in the process, most laying their eyes on such types of photos would have had difficulty limiting their thoughts to those of just any admirable nature. Dave was no exception. While resisting the urge of letting his eyes gravitate onto them, Jim took notice of his friend's efforts.

"Pamela's got a nice ass, huh bro?"

"Got no idea what you're talking about there."

Jim let out an incredulous laugh. "Bro man, you're so full of shit. After all the crazy shit the four of us [Himself, his ex-girlfriend Nancy, Dave, and Linda] use to do back in the day, I'm still baffled that lightening never came down and stuck our sorry asses—so I know you didn't just miss Pamela's ass there in front of you." He then sat quiet for a moment, grinning. "Yep, those were crazy times man, not a freaking care in the world. And to think I came out of it without ever needing a shot of penicillin in the ass or the dreaded umbrella. I'm surprised we outlived those times—no?"

Dave agreed, and then after reminiscing for a few minutes, Jim asked, "What's up with you, bro? Nothing but smelling salts should be keeping you awake right now. You're killing yourself, man. Something's on your mind—what up? Talk to me."

Pausing a moment and gazing towards the floor, Dave slowly raised his head. "Something minor—I don't know—maybe just our three thousand mile transatlantic trek, and before that, sailing to the Canaries [Canary Islands]—then beginning our trip from there."

The Canary Islands are located approximately a thousand miles north of the Cape Verde Islands.

"It's kind of been weighing on me as well," Jim commented upon a pause, adding, "and there's nothing forcing you to head up there first either. For instance, you could stay with us for a couple of months. Just tell them back home you got stranded here. You guys staying with us is anything but burdensome. God, Pamela and I are already attached to Heather and David. We love those kids and with this major undertaken lying before you, have you two given any consideration of not bringing them along?"

"Linda and I talked about it, but that's it, why?"

"Well honestly, when you first relayed that detail to me, I gave little weight to it at the time. I understand over here you're pretty much hidden from the radar for that sort of thing. But now that I've actually held your kids and played with them, the whole equation has changed for me."

"Remember me mentioning making a cross-Atlantic trip with my father-in-law to England, leaving port in Newport [Rhode Island]."

"Yeah, I remember."

"Well the North Atlantic isn't the most hospitably place, and that trip was no exception. Believe me, I state this being well aware that my role as a crewman then doesn't qualify me as that of any master seaman, but combine that trip to my resume of the last few years of coastal sailing between Newport, Rhode Island and Newport News (Virginia)—"

Jim took notice of the latter mentioned with Dave seeming to take the words out of his mouth. "Yeah, just further upstream from the Norfolk Naval Base where you were stationed."

"Oh, you saw my Second Fleet headquarters? That's cool. That place is what started my itch for sub duty. Now back to what you were saying. I understand your point, you got your feet wet—and?"

"Well at first we were torn about taking the kids along with us. They love sailing—even little David—and we've all been though some full gales together too. Giving that, I could say with confidence that together, both Linda and I make a pretty good team."

"Okay bro, pretty good is fine for recreational sailing, but you're crossing the freaking Atlantic, and with your kids, and in a new boat. I don't mean to be stepping on your toes here, but at least just do me a favor and please give what I just mentioned a little more consideration."

In tendering his friend more latitude than most others for such grilling, Dave chose to appease him for the sake of exiting the subject. His mind was set.

"I hear you, bro. You made a good point there, and thanks." Chuckling, he added, "Hey! If you don't hear from us within a couple months, it'll probably be because my dead reckoning was off and we ended up crossing the Straits of Magellan without noticing an entire continent [South America] to our right."

"Hey, Columbus is historically considered one of the greatest navigators, yet he mistook the West Indies for India."

"I thought it was Japan, Columbus thought he was on. Besides, Cook would have never messed up like that," Dave insisted.

"You and your Cook. Give Columbus a few hundred years and I might disagree. The man could have been your boy's grandfather displaced twenty generations. Your boy couldn't even swim. What was up with that—a captain that couldn't even freaking swim?"

"What was up with Columbus's so-called, discoveries? Give me a break. I'll stop there though. Not really in the mood for arguing history. My paunchiness must be kicking in—good sign, I guess."

"Better address that sleep soon, buddy. This shit can wait."

"Maybe soon. Not yet, though. Looks like you still got something else on your mind. What's up?"

"Okay, for the sake of argument you convinced me on the kids. But I've been wondering—why the Canaries? If you're going to be taking a tropical route to the States, then why there first? That's some major backtrack you're talking there. I mean if you were up there now, I could understand waiting around for the stronger late season winds. But heading there first? Don't get it."

"I guess at first glimpse it sounds a little crazy, I know."

"Hey, I admit that I'm no mariner, and the only cross-Atlantic experience I have is prowling hundreds of feet below the surface playing tag with the Russians. But why don't you just stay down here with us and head west in November. It's just we have a lot of catching up to do, and I'd love for you guys to stay here with us. I feel confident I can speak for Pamela as well."

"Well being late, I'll give you a quick synopsis. See, heading to the Canaries affords us a relatively safe way of getting accustomed to our new boat—you know, versus smoothing out any glitches in the middle of the Atlantic. Then by the time we arrive there, the winds will be more favorable to run with—a win-win situation."

"That's a lot of extra boating you know—two thousand freaking miles to be more like it. Why not hire some transport? I could hook you up with one of my connections."

"I never gave that a serious thought. At this point though in bringing it up, not sure of the insurance implications of doing so. Bottom line is I just want to get in that thing and go."

"Well in reference to heading north then, think about it. You could have more fun down here doing the same. We've got some really sexy beaches, and you can hone your skills with the four of us sailing around these islands to different beaches."

"I have to admit, that doesn't sound all that bad."

"Oh, it would be great. Sometimes the kids could come with us and other times stay with good friends of ours. Boa Vista for instance has some incredible dunes and it's probably just a short two-day sail from here. Man, can you imagine Pamela and Linda prancing around in strings? Linda looks great by the way."

"Thanks, and she proud of it. And your offer does sound worth staying for, but I'll have to take a rain check on it if you don't mind. I may never want to leave this place after seeing those two girls sunning together."

"That aint no joke, brother—but go on."

"Hey since we have plenty of extra time, I'm thinking of maybe sailing around these islands for some sightseeing first, even before heading north. That way we can hone our skills here while never being more than a day's sail from a nearby island—kind of like what you just suggested." Dave's statement caught his friend off guard in its impromptus debut. Then to Jim's dismay, his friend shrugged his shoulders in concluding. "Hey we have plenty of time, so why not?"

The addendum to his original plans was news to Jim, concerning him. In taking a stutter breath before letting his concerns fly, he instead put the brakes on it, preferring instead to keep his new anxieties under wraps.

"Is there something else? You were about to say something."

"Nah, nothing important." Jim responded, shaking his head. "It's just we haven't had a chance to catch up, and for a moment I forgot that we have the next couple of days for making up for lost time." Following a slight pause and then a more upbeat tone, he added, "nothing that can't wait till tomorrow, of which by the way you need to get some shuteye—and now, bro. You're killing yourself."

Jim's primary reason for having held back was his concern for Dave's sleep. He saw little to gain by speaking up, except possibly sparking some disruptive thought possesses that might cause further restlessness in his friend. What he came short of segueing into was the mention of Hurricane Elena menacing the warm fertile waters south of the Florida panhandle. Although the intense storm posed no threat to the Costas in their endeavors, its genesis as a tropical disturbance southeast of the Verde Islands was of great concern. In making the quick assessment a journalist such as Dave was likely keen to such acute tropical activity like Elena, especially giving the storm's impressive magnitude, Jim saw the futility of bringing up its subject. His primary concern was that the Costas initially circumnavigating the Cape Verde Islands during hurricane season further south than he would have been willing to venture with them stood to leave little wiggle room should some developing storm happened to overtake them while still unaccustomed to their boat. Avoiding addressing this, he changed the subject.

"Your father-in-law—what's he have to say about all this? I mean it's his daughter and grandkids you're *Lewis and Clarking* with."

"Hell, he's the one who took us to Kennedy. At one point though, he did pull me aside and said, 'Son, Godspeed.' He then went on to inform me that if I allowed even a single hair to be harmed on either his daughter or grandkids, that committing myself overboard still wouldn't be enough for evading his wrath. That's when I reminded him of our sailing excursion to England. He saw me in action and knew I could be trusted. You see, Linda was finally recovering from a long nasty bout of postpartum depression after David's birth, so she and her dad had had a heart-to-heart talk. They concluded such a venture would be a therapeutic outlet for me. He considered it an early Christmas present."

"Hell of a Christmas present, bro. Must be nice to have money."

"True, but believe me in my father-in-law's case. His stresses far exceed any benefits of his fiscal worth; I'm talking blood pressure that is. And referring to the irregularity of his generosity—Linda later told me that his unexpected gesture was actually a show of appreciation for having stood by her side through her really tough times—not having her committed, or whatever. Having said that, maybe his gift wasn't as disproportionate as it may appear on the surface. Believe me when I say that."

"What, you considered leaving her?"

"No man, the women had my kids, and her depression was her reward for David. Never crossed my mind. Well it's late and her depression's a story within itself. I'll only say she was sick and leave it at that for now."

"You were saying about your father-in-law?"

"Yeah, when all was said and done and we made port in England, he grabbed me by the shoulder and said, 'nice sailing son.' I'll tell you—coming from an intense man like him, that's quite the rite of passage. I swear her dad and mine were cast from the same mold."

"Wow! So when he said that to you, did it make your nipples hard?"

Dave shook his head with disapproval, restraining a grin no less. "That's just wrong, man. Can't you just keep shit like that to yourself?"

With Jim having treated his friend's question as rhetorical, still grinning, Dave extended his limbs in a stretch. "Man, this was great—needed it. Was on the way outside to take in some lung fillings of your clean Sao air, but I think I'm ready for bed now."

"Well if it makes you feel any better, like I told you earlier today, the boat is all set and will be docked at the slip in the morning. I managed to have gotten everything that you had asked for. I just need to ask one question though."

"Thanks by the way, and shoot."

"Where the hell did you get seventy thousand dollars to buy such a thing? That's a major luxury item. Are you telling me that you're doing that well as a local newspaper journalist?"

"We had help. You've seen the boat already. Think she's worth it?"

"Bro, she's a beauty—real sexy. Pamela took one step into it and was all over me—all night. That boat's an aphrodisiac I tell you. I mean I do pretty well here in comparison to others, but seventy thousand bucks—damn! I should have been in college with you guys, instead of the Navy."

"I though you needed the Navy. Besides, with the GI bill, college still isn't out of your grasp, is it? Hell, we're still paying off our freaking student loans."

"I figure that down the line I might give it some consideration. Obviously, my plate's pretty full right now."

"I can see that, and don't underestimate the value of your Navy experience either. That's the type of thing we boring journalist like to write about. Look, you've got Pamela. Also, don't overlook the insightful job you two did in recognizing the seller's urgency, of which may I say you exploited quite brilliantly. That's an extra fifteen thousand dollars you saved us—pocketed—not too shabby."

"Sure, make me out as some kind of shrewd capitalist." Jim responded with an underlining sense of pride.

"Hey, don't fret. No one else was biting on the boat, and I still need to sail the freaking thing across the Atlantic—never mind us needing to take time off from work to do so."

"You know with that fifteen thousand dollars added to the other sixty-five grand below its market value that they originally were unloading the boat for, that thing's a real steal. Maybe we really shouldn't be joking about such karma at the seller's expense."

"Not a big believer in karma or that sort of thing but agreed. Anyhow, thanks to you low-balling them, it tipped the scale for my father-in-law to cosign a loan via Linda's request. Believe me, he did his own inquiries before lending us any money. He knows more about the make of that boat than even I do. I mean if the old man were a reporter, he'd beat me on every news scoop. I swear too— the people that man knows could fill a freaking stadium."

The two friends began showing signs of fatigue, evident in the longer stints of silence.

"Jim, I need to ask you. What the hell are you doing up at four in the morning?"

"Are you asking sleeping habits—me? I get up when I want and sleep when I want. This is my life bro, and this room's where I conduct most of my business." Grinning, he leaned back. "That's when I'm not napping in this chair, that is. You know at first the locals were a little squeamish about letting some American have a shortwave radio transmitter like mine, but you know money talks."

Dave panned for a moment. "Nice, I could get use to this."

"Yep, I love the peace and privacy of night. Lot of times I just come in here to man the radio in the hope of hearing of any Ruskie [Soviet] submarine sightings, of which by the way I have a lot of eyes and ears out there, land and sea. They'll be keeping an eye out for you guys. They know your boat and are aware Linda and the kids will be tagging along with you too. Many of them also think you're freaking crazy for that by the way, but they'll have your back nevertheless."

"Appreciated, and by the way, I mean no disrespect, but does Pamela sleep naked?"

"Disrespect? I'm proud of it. And yes by the way, she does. Hell, if it weren't for the local laws here or church of course, that woman wouldn't own a stitch of clothing. Why?"

"Well I noticed she doesn't wear any more than necessary— damn! And I'm not complaining either. Nor should anyone with a set of eyes. Let me add though. Brought up a Catholic, I might wager that entering church pre-apple Adam and Eve style wouldn't be appreciated for the pureness in which it was intended to exemplify.

With that being said, what I was getting at is someone as sexy as Pamela is sleeping naked one room over and you're over here looking for Russians."

"Her sleeping is the only time I can recharge my batteries," Jim explained, grinning with pride. "That aside, on a serious note again, I'll be listening and networking with radio peers in the hope of receiving any tidbits of information about your whereabouts out there. I actually know of people who are out there right now."

"Thanks again, and I mean that." It was quiet for a moment before Dave broke it. "She wears you down, doesn't she?"

"Try wore, brother, but I'm not complaining. Still got a few good years left—I think. The woman's crazy."

Dave glanced at Pamela's revealing photos. "I can see that." He then stood from his old swivel oak chair intending to exit. "I can't pinpoint what was bothering me before, but what ever it was, it'll have to wait. I think I'll head back and try salvaging some sleep. Thanks buddy. And as far as Pamela's concerned, don't ever take that woman for granted."

"Even at this stage of my life bro, I still wouldn't take a blowup doll for granted. In fact I'd keep patch kit nearby, just in case. I imagine there'd be nothing worse than a case of the blowup doll, blue balls, no?"

"Ah, that's the Jim I once knew," Dave chuckled. "Good to see you haven't lost your sense of humility."

"Haven't changed much except now I have a beautiful wife. Just get some sleep, okay? We'll have plenty of time for more catching up tomorrow."

The two friends bid their "good nights" where afterwards Dave momentarily left the room before then peering his head back in again.

"So have you had any Ruskie sightings lately?"

"No I'm afraid not, bro," Jim responded, grinning with a sense of satisfaction. "I'm sure my boys of the Second Fleet must be keeping them in check."

"And we can all sleep well at night knowing that—seriously," Dave ended in exiting, there leaving Jim still leaning back and reclined. "Man the bad luck and shit—this is awesome."

Linda awoke a few hours later while Dave was in a sound sleep, laid embedded as if he were a reveal of a fossil's stone casting. She made her way to the kitchen with each approaching step bringing into greater focus the high level of her kid's excitement. Their enthusiasm resembled the glee of children in wait on a Christmas morning, eagerly scouting different presents wrapped beneath a tree. It was in contrast to their more frenzied energy displayed the previous day at trip's end.

Entering the kitchen, she was greeted by the fresh faces of her energetic children seated at the Woodson's modest kitchen table. "Hi Mom!" they both shouted in chorus.

"Sweeties, the men are still sleeping. Please keep it down."

Preparing breakfast at her kitchen counter was Pamela. There she stood notably dressed in a white cutoff tank top lacking the evidence of any underwear. Also catching Linda's attention were her host's scantly cutoff jeans revealing the entirety of her tanned model-like legs. She couldn't help but to be fixated on the only two items of clothing conforming tightly to her friend's gifted physique. Worn by most, that which might appear as either obscene or at best distasteful, instead for Pamela, mostly eliciting both admiration and envy. Gleaming with a genuine smile, she greeted her new friend.

"Hi, honey."

Smiling in contentment, Linda closed her eyes for a moment while drawing in the ambient mouthwatering aromas of breakfast. "Hmmm—Pamela, that smells wonderful. What are you cooking?"

"Just something nice for the kids and anyone else who happens to stroll out of bed—like you."

"I wouldn't hold your breath as far as Dave's concerned. He needed sleep more than any of us, yet I could have sworn he was up late last night. I was too far gone to care."

"You weren't imagining anything. He was up chatting with Jim. My husband loves spending time in his office alone at night. I think it's cute. It's his manly thing."

"And then you have my dearest Dave—wrote the book on sleep deprivation, you know."

"By the way, don't worry about the kids waking Jim. He's out at the marina right now. He wanted to be there when your boat comes in and help secure it to the mooring."

"Jim doesn't believe in sleep either, does he?"

"Oh, one thing that Jim love's about living here are siestas—his version of them, that is."

At the mention of his name and joined by her brother, Heather began slapping the table, shouting, "Jim!" repeatedly.

"Kids, keep it down!" Linda reacted in a restrained but firm tone. "Your father's still asleep, and don't slap the table either. It's not polite here or at home. And I want you to call Mr. Woodson, Mr. Woodson, not Jim."

"Oh I'm sorry, honey. He was playing with them earlier and said they could call him that. I hope it was okay."

Making her way to Pamela, Linda turned to her kids. "Okay, you can call Jim, Jim if you want, but everyone else is either mister or misses when they're grownups. You got me?"

Pamela felt embarrassed in believing she too had overstepped her new friend's parental authority. "Please forgive me, Linda. I also said it was okay for them to call me, Pamela. I hope that was okay."

Attempting to further reassert her authority, Linda gestured towards her chatting kids and then back to Pamela again. "And it's okay with me if you call her Pamela, but that's it. Next time you ask me first."

Schooled to their mother's parameters of acceptable behavior, the kids then focused their attention back to each other again with sibling chitchat. Linda turned to Pamela, grinning. "Kids, they're a handful. They can really push your limits, yet you love them a million times more than yourself. Don't mind me. Every now and then I just need to reassert who's boss to them. Sometimes they forget who their mother is."

"I think it's adorable, and I love those guys."

"Well thanks. My husband's a handful too, but I gave up on him long ago. You can't teach old dogs new tricks, you know?" Linda pointed to her children. "At least with them, there's hope."

Upon the kids finishing eating, Pamela approached her small dining table with Linda grabbing a washcloth, following behind. "Pamela, haven't you done enough already?"

Slightly offended, she reacted. "You're my guest. Our guests don't do housework."

Defiant still, Linda's insistence on clearing the table prompted Pamela to gently grab her upper arm to face her. She did so tactfully in front of the children, the meanwhile unexpectedly capturing her guest with grips of her eyes. It was the first time Linda would ever experienced such a reaction, no less with another women.

"Please respect my wishes. I can tell you're a nurturer like me, so I appreciate where you're coming from. Jim and I just love your kids, and we'd do anything for them. And that means you too."

"But you've already done so much for all of us."

"Listen, honey. You and Dave will have your hands full once you set off for the States. Meanwhile we're thrilled just to have you guys here. Jim's been like a kid since learning that you were coming, and believe me, he would have been crushed if for whatever reason you guys couldn't have made it here."

Humbled, Linda's shoulders sank. "Well if you need any help, please don't hesitate to ask."

Pamela then covered her new friend's lips gently with the tip of her index finger.

"I'll will—promise. Meanwhile you're my guest. That means no housework, sweetie."

Soon with the Costa children running to Woodson's backyard in loud cheers, Linda just shook her head in the hopelessness that her efforts of keeping their voices down failed in paying any dividend.

"You love them with all your heart, but if you're still enjoying your honeymoon with Jim, make sure you get any crazy aspirations out of your system first." Her statement was made with no idea to whom she was speaking.

Pamela motioned towards her small dining table, and this time Linda knew better than offering any assistance. She just sat in quiet observation of Pamela serving her breakfast. It included her host putting some final touches on a tea setup for the two of them. She then sat opposite a curious Linda, taking a quick deep breath punctuated by a sigh of relief. Hands rested atop her table with her fingers interlocked, Pamela motioned to Linda in a nod towards her food.

"Please, I ate already."

"Hmmm, smells great."

"Thanks, Jim cooks a mean breakfast too. We take turns. You know it's nice being able to just sit and chat like this. I love the folks around here, but it's been a while since I've been able to just sit and chat with another American woman—and in such layback setting like ours. It's quite refreshing."

Linda finished chewing. "Well I'm glad I can be that person, and hmmm, this is delicious. I noticed the kids like your cooking too. David didn't play with his food like usual."

"Keep eating, sweetie. I just love your kids. Little David is just so cute. I adore that little guy."

"Thanks, that's really sweet. You and Jim—you're both so great. Since Dave contacted your husband, we've really been looking so forward to this."

"That's sweet, and Dave's quite the handsome guy by the way. Jim had told me so much about him."

"He's alright. I guess I'll keep him."

"Yeah, you better hang on to that one. Don't let him get away."

Linda couldn't resist any longer. "Well you keep walking around showing off your assets like that, and Dave will find an excuse for backing out of the transaction tomorrow." Chuckling, she added, "Hell, he'll fly me back home without the kids."

Mortified, Pamela turned a shade of crimson as if exhibiting the acute latter stages of the bubonic plague. Her immodest outfit was the way she usually dressed, and while her scantly dress did at times raise the eyebrows of some locals, they'd quickly dismiss her appearance before warmly embracing her like any other neighbor.

"I'm so sorry, Linda," Pamela's voice cracked under the stress of shame. "I hope I haven't offended you, or brought disrespect upon your kids."

Linda placed her hand on Pamela's shoulder. "Sorry sweetie, I'm just busting you. It was a compliment—don't worry. Believe me, Dave would never leave me for anyone. He's loyal down to every fiber of his being." Grinning, she continued. "Plus he knows if he ever did, I would hunt him down and castrate him while still asleep with the bitch. After that he can have whoever wants him, once I'm done taking him to the cleaners, that is."

Briefly caught aback by both the violent nature and vengefulness of her comment, Pamela quickly regained her composure.

"Linda, thanks for the compliment." She then downplayed her temporary embarrassment with a mimicked gesture of a brushed forehead. "Whew, that was a close one."

"Hell Pam, if I looked the way you did, I'd be running around the house naked any chance I could." Smirking, she added, "but the kids sort of prevent that, I must admit. Not complaining though."

Pamela appeared bewildered at the modest nature behind her friend's remark. "But honey, you have such a great body—beautiful blond hair I would die for—and your lovely blue eyes. God, they're mesmerizing. I couldn't imagine you feeling self-conscious without any clothes. I'm sure you'd look awesome."

Linda couldn't believe Pamela's display of modesty or candor, especially in having made reference to Dave the previous day in likening her looks to that of a supermodel—"without anorexia". Resulted from such admiration, she didn't feel worthy of Pamela's compliments.

"Dirty blond. I'm not a true blond. My hair's dirty blond, but thanks."

"Oh, blond *shblond*. Linda, please don't be so humble. You've had two kids and still managed to keep yourself looking so great. I heard that's not easy to do."

"Honey, you don't know the beginning of it."

"I'm sure I don't, and with that said, it wouldn't bother me a bit to see you prancing around here naked as I usually do." Followed by a giggle, Pamela added, "That's of course if the kids weren't around. Yes sweetheart, I'm only dressed because of you guys. I hope you don't mind."

Having almost choked on her food, Linda was too dumfounded to interrupt. Meanwhile her uninhibited friend continued. "I guess if we were alone and you didn't mind, I'd be dressed the way I feel most comfortable, and then there'd be no secrets between us—assuming you were the same, no?"

Although Linda wasn't any prude, Pamela just took her to school. Embarrassed, yet flattered, she was nonetheless tongue-tied, the meanwhile not at all put off by her friend's straightforwardness. Attempting to get a handle on the sudden shifting moods without avail, resigned, she simply replied, "no secrets—that's for sure."

Linda gained over a hundred pounds post David's birth as a result of a severe bout of prenatal depression. Spanning a two-year recovery, both a regimented diet and workout routine led her to achieving an impressive level of athleticism. Stunned at such a metamorphosis having taken place before his eyes, Dave still found difficulty in convincing her that she looked better than ever, even more so than in her college days when nature graced her with the pleasing physical attributes normally associated with youthfulness. In spite of maintaining such an optimal level of physical peak for over three years beyond her full recovery, Linda's vanity was still in a fragile state, not yet having ever taken root into her self-esteem. That in turn left her somewhat vulnerable to the pleasing effects of Pamela's compliments. Feeling her emotions being juggled, Linda put the brakes on the flow of their conversation. She did so in sensing a suggestive tension growing in the room. What disturbed her most was the ease in which their conversation was doing so. Thanks to their husbands, the two girls knew enough of each other to be aware that such unchecked provocative dialogue could easily leave them both prone to a compromising outcome. It was quickly becoming evident by the fluency of their apparent chemistry.

Feeling as if her vulnerability was being held on display left only Linda scrambling to put the breaks on any further escalation of it. She did so, employing her husband's crude tactic of distraction, but in her case pretending to be choking on the tea she was drinking. Although an ungraceful way-out, a brief commotion of some non-genuine distress brought to light the usefulness of her husband's crude yet effective means.

Linda reestablished eye contact with her startled friend. "Sorry honey, I'm okay. So Pamela, how did you meet Jim? I mean you're such a sweetheart while he's got that bad boy type of attraction—pussycat aside."

"It's so cute when he tries playing that role."

"Yeah, sort of reminds me of *Tigger*." Following a brief laugh, Linda continued. "Was it the 'opposites-attract' thing? I mean Jim's really a great guy—cute too. Unfortunately his first impressions often rub people the wrong way—sort of like Eddie Haskell [*Leave it to Beaver*]. And the sad part is, it really doesn't reflect the great guy that he is."

The previous air of suggestiveness was lifted from the room. Cooled to a more even-keeled consistency, Pamela began with her accounts of first meeting Jim.

"I was working as a waitress slash barmaid at a dive called 'Benny's Bar and Grille' down in New London, Connecticut."

"Yeah I'm familiar with that place. Sorry Pam, I interrupted you."

"That's okay. Anyway, it was the first day of fall, Seventy-nine, and Jim was sitting alone at a corner table I was assigned to. At first he was just aloof—eating quietly, his mind seemed a world away—just looking down at his plate and gazing ahead into nothingness. I remember it clearly. He ordered his steak medium-rare, washed it down with an endless flow of beer, and when I cleaned his table, he barely nodded. I think that was his 'thank you'. Not sure. He continued ordering beer after beer and eventually began getting belligerent with me."

"Woo, this is hard to listen to, but please go on."

"Well I approached Benny the owner, in tears. I was the sensitive type you know."

Linda smiled affectionately. "No Pamela, not you."

Acknowledging Linda's remark with a brief grin, she continued. "Because he was a longtime patron of Benny's, the owner cut him some slack—let another waitress wait on him. She had known him for some time and didn't put up with his—I'd hate to use the word—crap."

"You mean 'shit', Pamela?"

Noticing her friend still in deep reflection, Linda apologized. Upon her recognition, Pamela picked up where she left off. "She told me that he was actually quite a nice guy—just struggling with some heartache. For the next few hours during free time she explained about how he went on consecutive tours for two years, and in returning stateside a mutual friend gave him the news his girlfriend of a couple years was seeing some doctor—go figure."

"That gold digging bitch! I didn't see that in her. I'm sorry, Pamela. I get a little defensive of Jim. After all, we all had some good times together, and I forgot how much I really love that guy. I mean he acts so badass, and yet the boy is so vulnerable."

"That's true, though I think he's matured since then. And the good times? Jim told me that you all saw each other naked, and many times. Is that true?"

Linda blushed with embarrassment. "Sweetie, we were young and drinking—just getting a little crazy, that's all. I saw Jim, but we never did anything. He's also a dead man."

"No hard feelings. Just jealous I missed out on all the excitement you guys had. That's all."

Linda's eyes bugged open at Pamela latter admission. She also refused to elaborate. Because both her and Dave had been waiting years for the information now being brought to light, she therefore had no intentions of derailing her new friend. Having taken notice, Pamela grinned slightly at her friend's reaction.

"Closing time came around, and I was left to check and make certain no patrons were still on the premises. Then when I opened the men's room door—oh God!" She grimaced. "The God awful smell. I was thinking, 'God, why me?'"

"Yeah, those men. They can get pretty disgusting. I've snuck into men's room on more than one occasion when the line was too long in the lady's. Never got any complaints—go figure."

"It's not what you're thinking. I found Jim face first lying in a regurgitated soup of beer and half-chewed, medium-rare steak. Well I stripped him down right then and there, stuffed his clothes in the trash, cleaned the god-awful mess in the stall, and then washed my hands obsessively afterwards. I grabbed a lining tablecloth and draped it over him before calling the owner over. I think Ben suspected that something was amiss. I mean the whole time this was happening he was balancing the register. He had to have known. I'm sure he could smell it."

"I hate to admit. Can't blame the man if you were already taking care of it."

"I guess. Anyways, with Ben's reluctant help, we both took him home and from there carried him to his bathroom where we laid him in his tub. I think by this point, Ben already saw way more of Jim than he cared to."

Both girls laughed. "At that point he stood straight, washed his hands, and told me I was on my own. He said, 'nice job, Pamela,' and something to the effect that I had just gone way beyond the call of duty for one of his patrons. He mentioned the next time I serve Jim, I better receive a very generous tip. Ben took off at that point."

"Well I can see that, giving his position. The man had nothing else to gain at that point. He was the bar owner, not Jim's freaking nurse—or potential squeeze."

"You're right, because next I uncovered him and bathed him under the shower. I think he saw that one coming and hightailed."

"Jim finally had a hot chick fondling him and was unconscious the whole time!" Linda belted with a mischievous laugh.

"Yeah, you could say that it was kind of like being Florence Nightingale, pornographic style. And thanks for the 'hot' comment by the way."

Linda was all smiles. "You are sister, get over it. So did you leave him there? The suspense here is killing me."

"No, the tub was too small. From there I dragged him into his bedroom where I left him to recuperate. I did stay awhile in case he got sick in his sleep, which he didn't, so I left. The next day in thinking about him, I remembered thinking then that he was pretty cute. Thank God for selective memory."

"I'll second that. So did he thank you? After all, you're married now. What happened?"

"A week later, Jim came to the bar, took me aside, and apologized for his behavior. He thanked me as well for what he referred to as my 'uncommon valor'. I was totally taken in by his humility and charm. He was a different person." She then giggled. "I also knew what he looked like underneath."

Fiddling with her teacup, Linda sat grinning, still listening.

"He had the whole package and I wanted him. For the next few months I got to know him better, and we became good friends. The other girls working with me were routing for us. You could say I was in crush heaven."

"So when did he finally officially ask you out?"

"I eventually asked him to join me for a walk by the beach."

Linda broke into hysterics. "That chicken shit!"

"No, no Linda, it's not what you're thinking. Eventually I was to discover that he was too ashamed to ask me out. He told me he felt funny about the way I found him in the men's room."

"Yeah, and you bought that. Listen dear, I know Jim well enough to safely say that for someone who carried around such a bad boy façade like him, when it came right down to actually closing the deal with any woman he was interested in, especially a looker, he was a pathetic wimp."

Still smiling, Linda grabbed Pamela's hand while throwing her a mischievous eye.

"You know what I'm going to ask you next?"

Pamela gazed at their adjoined hands before then locking eyes with her again.

"Either you're about to suggest we surprise Dave as he walks in on us naked and holding hands, or—"

Linda quickly became flush. While her new friend was only toying with her, she was also feeling her out. Pamela then casually pulled her hands away in an attempt of not putting Linda in any convoluted position where she might sense that her own intrigue was being exposed.

"—Or you were about to ask when we're going to have kids."

"Yeah, the kid's thing—that's it!"

In feeling as if having just been grazed by a bullet, Linda was well aware that others were likely to come her way. In addition, she was just able to witness firsthand how masterful her new friend was in controlling the buttons of her prurient makeup, like some chess master manipulating their opponent's every next move.

The reason Linda hadn't excused herself yet in avoidance of any further occurrences was with the knowledge Dave would take little issue to her experiencing such a side to herself. While he may have stated strong concern that she'd at least do so responsibly when the subject would be brought up, Linda never failed to be humored by the transparency of his obvious subterfuge. She understood the root of her husband's cause was a case where he was hopeful that her doing so might someday lead to a threesome. As to the query of having ever cashed in on such freedom granted by him, her new friend appeared to possess the faculties of being able to bring such an enigma to a head. In noticing beads of sweat building on Linda's neck and forehead, Pamela finally relented in her part of a cat and mouse game of seduction.

"We've decided to have kids when I turn thirty, and I just turned twenty-five. I'm ashamed to admit we're not ready to settle down yet, but after seeing your beautiful children and watching how Jim gleams around them, I wouldn't be surprised if that changes after your visit."

Linda was still wiping perspiration from her neck. "Hey, there's no shame in waiting until then, and I mean that's important. I speak for us in saying that I would rather suffer a thousand painful deaths before allowing even a single hair on either of my children to be harmed. They're gift from above and I have no regrets. That said, just after college, Dave and I were celebrating the last hurrahs of youth. We had no intentions on slowing down either. I mean we were completely out of control."

"Yeah, I heard," Pamela commented, giggling.

"I bet you did, and the contract's still out on Jim by the way. But what I was getting at was life for us was turned topsy-turvy when Heather began making me sick every morning"

"A shot gun wedding?"

"Yep, I guess the math is pretty easy. And I'll tell you this. Dave's a pretty tough guy to say the least, but boy did he cower when we broke the news to my dad. My father can be pretty intimating."

"Dave cower? I can't picture that."

"Well it was more a case of guilt with him. In my case, I figured that my dad knew beforehand I was some sort of hell raiser. He just didn't know to what extent. You could say my pregnancy was a smoking gun." Linda then gleamed with a radiant smile. "Ah, the first time he laid eyes on Heather, she melted that cold injured heart of his—real quick."

"That's sweet, and you a troublemaker?"

"Yeah me, but I've grown out of it—I think. You see when I drink, I kind of lose my buffers. Then again that's usually a given with most people. You see money was never an issue for my dad. Always wanted to throw me a big wedding—not some big ass shotgun one, that's for sure. The whole thing really hurt him, and I still regret it on many levels."

"How's your dad with Dave now?"

"Ah, the old man loves the kid. He knows Dave's a good husband, and dad. Believe me, he knows."

Finishing her breakfast, Linda stood and gave Pamela a heartfelt hug. "Thanks so much for breakfast, sweetie. It was wonderful. And thanks for sharing your story about Jim too. If you don't mind, I need to go and check up on the kids outside. Then I'll be back to help with the mess and feed Dave when he gets up."

"What did I tell you about that?"

In turning towards the back door, Pamela grabbed Linda's hand. "Please just do us this one favor. You and your kids are our guests, and you'll have plenty to worry about later at sea, so just relax."

Through the feel of the subtlest counter-pressures that were being exchanged between their adjoined hands whereby neither woman released in any normal timely fashion, such a compelling moment squashed any previous notion for Linda that she could continue playing denial.

Uneasy about the emotional rollercoaster she found herself

riding with Pamela, she was uncomfortable in having allowed her friend to be pushing her buttons so easily, especially as a mother. It compelled her to come clean about an overwhelming infatuation, one that only a half hour earlier was nothing more than intrigue. While her emotions were superficial at most, nothing more than the manifestation of simple chemistry, Linda also understood her present feelings were an undeniable force that quickly needed to be addressed.

Suddenly overcome by a newfound sense of confidence in her self-admission, she proceeded to release the hand of Pamela in a somewhat seductive fashion. Emboldened, she stared directly into her eyes, as if to cast a spell. While Pamela was bewildered at her friend's sudden change of demeanor, she wasn't as affected by it as Linda had hoped.

With deliberation, Linda then grabbed a chair and pulled it over to her puzzled friend. Pamela followed her lead. The two were soon seated opposite and facing each other with Linda starting, "I need to tell you something."

"Yes, what is it, honey?"

"One thing I noticed about you that amazes me is how you treat everyone like they're the center of your world."

"But they are. Maybe it just rubbed off from the locals here."

"Sorry, nice try. You just finished telling me how under awful circumstances you made sure that Jim would be okay—cleaning his puke—and he was still just a stranger to you then."

"Well it had to be done. No one else was around to do so. I didn't think he needed any ambulance."

"My point exactly, giving Benny was ultimately responsible for him. All being said, I need to give you a little background about myself. I mean we've only been talking about a half hour now, and I already feel like you're a soul-friend." Linda also wished to accuse her friend of ruthless manipulation while at the same time finding herself unable to excuse herself from the room.

"You listened to me and now I'm listening to you. That's what friends do, isn't it?"

"Well yeah, but I need to tell you about what happened after David was born."

Linda first needed to compose herself before continuing. "After his birth I fell into a depression which wasn't understood back then; hence, I got no help. Our family physician tried giving me some fucking pep talk like 'put on a fucking smiley face and you'll feel better. Life gets to us sooner or later but it all passes.' I was thinking, 'Yeah right! After I've blown my fucking head off, asshole.' The guy must have had some fucking ego, not one for specialists. He would have probably considered it some kind of failure on his part—or whatever. I know I'm ragging him pretty harshly, but I earned it."

Pamela was heartfelt at the anger her friend was displaying. "Why didn't you just go to someone else?"

"In retrospect I agree, especially considering our present doctor is pretty awesome. But in the midst of it all, everything just seemed so clouded. Plus back then we trusted that if anything could be done, he'd be the one to tell us about it. We were both naive to the wrath of a stubborn doctor's pride. The man was old-school."

"That asshole," Pamela exclaimed, no longer feeling the need to resort to any euphemisms, then apologizing afterwards.

"Don't worry, you're being nice. Anyhow, matters got worse from there. What I'm going to tell you next is still hard for me. You see, the next year following David's birth was hard on both Heather and Dave."

Voice cracked with emotion, Linda continued. "He should have divorced me after the shit I put him through. I mean I stayed in bed all the time. He'd work all day and then have to come home and tend to the kids—everything. Dave essentially ran the household; whereas prior to David being born we both worked and had someone clean and watch over Heather during the day. After his birth, I rarely got out of bed—never mind leave the house. Dave was ashamed of that, so he made a point of doing everything himself—shopping, cleaning, changing the diapers—everything. He did it all. At one point he even slept on the couch because I never showered. Actually, I finally would after being dragged there. It wasn't pretty."

Linda became watery eyed. "He's so sweet. Another reason he never went out other then for work and shopping was to keep an eye on me—make sure I didn't harm myself."

In taking a deep breath in relief of her admission, Pamela grabbed her hand, squeezing it.

"It's okay, honey." She also dried Linda's eyes with the backs of her fingers.

"I'll be okay, but I appreciate it. To this day, Dave still denies ever having had any affaires back then. I only asked him later out of curiosity, because he worked around a lot of hot woman and would then have to come home to my shit. It wouldn't have surprised me a bit had he done so. Back then I was just too far gone to care."

"But that wasn't the true you, Linda. You were sick."

"Sweetie, on the surface I know that, but there's a part of me that still believes I could have done more. It was all so hard on Heather too. I still have regrets about it with her—I mean I was pathetic."

"Linda, you couldn't have been that bad."

"Listen dear, I became a fat useless bitch with no sex drive, and I mean I was a bitch to Dave. I swear at times he must have thought he was road kill and I was some raven tearing little pieces off his carcass—bitch by bitch. Yet he was such a saint for hanging in there for me. I guess he took that 'for better and for worse' thing pretty seriously."

Also watery-eyed, Pamela expressed amusement at Linda's last comment. "Thanks for sharing this with me."

"Oh, you're welcome. I needed you to know all of this, because I figured sharing it would put more at stake into our friendship."

"I never underestimate what's at stake in any friendship, but I appreciate your openness nonetheless."

Linda acknowledged Pamela's declaration. "First of all, I want to apologize to you. My first initial thought in seeing you was, 'Wow, this bitch is stunning. Shit, she must either be some kind of bimbo or controlling she-bitch. God I pray I'm wrong for Jim's sake.'"

Pamela shook her head in awkward denial. Still listening, she regained her composure.

"All I knew about Jim's hard times was only based on vague information. That wasn't fair to you though. Then when I saw you with Heather and David, I felt like shit. My preconception may have been brief, but I still feel terrible for it."

"No harm, honey. I imagine if I were still back in the States, I might get more of that, especially the way I dress. I love the fact that you guys care so much about Jim. That matters most to me."

"Well I was lucky Dave hung in there. After the episode, we agreed not to have any more kids. It was he who offered to have a vasectomy. I was against it, but he was able to convince the doctor to get one anyhow without delay."

"Wow Linda, that's love. I give Dave a lot of credit there"

"Yeah, especially considering he wasn't initially giving enough Novocain."

Pamela winced. "I'm not a guy but yikes! That was love."

Linda smiled with a hint of mischievousness. "Yeah, he said it was like trying to play catcher with some Major League pitcher, blindfolded—and without a cup. In all actuality, he was just a horny bitch and was tired of rubbers. Anyways, now we're settled and I rarely drink—even with friends. One thing's for sure though. If I did per say get plastered at some shindig without Dave there, I can't guarantee what might happen, but with our kids depending on me, I'm pretty certain I'd never let them down. That I can attest to, for the most part that is—never really been tested."

In reflection, Pamela pulled her lower lip down with the index finger, eyes ogling. "Please excuse me for asking this, but say you were drinking right now and were certain no one would walk in on us, would you make a move on me?"

"I'll answer that by asking you, would you stop me?"

Anticipating a response and then returning a gesture of earlier, Linda motioned for Pamela not to reply by placing the tip of her index finger over her friend's lips. Feeling in complete control of her facilities at that point, she soon witnessed the shaky reign of such brief dominance crumble before her eyes. Giving their mutual attraction, it quickly became clear to her that she was out of her league when it came to toying with any level of flirtation with her new friend.

As if a switch was suddenly flipped into an on position, Pamela eyes took on a spellbinding appearance of a seductive temptress. Beneath the index finger of Linda, a mischievous smirk of almost demonic like character took shape as her lips drew her friend's pointer in against the succulence of their moist surfaces. Then with convincing control including some suction, Linda's finger was soon caught in the gentle grasped of Pamela's teeth. Grinning the whole time into the eyes of her stunned friend, upon full engagement, she gradually released Linda's finger from their grip, then eventually allowing only the firm suction of her mouth to resist in its exit. Soon freed from the hold of her friend will, Linda stood stunned, totally perplexed, nonetheless fully taken aback. While Pamela's usual kindhearted persona was a genuine one, when instead confronted with stimuli of any sensual nature, her persona would morph at a moments notice, almost as an involuntary reflex. She would do so as if suddenly being possessed by the will of some Aphrodite spirit.

Still locked in a seductive stare down with her stunned friend, grinning, Pamela eventually broke the dead silence. "Don't worry, I won't answer."

By then Linda had forgotten her host's question, having just experienced a hint of some climax resonating throughout her body.

Sill in an unrelenting mode, Pamela gently grabbed the shoulder of her helpless friend. Then in a sensual, throaty whisper to the ear she sent tingles throughout her submitted friend's body. "I'm glad you're not drinking. I'd hate to have to fight you off."

Linda could have either interpreted Pamela's actions as that of sensually engrossing or ruthlessly bewitching. Either way, every fiber of her was being inundated by host's will.

What further bewildered her was when Pamela suddenly pulled away and stood up straight as if nothing just took place. She did so as if the switch from before was suddenly flipped off again.

"Honey, we really need to behave ourselves, so to answer your question, lets' see how the next few days pan out, okay?"

Her unexpected comment was followed with a playful smirk and then a wink, one that sent Linda weak in her knees.

Once again she was floored at the ease in which her friend was able to push her buttons. Her last round with Pamela made her feel as if she had just taken a bullet, this time pointblank, and in doing so witnessed the light of utopia just to then be involuntarily pulled back from its bliss. Given a second opportunity to exercise some volition versus having just been subjugated to Pamela's will, it was a second chance that was just thrust upon her while at the same time was one that didn't lend itself to any sense of reprieve.

Meanwhile had both men been watching the events unfolding from around some corner, they might have resembled two of the *Three Stooges* in wait with one hovering over the other. In the hope of catching a forbidden glance of skin at any moment, they might have appeared as two curious teenagers jockeying for an equal peek, periodically pulling back at times and quietly exchanging high-fives in anticipation.

As for Linda no longer feeling the need to prove any sense of dominance over Pamela anymore and presuming it would have posed futile to even try, she resorted to a usual resigning tone.

"I'm going out to check on the kids now. Then I'm gonna take a real long—cold—shower."

"If you need any extra clean towels, just yell. I'll bring them over for you. Maybe then I can answer your question."

Ignoring the latter comment though not unaffected by it, Linda tittered.

"That's okay, I'll let you know."

With both her feet and arms crossed, Pamela just leaned back. Taking pleasure from what was just transpired, she just grinned in observation of her friend exiting, softly uttering. "I'm sure you will honey, and you won't have to say a word either."

While Pamela may have been able to control the level of racy interaction that just took place moments earlier between her and her new friend, she was nonetheless affected by it than was Linda. From then on, a defined relationship was established between the two women whereby afterwards, both of them were well schooled as to their parameters with each other.

What amazed Linda most was just an hour prior she was sound asleep and nestled against her husband, the meanwhile Pamela was immersed in the joy of being with her children. Dumbfounded, she just shook her head.

"Holt shit! What a freaking difference one freaking hour can make—damn that's mess up."

<< CHAPTER 2 >>

IN STROLLING ONTO PORTO GRANDE'S main pier later that Sunday afternoon, Dave was hesitant to make any such assumption that a beautiful craft with its towering mast just ahead was soon to be his own. Sensing his friend playing his usual denial game, Jim paused and pointed. "Bro, are you blind? You saw the Polaroids, didn't you?"

"You're shitting me," Dave reacted, hastening his walk.

"No bro, it's the real deal."

Halted dead in his tracks a few yards short of his moored boat, he panned its structure vertically to take in its full spender. He then turned. "You did it, man!"

Showing no reserve in the expression of a heartfelt embrace, the moment qualified as one where Dave didn't feel the need to spare any show of emotion.

"You have no idea what this means to me. Thanks man!"

Such a rare welcomed detour from his usual reserved self was one Jim first gladly let play out before then snapping his friend back to a more collected poise, one that he was both familiar and more comfortable with.

"Well don't you want to go inside and have a moment to yourself with her before the rest of the crew shows up? They should be here in a few minutes. If you want, I'll head back to the road and keep an eye out for them."

"Thanks. Not necessary though. I prefer this to be a group thing."

With everyone soon advancing out on the pier, Linda became increasingly enthralled with every step taken towards her new boat. "Oh...my...God," she chanted repeatedly in a soft undertone—bug-eyed.

In paying mind in avoidance of taking part in an embarrassing spectacle of cascading bodies finding the boat's cockpit together in a pile, everyone was laboring to maintain some stability in entering the boat's confines. Compensation of a slight undulation required deliberation on their part.

Soon admiring every bit of the vessel's forty-three foot structure bow to stern, both Dave and Linda couldn't help but to notice the elegance of its brass helm facing a likewise compass of vintage origin. Mounted on a binnacle, its elegance was yet overshadowed by the cutter's mast towering high above. Enhancing its grandeur evermore were two supporting stays swooping downward to their point of attachment, fore and aft. With the cutters two sails furled thereupon rendering the full splendor of the boat maximized, the Woodsons simply stood silent with pride, as they did so similar to somebody exhibiting a piece of original art.

From below, the group's meditative state was abruptly shattered by noise being generated there. Because the adults' slower advance failed in keeping pace with the more energetic children, Linda had allowed them to run ahead of the group on the promise of good behavior. As a result, the two siblings teaming up inside the boat's cabin to create a racket brought on the urgency for immediate adult intervention. Linda took on the roll by placing herself in plain sight of them from atop the boat's companionway.

"Hey sweeties, please keep it down in there! No horseplay on the boat!"

"But Mommy, we're in the boat, not on it!" David responded to his sister's amusement.

Assisting his wife, Dave stepped in as enforcer. "David, don't talk back to your mother like that! You know better!"

Soon below, the two parents were immediately taken in by rich earth tones encompassing their soon-to-be boat's interior. Now facing the living quarters and just off to Dave's right was situated a built-in desk and cabinets. Constructed of a rich mahogany, it was the boat's chart table, a location where its electronics, navigation, and communication equipment was laid concealed there within the luxuriance of its wooden cabinetry above.

What then caught his full attention there brilliantly contrasted against a lustrous mahogany surface was a pristine brass British sextant—a gift. Downplaying its significance, Jim jokingly pointed it out.

"In case the rough elements come on a knocking on your door, I figured you might need a paperweight for your charts." The item he so callously referenced as a paperweight was a precisely calibrated and still functional piece of navigational instrumentation. It was an impeccably preserved antique as well.

Following spending some time on the boat for verification of its general condition including giving the engine a test run, the group of six adult and kids then visited a local café where the Woodsons often frequented. Its laidback setting was one they preferred for drawing on for business deals. This led Jim to believe it would also serve as an ideal place for both the boat's present owner and their friends to finalize the last formalities of the boat's transaction because of its casual setting.

Subsequent to an exchange of money and paperwork, some polite small talk was exchanged before Linda, Pamela, and the previous owner's wife, Ruth, left with the kids to head back to the Woodson's place. It was apparent to them their husbands wanted to be left alone so they could then substitute the tea and coffee consumed throughout the transaction with a more celebrated gala of beer, homemade red wine, and spirits to nourish the mood.

Upon the woman leaving, Jim turned to the previous owner, a man in his late fifties named Richard, who preferred to be called Dick.

"Dick, I've never asked you this. I mean your wife's name is Ruth and yet your former boat is called Gloria. Can you explain that one?" Grinning, he added, "Is there something we should know?"

Dick, a soft-spoken man with pepper hair and a weathered complexion, carefully placed his newly filled glass of wine on the table before him. Masterfully milking the moment to its zenith, he did so emanating a grin, as if ready to divulge a bombshell of gossip.

"Gloria was our dog of 19 years."

Upon first exchanging looks of disappointment in his reply's lack of scandal, the two friends then broke into laughter.

"What's so funny? You relish in the lost of a man's best friend? The dog lived with us longer than our kids did. I don't really see the humor in that, do you?" A grin then ensued. "I do have to admit though. She's the only female dog that I ever knew of that ever humped peoples' legs."

"Maybe it wasn't female," Dave insisted.

"Or maybe it was a transgender dog," Jim added.

Half amused, Dick sat quietly, waiting.

"Are you two finished?" he responded, then pausing. "By the way Jim, I've seen many a transgender ever more beautiful then your wife. Are you sure she's not one?"

"I saw her nude picture pinned up on Jim's wall," Dave stepped in, "and believe me, she's no transgender. But may I add Jim, I do believe the man deserves a 'touché.'"

"Yeah, touché—whatever, though if Pamela is a transgender, no complaints here. Let's just leave it at that, okay?"

Dave then raised his glass of beer in proposal of another toast.

"Dick, here's to your late dog, Gloria. We eventually forget our X's, but never our canine friends."

Following the clanging of glasses and drink consumption, Dick changed his tone to more of a serious one. Noting his change of demeanor, the two friends played along anyhow in light of not being able to decipher when their quest might be toying with them.

"I want to propose a toast of a more serious nature."

Dick waiting as the café owner addressed everyone's drinks.

"Gloria's a beautiful vessel. We've taken good care of her, and likewise, she us. At night when her sails glide her gracefully through the waters and the ocean's darkened surface flickers in harmony as it mirrors the brilliance of the stars and planets above, and if you're lucky the moon joins in on the chorus of serenity as well, don't be surprised then to feel as if you're being carried along by a guardian angel—keeping you safe—journeying you beyond the boundaries of bliss."

Both Dave and Jim lifted an impressed eyebrow at each other, listening further in anticipation.

"It's as if she possesses the elegance of a ballerina and the sea is the vast stage upon which she dances. Like a seductive temptress, Gloria too possesses such graceful curves, pleasing to the eye. You don't control her. You can coax her in a way only she's will consent. When seated at her helm, she will rewards you the same way only a woman choosing to surrender herself to you can, allowing you take her anywhere you wish. Yet during inclement weather when the sea unleashes its full fury, she displays the unparalleled fortitude of a woman giving birth, hence, once again watching over you with the keen eye of a guardian angel. Gloria's wise. You just need to know what she's thinking, and together you can both forge ahead into the bliss like two lovers expressing their passion."

Visualizing the allegoric images Dick was expressing eloquently, Jim shook his head.

"Man I wish I could talk to Pam like that. In fact, right now I'm thinking about going around the corner behind *Emmanuel's* [Cafe's name] here and rubbing one out."

Dave did his best to constrain a grin. "Man bro, do have to be so crass?"

While Dick was less amused, he did appreciate Jim's comment in its compliment to his portrayals, despite its lack in finesse. He then focused his attention back to Dave.

"I understand you're taking your kids along and that concerns me, Dave."

Stated by a man who appeared to possess the deep wisdom of a seasoned mariner, this captured Dave's full attention. It also gave Jim an array of hope that Gloria's previous owner might be able to get through to his sometimes-thickheaded friend. Placing stock in the context of his words, Dave began feeling some doubt about his decision of taking his kids along. There he experienced a tinge of some apprehension.

"What do you mean?"

"Well son, this boat can act as an aphrodisiac, and there'll be long periods where your beautiful wife will be basking under the shower of the suns rays. In painting her body by the bronzing touch of nature's brush, she'll be doing so as our nearest star will be accentuating her curves without relent, thereby drawing you in like the scent of a Venus flytrap to one of its unfortunate victim."

Dave was laboring in in his effort of following where he believed Dick might be leading. Meanwhile, he was also reminding himself of the potential risks he might be subjecting to his kids.

Jim finally interrupted. "I think what he's trying to say is that you're going to want to get laid, but you wont have the privacy to do so. I'm surprised that one slipped past you, bro. I'd never let you play goalie for my soccer team—that's for damn sure."

Dave was still distracted with his mind seeming elsewhere. It was until realizing that Dick's statement wasn't any rebuttal to his judgment pertaining to his kids. In relief, he sighed before turning to his friend.

"First off Jim, fuck soccer!" He then looked to Dick. "Sorry about that. I can see your point Dick, but it's a big boat. I don't see the likelihood of what you're suggesting."

"Son, so you think. In such close quarters as will be afforded to your family over such an extended period of time, it's only human nature to be in tune with others occupying such tight quarters." He then grinned. "But keep believing that."

"Bro, you are so screwed." Jim interjected, laughing out loud. He then raised his beer for the others to join.

"Let me continue your toast, Dick. Here's to the Costa family and their safe voyage to America—and also to Dave's future bout with forced abstinence."

A slight wince, Dave shook his head in refusing to acknowledge Dick's words as any foregone prophecy. Showing reluctance, he joined in the toast anyways, having stepped up his consumption of alcohol to that of his favorite drink of straight tequila.

The three men spent the rest of the afternoon drinking, initially discussing matters pertaining to the boat and there stemming, seamanship. Proportionate to their blood alcohol levels reaching maximal saturation points, their slurred dialogue eventually consisted of nothing better than both a sloppy salad of locker-room talk and senseless viewpoints of a theoretical nature. That which was considered crass earlier became the subject of philosophical discussion. Such loud and infantile public behavior back in the States might have gotten the group told that they overstayed their welcome, but there in Mindelo's laidback setting, Manny the cafe owner gladly tended to their drinks until the men had had enough.

The following morning commenced with everyone squeezed around the Woodson's small dining table. The following day was the Costa's nine-year anniversary, and the previous day they had invited their friends to join them for a short maiden voyage in celebration of the event together. Concerned about bad behavior, it was arranged that friends of the Woodsons would watch the kids while their parents were away; they didn't wish for their kids to be subjected to it.

By late afternoon, fatigue finally convinced Dave that he was finished in his exhausted effort of scrutinizing every possible angle of his boat. Meanwhile their wives were also done stowing away some last items needed for transfer for the Costa's transatlantic crossing, celebrating in their own way with whispers and a few giggles following.

The provocative entanglement of suggestive interaction played out the previous morning with the girls formed a bond between them. With both still naive to their wives' interaction, it appeared to their husbands, who had no inkling to the exchange, that within just a day the women seemed to have transformed into a team of conspiring femme fatales poised to torment them with some sexy flirtation.

In completing their tasks and leaving in succession, each wife turned atop Gloria's companionway and peered downward to their husbands. In doing so, they both puckered and threw the men a kiss. In addition, Linda, who exited last, made sure neither of them missed her grabbing Pamela's buttock cheek in the process.

Jim grinned afterwards, shaking his head. "I'll tell you this. I never get tired of that ass."

"I don't make a habit of gawking at other women, especially my best friend's wife, but damn! Waving her buttocks from the top of the stairs like that I guess entitles me to take some notice."

"I meant Linda's, bro."

The words were no sooner exited from his mouth when Dave responded by way of a forceful but friendly backhand to a tightened abdomen of his friend. Jim had readied himself beforehand, still familiar with his friend's customary response to such comments.

"Hey! What was that about? I just complimented your wife's ass."

"After all the shit we did back in the day, I don't care about that. But come on—with someone as sweet and beautiful as Pamela, how can you even notice another's woman's buttocks? Are you that tired of her?"

"First off bro, your wife's ass is an ass. With all due respect, you can't call what I just witnessed, any buttock—a booty or bum-bum maybe, but buttock? No freaking way."

"Okay, Linda's got a nice ass. Are you happy?"

"After what I just saw, what do you think?"

"Okay, granted. But with some like Pamela, how can you even notice anyone else? The girl's an angel."

"For someone who did all the shit back in college as you have, you're pathetically naïve. Yes it's a given she loves children— puppies—kittens—and is a do-gooder—an angel even, but every fiber of that sweet angel's makeup exudes sexuality. It affects others around her to the point where they become stupefied with giddiness—sometimes women included. Hell, let her visit the Kremlin for a week, and I'd bet this whole Cold War thing would be over before you knew it."

"I could she that."

"Yeah, it's kind of like watching Mozart compose a symphony, or something"

"Mozart?"

"You know what I mean. You saw *Amadeus*, didn't you—the pool table scene?"

"Yeah, last year. And I remember that scene. Why?"

"I say this with all due respect being it I love Linda to death, but Pamela's like her back in the day, but without the attitude."

Dave smiled broadly in thinking affectionately of his wife. "Still has one bro, but I prefer to think of it as spirited or an edge."

"That's what makes those two so dangerous together. You just saw it displayed on the stairs. Together, they're like the Lennon and McCartney of tease."

"Lennon and McCartney? Better comparison, though I prefer not thinking of them in such context. Otherwise, nice job nailing it the second time. I'm still working on the Mozart thing though."

Dave then paused, viewing his boats interior with an exhaled sigh of relief.

"Jimbo, looks like we did it. Nice job brother. Thanks."

"Just did my job, man. You paid me well for it."

"Don't belittle what you and Pamela have done for us. There was a lot to be done, and you guys nailed it. We really appreciate it."

Ensuing a brief silence, Dave shook his head in disbelief. "Man I think your Pamela's been giving Linda lessons in eroticism the way she dresses, or should I say the way she omits doing so—and she it gets away with it to boot."

"That's the Mozart thing I just mentioned. Darwin in both his infinite wisdom and keen insight wrote the script. She just knows how to exploit it. By the way, Linda's got some serious potential too. She just needs more confidence, that's all. Does she work out?"

"Oh, she works out alright. I think the gym she attends needs to replace its treadmill belts after each of her visits."

"Man the bad luck and shit—she works out that much?"

"What's she's got, she's earned, and if Pamela could somehow instill more confidence into her, that would be great. Being a mother and working full-time hasn't afforded her much time for any playing, so for that reason alone I think this trip's well worth her loss salary."

"Well, good for her," Jim responded, pausing for a moment in reflection. "Remember the parties?"

"You mean the ones where Linda got drunk and chased you around naked? How could I forget?"

"Man the bad luck in shit—back then I was afraid you'd see us and kick my ass. And the naked part only happened twice by the way."

Dave grinned in thinking back. "Never saw you guys though. I was usually busy somewhere else. The four of us would have made Caligula proud."

"Yeah, add a little carnage and I think you might be right. I tell you though, that place was huge and had more nooks and crannies. You know if Nancy wasn't MIA all the time, she might have been able to help my cause with Linda."

"Or make it worse. Well considering how out of control she got when drinking and how nasty she got in not getting what she wanted, I appreciate what you did back then—you know, not giving into her. I mean that must have taken some serious willpower, and my Linda had a body for sex, not to mention a drive to match. Hell, I'm fourteen years past my prime and been together with her for over eleven, and she still manages to be able to push the right buttons. Just don't know how you did it, man."

"Fear, bro. Your boot up my ass and even worse, hers."

Jim began impersonating Linda. "'What the fuck Jim! I'm not good 'nough for you? Who the fuck are you, you scroungy pasty ass!' Hell bro, she was outright intimidating."

Dave broke out into laughter before straining to recompose himself. Still unable to speak, he broke out in yet another wave.

"I can picture you butt-naked running like gazelle from her in sheer terror. It's messed up, but freaking funny as hell."

"Yeah, but the way I was able to avoid her with her parents summer place being wall-to-wall people. And it was dark too. I'd prefer to think of myself more as OJ sprinting through the airport, leaping chairs [A popular commercial of the previous decade], except I might have stepped on an ass or two in the process. Who knows?"

"I'm sure they did, at least for a moment that is," Dave came back, chuckling.

Jim broke a brief silence. "It's a giving—all of us young, toasted, running rampant around her parent's place like a bunch of ecstasy driven, sex-starved monkeys. But why did you merry Linda if she was so much out of control? I admit that's a bit of a double standard, but just curious."

"And the scary part was she never took the shit. To answer your question though, it's simple. Remember tomorrow is our ninth anniversary—shotgun wedding—need more?"

"Man the bad luck and shit—I kind of thought about it, but didn't want to ask. Think you still would have married her anyhow?"

"I love that woman. Hey, I'm not claiming that our courtship or shotgun marriage resembled that of any *Rockwell* painting, but we were just lucky the ends justified the means. It was an unwitting roll of the dice that essentially worked out for us."

"Well based on the show we just got front row seats to, I can see why. Linda's got an even better ass now—though I was usually running from it back then. Never really got a good eye-shot."

"Your loss bro, and it takes a man to admit that too—it's squats, by the way. Linda does squats with weights and lunges," Dave proclaimed with pride, especially giving how far she was able to pull herself out from the abyss since her sickness.

"With Pamela it's genetics—ungodly genetics. Could you imagine Dick hearing us now? That man was old-school, traditional."

"Maybe so, but every man's got a story, and I can tell you this. Yesterday he held out on us. Did you see his tattoo?"

"Not really, why?"

"Didn't think so, it was on my side, mostly covered by his sleeve. Dick's a jarhead. He's fifty-eight. Do the math. The man's probably seen more shit than we could ever imagine or care to imagine. I highly doubt anything we could have said would have shocked the man." Dave shook his head, spelling disbelief. "In fact, we must have seemed like a couple snotty-nose delinquents to the guy."

"Hey bro, don't forget. He did eventually stoop to our level after boozing it up with us. Apparently he didn't mind being with us that much."

"True," Dave agreed, then taken notice of footsteps sounding at a distance.

Just then off the boat and unexpected, a male's voice rang though the open companionway. Recognizing it, Jim quickly pulled himself up to the entrance to check it out. There he witnessed his pastor standing less than surefooted on Gloria's floated slip.

"Hey Pastor John, come in and join us!"

"Hi James. I didn't see you or Pamela Sunday morning, but I'm glad to see you two are okay."

Viewed from Jim's perspective, his relationship with the pastor was underlined with dubious undercurrents on his part. While the pastor loved both him and Pamela coupled with the energy they brought to the island, without actually being able to pinpoint the evidence of any debauchee on their part, he was still uneasy by an air of moral indiscretion they projected. Both Pamela's freeness to normally wear as little as possible and Jim's endorsement of it was a dead giveaway to him.

In an effort not to appear too intrusive into their lives, the pastor would make unexpected appearances, masked as coincidences. He would do so like a shepherd keeping watch over a couple straying sheep from afar, there hoping in the process not to frighten the wandering animals completely away.

Jim motioned for the pastor to join them in the cabin. This was his way of appeasing the shepherd by not provoking any aggressive move towards a rescue. It was a delicate tactic that had served his agenda well to that point.

Ensuing formal introductions, the pastor gazed about the cabin.

"Nice piece of a nautical oasis you have here, Dave."

While always careful not to interject any talk of the Lord in the context of casual conversation with Jim, especially with a third party present, the pastor still often managed to slip in at least one discomforting comment of immoral implications, masked as a joke.

"I would offer to christen this vessel before your sendoff Dave, but I imagine Jim and Pamela have already done so."

While Jim took offence to the spirit of his pastor's comment, especially with his friend present, Dave in turn did all he could to contain his laughter. The clergyman continued fishing for more material to analyze. "Just saw Pamela and some nice women Linda who introduced herself to me."

Just then in making the connection that she was Dave's wife, the twenty-five-year-old pastor was taken aback. "Oh, I can see the good Lord hasn't deprived either of you men the riches of his creations."

In spite of an air of prurient linguistic intercourse still lingering from only minutes prior, Dave was nonetheless at ease with the uncorrupted spiritual demeanor of Jim's pastor. The clergyman began heading towards the companionway.

"Yeah James, I noticed this new boat sitting by your jetty, so figured I'd come out on the pier and check things out. I was actually waiting for a brother reverend who's supposed to meet me by the roadside. He's coming across the way from Santo Antao [A Verde Island just north of Sao Vicente] on a chartered powered boat to pick me up. He's got a small group of youths with him. I think the kids are really going to enjoy this trip."

"Yeah, I'm sure it'll make a great impression on them," Dave stated, enjoying the pastor's short visit.

The pastor exchanged parting words before pausing atop the stairs. "Dave, I'm aware of your voyage ahead and wish you the Lord's watchful eye. Until I hear confirmation of the safe arrival of you and your family back at the States, I'll make sure that my prayers and those of the congregation meet the listening ear of our maker."

To Jim's amazement, he then focused his attention back to him. "I'm sorry about my comment earlier, James. It was inappropriate. Please forgive me."

"Forgive you for what, Pastor?" Jim responded, brushing it off.

Heartfelt by the pastor's sincere concern for him and his family's wellbeing, Dave turned his attention back to Jim when certain the reverend was a safe distance away.

"Good man, *James*."

"Yeah funny—he has his moments, but I love him regardless." Jim paused a moment to assure there were no more footsteps on deck. "By the way, are you going to let Linda drink tomorrow night?"

"Man, the smoke hasn't even cleared yet, but since you asked, it's not for me to say. She really doesn't drink that often, and believe me she knows what she's like when she does. That's why we don't make a habit out of attending many drinking gigs, even in casual settings. As far as tomorrows concerned, I admit there's a part of me that's curious though."

"But what if she chases me around like before. What should I do then?"

"Keep your clothes on in the first place. Either way, you're a grown boy. You'll figure it out."

Jim had difficulty interpreting Dave's response. He also resisted the urge of asking for any clarification of it. Instead he experienced brain freeze until Dave stepped in.

"So we're going out on the boat tomorrow and let our hair down, something we haven't done since the good old days. I honestly have no idea what she'll do tomorrow, and I really don't care." Chuckling, he added, "though, I'm sure you do."

Dave's remark confused Jim evermore in receiving no definitive answer that he could in turn analyze.

"That's what I'm afraid of. I can fend her off, but damn, she didn't take rejection too well back in the day. Think she would now?"

"Bro, that was over nine years ago. I was there—remember? I appreciate you trying to take the high road here, but if somehow things workout where she chases you around again, corners you, or whatever, all I ask is that you'll at least make the effort of getting away from her. That's all."

Dave's response interested Jim evermore while still drawing no definitive line in the sand. The Costas weren't just another couple of players that the Woodsons had become acquainted with leading to the present. Instead, inserting his friends into the picture made the dynamics of the equation far more personal for him.

"Oh, I'll make an effort," Jim came back, chortling, "but what if she corners me again?"

"I'll probably laugh my ass off. But seriously, I just need to say this. Linda and I've discussed it. We know the risks and haven't changed much since college, except that we're responsible parents now. We haven't become prudes since then either. Listen, I would never want subject you to any position that might cause a strain to our friendship. Given that, I'm willing to take responsibility for what ever happens tomorrow. I also don't want to allow Linda to put herself in any situation where she might end up degrading herself either."

"I guess I'm making a lot out of nothing then."

"Not really, we have history. I guess feelings can resurface. I understand that. I hate to admit this, but that's what interests me most about tomorrow—the unknown—the dangers. Hey, if things somehow end up being mellow tomorrow, I might be surprised, though not disappointed—just glad to be with you guys, that's all."

Dave's approach to the conversation was naive in comparison to that of his friend's. Jim still had the momentum of his and Pamela's exploits working on him. Years prior, he did enjoy being chased by Linda. Dave the meanwhile was looking forward to playing the wait-and-see card on the matter, whereas Jim was feeling him out on the subject, the core of where his inquiry was stemming.

A brief silence ensued. Dave then snickered. "I need to ask you one thing."

"Hit me, bro."

"How did someone with such a pathetic approach to women as you manage to pick up someone like Pamela?"

"Thanks for that vote of confidence, bro."

"You know what I mean. You two deserve each other, but damn, the girl could be a supermodel for swimwear—lingerie too. That being said, the prettier they were, the more tongue-tied you would become. Did you get stage fright and vomit on her, or whatever?"

"Again, thanks for that vote of confidence, bro. That stated—you forgot centerfold. You're warm on the 'vomit' part though."

"Man, with you it's always something? What are you talking about?"

Upon giving his account of Pamela finding him face down in a Benny's stall, Jim summed it up. "To think I always placed so much emphasis on building the courage to approach women with the right lines when all I needed to do to was pass out face first in my own puke—and with my pants down." Shaking his head in disbelief, he concluded. "Man the bad luck and shit—poor Pam. Talk about a Kodak moment."

Dave just shook his head with a slight grin. "Anyone else, I would call them a liar."

"You know, not to undermine the saintly favor Pamela did for me that fateful day, 'her uncommon valor' which I referred to it as, but when I first met her, she didn't look the way she does now." This raised Dave's eyebrow. "Oh, don't get me wrong. Yeah she was as cute as a button—yep, a sweet, anorexic young lady with a pizza face."

"Hey, just like you, back in the day."

"Yeah, though not as bad. I still have shades of pot marks to remind me of it. Pamela's on the other hand has the silk completion of an angel."

"So you would like to have the silk complexion of an angel?"

"I would at least like to have the opportunity, yes, but that'll never be the case, will it? Anyhow, this friend of mine was an internal physician and things changed in Eight-two when a great new drug came out. It cleared me up for good. Then I let myself be the guinea pig for the two of us, and it worked wonders on Pam as well. I got her to work out with me, got her on a healthy diet which put some meat on her bones, and next think you know I now have a wife who's way out of my league. Hey even now I still have trouble holding my load with her, doggy style."

"Well I would have been better informed with that last detail omitted, thank you. But whatever happened with Nancy if you don't mind me asking?"

Jim slowly shook his head in reflection. "You know, you go to sea cooped up in a sub with 130 men for what seems to be forever—and twice, keeping the Free World safe from the tyranny of Stalinism. Next, you find out that the woman you love is being bodysurfed by someone else."

"Oh, I'm not condoning what she did, but maybe it had been brewing for some time. Distances kill relationships, you know."

"At first I gave her that, but doing so was more of a case of shock or denial. Looking in retrospect, I guess its better that I found out afterwards versus beforehand. I mean I would have felt so helpless down there in that underwater capsule beating my head against a nearest bulkhead while picturing those two going at it. Distractions weren't an option down there, never mind that."

"Yeah, that would have been brutal."

"Well besides a few scary moments where I sometimes had no idea what was happening and playing cards, it was mostly boredom down there. My MOS didn't always offer enough mental stimulation to keep me occupied every moment."

"You and your cards by the way. You're a poker bully, you know—sorry, you were saying?"

"Well I eventually survived the seven seas with everyone's cash just to find out from a friend that she was screwing some intern. You see, it would have been nice having been able to buy Pamela a bigger diamond, but unfortunately before I met her, I pretty much ended up spending a good chunk of it to buy some ass instead—you know, prove I still had it."

"Bummer dude—of course you've never told Pamela this, right?"

"Oh, what woman doesn't want to hear something like that that? That ones following me to my grave."

"You just told me though."

"Let me reiterate—make that our grave then, brother. Should I elaborate?"

"No," Dave answered, grinning, "We're good. But just wondering, with all due respect to Pamela, how much ass did you end up buying anyhow?"

A slight grin was hinted in Jim's expression. "Enough to have secured a third slip on the marina, bro. As you know, I only have two."

"Bummer again—I think. I mean that's a lot of ass. I'm assuming you're taking that to the grave too."

"No, I'm planning on saving that one for our Silver Anniversary."

"Nice touch. I like it. By the way, did you ever see the guy?"

"Did once. Didn't do anything though. Looking back, he wasn't a bad looking dude. Can't blame her."

Dave eyes widened as if suddenly witnessing someone breaking into a neighbor's home. "Man bro, you were on that sub way too long. The man was screwing your squeeze while you were stuck down there protecting their sorry asses. I'm not saying you needed thrash the guy, although in my case he wouldn't have had any use of his jewels when I was done with him, that's for sure. I'm just saying you don't need to praise the chump—that's all."

"Maybe so, but looking at it in hindsight, it's her I blame, not him. Besides, I have Pamela. You know, the best revenge is living well."

"True. The man holding the champion's belt rarely dwells on the few whippings received prior to its acquisition. And Pamela's one a hell of a tradeoff besides. You came out of that one way ahead, that's for sure. I mean Nancy was definitely a looker, but Pamela— man, she's freaking off the charts. I'm proud of you man. You're the alpha male."

Jim grinned. "Thanks for the sentiment, but you're the alpha male. You know that. I on the other hand am just some unbelievably lucky male, and I'm fine with that. Besides, apparently in Nancy's case I hadn't much of a chance of anything long-term anyhow. She unwittingly did me a favor, you could say. Who knows? I probably would have done the same in his shoes. After all, she was a great piece of ass. You saw her naked."

Denigrating his previous girlfriend to no more than some cut of meat was the only credit Jim was willing to grant his ex-girlfriend. While no longer hurt from the experience, he was still bitter at the passive means she employed in breaking it off with him.

Dave gave console for the purpose of bolstering his friend. "Don't compare yourself to such a chump like him, man. You could have never stooped to his level—stealing a woman from her man while he was at sea. You're better than that."

Dave was sincere in his declaration and no less was Jim in his quick response. "Yo bro, what part of 'great piece of ass' didn't you understand? I lost a third slip over the chick, remember?"

<< CHAPTER 3 >>

IT WAS YET ANOTHER breathtaking, late summer September day and a perfect one for sailing as well. Such conditions weren't uncommon for the Sao Vincente tropical region. All necessary stowing for the Costa's transatlantic trip was complete and extra provisions were also added to the manifest in anticipated of the short trip ahead. It was the ninth anniversary of the Costas, and anticipation of its celebration was as prominent as the trade winds filling the air.

Of the many secluded beaches that Sao Vincente equipped a sun worshipper, the one chosen for the day of leisure was laden with only the minor flaw of a slightly gritty volcanic consistency. To accommodate, extra blankets were being carted along to afford some isolation from its less than perfect consistency. While there were other beaches more accessible by vehicle that were instead solely blanketed with a silkier coral cover, the Costa's agenda for the day ahead was to take their newly acquired sailboat on its maiden voyage together as a group.

The secluded beach chosen over others was a distance of less than four nautical miles travel by sea and it was selected with the understanding that the Costas were planning on setting voyage the following morning, so they didn't wish to venture any further than necessary away from Porto Grande.

With everything aboard and poised for takeoff, the women basking under a blazing sun were also able to enjoy a refreshing northern breeze brushing over their bodies. As they relaxed reclined in Gloria's spacious cockpit, Jim the meanwhile assisted Dave in the casting of docking lines. Soon with them all released and the sails minimized, Gloria's engine was fired up for the purpose of maneuvering clear of the marina.

Once beyond Porto Grande's few buoys, cutting of the engine left both Linda and Pamela's bodies still buzzing from its previous vibration. Sails now set, Gloria moved underway cutting its track into the north breeze in a zigzag pattern towards the open sea. Soon persuaded by sail alone versus the noisier means of internal combustion, the only sound remaining as an obstacle to any intended conversation were whitecaps of small swells continuously beating up against the underbelly of Gloria. While the sound they emitted may have been soothing to the soul, it didn't pose as any impedance to any attempted dialogue despite its added volume.

Along with an exchange of a high-five, the two men shouted in triumph. Then to the girls' amusement, Jim followed with, "anchor's aweigh!"

Dave was less than impressed with his corny outburst. He first glanced downward as if in disgust, and then up to his friend again.

"'Anchor's aweigh', Navy man? Go sit with the girls. You're not worthy of being near this helm."

"Damn! A skipper after my own heart—yes, sir!"

Linda stood, steadying her balance by shifting her weight in compensation of the boat's heeling. Heading below, she announced, "I almost forgot something."

Soon in returning with the stems of four champagne glasses clenched between the fingers and a bottle of champagne squeezed under arm, upon noticing their friend struggling to maintain her balance, both Woodsons quickly jumped in, in aid of the toasting items.

With the three soon seated together, glasses in hand, Gloria's sails needed adjusting again before any toast could be made. Seated at the helm and facing the other three, Dave couldn't resist but to interrupt his friend. There he was seated between the two girls with his arms outstretched behind them.

"Hey bro, I'd hate to reinstate you at a time like this, but it looks like you're enjoying yourself too much with the passengers there. The sails need to be swung again."

In playing the act of reluctance to amuse the girls, upon standing, Jim handed Pamela his champagne glass.

"Ladies, please keep my seat warm."

Amused by Jim's debonair attempt, Dave snickered, imagining jumping back at a time where had his friend been sandwiched between two attractive women looking the way their wives were, especially in their strings, he would have been stumbling over his words like a drunken skier attempting moguls.

"Don't take long sailor," Pamela insisting, then puckering.

As if nine years never passed, Linda still found herself at ease with Jim in an open forum of bodily exhibition. In their more boisterous days, the issue then from his standpoint would have been the incapacity of being able to handle his sexually charged friend. An awkwardness stemming from her being his best friend's significant other didn't help the cause either. While the two had never actually engaged in any relations with each other before mostly due to Jim's ability of being able to outmaneuver Linda, there was still a common thread of intimacy the two shared. It mostly fringed in similarity to that of a dominatrix and one of her submitted subjects. With every intention to render Jim humiliated before Dave, Linda canvassed Pamela's near naked body, and she did so while also ogling at her old friend. In keeping his attention, she added more torment by wetting the full perimeter of her lips in a seductive manner. "Yeah, we'll be waiting," she stated in a throaty whisper, adding, "Jimmy boy."

Linda's unexpected action of dallying took its toll on Jim who was facing everyone with his vulnerability being displayed by the evidence of involuntary activity apparent below. In turning away to perform his task in an attempt to hide it, the girl's giggling did little to afford him any reprieve or dignity. It included Dave who was on the brink of laughter.

"Man the bad luck and shit, bro—your cover's blown, dude!" Seconds later, he was in tears.

While it is possible for the pressure of performance to pose as a factor in an unexpected bout of impotence despite whatever strong desire one might feel at a giving moment, Jim instead experienced the opposite effect. His wish of bringing about a stint of temporary impotence in avoidance of embarrassment was only worsened by the pressure of the need to avoid it.

"Hey girls!" Dave shouted. "Can you please pour the boy his champagne? Looks like he could use some."

Contorting his upper torso in the voidance of exposing the invalidity of his façade being his present inability of being able to exercise control over his faculties, Jim went on the offence.

"Dave, you're over there taking cover behind the helm you chicken shit! Girls, give him a show and see what happens then!"

"Don't listen to him—only I give orders here!"

"Pussy!"

The two continued bantering each other, eventually breaking the air enough for Jim to be able to face forward again. Linda then shouted. "Okay guys, you asked!" As if cued by a director of some adult flick, she slid over to Pamela and slipped her arms around her before engaging in a steamy kiss there afterwards. Both men were stunned at the unfolding event. No less was their bewilderment in Pamela having reciprocated in kind, not missing a beat. From both of the men's standpoint, Pamela, who it seemed should have been taken aback by Linda's unexpected display of affection, made them believe their wives' unrestrained actions indicated more than that of just any playful act of teasing. To both men, her reaction wasn't representative of a shaky hand that had never fired a pistol before.

Like deer caught in headlights, the stunned men were frozen in watch of the unfolding events. Linda the meanwhile kept a blurry eye open in observance of their reactions. She took no issue to continuing her steamy display with a collaborating Pamela, and did so until it became apparent to her that their husbands were totally befuddled. Soon with them exchanging looks and shrugging their shoulders at each other, she backed off of Pamela. Considering their strong preference for such a fetish, what should have panned out as an arousing moment for both of them, instead played out as surreal, Jim no less.

As stunned by the sudden onset of their wives' behavior the men became, the two were as equally bewildered at how quickly their spouses stopped. Linda then quickly slid back to her original position where she wiped her lips with the back of her hand like some wild predator having just devoured a fresh kill.

"Hey guys! Are you hiding something now?"

Pamela giggled at her friend's baiting.

Left standing stupefied instead of having been able to embrace what should have been an arousing moment, Jim shook his head in disappointed of himself; there was no involuntary activity on his part to hide.

"Dave, did you see what I just saw?"

"If you sports lovers would like an instant replay, we'll gladly roll again," Linda interrupted, "right Pamela?"

With her friend responding in an affirmative nod, still fixated on her and eagerly awaiting more, together both men vociferated "no!"

"Do you want me running this thing aground?" Dave elaborated, then grinning at Linda. Can you please bring the champagne back to the fridge, honey? We don't need any orgies breaking out before we even get to the beach. It's our wedding anniversary, remember?"

Still without her sea legs, Linda straggled her way towards the companionway, champagne still corked and all. In her attempt to do so, every move she made was executed with the intent of teasing her husband. Meanwhile due to the movement of the boat, what might have otherwise come across as some erotic exhibition of lechery, instead simply played out as a comedy of missteps.

Both grinning and shaking his head at what just took place, Jim approached Pamela and kissed her.

"Damn!" He then looked Dave's way, shaking his head. "I guess I better get back to the sails before we end up grounded. And you keep that wife of yours under control as well. You're the skipper, so maintain order, sir!"

Dave just sat back grinning in contentedness.

"Well aside of Linda being the skipper of our marriage, I didn't see that coming either. You've got to love it though. I have a gut feeling this anniversary's going to out stand out from the rest, and the days still young—damn."

As the group settled in for the short trip ahead, the men were eventually able to concentrate on their efforts of sailing again. Beforehand, both women summoned their respective husbands to spread oil on them; everyone was well aware of the risk any mutual exchange between them stood to pose. In removing their tops within the relatively safe confines of Gloria's safety rails at its bow, the two women eventually dozed off. Meanwhile their husband's were seated by the helm. There, Jim nodded his approval from the cockpit, speaking softly to Dave." "Doesn't get any better than this, does it, bro?"

"Understatement. I mean our mostly nude, beautiful wives—the cliffs, simple existence with the elements, the sea air—damn." Dave paused for a moment. "Linda's in rare form. It's great to see her playful like this again."

"Do you think that kiss had anything behind it or were they just messing with us?"

"It's funny you should ask, because Linda hasn't had anything to drink yet. It's tough to tell though when it comes to women. They're so are much different from us guys when it comes to sex. I mean for us its simple math. Mutual attraction and nudity equates to sex, and you know Linda's an admitted bisexual. I've also gathered from our short stint here that Pamela's looks can be pretty provocative when she employs them."

"Oh, you just figured that one out, huh?"

"Well out of respect for you I've tried to ignore it—wiseass, but back to the girls. My guess is they might have some sort of soft spot for each other and they're just figuring it out—or haven't told us. The thing is this. I can size up almost any man in character, but still after all these years I sometimes still find myself out of sorts when it comes to figuring out what makes that woman tick."

"Yeah, seeing them over there reminds me of puppies."

"Mozart—puppies? This has to be good."

"Yeah, check it out. Right now they're over there looking all cuddly and peaceful, lying, napping, recharging. Then when they awake, all hell's likely to break loose again."

"You're right except about the cuddly part. My parent's dog had several litters and I don't remember ever wishing to pounce any puppy like I do with those two over there."

"Your fault—just needed to get to know them better. That's all."

"You know Jim that's messed up."

"What's messed up is you just admitted to wanting to pounce on Pamela. How could you even think that, Dave?" Jim played a perfect poker face.

Buying it, Dave took the defense in gesturing over to their wives. "Sorry bro, but look at those two over there."

Jim broke into a slight grin without speaking.

"You know you're an asshole," Dave asserted. Sitting quiet for a moment, he eventually conceded. "Okay, funny, you got me there."

"Funny yes, and your slipup was also a Freudian. Deny that and see if I buy it."

"Okay, whatever—granted. But let's get serious for a moment, okay? I just want to say that I don't think we have any control over what might happen later. It's as if I subconsciously set this whole thing up with the hopes of the risks—you know, the dangers. I mean it seemed intriguing at the time when we planned all this, but now it's all so real."

"Real's an understatement, bro."

"Agreed. What I'm getting at though is things could get heated up if my vibes about Linda are right, assuming she's not just toying with us. That stated, if you and I can both agree that we'll accept whatever happens later, I say let it fly. If you instead have any reservations about the risks we're assuming, just let me know. We'll head back—simple."

"Well thanks for your concern, bro. In those parties back in the day, outside of hangovers and spinning rooms afterwards, I never had any regrets—even running from Linda."

"Regrets? How could anyone not enjoy that, the latter that is? So should we reverse course or are you cool with all of this, especially considering what can possibly go down?"

"Damn straight I am. I could watch those two going at it all day."

"You mean like the two stunned losers that we were?"

"Bro, speak for yourself." Giving further thought, Jim retracted. "Yeah, you're right. But they did catch us off guard. We've got to at least give ourselves that."

"Granted, though try selling that to the old drinking buddies and see how that works out."

Jim agreed, and the two mostly remained quiet for the duration of the trip with the intent of just sitting back and enjoying the scenery.

In keeping Gloria to a more coastal route, the sea there offered a smoother rhythmic rolling motion versus a rougher ride stirring further away from land. In creating the soothing effects of both a sound machine and rocker, small breakers interacting with Gloria's underbelly inherently induced a similar type of hypnotic effect on their wives. It caused them to slip ever deeper into their sleeps. In the meantime, both men kept a keen eye on them to assure they didn't either roll overboard or atop each other.

The next hour of coastal sailing elapsed without incident. The provocative events of earlier were temporarily cloaked from the men's memories due to the distraction of a picturesque view of Sao Vicente's rugged northeastern terrain. Protruding out from land were numerous uprisings of jagged, stony inclines covered with a sparse mix of scattered vegetation.

Outside of matters connected with sailing, most dialogue for the balance of the trip was limited to small talk. Only Jim ventured briefly to a personal note. Gesturing to Dave, he pointed out Pamela peacefully lying prone on her towel.

"A lot is to be said about Pamela's unprecedented looks. They overshadow what that sweet woman's really about. I mean she's the type that if she somehow lost her footing—say on one of those bluffs over there (pointing), and then tumbled down one of those embankment of jagged edges resulting in permanent disfiguration of her face and body, she would still be the free spirit you've come to know the last few days."

"Hey, nice thought, buddy. You're almost as well spoken as Dick. You'd make the man proud." Dave took brief pleasure in Jim's show of disapproval of his comment. "Bro, don't worry, I know what you're saying. I can see that in her."

The two sat silent, staring at the landscape in reflection. "Hey, Dick's the man, yes?" Jim attested, breaking the silence again.

"Right you are, bro—right you are," Dave agreed, just leaning back and grinning in a pondering state of meditation.

In rounding a small peninsula, the final leg of their short voyage, a small, secluded beach there came into view. It was the mouth of an ancient volcanic river with its debris lying static, frozen in time. A terrain that appeared increasingly unstable leading to the summit of the volcano, in turn lessened in volatility swooping downward towards its base before eventually consisting of a finer beach cover nearing its shore.

In entering the natural harbor with the intent of anchoring there, the men brought their wives back from their apparent state of hibernation. Jim gently shook Pamela's shoulder, whereas Dave took a lesser subtle approach of forcefully striking Linda's backside. Quite familiar with but never used to his method of awaking her, wincing, she quickly turned to avoid a repeat of the other cheek.

"You're an asshole! You're really going to pay for that one!" Her reaction was a usual one he always aimed to elicit.

Appreciating the spectacle sound and all, Jim couldn't help but to feel Linda's pain. Almost believing the slap could be heard echoing back from the summit a mile away, he cringed. "Man the bad luck and shit—that had to have smarted!"

Looking towards her husband, Linda lashed back. "Jim, you tell your friend he better cool it with that shit or I'll stop doing squats! See what he thinks then!"

"Uh-oh, Dave, you're a third person now."

Linda then turned to Jim instead. "Oh, let's side with Dave and maybe he'll let me kiss his ass—pussy!"

"Wow, now Linda's got an identity crisis."

"You're the one with an identity crisis!" She retorted. "You're the asshole, asshole!"

Amused, Dave stepped in. "Can we get on with business? There's a lot to do here, you know." He then just shook his head in disbelief, grinning at the same time. "Damn, it's as if ten years had never passed with you two, I swear."

Jim conceded with a hint of sarcasm. "Sorry Linda, I still love you."

She then blew him a kiss laced with the same spirit.

Linda was fire and ice. Her being able to cool, quickly paved the way for the four adults to work as a team in the handling of the sails with the general mood aboard taking on a more businesslike air about it. Meanwhile, the dragging Gloria's anchor took longer than anticipated before it finally held ground, and while it doing so did cause some need for concern, Dave refused to spend the rest of his anniversary attempting a perfect grab.

Quick work was then made of unloading everything ashore. Once established, Jim pointed to the volcano summit.

"Just think, on the other side of there is our beloved village of Mindelo, yet we have all the privacy in the world here. Bad news is that the local new government doesn't condone any open display of lewd behavior, and it shouldn't. Every society old and new has the right not to be subjected to such a foul public display of indecent behavior."

The other three rolled their eyes as Jim continued. He then pointed towards their cooler. "Good news—beer, wine, champagne, and some hardcore hooch to enhance our celebration."

"Do we need to spend all day listening to your hole?" Linda objected.

"Patience my female friend. Okay girls—let's see what you're made of now, or can we all instead just start acting more like a group of responsible adults. That means you, Linda and Pamela."

In response, Jim was expecting a snicker or sarcastic comeback at most from his old friend. He guessed the activities to follow would likely consist of everyone pitching camp and making way for a casual get-together. Instead heeding his remarks as a dare, Linda intended otherwise. She approached Pamela.

"I've been playing to life's freaking conformities for nine years now! Conform this, guys!"

Without hesitation, the two girls tore each other's bathing suits off to the dismay of their husbands. With both men again left frozen and standing stupefied, they observed Linda tackle Pamela and moments later witnessed their wives rolling around completely naked. Totally taken aback at the sight of them locked in excessive petting, the men were then able to qualify their wives' actions as all-out sex, unlike earlier.

Snapped out of shock mode, it took Dave some effort in peeling Linda off of Pamela. While doing so, she fought him off like a crazed person engaged in a fight, only focused on their foe. When she finally calmed, Dave fetched a towel and draped her with it.

Having also aided in the separation, Jim covered Pamela with a towel as well. The two then settled on some twisted blankets where they snuggled up to each other.

A still defiant Linda objected. "Dave, I thought this was a fantasy of yours!"

"Damn straight it is," he responded, "and I have no freaking clue of why I just stopped you two. I think maybe it's because if you continued and we all got involved, we'd all soon be finished, and where to go from there? I mean we just got here. I do have to admit that I'm at a loss for words except—holy shit there girls!"

"I'll second that," Jim added, still slightly awestruck. "I love the fireworks, but there's not much to stick around for after the grand finale. That's my best guess." Kneeling next to his wife, he then embraced her from the side. "I'll tell you one thing though, that was one hell of an icebreaker, you two."

Pamela giggled at her husband's comment, turning to kiss him. This wasn't unfamiliar territory for them. "Dave, to answer our earlier question. I'm pretty sure that was the real deal this time."

Both grinning and agreeing, Dave released Linda to retrieve her bathing suit from an entangled mesh of blankets where his friends were seated, those still bearing the scars of the girl's outbreak.

In approaching Linda again, he handed her back her bathing suit. "I'm not going to ask you to put this back on, but here. Otherwise, if you instead want to prance around here naked all day, I'm sure no one will object."

With Jim adding, "no objections from this corner, bro," Linda mimicked another kiss at him, as she would often do post their many quarrels.

"You mean you're not going to run from me naked this time, you handsome devil?" She added.

Even in all his many present bouts of swinging, Jim was never confronted by any women as roguish as Linda, still able keep him off balance. "And you ran from me more than once—chicken ass."

Dave and Pamela joined in on the teasing. Jim was one who wore his vulnerability on his sleeve. For the sake of everyone's collective entertainment, he had an unselfish disposition of tolerance to align himself as the brunt of all jokes. Not only didn't he mind leaving himself prone to such taunting when certain its spirit was only banter, the meanwhile taking some pleasure in the attention he'd received from it, to a certain degree he thrived on it.

Still embracing him, Pamela jested. "Please stop picking on my baby. He's very sensitive."

Dave grinned in response before kissing Linda atop her head.

"Sweetheart, there's nothing we'd enjoyed more than seeing you two girls rolling in the sand the way you were." He then glanced over her shoulder towards the Woodsons. "I hope I'm not being too presumptuous, bro."

"I'm right in lockstep with you there, buddy."

"Good. Then can we at least settle down and have a brew. Maybe chuck some Frisbee—talk, whatever? This'll be the last time we'll get to hang out, and I want it to last."

A subtext provoked by his comment caused the others' faces to drop. Then in recognizing the other's subtle, disheartening change, Dave lifted the mood again. "—The last time that is, until next year."

Relief spilled over everyone upon hearing his addendum.

"I think it's quite apparent by now that normal social rules aren't applying here."

"Understatement, bro."

"Glad that you agreed. So could we at least try to regain a little normality—make this afternoon last?" Dave leaned his forehead against Linda's. "My honey and Pamela have twice tried to turn our ninth anniversary into the shooting of some skin flick. Girls, you want to exhibit? Be careful what you wish for."

"I'm confused bro, what are you talking about?"

Every eye was fixed as Dave lifted his jean bottom in access of a sheath strapped to his ankle that contained both a mariner's knife and marlinspike. In extracting the former from its casing, he then grabbed both pieces of Linda's bikini away from her. Everyone's curious eyes were glued to his next move as he severed all its strings, rendering both pieces unfit for wearing.

"Why did you just do that? I loved that bikini!"

In Jim gesturing, "bro, over here, buddy," Dave tossed his knife short of his friend's feet. With no objections from Pamela, he did the same.

"Maybe if you girls look at each other long enough, you'll grow some immunity to each other." he explained.

While understanding that his method was a risky approach to habituation, nonetheless a trashy approach of making his point, Dave was simply caught up in the moment. A presumption it was highly unlikely either Pavlov or the like of him ever had a naked Pamela standing before them while conducting their behavior experiments was irrelevant to him at that moment.

"Well then, why don't you guys bare it all?" Linda demanded, trying to ensnare Dave with same logic. "It always has to be us chicks doing the dirty work."

"Yeah guys, show us you're stuff!" Pamela shouted, agreeing emphatically.

"Sorry girls, and the 'dirty work?' I don't recall Jim and I being the ones who just tore each other's clothes off and tackled each other a minute ago—and your make out deal earlier. Besides, this is our anniversary. Can I at least be able to enjoy checking out my wife? Fair enough?"

Dave then locked eyes with her. "I mean I'm proud of how hard you've worked to look the way you do and even more so that you've grown back into old self again." This was followed by a kiss to the forehead. "I love you."

"Well thanks and I love you too, but don't try pulling the wool over my eyes. You'll be checking out Pamela too. I'm sorry, but look at her. That woman exemplifies the quintessential epitome of a sex goddess."

At that, Dave was highly intrigued at both the abandonment his wife was displaying in general and the conviction to which she just declared her attraction towards Pamela, especially in front of the others. He was also almost as impressed that she was able make such a statement without getting tongue-tied. The general behavior of the group the meanwhile was no anomaly to Jim, since his wife's usual effects on others was the primary reason the couple was so firmly embraced in every circle of the alternative subculture.

Jim panned his attention from his elated wife back to Dave again, breaking into a grin.

"Man the bad luck and shit." His comment was made in reference to the nostalgic feel of the moment related to their youthful days.

Soon afterwards and without interruption, the group set up a camp of two small tents and a fire pit. At first it took some effort for the men to be able to avoid the distraction of their spouses in doing so, but their goal of remaining on the beach throughout the day and evening by bringing nothing to a climax warranted the need of exercising some level of restraint.

Such an agenda posed most practical for Dave versus the others. Unlike in his more youthful days, he especially wasn't interested in spending such a significant day engaging in a marathon of carnal activities only for the sake of doing so. Subconsciously, he was also concerned about later regrets.

Linda eventually slipped on a long white tee shirt and wicker hat to prevent succumbing to the strong tropical sun. Pamela instead took advantage of it for augmenting the bronze tone of her olive complexion. Before the softening hues of dusk would prevent her from being able to do so, she wanted to exploit a full day of nude sunbathing with the hopes of eliminating any possible remnants of tan lines still remaining from previously worn bikinis that she reluctantly needed to wear prior on populated beaches.

Given the scarcity of firewood available on the island, only a few logs were carted along to enrich the camp's smothering charcoal with the soft emanated glow of a fire. Such was the case as the moon approaching its latter quarter stage was for the time being relinquishing its nighttime reign in the early evening hours to the thousands of pristine speckling stars stretching across the near panoramic celestial display.

As dusk fell, beer, the day's beverage of choice, eventually paved the way for shot glasses. With them carried in the consumption of gin, vodka, and tequila. To avoid affixation, the four adults were huddled together on a single blanket favoring the upwind side of the burning coals. They did so as the alcohol continued flowing freely and the evening progressed.

With the intoxicant flooding Linda's bloodstream and as a result negating any of the social buffers that she was previously able to exercise beforehand, disposing her white tee shirt into the fire at one point to aid in its combustion only reflected the slippage of any remaining social bearings on her part. Her next act of choosing to maintain possession of her straw hat while explaining it still provided some sense of modesty only furthermore reflected her decaying sense of judgment.

Even in the avoidance of focusing on Pamela, Dave still wasn't able to ignore the riveting sight her freely prancing about naked all day. In turn, while assuming no guilt in enabling Linda's pageantry of doing the same, his encouragement of her exhibition was intended merely for the purpose of good fun versus that of any sexually based agenda. There was genuine appreciation in being able to observe is wife feeling her oats about herself again.

In contrast, even in consideration of the parameters of their immodest setting, Dave was still uneasy about Jim's rational for Pamela doing the same. He was torn in the belief his good friend was courting her to have relations with him, thinking it wasn't the natural course to which such possible events should evolve, should they at all.

Rather then with any established friends with history, the few swingers Dave knew preferred mingling in such encounters with either strangers or exclusive acquaintances typifying the same interests. He therefore found the former unsettling, leading to his paradox.

It was becoming apparent to him that Pamela wasn't off limits, neither in the eyes of Linda nor Jim's if his premonitions were correct. It was the perceived spirit behind everyone's intents that was increasingly making him uneasy. It led to his paradox.

With nightfall's onset and the trace of all decency having faded with the sun, the stakes were no longer just some figment of reflection on Dave's part. His paradox was the need to deny himself the option of giving into Pamela while the others in turn would likely raise no objection to him being with her. It was therefore clear to him that the only fine line standing to keep him at bay was his resolve. Making matters worse, it needed to be maintained in the face of either offending or embarrassing Pamela, her the meanwhile possibly misinterpreting the intentions of his inaction. There laid the dilemma Dave faced.

Any prior strategy was rendered futile with the waning of daylight. Earlier, Dave was able to downplay the other's goading in the hope they might eventually relent, whereas later he was faced with the reality that playing a passive role was no longer a luxury. Instead of wondering how his wife should be courted into some celebrated lovemaking on their nine-year anniversary, he now foresaw the likelihood that at some juncture he might need to refuse the advances of his beautiful friend. It came with the understanding that Pamela would likely render his already compromised convictions impotent at any moment by simply approaching him au natural. It was a look to which he never became acclimated, once believing otherwise.

Aided by the catalyst of hard liquor, the fervor of the group eventually reached a fever pitch. Meanwhile Dave's mind was still racing with ways of being able to tactfully reject Pamela. He was wondering how to do so without either appearing unmanly in front of Jim, or oddly the same with Linda.

Muddling in the torment of moral indecisiveness with the spice of the evening's dialogue growing ever hotter, Dave finally relented.

He chose instead to openly participate with the others but only for the time being. Taking it a step further, he disrobed in front of the others to full nudity and raised his shot glass filled with tequila. Then with his free hand, he tossed his clothes into the fire.

"Here's to the cover of darkness, who needs those? Come on, surf's waiting!"

Dave was at first silhouetted from behind by the camp's bright lantern, not enough of a deterrent to prevent the woman from attempting to canvass his body. He quickly swigged his drink and headed towards the water, soon fading from the other's sights.

Meanwhile with Linda and Pamela both exchanging raised eyebrows, Jim instead verbalized his own approval. "Man the bad luck an shit—that was awesome. Didn't know the boy still had it in him."

As if defying gravity, he catapulted from his blanket, disrobed, and reached for the hands of both women. In assisting them from their seated positions, the three then headed towards the water with Jim leading, their hands adjoined.

Such an unexpected action by Dave was part of an impromptu plan devised through the filter of alcohol manipulation, there viewed as some foolproof tactic. His ill-thought-out plan was to let loose with the others and in there doing perpetuate whatever dilemma he believed was inevitable to arise. Guessing it would then be simpler to deal decisively with it while still intact with his faculties, he also believed giving in stood to serve everyone's best interests by not bringing down the general mood of the group. His dual-purpose plan conceived under the influence of impaired judgment led to overlooking a simple reality. When it came to pushing the right buttons, Pamela's was masterful at applying the right touch when it came to cajoling.

The only available light being a bright glow emanating from the camp's hissing propane lamp was revealing both the toppling crests of small breakers washing ashore and the glimmering contours of everyone's wet bodies. With the group of four engaged in the bold horseplay of bodies being tossed about, both individually and in group efforts, Dave was still able to avoid getting too close to Pamela. For him, employment of lesser evasive straight-arm tosses was allowing the moment to be enjoyed without reservation.

In the confusion of everyone's indiscriminate grabbing of each other whereby nobody was paying any mind to either their own modesty or that of that of the other's, matters suddenly took a turn towards the unexpected for Dave. It seemed for him to strike like some unexpected flash of lightening as he was standing waist deep in the restless water gazing towards the camp for a moment. In hearing Linda belt out, "Down yer go bitch," he was unaware that right afterwards Jim had grabbed his wife and threw her over his shoulder. It in turn left Pamela alone, still on the attack.

Based on her voice's previous trajectory, Dave quickly turned and lunged forward blindly to where he guessed Linda should have been. Seconds later, he stood frozen in time, locked in a sultry full body embrace with a soaked and wanting Pamela.

In the chaos of the noise and darkness, he still believed it was his wife melded against him. As a result, Dave made no effort in containing a physiological reflex of appreciation cropped up against both Pamela's soaked body and his own. With everything still racing around like a debauched whirlwind, she then slid her hands up his upper back until fully gripping the back of his shoulders. The two were left waist deep in water with Pamela's legs wrapped tightly around Dave's lower torso in full support of her weight.

With passion propelling the two of them into a frenzy, Pamela initiated a devouring kiss in the midst of a miscalculated train of events that seemed to be unfolding in a blink of an eye. In reaction, it left Dave beside himself when he ran his hands through what should have been Linda's long wet hair. Pamela hairstyle was that of a buzzed nape-trim—short hair. With his fingers failing to grasp an anticipated handful of any hair, anyone less principled than him might have just tossed in a white towel at such a moment. They would have been unable to foresee the repercussions of doing so through a blazing stare of Pamela.

Dave gave a quick glance ashore and then back again just to find himself caught in the beams of Pamela's bedroom eyes radiating into his. No sudden cough stood to help his cause this time. If there was ever a worst-case scenario that he could have ever imagined beforehand, presently leaving him subjugated to extreme feelings of lasciviousness stirring inside and furthermore stretching the bands of his normally unwavering scruples to their failing points, then those short few seconds in which both his and Pamela's bodies were locked together as one exceeded any previous notion that he could have ever been able to fathom there prior. Embracing an obsequious wet and naked Pamela against his like self left no such notion in doubt.

Dave was helplessly caught in the riptide of his new friend, his mind racing. Alcohol had already eradicated what little trace of resolve he was previously able to keep at bay. The notion it was futile to resist Pamela's unyielding currents any longer was quite apparent to him. Countering such an idea was the belief that engaging in sanctioned copulation with his best friend's wife wasn't an option either. Dave's devotion to Linda was no less of a consideration either. This left the two opposing forces of his paradox struggling for dominance.

Still unaware Pamela would only meet any meager objection with both compellingly verbal and aggressive physical persuasion, his only exit strategy to a desperate predicament bordering a sloppy exit at best became clear in its potential for success. It arose in surmising the best way of escaping a riptide is by riding one out. He just needed to figure a way of making it pertinent to his cause.

On the brink of surrendering, Dave's cause wasn't helped any when the beautiful woman, one who he had held in such high esteem since meeting her and even referred to her as a saint several times, stared directly into his eyes with an intensity seeming a thousands suns.

"Let's fuck," she insisted with a voice of an angel.

It was at that defining moment the weight of his paradox shifted across its fulcrum. In persuading Pamela's wet body off of his, which in itself required both invasive and incidental probing whereby no objection was sounded, Dave then grabbed Pamela's hand.

"Honey, let's go to the fire."

Filled with joy while eagerly following him to a dwindling campfire, Pamela did so in the hopes of soon sharing her strongest craving with a man to whom she had become so enthralled over the previous several hours. Grinning, Jim the meantime checked out the two from the water while grabbing Linda's arm.

"Looks like you met you match, bro!"

Unfazed and becoming increasingly belligerent, Linda also took notice of the two. She did so, yanking Jim's hand off of her arm.

"Don't think this means I'm gonna fuck you, you bastard!"

"No no Linda, I don't want to have sex with you!"

"Whatta you mean you don't want me—to do me?" she slurred, adding, "yer think cause your wife's so beauriful, I'm not good 'nough fur you?"

"No, that's not what I meant. I think you're hot as hell, Linda." Jim declared in defense, attempting to appease his friend's shifting moods the meanwhile.

Then, in displaying an array of spasmodic gyrations of her upper body, she approached her old friend in a pathetic attempt to tease. With Linda's advance appearing comical to Jim in spite of her impressive figure, in scrutinizing her approach and fearing bodily harm in the process, he protected his privates while laboring to contain his amusement. Then in the same way Pamela had latched onto Dave, Linda did the same to a rigid body of Jim. It in turned triggered many discomforting thoughts and feelings to overcome him. They ranged from unavoidable arousal to the confusion of Linda's unification with his friend. A more imminent fear of impending harm was no less a concern either.

"Dave's gonna kick yer ass when he sees us, so let's do it anyhow," she taunted him, grinning deviously in the process just prior to probing his ear with her tongue.

As if a decade never passed, such a recurring moment prompted Jim once again the need to elude his inebriated friend by slipping away from her. He then coaxed her towards the safety of land, just keeping ahead of her. Although their means lacked the modesty normally associated with the term, to that point both men had tried their best in maintaining some level of chivalry.

Unaware such a disruption would have been a remedy to his friend's cause, Jim diverted his dealings with Linda away from the makeshift camp. He wanted to offer the other two their full privacy.

Meanwhile seated toe-to-toe with Pamela who was brimming in sexuality, and no less still naked like himself, a barely resolute Dave continued digging through his creative archives in search of any action that might release him from her. Feeling the fingers of her will drawing him closer like the increasing currents at a waterfall's edge, he recognized any ability to fight it any longer would be a lost cause on his part. It in turn triggered an empty bottle of vodka lying nearby to catch his attention, prompting him to then approach their cooler and to retrieve an unopened bottle of tequila instead.

A notion that little could compared to the raw gratification of anyone wishing to impose their will on a receptive Pamela, ready to please them in turn, would have made it a stretch to state Dave's preference for tequila could replace the wonders of which she was both willing and capable of journeying him. Fortunately for Dave, such truth was irrelevant to the latent success of his last-ditch, precipitous plan.

"Do you like tequila?" he asked, further milking the moment.

"Oh yeah," Pamela replied in a submissive tone. By then, she would have been willing to follow Dave overboard, mid-ocean.

"I was saving this for later, but I guess you are my later. This is the good stuff." He handed her the bottle, now opened. "You first, but be careful, this is the 150-proof stuff. It'll knock your socks off."

Pamela took a swig, whereby afterwards it didn't require any breathalyzer to determine when the drink was entering her system.

Her body became flush as she wiped her mouth, her eyes still widened. "Wow!" She then paused for a moment as a sensation of warmth overtook the rest of her body. "Dave, I want you so bad, it hurts." Pamela then smiled. "You next."

Dave then grabbed the half-liter of potent tequila, less one swig. "Sweetheart, please forgive me for what I'm about to do." He then shrugged his shoulders in defeat. "I simply can't resist you any longer. You got me."

A feverishly horny Pamela was seated toe-to-toe with him again. Her sand coated feet were crossed, hands placed on opposite knees. She was also fixed in an unwavering stare down with her new friend, almost hyperventilating. "I'm sure forgiving you will be the last thing I'll need to do, honey. Bring it on, already."

With a smitten Pamela following the tequila make its way to Dave's mouth, her expression then changed from that of an extreme wantonness to one of total disillusion. There she just sat helplessly bewildered in witnessing his full consumption of the balance of his favorite spirit in its entirety. Although not a true demonstration of restraint, it did work. It was a price that he felt inclined to pay for averting the repercussions of his earlier indiscretions, led to the moment.

Following, Pamela just helplessly watched her former subject slip away until he lied still on their blanket. Then after only a brief moment of confusion, perplexity gave way to joy. It occurred in becoming clear to her what was truly behind Dave's actions.

Grabbing a large towel lying nearby, she draped him with it before then checking his breathing. Gently stroking the side of his head, she whispered in his ear. "You can die from that you silly, but I know what you did, and I love you for it. I would have taken you to heaven and asked nothing in return, except your pleasure. Instead when you wake up, you'll probably really feel like shit."

"Sweet dreams, baby," she whispered, kissing his forehead. Next in doing so elsewhere out of curiosity, nothing happened. This left Pamela confident that her new friend was gone for the night.

Meanwhile with the other two still playing out a familiar scene reminiscent of years back, Jim glanced back towards their small camp to be taken aback at the puzzling sight of Pamela standing over Dave's still body. This prompted him to sprint towards them with Linda playing catch-up, straggling behind and yelling.

"Where the fuck you goin, bitch?"

"He's okay honey," Pamela explained, recognizing her husband's startled expression. "Just passed out—I'll tell you about it later."

"That bitch killed my Davy," Linda charged, hysterical and just approaching, "Now I'm a fuckin widow, yer asshole princess!" she insisted

Pamela and Jim exchanged smiles. "He's not dead sweetie, just passed out."

To Jim's bewilderment, Pamela summarized what took place leading to the moment. He in turn found it difficult fathoming anyone would have purposely avoided having sex with his wife. It was in ignorance to his friend's issue of being encouraged to pair up with her earlier. Jim had misinterpreted his intent of going along with the spicy carousing just to pacify the spirit of the moment. As a result, Dave ended up paying the price for having ridden Pamela's wave for too long.

Later with Linda lying on her side and passed out next to them, Jim just grinned. "It doesn't get any better than this, huh Pam? That's all I have to say."

"I had fun, though obviously I didn't get lucky with Dave. Did you get a chance to enjoy a taste of Linda's fine ass, honey?"

Jim grinned in disbelief. "No, some things never change. At least I can look at Dave in the face tomorrow without feeling like shit. Apparently we made the mistake of assuming our good friends were like us."

"You know maybe back in the day based on what you've told me, but their devoted parents now. Do you want me to take care of you? I'm all primed up, thanks to Dave."

"Baby, I'm one step from feeling like Linda. Otherwise I would have been all over you by now. I'll take a rain check if it's okay."

"Shit! Two beefcakes, and I got nothing other then kissing Dave, you know where. That was after he was passed out."

"Man the bad luck and shit for him." Jim chuckled. "My boy didn't know what the hell he was missing. We'll make up for lost time tomorrow. How's that?"

Giving witness to some degree of coherency, the soft undertone of Linda's calmer voice rang out from beneath a blanket draped over her.

"I heard you two by the way. Your cover's blown, guys."

In spite of an abandonment reflected by the group's behavior over the previous several hours, both Jim and Pamela were no less discomforted by the way their secret was just exposed. "What was that, Linda?" Jim asked, hoping he heard otherwise.

"You heard me right. And I'm telling Dave if he hasn't figured it out already. And Pam, I'm also letting him know what he missed with you as well. Oh, by the way—sorry about the bitch-princess comment. I still love you, sweetie."

Jim jumped in. "You're not really going to say anything to Dave, are you?"

"He's my husband. What do you think?" Linda lay silent for a moment before finally adding. "But I'll wait until we're underway. It'll break up some of the monotony that way. Now I just need to clam up and recover. Shit tomorrow's going to be a really long day."

Jim rose and headed towards a nearest tent. "Well at that—night, Pamela—night, Linda—unless Dave's got something to say."

A slight pause elicited no response.

"Night, Dave. I hope you're okay tomorrow, bro. Hell of a night, huh girls?"

"Just like old times, chicken ass," Linda's voice rang out.

Amused by her friend's comment, Pamela then reassured her husband. "Sweetie, looks like you're about to drop. Go inside and I'll make sure these two are okay. I'm thinking of fixing me and Linda some tea."

"I threw more charcoal on the fire. Looks like it took. And please do keep an eye on my boy. I'm worried about him. Night, girls." As Jim headed towards a nearest tent, he shook his in disbelief. "Holy shit, bro—a half a liter of 150-tequila—good luck tomorrow, dude."

An hour after sunrise, the sunlit side of Jim's tent was flapping without relent against a constant sea breeze spilling in from the small secluded harbor. From the senseless imagery of a dream to the desolateness of his tent's flailing canvas, its empty tone was reigning in a sad reality for Jim that within the next few hours he would soon need to bid farewell to the Costa family. It was such a sad finale, especially giving the previous few days resulted in the reestablishing of an old bond.

Further deepening Jim's regret was in the supposition that the transatlantic crossing of his friends carried with it the possibility of perilous consequences. Puzzling him furthermore in awaking was the realization that it wasn't Pamela snoring next to him, but was instead Dave. Unable to remember how he ended up being there while for a disorientating moment struggling with no success to scrape up some recollection of the previous several hours, Jim spent the next few moments deciphering his surroundings while also hatching possibilities in a triage of worst-case scenarios.

"Man bro, glad you weren't spooning me," he uttered, still unable to remember anything.

Jim then exited his tent to visit the girls. In doing so, the cooler outside air provided some relief for a mild hangover at the same time the rest of his exposed body took notice of a brisk, sustained sea breeze. In lifting a partially unzipped flap and peering inside to account for both women, his relief was soon segued into rapture. Behold his eyes was the sight of Pamela spooning Linda.

In addition to laboring to make some sense of the events leading to the moment, Jim was also struggling to pinpoint what was haunting him. Meanwhile in correctly surmising both Pamela and Linda were likely still naked beneath their sleeping bag, he contemplated waking them for the sake of a cheap thrill. He figured doing so would still be justified under the spirit of the previous night's festivities. While his assumption the girls might welcome such an intrusion wasn't unfounded, a blast of adrenaline suddenly shot through his veins. Aside from their dinghy pulled ashore, the natural harbor was empty, void of any signs of Gloria.

Jim knew his only recourse was to wake Dave, who was neither a morning person nor someone who would relish the news that his boat with a market value of $150,000 was missing. If missing Gloria wasn't enough of an issue for the group to be face with, subsequent to waking his friend, an increasing volume of an approaching vessel could be heard, still a distance away.

With it not in sight yet, Jim didn't hesitate in waking Dave. In groaning his way back to consciousness as a result of a stifling hangover, he covered his head with a pillow in the avoidance of sunlight. His demeanor quickly changed when the troubling words "the boat's gone" rang into his ears. Then as if suddenly possessed by an entity, Dave spun his head by the same shot of adrenaline that also caused his debilitated eyelids to shoot open.

"How are we going to get everything back to Gloria? I want to set off by early afternoon, and this isn't a setback we need!"

"Bro, Gloria's gone, not the dinghy!"

Within the short timetable of Jim summoning his friend and the two exiting the tent, a large powerboat approaching the harbor had already come into full view. While it appeared to Jim as some prowling adversary readying for an invasion, for Dave, he viewed the boat's debut as an array of hope. He first then leaned over momentarily as a wave of nausea began overtaking him before then standing straight again, sighing.

"Whew! That was close, but I think I'm okay, at least for now. This freaking head though—Jim, we need to go and meet these people. Maybe they saw Gloria."

"Like this? Apparently total public nudity doesn't bother you. And besides, the two of us here standing alone naked like this is gay, even for me."

"Oh, big whoop. There's more pressing issues here if you haven't noticed. I mean I've sailed my seventy thousand dollar investment no more than five miles since owning it, and I've already lost the freaking thing. My head also feels like it's going to pull a *Scanners* [1981 horror movie] at any moment." Quiet for a moment, he then turned back to his friend. "What did you mean 'gay, even for me?'"

"What I meant is we need at least one of the chicks over here to validate us like this. I also don't feel too confrontation this way either. What if they have guns?"

"You know the Celts used to enter battle in the buff to freak out their enemies. In fact, doing so often terrified their opponents into submission. What do you think about that?"

"What's this, freaking *Trivial Pursuit* time? And I'd also venture to guess they didn't have to worry about guns back then either, did they? In addition, I'd also wager they weren't standing alone on the beach like this either, do you?"

Half ignoring Jim in his fixation of the boat, Dave pointed out activity aboard it as it slowed its approach in entering the nature harbor. Viewing nothing indicating any signs of malice, he first addressed Jim's last comment. "No, probably not. But look, they're coming to meet us, and it's not some freaking beach invasion, okay? Just relax, man. I'll grab a towel by the fire pit, and I'm sure you can find something inside the tent."

The two friends were soon both together outside again with Jim having employed a pillowcase and Dave a towel, the two items secured to their waists by means of a crude knot. Taking solace in the hope the visitors might know the whereabouts of Gloria, Dave took notice of Jim clenching a baseball size stone. He laughed. "What do you plan on doing with that if they happen to have guns?"

"You can never play it too safe, buddy. I also have sand in my other hand."

Feeling optimistic about the future, a lighter Dave held out both arms in submission, facing him. "What are you so worried about? *(British accent) Cor Blimey, mate. Donned like this, we're ready for any encounter.* (His regular voice) Hey, how about checking to make sure that the girls are okay? In fact, stay in there. It's my boat. I'll meet these guys. The last thing I need now is bending over with this freaking hangover. I'll probably end up puking all over the girl's tent. I'm sure that would be a sight to behold from inside."

Jim didn't need any more convincing. He quickly raced over to join their wives. In watching, Dave just placed his fingertips on his forehead, half in pain, half-amused.

"My badass friend," he uttered, shaking his head. "It's always a comfort knowing you have my back there, buddy. You'd make the most noble of samurai warrior proud."

In approaching the two men exiting from their rowboat and

recognizing one of them, Dave quickened his pace. "Dave! I'm so happy it's you. I think you're missing a boat. It was adrift, but we secured it just around the bend."

Able to ignore his hangover for a moment and still approaching, Dave celebrated. "Pastor John, what a sight for sore eyes! Sorry about my appearance!"

"That's not important. We just need to reunite you with your boat again. If you need some clothing, I'll go back and fetch some for you—and for your wife too if she needs some. Please forgive me if I appear curt on the matter. Nothing personal. Three of our youths are there now overseeing your boat. They're at a very impressionable age, you know? I'm not being judgmental, just protecting them. Please understand that."

The pastor could have shot accusations of condemnation at Dave threatening brimstone and fire, and it still wouldn't have lessened any of his euphoria. In also taking slight notice to a second tent erected, the clergyman preferred not reading any further into it.

Concurrent to the men's cordial interaction taking place ashore, back in a more serene location of girl's tent, the need of the Pastor and Dave to converse over the sounds of an active surf caused Jim to misinterpret their elevated voices as possible confrontation. Meanwhile the girls having no incline to the goings on outside instead found amusement in teasing him with some racy flirtation.

"Ladies, any other time or place I'd tear this tent up with you, but Dave needs me outside."

In his exit, both Linda and Pamela shared looks of teaming conspirators, shouting, "Jim!" repeatedly in unison. Still in the buff, they both began following him out. Then, just as Jim was mostly exited, Linda got a hold of his feebly secured pillowcase and yanked it off of him.

"I'll show you tear up baby! Now come back in here and show us what you meant by that. It's about time you and I close the deal after all these years." She meant it.

"Yeah Romeo—that's if you can handle the two of us chicks!" Pamela shouted, adding, "or maybe I'll just watch instead!"

Totally aroused by both their comments, Jim entered a state of paralysis in seeing the three men ashore, two whom he recognized as Dave and his pastor. In turning back to reenter the tent, the two girls still naïve to events unfolding outside blocked his escape inward. Then in slipping out themselves, they began fondling him in clear view of the shore.

Dave couldn't believe his eyes in witness of the X-rated spectacle of the three playing out before him. "Oh my God," he muttered in a soft undertone, then even quieter, adding, "bro, you are so screwed, you poor bastard."

Apologizing just prior to succumbing to hysteria, Dave's doing so prompted Pastor John and his fellow brother to commence their exit. In facing away, the pastor shouted in a formal businesslike manner. "Like I said, we'll be back in a bit!"

As the two hurried off as if to avoid the wrath of God soon raining down, Dave broke his laughter. "Man the bad luck and shit for you Jim, but that was freaking priceless."

The pastor made good on his word, eventually returning with clothing in assurance that the modesty of his flock would no longer be in question. Had it been either couple stranded alone on the beach naked, he would have overlooked it, respecting their marital rite of expression on the secluded beach as a celebration of their shared passion. Such wasn't the case though. Viewing Jim being groped just outside their tent in an entangled exhibition of lechery made such a notion quite clear to him. Meanwhile Dave's lack of objection to his wife's willing participation in act wasn't any less a contributing factor either.

Although Dave may have found the whole scene highly amusing, the Woodsons in turn knew the shaky fence on which they had been lingering to appease their pastor was just shaken violently. It was at that moment they also understood their relationship with him was about to take on a new face.

During the actual clothing transaction, Jim and the two girls retreated back to different tents while Dave finalized the exchange. Upon dressing, he joined the pastor in returning back to Gloria while the other's cleaned and broke down camp.

For Dave, the trip to his boat accompanied by the two clergymen was both long and quiet. With its silence only being broken by his intermittent violent bouts of puking over the side of the dinghy, his doing so rendered nothing in cause for improving the report of the three men.

In their return to the small town of Mindelo, both choppy seas and hangovers equated to seasickness for the Costa couple, who drank the heaviest of the four adults, especially Dave in having capped his day's consumption off with his heavy binge. While both Jim and Pamela may have been faring better than their friends physically, they in turn had other colossal concerns to contemplate pertaining to their pastor.

What was supposed to be a noon launch for the Costa family upon arrival in Porto Grande was postponed to the following day. Meanwhile, while a private consensus might have led everyone to understand that someday they might all be able to look back at the previous twenty-four hours and would be able to laugh about it, for the time being, nobody was in any shape to be doing any laughing.

<< CHAPTER 4 >>

THE NEXT AFTERNOON, September 4, a Thursday, tears were spilling down Pamela's face like rain over a windshield. With her emotional torrent showing no signs of relent, little David asked from the grips of her arms, "Why you cwying?"

Too distraught to respond, Jim came to her rescue, taking the little boy into his arms.

"Buddy, Pamela's always cries when she loves kids as much as she loves you and your sister."

With his gesture being reciprocated by way of an affectionate squeeze to the shoulder, Jim, who was able to outwardly contain his own gloomy spirits in limiting their effects to watery eyes and a burning fixed lump lodged in the throat was no less overwhelmed by emotion than his wife.

Dave and Linda were meanwhile preoccupied. Both understood that anything overlooked could potentially leave them all prone to catastrophic implications down the line. Figuring there'd be plenty of time to grieve later, Linda's ability to maintain any composure was far more fragile than that of her husband's. She was on the verge of tears the whole time.

A belated departure was also bringing the Woodsons ever closer to the brink of a looming Sunday. They recognized their pastor would likely focus his rescue on their souls in having allowed two of his straying sheep to venture so far from the flock for too long.

An extreme binge of tequila two nights prior coupled with both underlying feelings of melancholy and concerns for their trip was still taking its toll on Dave. It was rendering him off and as a result ornery with a slight onset of added depression being no less of a contributing factor to his negative state. Only setting sail stood to subdue any of the negative effects of his present condition.

As for Jim, the day's takeoff was especially provoking some deep emotions. He once again needed to let go of two important threads from his past that were just woven back into his life again. In anticipation of a void likely to be engendered from their departure, he was also sober to the ominous undertaking laid before the family, especially in the case of their two children.

As a result of regret in seeing his friends leave coupled with haunting premonitions of impending dangers lying before the family, in gazing from the mooring towards the ocean behind them, Jim began feeling the teeth of time's passage lessening any probability of making any definitive appeal to dissuade his friend from taking his kids along. An unfathomable scenario of the Costa family perishing at sea left him standing helplessly numb. There he viewed them as ill-fated souls scrambling about their activities, similar to viewing some old grainy home movie—an only vestige representing a family's memories playing out before him. Refusing to take any refuge in the cover of procrastination any longer, he couldn't help but to summon Dave for discussion a short distance away from the others. A direct approach versus trivial persuasion like he had tried a few days earlier was the only viable means he concluded was left in convincing his friend not to circumnavigate the Verde Islands prior to heading north.

"What part of December's the best time to catch the winds up north?" he asked, first taking a lesser direct approach while also searching for a way of segueing into his concerns.

Jim was getting further frustrated in wondering how to bring his concerns to the forefront without either alarming or roiling his friend. Worse, concerned about perhaps infusing hard feelings with no time to reconcile, his torment of vacillation soon hit a wall in hearing Dave's new intended course. It arose in his omission of heading north altogether and instead sailing due west upon first visiting the Verde Islands.

Similar to a wild animal suddenly being cornered, Jim's attitude quickly changed. He no longer felt the need to tap dance around his concerns any longer. Now feeling the urgency of offering a caveat to Dave's new intended course, his underlining worry for the children far exceeded any desire to appease him any longer.

"Dave, we need to discuss an important matter by the shore, away from the others, please."

Meanwhile the women were too involved with each other and the kids to pay their husbands any mind.

Prepared to take a stance, Jim felt some relief in finally having ended the inaction of silence. Now near the shore and without yet sensing his friend's degree of disapproval, Dave spoke first.

"Before you start, please know that we can't begin to thank you and Pamela enough for your hospitality."

A forced grin, his cerebral wheels burning rubber, Jim continued feeling his friend out.

"Well as long as you're still around these islands, you'll be within the range of my two-way. You'll also have that capability on Gloria's shortwave for transmission, but you'll need luck getting a hold of me there. Before leaving these islands, I want you reconsider our offer."

Feeling his last chances slipping away, Jim was frustrated about still taking a passive approach. Noticing Dave growing antsy, he glanced towards Gloria in observance of Heather and David's little bodies both standing innocently, there reminding him of why he insisted his friend venture away from the others to speak in the first place. Pleasantries aside and well aware of how obstinate his friend could be at times, Jim insisted that Dave follow him to a nearby side street where some old Portuguese structures would screen any anticipated heated discussion from the others. Slightly bewildered, Dave reluctantly obliged. His body language showed it. Although still listening, he stood both fidgety and distracted.

"Bro, I'm no expert on navigation, but I can tell you that heading west now isn't a good idea."

Still in a bit of a funk being a residual leftover of a hangover, Dave's sometimes-quirky propensity reared its ugly face. Although normally levelheaded, he was at times prone to defy reason once his mind was set. Believing both Linda's and his portfolios were sufficient to their undertaken, exception was therefore taken to his friend's questioning of both their abilities and judgment.

"That's right you're no navigator, or sailor! You're also out of line for pulling me aside like this and questioning our course. That's our business, not yours!"

"First off if you're going to be condescending, then you better know what the hell you're talking about." Ignoring an interruption by Dave, he continued. "Listen! I've also served aboard a naval destroyer on the open sea, so don't give me any crap about me being no sailor. I've seen more of the open ocean above and below than you will ever in a lifetime, so don't delude yourself with some pretentious notion you're some expert sailor and I'm just some yokel on the subject. I've seen waves that would fucking swallow your damn Gloria. You're fucking crazy for taking Heather and David along with you during this stormy season."

"Okay, big whoop. You sailed on some big ass, state of the art Navy vessel. Smaller boats react much differently than those larger ones—like that damn frigate of yours."

"You mean like getting crushed beyond recognition?"

Dave paused in having gotten caught off guard.

"So what to you expect me to do, just hang out?"

"Bingo!"

"No way. I appreciate the offer and I know you mean well, even though you're way out of line here."

"You might say that I'm out of line for challenging you as a non-parent, but I say you're out of line for taking your two young kids along with you, especially during freaking hurricane season. You're supposed to protect them from such poor judgment, not throw them in the middle of some potential goddamn quagmire as a result."

"Your basis is postulate, so don't start giving me any lessons about my kids unless you really want to start pissing me off."

"Hey! If the ocean has its way, that'll be irrelevant—*postulate* or not. I'm serious. I'll walk to the damn bank now and give you back every cent you've paid me so I can then wash my hands of this one. I'm sure Pamela would concur too."

"No way, you earned that money—I won't take it back."

"Well then I'll wipe my ass with it instead, because it's blood money to me now. Bro, please don't head west yet. Stay with us. If you do go, at least leave the kids with us. I'll fly back with them personally and meet you guys later."

In making his way back to Gloria with Jim still insisting, Dave stopped and turned to him, his index finger pointed.

"Were going back now and pretend none of this happened. I don't want to hear another damn word on the subject, got it?"

"Sure, but I just need to ask you one question first."

"What is it?" Dave snapped.

Jim's voice calmed. "God forgive me for even implying this. But say Gloria's getting shredded up by either some intense tropical storm or maybe a hurricane like Elena, which essentially took the same path you're taking, will you be able to guarantee Heather and David's safety then?"

Dave hesitated for a moment. "Are you finished?"

"By your lack of response, I would say yes. My mind's spoken and I stand by everything I said—though I don't feel any better for it. Thanks for introducing me to your kids, because this shit is really ripping me to pieces."

Crushed, Jim gazed downward and concluded. "I have nothing else to add—and may God help me if I'm right."

The two then made their way back over to the boat with the understanding of masking their differences for the sake of the others.

With everything accounted for and all tanks topped off, Dave felt that the only item preventing them from launching were bids of farewell. His stubborn state left him little wiggle room of being able to express any well-deserved goodbye to his old friend. Meanwhile, while Jim may have been annoyed at Dave's display of inflexibility, he was mostly saddened just to see the Costas go. There was also regret such differences between him and his longtime friend could rupture their relationship, especially at such a pivotal moment.

Each giving mutual comfort, both women were drenched in an endless deluge of tears. It was as if their emotional farewell bids were preceding some foreboding tragedy and letting go marked the inception leading to it. Although Pamela was generally oblivious to any such notion, she was still able to pick up on the appearance of her husband's mien. In there doing, she was able to sense that something troubling likely just occurred between him and Dave.

Meanwhile still caught up in the inflexibility of his indifference, Dave expressed a lukewarm regard to Pamela and an even lesser one to his troubled friend. He then hastened the events to proceed in a cold manner with the tasks of tending to Gloria being his only order of business.

"Linda! Kids! It's time to get going. Please get on the boat!"

Dave stood on deck with the cold-blooded stare of an assassin. Not wavering to any emotions stirring in the others, he was caught up in the vortex of his sulking.

"I think I'm being summoned," Linda muttered in a broken voice, directing her comment at her friends. "We need to go."

She then approached Pamela, wiping the tears from her cheek.

"Save these for the tears of happiness when we see each other again." Pamela replied likewise, to which Linda kissed her atop a drooped head.

She then gave Jim a heartfelt kiss. "As much as you sometimes get on my nerves, don't ever forget that I do adore you. You're a beautiful person you—" her voice cracked, "—you sometimes pain in the ass."

"I don't want to keep the skipper waiting," he responded, deeply moved by Linda's remark. "Keep an eye on the kids for us, and both of you be safe as well. You better get going now."

Meanwhile the noxiousness of Dave's aloofness hung adrift in the balance heavier than the bluish fumes being expelled from Gloria's diesel exhaust, of which conversely, the deafening volume of its engine sounding paled in contrast to the silence of his detached character.

Linda boarded their boat with the kids in understanding Dave would soon employ her services for the tasks of getting underway. Meanwhile there from Gloria's deck and refusing to acknowledge any initial orders by him, she faced her friends. Viewing them snuggled together, she could spot their distress through the transparency of braved smiles. Linda then swooped a methodical rainbow motion from Gloria's deck and returning the gesture, Pamela did the same, lip-syncing "I love you."

Especially getting the better of the Woodsons were the children standing next to Linda, also waving. It prompted Pamela's body to go limp in grief with only Jim keeping her standing upright. The little squinting five-year-old David, so small in frame, particularly got the better of the two, there projecting in his innocence an inability of being able to clasp what might lie ahead.

Jim viewed him a small boy facing a vast ocean in a small vessel, believing his superman dad, who could protect him from anything, was merely taking him for some joyride. It was both the boy's introverted nature and uncorrupted mind that the Woodsons were able to peer into the previous few days which made it so difficult for Jim to witness such innocence being prematurely placed against such colossal risks—ones capable at times of challenging even the most well-trained seafarers endowed with the most sophisticated maritime vessels and equipment. Numb inside, both he and Pamela just gazed at Gloria fetch her way out of Mindelo's bay. Once it reached the open waters, Jim refused to continue dwelling on something he was powerless to effect.

"Come on sweetie, it's in God's hands now. All we can do is wait and hear from them again."

Before heading home, the two visited their local café for a few drinks.

Heading northeast and with Mindelo Bay behind them, the same route taken on their anniversary, Linda directed the kids to grab a snack below. She instructed them to stay there. Still in a sulking mode, Dave snapped. "Why are you having them snacking so soon? We've got over three thousand miles to sail and we haven't even covered one yet."

If his earlier behavior wasn't enough to have ignited Linda's fury, Dave's latest remark was more than sufficient to initiate its burn.

"I need to know what part of the Woodson's hospitality made you feel the need to be such an asshole to them? You embarrassed the hell out of me. I kind of felt something had happened by the shore between you and Jim. But when you came back and were quiet afterwards, I have to admit—I could have never imagined beforehand that you could have ever been as cold as you were in saying goodbye to them. I mean what was the rush? Would another few minutes have made that much of a goddamn difference? I mean are you such an incredible navigator that you've charted our course down to the goddamn, freaking second?"

In his avoidance of direct eye contact, Linda snapped. "Look at me you bastard! You had your say before with your pathetic attitude. If you plan on copping some kind of goddamn attitude with me now, we'll turn this freaking thing right around and you can just as well let us off. I'm not making this trip with you being like this. Every once on a blue moon you get this way, but I usually have a place to get away when it happens. Now talk to me."

Listening, Linda just stood, steering fiercely at her husband.

"Jim was an asshole," he finally blurted.

"Oh was he? Was it because he opened up his heart and home to you, and as quirky as it may be, entrusted his wife to you the other night? Jim may be slightly weird at times, but who are we to talk? He's also one of the sweetheart guys I've ever known. I need better Dave or turn this fucking thing right around, and now. I'm not kidding. I'd skip overboard, but that would leave the kids to have to deal with you alone."

While getting Dave's attention, the meanwhile leaving him both seated quietly for a moment and questioning his earlier actions, he was still unwilling to concede.

"Jim had the audacity of questioning my motives about heading west so soon. The boy's worried about some freaking hypothetical hurricane."

"Oh, so you made an ass out of both of us because Jim loves our kids and voiced his concerns for all of us. Good one! Sorry, your means didn't justify the end, which basically sucked. Not even close, you asshole!"

"You don't get it—"

"—Oh, I've got to hear this."

"He pretty much insinuated that I was a fool for doing so and kept insisting we stay with them. What pissed me off was the boy wouldn't back off."

"Oh, got it—now it all makes sense! He offered his hospitality, and then you just turned around and shoved it right back up his ass. Hmmm, that does make sense. Giving you were right, which you weren't, I'm sorry, but you just couldn't have just taken it for face value and let it slide right off of you like a mature adult. Instead you needed to climb into your shell and not give a shit about anyone else. Heather picked up on it as well."

"Yeah right, Heather didn't pick up on anything."

"Yeah? You were so caught up in yourself, I don't think you would have picked up on her falling overboard, you prick."

"That's ridiculous, and can you cool it with the assholes and pricks?"

"Oh, you got feelings. There's hope after all. I'll tell you what's ridiculous. It's ridiculous we're even having this conversation. I'm beating a dead horse with you, but at some point you need to own up to your actions, and you know it—or better figure it out, and soon. One more thing—even if you were upset at Jim, which I don't believe you were warranted, you could have at least spared a lot of people a lot of harm by considering your actions beforehand, especially giving the circumstances. The balls in your court now, so do what you gotta do. Either rethink your actions or turn this thing around. It's your choice, Dave."

Linda then approached the companionway before looking back towards her husband.

"You're on your own for a little while. I'm heading below with the kids. This whole emotional rollercoaster has taken its toll on me, and I need some rest because of it."

Satisfied in having convincingly made her point, she retired below. Leaving Dave alone to lick the wounds of his pride, he also understood such another like tirade by his wife wouldn't stand to be in his best interest.

En route to the most northeastern Cape Verde Island of Sal, his bout of sulking began melting under the tranquility of the warm tropical sun. Dave could now see his friend's need to have so vehemently conveyed his sagacious concerns earlier. It was then he succumbed to the realization that although rarely reacting in debate as some a wild animal as he had just done, there having senselessly lashed back at his old friend with a take-no-prisoner position in respect to the solemn enormity of everyone's sad farewell state of affairs, such a rare event of having demonstrated such a repugnant mood to such an excessive degree only sharpened the sad irony of its infrequency.

In approaching some familiar stony ridges marking a harbor, the place where everyone enjoyed its comforts two days earlier, Dave's heart sank. Remembering the extremely embarrassing events of his friends there the previous morning left him seated quietly with a pondering grin. As the last stretches of Sao Vicente extended its reaches eastward, it gave the small island an appearance of drifting gracefully to the west. In observance of its steady shrinking into the horizon, Dave understood that their brief stay on Sao Vicente was officially over. It was time to forget about the past and move ahead.

Hoping his two friends would both forgive and forget his actions, he considered the notion that absence might eventually abate some of the foul taste left behind, and that time in turn would sweeten the pallets of their memories with the good times shared.

Filled with humility, Dave cringed in seeing Linda re-emerge from below. Unlike before, he noticed the fire in her eyes appeared to have subsided to their normal softness of blue. Denying any chance of a first strike, he preempted by speaking first.

"Linda, you're married to a complete asshole."

The two approached each other.

"Honey, what happened, happened, and I can see you've been beating yourself up over it. You know I don't like getting upset at you and I'm sorry I snapped like that, but you left me no choice."

"Well you did me a favor, and I deserved it," He then paused, softly clasping Linda's hands. "You're a sight for sore eyes, and I'm sorry about earlier. I only wish our friends knew the extent of my regret."

"Well if this makes you feel any better, Jim adores you, so he'll forgive you I'm sure. As for Pamela—you could try running that girl down with a car and she'd still try to find some good in it."

Dave grinned in response, the meanwhile also taking notice of Linda's skimpy outfit.

"You're looking pretty appetizing right now."

Their new sense of reconciliation was one whereby Dave was playing denial to Dick's references of their boat's relatively tight quarters. In contrast several miles to their east, Jim was rested atop Pamela after having just collapsing onto her; a fate he too would have met had he not binged himself into an induced coma a couple nights earlier.

In a desperate attempt to breathe more freely, Pamela slid her arms around her husband's sweaty body. Then with great effort, she rolled his 190-pound lean frame to her side. There they lied facing each other.

"Honey, you're all sweaty. I'll get a towel and I'll be right back."

In snatching one off a heap of others thereby allowing gravity to release the remaining towel from its fold, Pamela then felt its weight suddenly lessen. Feeling an object make contact with her bare ankle concurrent to striking the asbestos floor below, puzzled, she picked up the bulky envelope. Its seams were secured via a generous amount of plastic packing tape. Carefully examining both sides and squeezing its contents, she then carried it to Jim, who first sat up to towel his upper body dry.

"When was the last time you did the towels, honey?"

"Last night. I wasn't sure if I'd be up to it today. Are you going to open it?"

"Damn straight I am."

Jim first made a few attempts of finding a weak point to tear the tightly wrapped enveloped, but when the hassle of his futile attempts exceeded his intrigue, curiosity yielded to impatience.

"You open it. You've got the fingernails."

Matching her decked out toes, Pamela employed her likewise fingernail's to breach the envelope. She soon had it dissected at different sections.

Jim grinned. "I'm surprised it doesn't have 'Classified' stamped all over the damn thing."

The mood soon shifted from a calm inquisitiveness to that of celebration as the couple became awestruck at the sight of stacks of freshly crisp fifties intermittently spilling out of the partially mutilated envelope's few openings.

With the two beside themselves, Pamela made reference to a dollar amount stamped on each of the paper ribbons securing the bills together into their separate stacks.

"Are each one of these a thousand dollars?"

"I think so, and I'll tell you something else. This has the Costas written all over it. Man those two are something else. It's as if they read my mind about the stereo."

Pamela didn't catch onto the meaning of Jim's last statement. Instead she was focused on gathering the stacks of bills spread about their entangled sheets. In doing so, she noticed a note tucked with one of the ribbons. In pointing it out, Jim requested she read it. She did.

"We want to thank you for a job well done and can't thank you enough for your gracious hospitality. We've also never had as much fun acquiring hangovers, as was the case with you guys. By the way speaking of which, good luck with Pastor John."

"Screw you Dave," Jim commented, also laughing genuinely and shaking his head. "Leave us with that mess to clean."

Pamela continued. "Had you gotten the owners down another five G's, we would have needed a larger envelope. Left cash for a bonus. Know you would have torn up a check. Sorry. Love you both, sincerely, the Costas XOOXX. See you soon."

Dumbfounded, Jim sat quiet for a moment before expressing with an air of affection. "That jerk. Now I feel like the moron. If he were here now, I'd kick that stubborn Portuguese ass of his."

"But honey, Linda had a part in it too."

"Yeah, but she'd kick mine instead," he snickered before adding, "besides, I'd like to think it wasn't Dave who left all those X's and 0's at the end there." He then grinned deviously. "You know what we should do with this money?"

"Run to the bank with it?"

"Yeah right!" Jim shouted while suddenly propelled himself onto her. "Try a second round on it, baby!"

"You're sick and I love it!" she reacted, giggling and welcoming her husband's unexpected move.

Miles to the east, Dave wasn't as fortunate to be able to capitalize on an anticipated round of makeup sex. His kids had awoken from their naps just minutes after Linda. Their appearance on deck substantiated a wisdom Dick now seemed to possess. It would later lead him to self-induce flashbacks of his drinking gala with both Gloria's previous owner and Jim. In doing so, he would scrutinize his memory frayed from the effects of alcohol in an effort of recollecting other insights possibly divulged then that might later pose beneficiary to the voyage ahead.

Concerned about how his children were faring in the trip's early stages, Dave placed each of them by his sides. He began by rubbing David atop his head. "How's my favorite sailor doing?"

As a precursor to his son's possible non-enchantment, a less than encouraging sign was indicated in his response. "Dad, when are we goin home?"

"We'll be home in about a month, buddy. Don't you like sailing? You did last year. Do you remember that?"

"No, I can't wemember. When am I gonna see Puff? I miss him."

"The Nelson's next door are taking care of him," Linda explained, having stepped in. "He'll be okay. They love Puff and will make sure nothing happens to him, sweetie."

Puff was an outside cat whose occasional rub against ones ankle or arching of its back to greet its feeder was the only extent of human contact it desired. Now with the Costas away, it would instead have different ankles where to leave its scent, and the Costa's absence also stood to provide it a short reprieve of not needing to worry about being carried submissively around in the backyard, upside down and hanging only by its hips.

"How about you Heather. How are you doing? "

"I'm okay dad. I like it out here. I love the sun."

Dave turned to David. "Hey buddy, how would you like to look at a few things on the boat with me? You can be my first mate."

The boy's face then lit as it would always do at the prospect of being able to emulate his father, especially when involving tasks appearing as official business. Dave the meanwhile welcomed such episodes of enthusiasm on his son's part, not to mention the added benefit of when they would lead to him holding a flashlight for him in tight areas. Both parents also understood their boy's preference of staying out of the sun lessened his desire to venture out from the safety afforded below. In general, David was contented just to keep busy playing with his plastic GI's, now especially being able to take advantage of a full array of the nooks and crannies provided by Gloria's interior. Included was wherever else he would be able to stand his plastic figurines when the ocean would allow for it. An endless supply of the strong trade winds stood to hold the final say in the matter.

Outside of her homeschooling, Heather's approach to keeping occupied involved a little less simulated carnage than that of her brother. She mostly enjoyed reading, underlining to the parent's notion that with her the apple hadn't fallen far from the tree. Pertinent to her brother, the clock was still winding down for them to be able to gauge the same for him. His quieter introverted nature made it difficult for them to decipher what level of intelligence was actually laid buried deep within his concealed mind, still after so many years.

Later that evening in the sun's descent beyond the western horizon, a combination of Sao Vicente having done so earlier and Sal, Cape Verde's most northeastern island, yet to emerge from the east, provided the Costas a full panoramic view of the horizon.

Both Dave and Linda were snuggled up to each other in full appreciation of the surrounding Atlantic. It could be added to a few times back in the States when they were also able to relish such a view. Unlike then, what added more to the present splendor was the absence of any light pollution. Even the moon making its debut in several days passively cooperating by way of its absence. It gave the relaxed couple an unblemished shot of the heavens.

Resting her head against Dave's shoulder, Linda couldn't help but to appreciate the feel of his warm body. She once stated that if he ever lied on a glacier, the concave of his icy imprint would linger indefinitely until eventually breaking away into the ocean.

Gazing into the darkened sky while nestled close to each other in the cockpit, Dave couldn't help but to point out the planets, constellations, and individual stars all collectively blanketing an unobstructed sky in brilliance, horizon to horizon. Included were both the glowing Milky Way appearing as a glowing mystic cloud rich in speckled luminaries and several satellites moving at hypersonic speeds, yet appearing below as points of light gracefully journeying among the stars.

Dave also didn't neglect to explain the mechanics of shooting stars materializing out of nowhere, as they would streak into the atmosphere traveling at hyper-bullet speeds just to then meet their violent fate, vanishing quietly into the darkness as viewed from below. While appreciating the poetics of Dave's spoken tour of the heavens, Linda took less interest in the infinite enormity of the mind-boggling facts he was conveying. Instead she simply chose to appreciate the spectacle above them in the same light as some extravagant firework display, there savoring the peaceful moment with her husband. Free of all human induced stresses and dramas, civilization seemed as far away to them as did the stars and planets above.

Dave's inability to have harvested even one good nights sleep over the previous several days finally caught up with him. With Linda's head resting comfortably against his shoulder, both a lack of muscle activity and cadence breathing indicated to her that the marathon of activities of a few days prior was finally taken their toll. She affectionately ran her hand over his left cheek in gentle strokes of his short black hair.

"Oh, sweetie, you've had enough. We need to get you to bed."

At that, she reluctantly woke him. "I'm sorry honey, but you need this sleep. That means in a real bed."

"What about the sails? We—" A drowsy Dave began asking before then getting cut off by Linda.

"They're not rocket science, honey. I can manage them. I'll also get you up at three. I'd let you sleep a little longer, but I know how much you really wanted to see Sal [Cape Verde's most northeastern island] as it emerges."

No objection was raised at the prospect of turning in below for a well-deserved sleep. After an exchange of a kiss, a lethargic Dave descended below into Gloria's cabin for his short rest. Soon playing helmswomen while seated in a reclined position and facing south, Linda's legs were stretched across the helm in doing so. There she took in a full inhalation in appreciation of the moment's purity.

"Thanks Pamela—thanks Jim. It doesn't get any better than this. This is heaven."

Arising just a few hours later from an extended nap, Dave was then able to relish the twilight sky brightening with an iridescent brilliance of a deep indigo, there highlighting Venus standing alone in dominance of a waning night. Early dawn also gave relief to the distinct silhouettes of Sal's several volcanic peaks protruding from the horizon. It was a sight Dave had been anticipating and planned on being awake for its emergence.

Later that day heading south, upon admiring the picturesque white dunes of Boa from just beyond its west shoals in deeper waters and then heading southwest to make a flyby of its sibling island of Moio, Linda eventually assumed the helm in relief of a highly exhausted husband. Subsequent to overshooting Cape Verde's Moio and still heading southwest, she was eventually able to set anchor off its neighboring island of Santiago later that night. There off its west coast and near the island's northern tip, she was then able to join in what would become a rare night's sleeping event for the whole family.

Upon waking, everyone was able to savor a traditional American breakfast in Gloria's cockpit, the meanwhile doing so with a rich view of the historically affluent town of Tarrafal as a backdrop. In dining there that serine mild morning and projecting far into the future, it rang to the parents as an ideal setting for everyone to be able to bond as a family. With Tarrafal's impressive view as a backdrop, they hoped that doing so might instill into their young impressionable children fond memories through which someday they might be able to look back and clearly recollect the innocence of that private event as one of the good old days.

The family then headed further southwest with their eyes set on Santiago's neighbors, Fogo. In arriving there, they took a hiatus a couple miles off its east shore to marvel at an imposing Mount Fogo rising over a half-mile out from the water. There the family was able to enjoy a late lunch before Dave decided upon spending the remaining daylight hours conducting an extensive inspection of Gloria. He regretted not having done so earlier while still moored at Santiago's Tarrafal following their breakfast for reasons that once circumnavigating southwest around Fogo and then heading due west, south of its neighboring Brava, the much smaller island there stood to offer little recourse should any extensive repair need to be made to their boat.

Beyond Brava lay the U.S. and over three thousand miles the Atlantic in between. Dave was well aware such a significant span of ocean wasn't just some common itinerary of standard practice that should simply be brushed aside without regard. He also considered the notion that what lay ahead between them and the U.S. Seaboard where they would then head up north towards Rhode Island, lay possibly anything from that of the expected to the epic of the vast unknown.

Sailing south of Brava later in the stealth of darkness provided the Costas an impressive yet unsettling view of the southern coastal mountainous terrain of the island. The blackness of its shadowy representation was in stark contrast to the starlit sky appearing above. Less than an hour shy of midnight, Brava's black unearthly coast lurking just north of Gloria's starboard side appeared as some darken void silently drifting east. It struck Linda as some herald of darkness searching for its next victim to prey upon, even unnerving Dave. Both also viewed it as some harbinger wandering in from the open ocean, prognosticating by way of its eerie silence.

Even in sparsely populated stretches of a friendlier US coastline, the two were accustom at any time to at least be able to expect even a slightest glow of a secluded light seated there within a terrain's darkened silhouette. Unlike with the pitch-black Brava seated before them, it would let the passerby know that they needn't feel alone.

Meanwhile like NASA's *Voyager 1* as it would turn back to the Solar System years later before then leaving both its eight planets and a faint Sun behind forever into the cold, darkness of space, the Costas could now only look ahead and know that they too were facing the unknown. Gazing upward, the family was at a similar vantage with *Voyager 1*—together, both staring into the same infinity of space— independently, both forging ahead into a vast unknown.

<< CHAPTER 5 >>

HEADING WEST, THE VERDE ISLANDS were now behind the family. The last reaches of Brava slipping into the darkness punctuated the reality that Gloria's 43-feet of real estate was now the Costa's soul link to home and safety. Linda was once again rested against her husband's seemingly perpetual warm frame. Nestled together, the couple were able to feel the apparent wind's influence as felt aboard brushing over them. With a more assertive breeze propelling their sails forward with its thrusting action, thereby allowing them to run with the eastern trade winds, the family found themselves moving along west at a generous clip. Seated quietly, both in meditation, Linda finally broke the silence in reference to Brava.

"Now that was eerie."

"Yeah, I thought it was just me. It was kind of like watching a tarantula from a bug's perspective. I hope it wasn't any bad omen."

With the couple nestled together on the port side of the cockpit and facing north, Dave pointed ahead. "Just about eighty miles north is Sao Vicente. Jim's probably snuggled up to Pamela right now wondering where we are."

"No Dave, I would wager he's up against her right at this moment doing something else instead. Wouldn't you think so with those two?"

"True, but alone or with company. I think those two swing."

"Oh they do," Linda came back, smirking. "I heard them talking when they thought I was passed out. I have a feeling when day breaks, Pastor John's going to shake their world up a bit."

"No doubt. And based on the other night, I'm not surprised about them swinging. It's just a little weird initially hearing it about your friends—that's all. One thing's for sure though. I definitely can't picture anything good coming about when the pastor gets a hold of the two of them."

"That's a matter of perspective, isn't it?"

"True. I'm not justifying what we used to do, but being outright swingers? That's bizarre. I guess if you have the temperament for it, I can see the intrigue in it. I know people that do that, and there aint nothing uptight about them—at least not on the surface."

"Sounds to me like you wouldn't' mind going there."

"In fantasy, maybe, but..." Dave then grinned.

"Okay, what is it? I mean we've sort of been there before. I sure I wont mind whatever you have to say. Come on please tell me! Please, please, please!"

"Well if and when they come and visit us, we better make sure we're at Logan before HAZMAT gets a hold of them."

Dave's comment was met with a grin and then a quick backhand. "That's terrible, honey! How could you say that about those two? And besides, it's not like we were any better before. I do have to admit though, that was pretty funny—you sick shit."

"Can you imagine those two coming out to meet us all primed for sex, and we're dressed in Tyvek?"

"I can't hear this anymore," Linda cried, yet grinning at the same time. "Those two are sweetheart. And beside, if Pamela came out greeting you in some negligee, you wouldn't care if she had just walked out from the city sewer covered with shit. Let's change the subject, please?"

"Okay—hey, remember sweating it out before the blood test results came back on Heather?"

"Nice change of subject by the way," Linda cringed, adding, "and don't remind me. Can you imagine me explaining to my dad had she not been yours? It was bad enough otherwise."

"Can you imagine introducing Heather to her half-brother?"

Linda cringed again, this time shuttering. "Okay, enough already. You just don't know when to quit, do you? Sometimes you're worse than Jim."

There was a pause for a moment before Dave broke the silence. "I'm thinking of those poor guys in pure view of Pastor John and his brother reverend next to me. I mean I looked up and there behold my surprised eyes stood the three of you all naked, especially with Jim supporting a woody. Man, my heart really went out to that boy. I also thought it was probably one of the funniest things I've ever seen in my life."

"Hey jerk, you're forgetting—I was one of those three! I was humiliated! Still am."

"Ah, don't get me wrong, honey. The sight of you and Pam naked together is anything but funny, but it did resemble some sort of pornographic sitcom if you could imagine such a thing."

It was quite for a moment.

"Dave, while I know you're usually up late at night [at home] watching the girls on that Spanish station, I'm sure these long nights of helming will still test your ability of keeping awake."

"No, not necessarily Linda. I'm figuring that the later time zones should somewhat compensate for the long nights."

"Okay granted. But you can't deny that boredom will eventual cause you to fall off every now and then, and we don't need that, especially when you're outside." Dave agreed as she continued. "This brings to mind, Pamela. I mean there was nothing preventing you from having sex with her the other night. Jim wouldn't have mind, and I have to admit, me neither."

"Holy shit!" Dave exclaimed to Linda's amusement. "I didn't see that coming. But to answer your question—two reasons—you and him."

"Not sure if you're gay, sick, or just still madly in love with me, but I really appreciate it to say the least. I mean that."

"You've forgotten committed. You remember that nine years of marriage thing? That was supposed to have been the emphasis of the other night, and you're appreciation is noted by the way. All being said, you're welcome."

"Well I won't forget it, that's for sure. I still need to ask you this though. I mean look. There you were with the sexiest woman on this planet naked and wrapped around you in the water. Based on what I saw, the alignment seemed pretty fitting for the billing. It's therefore hard for me to believe you didn't slip one in on her. Believe me, Pamela really wanted your ass, you sexy devil. She had told me earlier that morning."

Again taken aback, Dave was becoming uneasy. "I'm not going to lie. I was tempted and giving the situation, can you blame me?"

"Honey, please—I'm not trying to entrap you."

Linda then stood up to head below. "So you're telling me you and her didn't have sex, either in the water or by the fire?"

"Honey, I didn't. And if I did, I'd be feeling like shit right now."

"Please don't lie, at least not on my part. Had you two ended up together, that would have been partially my fault; though I don't believe fault is an appropriate term here."

"Well in light of that provocative thought and my appreciation of your open-mindedness, please read my lips. I did not have sex with Pamela."

Knowing the kids were asleep, Linda lifted her favorite turquoise thigh-length cotton tee-shirt to almost full nudity in approaching Gloria's companionway.

"Well at least that makes one of us, and I'm not referring to our little outburst on the beach that you and Jim had your front seat showing to either."

In letting her shirt then drape back to her thighs again, Linda turned back and approached her stunned husband. Subsequent a devouring kiss, she gave an admission upon gently biting his lower lip.

"Looks like I finally cashed in on that woman thing. I hope you don't mind. I was in the shower and needed my back washed. That may sound a bit cliché, but what I experienced with Pam was anything but cliché. By the way, the kids were playing next door and you and Jim were on the boat at the time. Bummer, huh?"

In strutting to exit again, Linda gave Dave no time to respond. "Just didn't want you falling asleep at the wheel, so I figured I'd tell you." Upon a wink, she disappeared below.

It led Dave to conclude that if his wife was able to shed all but the last few remnants of any uptightness over the several previous years through workouts and eating healthy, then whatever lack of confidence that might have still been hindering her prior to their Sao Vicente experience had all but been shed in just those few days spent with Pamela. Dave was left speechless, only able to utter to himself. "And you called that thing on the beach with Pam, a 'little outburst'? I can only imagine."

Linda's means of distraction were quite effective. The last thing on her husband's mind at that moment was any desire for any sleep.

In many attempts made throughout the night to contact Jim, Dave ended up doing so instead with an American couple heading their way. In approximating their intercept at two and a half days, both planned a rendezvous, putting him on the hot seat in testing his navigational skills. Meanwhile a precedent established between the two placed Dave as night watchman while Linda in turn would cover the pre-afternoon hours. For her, doing so would also require juggling Gloria's many household functions. Pertinent to their kids, the two parents could only imagine what might ensue if either David happened to exhaust every possible battle configuration with his plastic military figurines or outside of her homeschooling, Heather ended up reading every available printed word contained aboard Gloria.

While grappling with his radio the next morning, predawn Monday, Dave was able to hear Jim attempting to establish contact with him. While the antenna atop his towering mast gave the radio a decent range of transmission, it still wasn't as fitted to guarantee any consistency of success like Jim's land based antenna was. The two never spoke.

Up until that morning, the family needed to deal with one violent thunderstorm in which Dave needed to cope with harsh weather and sea conditions outside. With an onset of a larger regional disturbance both weak and unorganized, he was nonetheless bothered that at some juncture it was likely the same benign mass of inclement weather probably impacted the entire Verde region previous to them. As a result, he wished to speak with Jim evermore and reassure his friend that everything was fine.

Well after dawn that inclement Monday, Dave was joined by both Heather balancing a cup of freshly brewed coffee and Linda emerging from below carrying a welcoming plate of scrambled eggs and freshly seared bacon. Cold and hungry, his appreciation of everything ranged from the mouthwatering aromas filling their temporarily sheltered cockpit to his wife and daughter's service with a smile. He likened their attention to that of a victorious commander being greeted by the townswomen in returning home in Old Europe.

Linda was all smiles as she and Heather took residence next to him. "This is great—my two favorite ladies. Where's the little prince, commanding his plastic armies again?"

"No, he's still eating. I told him he could join us when he finishes. You know he likes to play with his food."

"Come on, let's cut him some slack and let him join us. This doesn't feel right."

"Yeah you're right. He's probably tucking his food under the cushion as we speak. It wouldn't be the first time he did that, that's for sure."

Thereafter being fitted with raingear and a life vest, David was soon seated next to his father under Gloria's protective canvas dodger. There Dave expressed his approval of the moment by affectionately squashing both his kids against his sides. Dividing his attention between them, he directed his first comment at his son. "So isn't this like being at Riverside Park [A popular amusement park that was located in Agawam, Massachusetts prior to being renamed after 1999]?"

David nodded in an affirmative manner while at the same time being unable to formulate any comparison from his fragmented recollections of the amusement park. In turn, his more pragmatic daughter voiced her opinion instead. "No Dad, Riverside had a lot of rides, and it was sunny. When's this rain going to end? It's boring."

"Nice try, hon." Linda smirked.

In getting her daughter's attention, she explained. "It might be like this all day sweetie, but it should all pass by the end of today. Right Dave?"

The proud dad was taking aback by his wife's relay of a repeated weather forecast. In response, she grinned at him. "I know how to operate a hand radio too, so there." Upon sticking her tongue out, both kids giggled.

While the adults were able to savor the pure harmony of being one with the sea, there exempted from the everyday bustles and worries of society, for the children, the novelty of their new surroundings carried with it the threat of losing its full head of steam. The two were at the mercy of a few board games, those that posed a challenge to David's attention capacity.

The large weather mass engaged the family for the remainder of the day. With the onset of Tuesday morning's sunrise, Dave was able to readjust his course latitude and verify their position longitude via his chronometer. Doing so without the later use of GPS took diligence, for being off by only seconds longitude in calculation could stand to leave the family dangerously off course. Such a discrepancy might be discovered the hard way in failing to reach an intended target, making doing so either a regrettable blunder or at best an extreme inconvenience.

In crunching the numbers, Dave was able to approximate that they had covered 350 miles since witnessing the eerie spectacle of Brava's darkened coast.

That same morning in relieving her husband earlier then usual for extending him extra sleep time, Linda did so with the hopes he'd be better suited for joining in search of the other boat they were expecting to join in a rendezvous. Prior to turning below just after dawn, Dave's use of a pristine sunrise in establishing a fixed position revealed that if the other boat happened to maintain the same margin of error as they were, then the two stood to be on a same visual plane in the near future. During his rest, Heather assisted her mother in tidying up Gloria's interior, whereas little David's main task was limiting his own ability of undoing their efforts. There was excitement aboard, even for the little boy who understood someone would soon be visiting.

An underlining enthusiasm caused Dave to awake earlier than he was anticipating, choosing then to make use of the extra time afforded by manning the radio and panning the horizon. In carrying out the former, thrill was realized at the sound of a deep male voice resonating over the airwaves.

"Unless there's someone else crazy enough to be hanging out here, I would venture to say that it's you guys to my southeast."

Upon excusing himself, Dave was quick in entering the cockpit to survey the northwest horizon. In panned it with his binoculars,

Linda instead spotted the other boat with her naked eyes.

"Holy shit, Dave! Is that them?"

He panned a bit. "Yeah, I see them, now. I'll tend to the rigging. If you wouldn't mind, get the helm for me."

Dave took notice to Linda's tight cutoffs and snug braless tank top. With the latter cut off above the naval, it was an outfit she would have never considered wearing in public prior to meeting Pamela.

"Honey, if the guy sees you like that, we might end up colliding with them."

In spite her run in with Pamela, Linda's level of self-confidence was still a fragile one.

"You're saying this is too slutty?"

"I wouldn't encourage you to attend any PTA meeting that way, but this aint no PTA, so no I'm not."

"So is it okay?"

"Are you cold?"

"Are you kidding? I'm sweating. You can see that."

"If that's a 'no,' then I guess you're dressed appropriately, my dear. Now let's meet our new acquaintances."

With Gloria soon idle in a static tow downwind from the other sailboat, both Dave and Linda were fixated in admiration of a fifty-two foot ketch sail yacht. Its impressive three sail configuration dwarfed even a respectable size sailboat such as theirs. Its two occupants were friends of Gloria's previous owners, Dick and Ruth. It was through their association whereby they also came to know the Woodsons. They were some of the people Jim spoke of with Dave in his alluding to the "ears and eyes" cognizant of their crossing.

Soon with everyone aboard the larger sailboat, its twenty-nine year old co-owner pulled out both shot glasses and fourteen-year-old scotch for toasting. Right off the bat Dave liked the style of his new acquaintance. The six-foot-three burly framed co-owner, Randy, projected an apparent lack of vanity by both his unkempt, long blondish hair and non-addressed receding hairline.

Dave and Linda couldn't help but notice his frumpiness was no turnoff to his attractive wife Carolina, who instead carried a hint of class. Together they projected an air of "what's mine is yours" mindset, a common thread seeming to link everyone together who they met since landing on Sao Vicente.

A slender bodied Carolina was also a deeply bronzed ravenous woman—half Portuguese, half French, and Brazilian-born. At an inch shy of six feet, she too projected an impressive presence like her husband.

To put his guest at ease, Randy toasted.

"Here's to my old friends, Dick and Ruth, and our new friends, the Woodsons, making this all possible by placing you in our path."

Impressed, both Dave and Linda shrugged in agreement before raising their drinks to the other couple's. Upon doing so, the four clanged their glasses and together swigged their respective drinks.

Randy then wasted no time in grabbing little David's tiny hand. He did so while patting Dave on the back. "Let us men check out the rest of this boat."

In comparison to Gloria's relatively roomy interior, size wise, the larger boat's main cabin area seemed likened to some land based dwellings that were constructed decades prior. Although not as finely embellished in rich earth tones as Gloria's mahogany interior was, the ketch sail yacht carried with it a touch of European elegance. It hinted accents of Victorian, England.

Everything about its interior spoke class down to its affixed crystal lighting fixtures. Its living quarters that had been stripped of all original manufacturer stock items and replaced with authentic mid-nineteenth century Victorian décor didn't go unnoticed by Dave. He couldn't help but to make mention of the painstaking attention to detail that reflected an effort whereby no stone was left unturned.

"I'm glad you can recognize and appreciate true authenticity and quality when you see it." Randy reciprocated.

With his wheels spinning in curiosity at what his new friend did to make a living in order to be able to afford such a vessel, Dave preferred not asking directly.

"Did you design this interior?"

"No, my wife does it for a living. This surprises a lot of people, but she the real breadwinner here. You might refer to me as her oversized worker bee, and a lucky one no less if I may add."

"Oh, she's an interior decorator, and quite the good one at that. I'm impressed."

"Well thanks. When Carolina visited her aunt in France at twelve, she did so while she was redecorating her old brick chalet. It still showed scarring from the Second World War—even the interior. To make a long story short, one morning Carolina approached her with some detailed sketches of how every room should appear, furniture and all—and the exterior—colors even. She had drawn them up overnight and her aunt was floored. Next thing you know a prodigy was born. A local article went out, and soon everyone from Europe to Brazil was seeking her services. You see, I'm just her Carpenter."

"Great story—and man, you both do some great work. How did you meet her? I mean you seem as American as apple pie, and she's—"

A robust laugh filled the cabin, "—so exotic?" Randy inserted. "You got that right. Making a long story short—again, I was in the Army and on leave from West Germany. I was visiting the Azores where I met her on a beach. Of course she was stunning in her bathing suit, but her French/Brazilian accent is what really hooked me."

In pausing a moment and grinning, he continued. "I was a little more presentable back then believe it or not. Still, talk about opposites. People always tell us that."

"Well first add me to that list. And second, you two did a phenomenal job here. My boat's modest in comparison."

Randy suddenly took on a stern expression. "Thank you, but don't say that. Gloria's a gem. I love that boat." He then squared off to Dave, though not in any aggressive manner.

"It's brilliant what Carolina has done with this boat, but do I look like some Victorian antique type of guy to you?"

Dave grinned as Randy continued. "That's Carolina's forte. Me? I'm a scotch and a big beer drinker on Sunday afternoon when it comes to watching my Bears. By the way, what teams do you like?"

"I'm a Giants and Yankees guy," Dave responded with pride, adding, "all New York for me, my friend."

"Well given your Giants are improving, they're still no match for my Bears. Word out to those Pittsburg, Dallas, and San Fran fans, my Bears are mean and hungry."

In pausing a moment, Randy caught himself. "Oh, excuse my ranting. I get a little overzealous about my Bears. I wish I could do the same for my Cubs, though the Bulls might have some promise. I heard they have this new dynamic player, but his name slips my mind for whatever reason. It doesn't matter though. I mean I'm not really sure what difference any single player could make for a team anyways."

"Yeah, you're probably right. And I forgot its football season, being out here. In fact being out here I've forgotten about the whole sports scene altogether, and this is coming from a football junkie."

"You're all Portuguese, you told me. I would have pegged you more of a soccer fan than anything. They love that shit in Europe."

Dave grinned. "Nope, you could say I'm a little nonconforming there—American born and raised. No soccer in this blood—drives my relatives nuts."

"Well about what you said before. You seem to be in the right frame of mind, because being out here is sports my friend—living on the edge. It sort of puts things into perspective, doesn't it? Getting back to the boat—in case you haven't noticed, Dick had Gloria custom built by the manufacturer. That included having its structure beefed up for extra durability."

"I didn't know that. Why wouldn't he have mentioned it? You'd think disclosing any kind of plusses like that would have been advantageous in negotiating—not that I'm complaining."

Randy grinned. "Well you see, Dick's a bit of an eccentric. You could even call him a bit bohemian. You see the man doesn't need the money. If anything, he probably got a kick out of you guys knowing nothing about Gloria's bells and whistles. Speaking of which, what do you think of that the kickass stereo system he had installed in her?"

"Stereo system?"

"Yeah, stereo system. I can't believe Jim didn't tell you about it. It's an incredible system—good stuff throughout."

He then paused for a moment. "Didn't he show it to you in the cabinet, above the chart table?"

"We were both in there, but I didn't see any stereo," Dave replied, shaking his head and adding. "Man that boy's something else. I'm glad he doesn't design rockets for NASA. 'Oh, those wires are probably for some stereo this baby use to have,'" he stating, impersonating Jim.

"Interesting, can't imagine him shorting you like that. Maybe it was broken and was still being fixed. Jim's too honest and with that being said, there was both a receiver and cassette deck in there. I'm really sorry to hear that—how unfortunate."

Dave then pieced it together. "I think the receiver's still there now that I'm thinking about it. I'm not very well versed in that type of thing, so I just didn't want to start hooking up wires I wasn't sure about. I mean there has to be some logical explanation, because you don't get any more honest than Jimbo."

"Agreed. Anyways, we'll go over to your boat and I'll show you where the hookups are. The external speakers were installed aftermarket and are totally concealed from the elements, but you can still access them from below. You lose some of the higher tones outside, but it's still an impressive sound from above. I don't know why he chose to have them installed that way, but then again we're talking about Dick. I love the man."

Dave's eyes widened with every added bit of knowledge being mentioned about Gloria with Randy continuing. "Our boat has a system too, but not like yours. Like I said Dave, Gloria's a gem and she'll never let you down."

The two men returned there, and while going over some of the Gloria's features, Dave asked, "Was Dick involved in the Pacific during World War Two?"

"No, Korea. He was involved with the First Marine Division at Chosin Reservoir. Are you familiar with that?"

"Quite familiar—damn!"

"Yeah, he doesn't like to talk about it. I did some reading about it after he mentioned it, and then I knew why. That man was in hell— a fucking frozen hell, that is. He's a great guy and hides it well. You'd never know it."

Dave let out a slight laugh. "I'm not laughing at that, of course. I'm just laughing at what he predicted for me."

"Ah, Dick and his predictions. That man's something else."

Dave explained about his prediction in reference to Linda's attractiveness and how problematic it stood to pose with the children always being in close proximity. Upon offering a few examples of her sunbathing, sometimes nude, Randy interrupted. "Are you telling me you two haven't done anything on this trip?"

"Try two weeks, my friend," Dave winced. "She's afraid of the kids hearing her and walking in on us—or something."

"What, she's a screamer and can't keep her voice down?"

"It's not that—just paranoid. I partially can't blame her, but this is killing me nonetheless."

"Well maybe you're killing her too and you're just not giving yourself enough credit. I say screw this boat. We need to fix your problem, and now. I mean you can't be an effective sailor in your state. I'll tell you if Carolina were prancing around wearing what your wife is, I'd be going ballistic if I couldn't have her."

While appreciating Randy having his back, Dave found his admission to be too much information.

Linda was in the dark as to why she was being ushering back to Gloria without their kids. Once there, she caught wind of Randy in leaving, giving them both a thumbs up.

"Enjoy!"

Dave understood their plan came with the risk of his wife being mortified in discovering their new acquaintances were onto their sexual dry spell. Meanwhile with his thumbs up and some words of encouragement, it was at that point Randy blew the cover off of their coy plan.

"What the hell was that about? They know, don't they?"

"They know what, honey?"

"They're going to know were over here doing it, or at least think so. That's what. This is humiliating!"

Hearing their commotion, Randy glanced back for a moment, amusement written across his face.

"He just grinned at us. He knows! Dave, you're an asshole. Don't go around blasting your mouth about our sex life to everyone. That's our business. We don't even know these people."

"Well apparently we knew them well enough where you didn't have the kids come back with you!"

Linda was caught speechless for a moment, only able to pan. "Go inside now. I don't want to fight in front of Randy."

She struck Dave on his backside as he was ducking into the companionway, his mind racing in search of someway of defending his position once they were to square off below. Once there, she grinned. "Got you going, didn't I? What you did was messed up, but brilliant."

Linda then thrust forward and wrapped all four limbs around Dave before then engaging in a devouring kiss with him. Then in jumping back to strip down naked, she demanding he do the same.

"I know I've been teasing you, but you better make this fucking worth it. If not, then you're really going to have a bitch on your hands for the rest of this trip, and don't need that, do we?"

Dave normally held his own quite well in the category of staying power, but a tension accumulated over the previous two weeks and enhanced further by the way Linda had just come onto him didn't guarantee any lengthy session of any lovemaking. It in turn left him concerned his state of questionable self-control might consequently leave her unsatisfied. Dave hoped that tapping into her bisexualism might assist in evening out the score.

"What about that Carolina. What did you think about her?"

"She's okay, but not my type."

"What do you mean, not your type? Are you telling me if you were on some hot secluded beach and she requested you spread oil over her tanned body, you'd say no?"

While not a womanizer and well aware anyone, especially one as well carried as Carolina, deserved better recognition than that of just some fine cut slab of meat, once the clothes came off and agenda for the moment was sex, then the subject of described superficial attributes usually became the benchmarks of Dave's discussion. Linda understood this, enjoying that lesser reserved side to her husband's usual deliberate nature. Meanwhile her response did little for the cause of leveling any playing field.

"I didn't say that." She then threw him a sexy look. "Don't get me wrong. I would have no problem spreading oil over every *nock and cranny* of her *naked* body if she asked. It's just doing so would be no major whoop for me. Sorry baby, nothing else would happen. Oh don't get me wrong. She's quite attractive, just not my type—too polished. There's something else you wouldn't understand either."

"Understand what?" Dave asked, perplexed.

"I'm probably wasting my time, but did you see her shoes?"

"Didn't really give it any thought at the time. What's that have to do with anything?"

"See? Didn't expect you to understand. Your eyes probably never made it below that tight little ass of hers with her painted on designer jeans—so let me enlighten you."

"Oh please do." Dave came back, " his curiosity almost rivaling his need for sex.

"They screamed pretentious. She probably purchased them at Saks Fifth Avenue or whatever."

"Her shoes or her jeans?"

"Dave, the jeans looked fine on her. It's her shoes we're talking here."

"So what's the big deal? You have expensive shoes too."

"Yeah, but you don't see me wearing them in the middle of the freaking Atlantic, do you? I told you, you wouldn't understand."

"You got me there." Dave responded, somewhat amused, but also at his wit's end. While he knew of other means of bringing his wife to a climax, he also understood her present itch mostly craved the likes of raw copulation to satisfy it. Both perplexed and feeling helpless, he listened as Linda concluded.

"Now if you want to imagine such a thing, then go ahead, sweetie. Carolina is very pretty—nice figure too. I can see your intrigue in her for the most part. But those shoes—what was that woman thinking?"

"I'm sure if it was Pamela who was wearing those same shoes, your attitude might be a little different."

Linda's tone changed to that of a defensive one, her appearing ready to snap. "Had to play the Pamela card, didn't you. First off, Pamela would never try to make any such fashion statement, and second..." A slight grin overcame her expression. "Now if those shoes were the only thing that Pam was wearing, I might be willing to overlook them."

Dave exhaled a sigh of relief "Holy Shit!" with Linda elaborating. "Now ask me to cover Pamela with oil, *shoes or no shoes*, and now we have a conversation. Let's continue this discussion on the floor."

The scene couldn't have been scripted any better for their erotic stage. Even with no chance of their kids walking in on them, there was still an element of forbiddances adding to Linda's excitement. She was so sex-starved by that point, her eventual expression of approval would have left even the most meager of men feeling a false sense of sexual prowess. With Dave not fitting such a category, she ended up having no reason for resenting him afterwards. Whales listening miles away would have found just cause for concurring.

The two lay in each other's arms the ensuing minutes following. There they labored to catch their breaths again with their skin bearing the mirrored relief of Gloria's teak floor.

Linda planted a kiss of approval on her husband. "Holy shit! That topped them all. I guess we better signal our friends now. I assume you've taking care of that already, you dirty dog, you."

Dave stood to gather his clothes. "If hand signals don't work, I can get them on the handset. We're locked in on channels." He then grinned in realizing Linda's statement was only rhetorical. "In other words, yes I did, dear."

"After the way you were just squeezing my ass, I'm not sure you'll have any strength in those paws of yours for squeezing any handset, you fucking animal, you."

In redressing, she reflected on their return back to the others. Doing so caused the luster of her sweaty experience to quickly dissipate.

"This is going to be quite awkward."

"Maybe so, but damn worth it, I say. When we return home, we should send these guys a thank you card."

"This doesn't bother you, does it? Don't get me wrong. I loved it, but now it's embarrassing as hell. I really do feel like a tramp right now."

Dave just grinned in response.

"Men!" Linda blurted. "I'll make sure I get you a trophy when we're back to Narragansett. Maybe that'll satisfy your freaking ego."

Back with Carolina and weighed down with humiliation, Linda apologized to which her gracious host laid it to rest for her. "Don't be embarrassed, dear. You may not look it, but I now believe you have some Brazilian in you. I was glad we could do that for you." Again Linda became weighed down with humiliation, but for different reasons than before.

The group soon called the gathering a wrap with Randy having become uneasy about the Costas being idle for so long in the middle of the Atlantic. With his and Carolina's sail to the Verde Islands only a couple days travel added to heading in a direction where any tropical storm activity would at most be in their infancy, she remained behind while her husband transported the Costas back aboard Gloria. There, Randy took on a more businesslike tone.

"Remember what I told you about the tiller, rudder assembly, hardware, springs, and anything else that either moves or fastens. It's all new. Dick didn't mess around when it came to fortifying Gloria. What he didn't replace was left for Jim to take care of. He and I had long talk about this, and as long as Jim didn't make any of the changes himself, you should be fine."

"He hired a marine mechanic friend. I just hope he didn't play his apprentice."

"Well as long as your friend kept his entrepreneur hands off of this gem, everything should be fine. Gloria is more seaworthy than any of its stock sisters. She's suited to the kilt. You keep the ocean out of her—she'll keep you out of it. Just stay aboard and she'll get you to where you're going. I'm not trying to alarm you, but this ocean can kick up before you know it. Never underestimate it's potential, and I mean—never."

Dave glanced down to his feet momentarily in reflection before reestablishing eye contact with Randy.

"Can you do me a big favor? I've been trying to contact Jim, and at one point I even heard him on the shortwave. I couldn't step into his signal though. Could you please tell him I'm sorry? I sort of had falling out with him before setting off, which was my fault."

"Jim can't stay upset at anyone, but I'll tell him anyhow. That Pamela of his is something else though. She and Carolina were inseparable the whole time together."

Dave broke into laughter at Randy's disclosure; Linda didn't. Instead she appeared as someone who just discovered that they had been cheated on. He then apologized for his outbreak in the face of his wife's leer, and taking note of the Costas mannerisms but ignoring them, Randy continued. "Anyways, I hope to get in range of him soon and bust his ass about some poker money he owes me."

"Interesting, I've got to bust his chops about that, too—Mr. Poker he is."

"Oh, don't get me wrong. Your boy's good, but I detected a slight tinge in his pinky when he was bluffing. I tell you, that game's brutal."

"Well thanks for that tidbit. It'll serve me well in the future. I'm sorry about derailing you there. Please continue. You were saying?"

"Thanks. I need to get serious with you for a moment, so please hear me out. It's relatively quiet out here now, but you need to get your asses back to the States, and as fast as possible. At least near the Caribbean. I mean think about it. This front that just overtook you—it was a weak system, but overtook you nonetheless. Elena's tropical wave came this way just a couple weeks ago. Fortunately we were north of it, though we did catch its wake. Had it veered our way, which isn't uncommon, it could have become a dangerous situation for us. Also, the 1935 Labor Day Hurricane came this way. And growing up in Connecticut, I'm sure you heard your parents talk about the Thirty-eight Hurricane or the Long Island Express as it was sometime affectionately referred to as. It came this way too. Those were some two nasty storms."

Even though both his parents were living in Portugal at the time, Dave nodded. By way of many firsthand accounts, he was well schooled to many of the influences the 1938 storm had on New England and as a result the extensive damage it left in its aftermath.

Randy continued. "I think the low pressure system that later became Camille came this way before feasting on the warmer shallower waters heading north through the West Indies. Right now we're sandwiched right between those dates as they occurred over time. Can you imagine getting caught up in either something like Camille or The Great Labor Day Storm? Gloria's a great boat, but monsters like those two would have shredded this sweet gem into pieces—in seconds."

"You seem to know your hurricanes."

"I'm fascinated by them. Also, with this being our playground, it doesn't hurt to be an expert on the subject either. Actually I'm no expert, but I know enough about them to keep my ass out of this area between June and November."

"But you're here." Linda added.

"Yeah, and as you can see, we're getting our asses out of here." What he wished to have added but omitted in the presence of the two kids was the fact they didn't have any children aboard. Such a factor alone lent more latitude for risk on their part.

Randy continued. "That reminds me, Dave. In my tack patterns, I usually don't come this far south. I only did so to meet you guys. That stated, I understand you're not familiar with these waters, so I need to tell you incase your haven't already heard. The doldrums for whatever reasons are encroaching further north by the day. I've heard this through the grapevine. I need to remind you then that you're already venturing way too dangerously south, although at least here you still seem to be okay. Being from Connecticut, I'm sure you're aware that when driving in the snow, that veering off onto any unplowed payment can easily get you sucked to the roadside, and then you're stuck. Know what I'm talking about?"

"Yeah, it's one of the first things my father taught me when winter driving—that and 'Steer away from spin, Davi! *A árvore* (Portuguese-*the tree*)— A árvore! — A árvore, Davi!!!'"

Well the doldrums will do the same to you if you're not careful. I've heard a couple horror stories about it.

Linda was appearing alarmed with Randy catching wind of her concern.

"I'm not trying to frighten you, Linda. Just respect where you are and get to where you're going. I feel it's my responsibility though to suggest that you should really start heading north as you run with these trade winds. That stated, I'm curious as to why you're crossing the Atlantic now. It would have been better waiting another couple months, no?"

"Dave's impatient. He wanted to bring his prize home."

"Well guys, let me sober your complacency a bit. First get your adorable kids home quickly and safely. Carolina and I really like you guys, so we were thinking maybe next year we can all get together with Jim and that saintly wife of his—you're welcomed to join of course."

Linda and Dave traded smiles in the reference of 'saintly' being made about Pamela. Randy picked up on their ocular exchange. "Don't get me wrong. I know she's a bit jaunty, but I've never met anyone as austere as her. That girl doesn't have malicious bone in her body either. Believe me, my Carolina adores her. Most of the time visiting, I never knew where those two girls were."

Dave was unable to contain his comment with the knowledge of later likely repercussions. "Looks like you've got some competition, honey."

Linda in turn responded with a fake smile. Uninterested in the gist of their banter, Randy only cringed inside in fearing that his warnings weren't being taken seriously.

In recognition of his rudeness, Dave chimed in, "You guys are great by the way. We appreciate everything, and believe me, your warnings aren't being taken lightly."

"I was afraid there for a moment, and I hope you're right. Your lives may depend on it. Hey listen. Please don't misinterpret what I'm saying as anything foreboding. Just continue your steady pace, and you should be fine. Just get yourselves home so we can meet next year. Meanwhile, I'll relay your regrets to Jim as well. If you want to socialize more, let's do so over the radio. Time's a decaying commodity. And like I said guys, start thinking north, okay?"

Once the two sailboats were freed from each other and goodbyes were bid, the two boats then drifted apart. Soon appearing as only specks on the horizons to each other, the Costas knew they were on their own. Both Dave and Linda understood it was highly unlikely they stood to bump into anyone else, there in middle of the Atlantic.

The kids were soon below deck. Outside and grinning, Linda affectionately backhanded Dave in the stomach. "I'll show you competition. And by the way, maybe I changed my mind. If Carolina and I did get together with Pamela, maybe we would have a nice slumber party omit the pajamas, and do so secretly so you can't watch. Remember what you said long ago—as long as I eventually tell you about it?"

Although only toying with him, he couldn't be certain anymore. In spite of its slight impact, Dave did his best to downplay Linda's comment.

"Sounds great in theory, but as far as all three of you together is concerned—too many arms and legs—couldn't keep track. Sounds like a long shot anyhow—like Randy would really go for that."

Dave was still mellowed from their earlier lovemaking, leaving him less prone to the effects of his wife's teasing. In spite, Linda still wasn't willing to go down without swinging.

"Yeah, a mesh of entangled flesh made up of a naked me, Pamela, and Carolina. And as far as any long shot might be concerned, never underestimate what us chicks are capable of. You heard Randy state it with him having no clue of the girls' whereabouts. I'm sure you'd choose watching your Giants over that, wouldn't you?"

"Divisional rival aside?" Dave came back, smirking.

Linda grinned with affection. "Looks like I need to start working on you again. And by the way, Carolina and Pamela might be a long shot, but do I know girls at the gym—we do talk." She then winked.

"Great. I'll be at my gym trading kicks with some of them landing me to the floor while you'll be planning some sort of private bathhouse get-together with your gym mates."

Linda then squeezed his hand. "You got a problem with that?"

"Yeah, as long as it's not my noggin getting smacked around in the process. You know how much I hate that." Grinning, he added, "Does that answer your question?"

"Well I'm going to join the kids below. And by the way, who said anything about private? They've seen you before and would have no problem with you joining. That I know for a fact."

Upon another flirtatious wink, Linda disappeared below. This time her comment did catch Dave's attention, leaving him alone and shaking his head.

"Pamela, you've managed to accomplish more in three days than what I have in eleven years—damn."

Gloria resumed its previous course west with the Costa family going about their normal activities. In scanning the airwaves pre-dawn Thursday in aim of linking with anyone, the chatter of distant voices echoing plenty of activity elsewhere in turn left Dave feeling isolated. Throughout the darkened hours he was twice able to make out the distinct luminosity of different supertankers, their deck floodlights highlighting their massive spans from afar. The floating cities glowing brightly yet dwarfed by the vastness of the dark horizon each came into view from the southeast before then fading in the west. Mesmerized, Dave used those long drawn-out events to break up morning's monotony by getting absorbed in the splendor of the two lucid ships' steady advances.

An eventual intermitting thumping noise emanating from below prompted him to peer down the companionway. There he was able to witness his still groggy wife wandering about sluggishly in Gloria's small galley. She then strayed to the main living area and began picking up a few mislaid items to buy more time for her mind to sharpen.

Witnessing his usually active wife lethargically meandering about in her favorite thigh-length, turquoise jersey reminded him of a time he once uncovered an inhabited hornet nest one brisk autumn morning. He did so just to find himself face-to-face with dozens of temporarily semi-sedated hornets still shaking off the night's chill. Had it been an hour or so hour later, Dave would have likely found himself in an emergency room instead.

Like the hornets sure to soon come to life, so did Linda. Fully awake, she was soon busy juggling the boat's activities including serving breakfast to her very hungry and fatigued husband. The former was more a result of the latter, and the latter was the dual result of both staying awake all night and his body being subject to a benumbing cooler breeze throughout its course.

Early afternoon and still wearing her favorite jersey and travel sun hat to match, Linda caught wind of Dave below linking up with someone. She quickly approached the companionway as he was establishing contact. Feeling her hovering over him, he shouted, "Honey, I've got Jim!"

Dave was overwhelmed by the event's improbability. In many attempts to summon his best friend over the previous several days, he was only to succeed after finally having given up all hope.

"Jim, it's good to hear from you, buddy."

Piggybacking that of her husband's, Pamela's voice rang in the background. "Hi everybody!"

"Bro, tell everyone I miss them. I love you Heather and David if you're there, and Pamela says 'hi' too, which you probably heard."

"Hi Pamela. I heard you. Jim, I want to apologize to the two of you for being such an ass and to also thank you guys for everything on behalf of me and Linda."

"Think nothing of it, bro. Friends sometimes fight and then afterwards they drink a beer over it. Down a cold brew for me and we'll call it a day. Besides, I spoke with Randy yesterday, and he relayed your mea culpa. I also learned he needed to escort Linda back to your boat so you two could finally score with each other. And how about his wife, Carolina, or should I say, Miss Legs? She and Pamela were like two peas in a pod together—two peas in a pod that is with smoking legs and killer asses. The two were mostly MIA though. I can only imagine those two sexy women together."

Both grinning and shaking his head, Dave then stepped on Jim's signal with Linda ushering their children away from the radio. "Thanks Jim. That's something I'm glad you could share with me and the family."

Linda took further exception, yelling from across the cabin. "No! Thanks Dave for not hitting the button sooner!"

The airwave was quiet for a moment before Jim spoke again.

"Oh, they're there? Sorry, bro. I guess Dick was right about the tight quarters. Hey, where are you anyhow?"

"In the middle of the freaking Atlantic, that's where," Dave responded before then following with their actual coordinates.

"Damn, I can' believe we're still in contact on this frequency. If Randy hadn't told me where you guys hooked up, I would have guessed you were still lost around these islands. I was worried there for a moment. Well the good news is everything's clear off the African coast. Just keep your status quo, and you'll be okay."

"Thanks bro. I have no intention on hanging around here, that's for sure. Randy reiterated that point to me."

Just then, Linda stormed back and grabbed the mike away from her husband. "Jim, you're a dead man!"

There was no response, only static. Linda's warm perspiration of vexation quickly cooled to that of a cold clamminess. Repeating, "Jim? Jim?" she then turned to Dave in dismayed. "We lost him."

Jim was no less disturbed on the other end, turning to Pamela. "I heard Linda say my name and then she was gone. I didn't even get a chance to thank them for the money. Even worse, looking at my charts here again, I'm not sure if Dave's been taking Randy's advice either. God I hope I'm wrong. I wish I had said something, but I was caught up in the moment—dammit! Pam, if only I had just said something—too late now."

Pamela approached her husband and in leaning to embrace him, rested her head against his. "That's okay, honey. At least you got a chance to talk to them and know they're okay."

Staring eerily into space, Jim affectionately placed his open palm against her face. "I know, Pam, and thanks. Maybe I'm wrong about the south thing. At least I hope I am. It's just that if Dave was able to nail the Doyles [Randy and Carolina] in the middle of the Atlantic, then it's highly unlikely he would have just given me some wrong coordinates just now."

<< CHAPTER 6 >>

FOLLOWING THE EERIE FEELING hung in the air upon losing contact with the Woodsons, Dave cheered the mood by making the necessary hookups to Gloria's sound system. His efforts paid off with an impressive projection of sound; it was static as they never heard it before.

Positioned at the helm that night, he sat gazing at the rich offerings of a panoramic celestial display blanketing the night sky with a vividness likened to that of Van Gogh influence. Although such stargazing lacked the substance of occupying every moment, he nonetheless didn't mind consuming many hours doing so in meditation. Relaxing in the seclusion of the open sea and immersed in the splendor of unimaginable distances to where his eyes were journeying him, Dave was simply savoring being in the moment.

There in deep reflection, his wandering mind fell victim to the sandman, the one entity that he was unable to elude there within the obscurity of the open sea. It was both a well-deserved and unexpected doze off that in turn feels so gratifying in ones onset.

Doing so also went against Dave's belief system. Beforehand, extra diligence had been paid in keeping awake when at the helm.

Occasional trips below didn't hurt the cause for breaking up the scenery including sometimes preparing hot coffee that could be appreciated in the cooler nighttime climate outside. He understood making a habit of napping while averaging eight plus knots for any extended period could leave him prone to waking just prior to making contact with the unyielding outer steel skin of some giant supertanker's double hull. Even in surviving a collision with such a colossal moving wall, the prospect of then getting sucked beneath the floating city and getting chewed up by its giant propellers would have given credence to the dangers of catnapping there in his position. Awakening to such a mishap would qualify as a worst-case scenario, even rendering benign the ruthless manic energy of a drill sergeant rudely welcoming their new recruits into military life—proceeded by the memorable early morning flick of the switch.

Dave eventually awoke. Fortunately for everyone aboard, his doing so wasn't the result of any clashing hulls spelling an ending within the ensuing seconds. Nor was it the brim of some drill sergeant against his forehead and the excruciating decibels of their trained voice sounding only inches away. Instead it was something far subtler, yet no less objectionable than the latter. Dave awoke to the soft sound of his sails flapping from the lack of leeward wind. As a result, their boat was barely being nudged along.

Gloria's previous progress still left him mostly unconcerned about any potential storm activity possibly originating off the West African coast. However, a deficiency of wind stood to change such an equation in keeping. Dave therefore wasn't thrilled about the prospect of sitting relatively idle for any duration with the potential of some developing storm planting its feet firmly in their respective starting blocks, waiting for the sound of a pistol to sprint west.

Using Gloria's knot stick, he estimated her speed at two knots. Also figuring in the westward sea current, which was undetectable since they were part on it, Dave estimated he was netting three to four knots, or a walking pace. It in turn did concern him with the understanding that neither tropical storms nor hurricanes ever stroll across the Atlantic at any leisurely walking pace.

With morning only three hours into the making, its onset tested Dave's belief as a realist. In an unwillingness to acknowledge the concept of either superstition or karma, several hours earlier he and Linda had poked fun about the upcoming day mocking people's beliefs whereby they sometimes attached so much emphasis to it. Though still not sold on the concept, he couldn't help but take notice of the coincidence of his present predicament. It was Friday the Thirteenth, and although still refusing to acknowledge any notions related to myths, the date's timing was nonetheless still unsettling to him.

In response to Gloria's rhythmic undulation having changed to that of a more ill syncopated vacillation, unlike her husband with the sounds of the sails, Linda instead awoke to the different character of the sea interacting with their hull. With Dave utilizing his face's many nerve endings in detection of the slightest wind variations, Linda startled him as he was facing sternward.

"Honey, what's happening?"

"The wind let up. It appears we're covering about three knots."

"Is this what Randy was talking about?"

"Maybe. I mean you know since that conversation we've had the sails slightly in a broad reach. I could have sworn the numbers indicated we were venturing somewhat north."

"Maybe it wasn't enough to compensate for the current."

"Good point and regardless, I just don't get what happened to the numbers."

"Well we are where we are, so what are we going to do now—use the engine to head north?"

"Too risky. I want to save all the fuel I can as a last resort—like storms and really rough seas. Can't risk that yet. Instead we'll see if we can suck more thrust out of these sails and also conserve water the best we can, I guess."

A day and a half of idleness carried the bored, discourage, and somewhat edgy family into mid-afternoon, Saturday the fourteenth. While a hot sun did offer a perfect sultry setting for Linda to pour on her erotic display for Dave, the deficiency of Gloria's progress in turn contributed in the dampening of her powerful libido. It was instead replaced with nervous energy.

In ransacking the premises below in aim of restowing everything for a net of a few unnecessary extra cubic feet of storage space, Linda did so while her two bored children moped about the cabin.

In hearing them sound mumbles of discontent, she waved any reprimand of their sulking in feeling some responsibility for being the cause behind their disgruntlement.

Meanwhile still fidgeting with Gloria's lines in frustration, Dave took notice of his upbeat wife suddenly summoning his attention below. With his boat still drudging along at a walking pace, any excitement either good or bad elicited an instant response.

He entered below to find her attempting to extract a box from beneath their owner's berth. Tightly wedged in its drawer, Dave assisted with its removal. Soon like kids gazing at unopened presents Christmas morning, everyone was huddled around it, standing wide-eyed. There were no markings on the box indicating any origin.

"Didn't you see this when you packed the cabin?" Dave asked.

"I swear, I packed every square inch of this place and saw nothing of the sort." They then both exchanged looks at each other, shouting in unison, "The Woodsons!"

"They left us a care package," Linda added. "That's so sweet."

Pausing a moment, she threw Dave a mischievous grin. "Can I open it?"

In response to his nod, she began opening the package, tearing its taped seams with her fingernails. Then in grabbing each of its two main flaps, she hesitated.

"Why are you stopping?"

"Dave, should we open this in private just in case?" She then whispered. "Our friends are swingers, you know."

"Honestly, at this point I don't care if some blowup doll springs out. Let's just shoot and ask questions later."

"Well I'll take a leap of faith here, and if this happens to be some sort of distasteful joke, Jim's a dead man. He still on my shit list for the comment on the radio."

Dave grinned, shaking his head. "It's a good thing I met you before he did. Otherwise, you'd probably be doing life in Somers [A Connecticut town referenced for a State Penitentiary located near its border]."

In removing the contents of the box, Linda's worse fears were replaced with jubilation. Uproar filled the cabin. Contained within were coloring books, crayons, reading material, a diary, a fountain pen, and ink in a bottle. There were also a couple Hot Wheels and a

Transformer for David. Meanwhile for the parents, there was a bottle of Sao Vicente homemade red wine and a note attached to it indicating a location where Jim had hidden their cassette player.

"The wheels in that boy's mind never stop spinning, do they?" Dave commented, laughing.

"Look who's talking, Mr. Fifteen thousand dollars."

Realizing that Jim likely forgot to mention the money in the excitement of their unexpected radio contact, Dave joked. "I hope he didn't end up mistakenly drying himself off with the money."

"Yeah, he's probably covered with paper cuts as we speak."

"That's not nice, though with him I could see it."

Savoring their windfall of gifts, the family's mood became more of an upbeat one. With Dave having interconnected their tape player and receiver thereby completing the final touches on their stereo system, the family was now afforded a better variety of sound versus that of just static.

As far as little David was concerned, the commanders of the mid-twentieth century could now retire. Furthermore, the little plastic figurines whose represented lives he had so callously exploited could now intermingle with their foes in some darkened shoebox.

After Heather finished examining their bottle of homemade wine, Linda secured it to a safe place where Gloria's movement wouldn't serve it up as some salad of red wine and glass. Also found concealed with the cassette player, she examined some recorded tapes of which Jim knew from years back she and Dave would be able to enjoy. Although the Costas were still stagnant in posture, the morale of the family was mostly still intact, despite of it.

The previous afternoon and approximately three thousand miles east, a solidified soil baking beneath the bare feet of a northern Nigerian farmer was the result of an endless flow of arid air being subject to the constant effects of an unrelenting blistering sun. Countless years of the sun's subjection bore its mark on the man's face leading anyone to believe he was likely twenty years beyond his actual age. There he stood still, hopelessly inspecting his barren land that in recent years had been yielding to the indiscriminating desertification forces of a relentless southward expanding Sahara. It was encroaching southward from his northern neighbor of Niger, whose citizens knew all to well the harsh realities of desert life.

Submitted to the reality he'd eventually need to relocate further south, yet still holding out as long as possible on a thread of hope, the farmer simply gazed upward into a blue sky. There he noted an absence of fine Sahara dust that at times would obscure the sun with its rusted ruby cloak, the meanwhile him being in constant subjection to an unrelenting rush of heated air interacting with his body.

Several hours later and hundreds of miles southwest, his fellow countrymen needed to fix their eyes upward to witness the same convection of dryer air. Now miles above them, it was interacting with more humid air spilling in from the Gulf of New Guinea further south. As the farmers' countrymen were sweating it out below in their balmy surroundings, clashes were taking place several miles above their position thereby causing outbreaks of scattered thunderstorms to be spawning throughout the region. Several hours following, the same air the Nigerian farmer felt harmlessly brushing up against his body was now joining forces on a massive scale, destabilizing everything in its westward track.

Little did that modest Nigerian farmer know at the time as he was scrutinizing his barren soil hours earlier, nor would he ever, was that the same flow of heated air he experienced interacting with his body on that blistering day would eventually seat a seed that in turn would grow into an entity, of which in time would become a mimesis of monumental proportions. What the humble unsuspecting farmer was in direct involvement with that particular day was the genesis to the birth of a meteorological monster.

Later the next day with the Costa's stereo system hooked up and the family making the best of their stagnation, the same air that the farmer took into his lungs a day earlier was now traveling west through the mid-tropical region of West Africa. Gaining mass, it was doing so similar to a snowball gaining size, proliferating in its advance while also taking on a regional counterclockwise rotation as well.

Because the easterly wave hadn't reached the West African coast yet, it therefore didn't warrant enough attention for the maritime meteorological community to broadcast any verification of it. That was because many such developing storms like it were prone to dissipation, amounting to little of any significance.

What the farmer did notice the previous day was that a bright blue sky above revealed an absence of any reddish hue. With only a negligible quantity of fine Sahara dust spilling west in the upper atmosphere, conditions were therefore more favorable for a developing storm to flourish. Opposed by negligible impedance from above as a result, one could then feast upon an endless supply of humid air made available by a mild ocean below.

As the result of the care package left by the Woodson's, the pre-stagnant activities aboard Gloria were once again of a more routine nature. Meanwhile, while Dave's mood was far improved there seated at the helm on the afternoon of the fifteenth, he was nevertheless still uneasy about their rate of progress. It came in the face of being unaware that a substantial tropical wave had just firmly planted its feet in its starting blocks off Africa's west coast and it was there poised to head west towards the Americas, placing him and his family directly in-between.

By the time Linda was ready to turn in prior to midnight, the large easterly wave had already left the West African continent behind and was heading their way. Capping the evening by sharing their homemade wine, Linda went straight to bed afterwards. Dave instead chose to chase it with a couple of beers, and in there doing, inadvertently dozed off while resting his head atop some charts.

Waking a few minutes later brought on an urgency of manning the helm, doing so rather than checking the latest meteorological broadcast made available. Concerned they might pick up at any moment with Gloria's sails still maximized, the idea of ignoring the outside elements for any duration didn't settle well with Dave. His uncharacteristic neglect of checking the shortwave that evening was catalyzed by a confidence that all the previous meteorological activity reported to the present juncture indicated that the coast was still clear behind them.

Twenty-four hours later, a sufficient amount of sleep left Dave feeling no need to rest his head again as he did the night before. If Linda hadn't placed her full confidence in him for checking the weather, she instead would have done so herself. But between watching over the boat during her husband's resting period and overseeing the kids, notwithstanding running the household and homeschooling Heather, her plate was far more demanding then that of her husband's. It was Dave's willingness to play night watchman of which she wanted no part that kept him off the hook of most of the household chores. In general, complacency was becoming a dangerous habit on the duel's part.

In finally checking the weather report, the tail end of a repeated forecast revealing a regional disturbance of decent size provided Dave the luxury of being able to ignore it. Both its moderate character and location further north allowed for his doing so.

He also noted the mention of the dominant Azores High as trivial. The large mass of regional air was a summer staple of the North Atlantic and posed no threat in itself. Any such details supporting a status quo suited Dave just fine.

What caught his attention next didn't. The mention of the large benign air mass in turn segued into its direct influence on an impressive tropical disturbance of which he held no prior knowledge of the latter. The high was a steering force that was now directing the foul weather directly towards their position.

Dave listened unnervingly to the news of the ominous genesis lurking only days behind him. He was then able to estimate its present location at less than a hundred miles south of where he and Linda witnessed their unnerving experience of Brava. Its eerie reference sent chills down his spine in remembering traversing just north of those waters eight days prior. Also offering no peace of mind was the knowledge that a storm that he just learned about was now heading his way far quicker than he could ever wish to be distancing himself away from it.

In believing Gloria was well up to the task, Dave was still confident in his abilities of being able to ride out such a storm. While refusing to accept Jim's warnings prior to takeoff might have just substantiated into reality, he chose instead to label any impending rendezvous with the new storm presently in its infancy as worse case, problematic. Any alarm on his part mostly stemmed from first hearing of its existence, because with the exception of the previous day, diligence had been paid in the monitoring of all available weather updates.

Checking charts and mapping different courses in projection of their progress against that of the storms supported the belief that the Caribbean region might still be attainable before the ensuing storm would catch them. Such a premise was hinged under the conditions that the surrounding winds would pick up within the next couple days. In believing a plea for help would likely be received in such close proximity to the islands if he should happen to reach them beforehand, Dave therefore presumed that hope for rescue could then be considered a forgone conclusion at such a juncture.

In further brainstorming, he surmised with both his wife and kids then removed from Gloria's dangerous confines, it would then free him up to remain aboard her at the risk of his own safety. It was in guessing his boat's durability would then be better put to task out at sea versus dry-docked or moored like some sitting duck in some foreign marina.

Shy of sunrise, Dave had just returned to the helm following hearing the latest weather update. In hearing Linda clomping around below, he viewed it as an opportunity to make a preemptive strike. There he returned again with the hope of catching her while still in the early stages of consciousness.

"Honey, there's something we need to discuss before the kids get up."

While his words weren't enough to have snapped her of her morning funk in spite of being stated in the middle of the Atlantic, Linda still took notice in her own quiet way. She greeted him with a sticky lip, good morning kiss.

"This has to be good. If it can wait a minute, I need to freshen up. Then I'll fix some coffee and join you on deck, okay? Don't worry—no funny business."

Soon sitting by Dave at the helm and sipping her coffee, her legs crossed, Linda spoke first. "What are you about to tell me—some hurricane's coming our way or something?"

"I don't know how you do that, but to answer your question, right now it's only a something, not a hurricane—thank God." He then paused, adding, "a tropical depression, to be more specific."

"Didn't we just spend over a day in one of those things?"

"No that was just a disturbance—nothing organized. This one on the other hand is a little more substantial. The good news is new data indicates it hasn't intensified. I just learned that before you got up."

"I heard you. That's what woke me. And what do you mean by,

'substantial'?"

"Around thirty knot winds, some scattered thunderstorms, and it's rotating regionally. You could say this one's breathing."

Based on their present course and assuming the status quo of their present position wasn't going to change, Dave was candid in explaining when the storm was likely to overtake them. Although Linda wasn't pleased at the news, he was nonetheless impressed at how well she maintained her composure in hearing of it. Like him, her greatest concern was for their kids.

Next in mentioning policing Gloria post her and the kids' rescue, Linda shattered her husband's previous reasoning.

"That sounds great. I'll be comforting the kids while you're out on some suicide mission seeing after the boat. And if you do make port in Rhode Island without killing yourself first, I'll make sure a moving truck's there with all your belongings waiting for you." In snapping, she added, "I'll even rent a storage spot for you just incase you need some extra fucking space! How could you even think that?"

In such a specific case where she so vehemently expressed an expletive in such a manner, Dave could then be certain that it was unlikely his wife was going to stand erect at any moment and lift her thigh-length tee shirt for any booty show.

Once she cooled down, he was at least able to provoke one cynical laugh from the events unfolding, slowly shaking his head in perplexity.

"Here's the interesting part. When you mention the name, Gloria, make sure you're differentiating between our boat and this damn storm breathing down our necks."

In such a light moment of trivialization, Linda smiled in both amazement and denial. "You've got to be shitting me. The storm's name is Gloria? That's not interesting—it's more like fucked up."

Dave just shook his head slowly with a pondering grin. "Not the type of symmetry I can appreciate. And you know honey, against everything I believe, there still seems to be something quite clairvoyant about Dick that just seems to keep resurfacing. It's weird."

"Maybe you should start rethinking your stance on the concept."

"Yeah, maybe."

With neither of the two in an immediate panic state, an option of heading north days prior to the ominous weather system possibly overtaking them didn't sit well with Dave. He understood storms like Gloria had the tendency of traveling unpredictable paths, and therefore deduced such a mass of foul weather would do little in rendering those already treacherous waters further north any less so, even hundreds of miles away.

He and Linda seized their lull as an opportunity for checking the condition of their boat. They also coordinated plans in the hopes of minimizing confusion in case of finding themselves face-to-face with the ensuing storm. Upon doing so, the fruits of their labor left them both feeling somewhat confident that all possible survival methods would be able to be implemented in the face of conditions they had no control over. Both manning their radio for Mayday purposes and keeping hunkered down were the only viable options the two believed was still left at their disposal.

News of the developing storm back in Sao Vicente fell hard on Jim. In keeping atop it, he did his best to keep his anxiety from Pamela. She the meanwhile wrote his lack of passion off as general concern for his friends leading to the moment. If getting caught in humiliation with his pants down in front of Pastor John and then the talks that ensued afterwards wasn't enough to have swayed him to atone for his ways, news of the tropical wave leaving the West African coast behind was.

Based on some latest stats, Jim believed his friends needed every prayer they could muster in having calculated that an upgraded Gloria to that of a hurricane was finally upon them.

Any plans the Costas implemented were simply no match for an eventual *Category-Three hurricane* (The Saffir-Simpson Hurricane Scale). Its 120 mph sustained winds producing both driving rain and sea spray were together pelting Dave like unending waves of bees assaulting his body. They were also surrounding him with mountains of water, some of which he could barely traverse.

Even with their sails furled to minimize the wind's effects, Gloria continued heeling dangerously until one particular swell caused it to slam into the water. With her mast then getting snapped off footing, she rolled a full summersault and returned upright again due to her heavy keel and upward buoyant momentum. With Gloria still floundering about, her helm only bore witness to a snapped tether line—but no Dave attached.

Below, Linda had loss consciousness in striking her head during the roll, thereby leaving behind her terrified children rolling about helplessly and holding each other in shear terror. Around them their surroundings appeared as if an explosive had just detonated there. Their extreme trepidation was short-lived when a much larger wave carried Gloria halfway up its crescent wall before then crushing it into pieces, killing everyone remaining.

At the moment of such a chilling scenario playing out, Jim shot up from an overactive REM state gasping for air and soaking of sweat. It caused Pamela to also jolt upright, first turning on a lamp next to her and then grabbing her distraught husband's moist arm.

"What is it?"

In waiting for his hyperventilating to subside, Jim just stared downward for a moment. Then with Pamela affectionately brushing his damp hair, he finally spoke.

"Sorry Pam. There's stuff I simply needed to keep under wraps from you, because in all reality it could all amount to nothing."

"I'm all ears honey, and tougher than you think."

"You are, but you're a mush ball too."

Jim summarized about the storm while explaining its potential for further development. He then related it to his concerns for the Costa family. Now also concerned, Pamela asked, "what was your dream about?"

"Them—our Costa friends that is. Although they could be in some danger, they should be able to make it to the Caribbean before the storm ever reaches them—and have time to spare. At least there they'll have a better chance of finding safety."

"Well that's good to hear honey, but the dream, that wasn't any ordinary dream."

Jim hesitated before answering.

"When I was on a naval frigate we were in some nasty seas and out of nowhere this huge wave just appeared. We only caught its fringes, and that in itself was unpleasant enough. I mean you could feel its presence. It was as if hell was opening its mouth and even out of its full path, it still rocked us sideways pretty violently. When all was said and done, I was lying flat on my ass wondering if I was still alive. You talk about disorientation. Damn that was fucked up!"

Pamela was unnerved. "But you were in a naval vessel you told me. Aren't they designed for that kind of thing?"

"Honestly Pam, I don't know—maybe carriers or larger ships. In our case you could see that the freaking wave was towering higher than any point of our ship. It was messed up. It just grew up out of the water as we dropped and at the angle we were to it, I think it could have capsized us. Its main crest just missed us, and who knows? Hadn't it done so, I might have been one of the lucky ones. I was briefly on the weather deck when it emerged. Instant death—no suffering—you know?"

In snuggling closer, Pamela was disturbed.

"I'd hardly call that lucky. You never told me this."

"Well it's not one of my top ten fondest memories to rehash. Experiencing one of those things surely was never part of my bucket list either. I mean I just froze in complete terror—couldn't react. Like I said, you could actually feel its presence."

Pamela's normally tanned complexion showed little evidence of any of its usual rich hue. "What do you mean by feeling its presence anyhow?"

"Hard to explain—maybe all the air that was being displaced around us—I don't know. And the sound as it grew. It was eerie as hell. You could actually feel it growing. You know I was so freaked out afterwards that that when my adrenaline finally wore off, I swear, I'm surprised I didn't end up puking my toenails up in addition to breakfast—and my intestines, and liver—get the point? Me and others guys too. It was a freaking puke fest—such a lovely moment. I miss those days. Such comradery."

Jim grew uneasy in continuing. "In my dream, Gloria appeared as a small toy boat in comparison to the wave, which in reality would be the case."

Pamela then held her husband until both felt comfortable enough to turn the lights back off. After a brief period of the two feeling amorously in sync with each other, she broke the silence. "Do you think they'll be alright?"

"Oh I hope so, Pam. I love Dave and Linda. I mean they're my longtime friends, but the image of David and Heather so innocently standing on deck and waving back to us—their naïve faces still haunt me every freaking second."

"But you said they can outrun the storm."

Jim lied silent for a moment before responding. "The truth is they don't have much of a choice. I have a bad feeling about this one. I mean I've followed storms like this before, and with both the warm water out there and a lack of shear winds to the north, they just don't go away. The thing is strengthening too. And from what I've extrapolated, my guess is they need to outrun it, because that damn Azores High isn't giving them any other choice."

"What's an Azores High?"

"Right now, my biggest nightmare. Can I tell you something else that's a little bit on the freak side?"

"Of course honey, please do so—no more secrets."

"The American forecasters are calling this one "Gloria." Damn, go figure, huh? That's freaking crazy, hence my bad feeling."

What Jim was unaware of, which in turn would have further posed him little comfort, was a somewhat weak 1985 El Nino that particular year translated to all tropical activity in the Atlantic that season being less predisposed to the disruptive forces of wind shear being driven in from the west.

Meanwhile, instead of Jim feeling better as a result of having shared the news of Storm Gloria with Pamela, her having guessed beforehand that his doing so might lighten the load for him, instead both the information and imagery he ended up sharing with her in turn left Pamela feeling no less apprehensive than he already was.

<< CHAPTER 7 >>

DAVE WAS JUST RISING up out of bed early Wednesday afternoon, September 18, Cape Verde time zone plus two *UTC* (Coordinated Universal Time). Against what would have been his best wishes, Linda had sabotaged his alarm clock to grant him extra sleep. She did so in understanding his likely role in the days to follow would include riding out violent weather for a prolonged period. Unlike him, she considered her husband's state of rest no differently than any other means of preparation for what was upgraded from tropical depression to that of a tropical storm.

Dave eventually strolled out onto the deck after finishing playing with his children. He made a point of spending more time with them in the hope of squashing any suspicions of which they may have already formulated, especially in the case involving his bright daughter. Having noticed a different feel to Gloria below, he exited outside to witness Linda seated at the helm grinning. Her look resembled that of someone who just won the lottery and was holding out on the winning ticket. With Gloria's sails in full capacity and its progress west at an impressive rate forward, he simply faced sternward in appreciating of the rejuvenated winds.

"Oh, that's awesome. Have you checked the storm? Last three reports I received say that it's increased its pace towards us."

"Hey, don't sound so bleak. Look, we're moving along again."

"Oh, don't get me wrong. This is exactly what the doctor ordered. I just hope it's enough to make up for any of our delay. I'll crunch the numbers to make sure."

"Well, with the kids and everything I needed to be careful with Heather. I only got bits and pieces on the storm."

"Good call with the kids by the way. Thanks"

"Hey, not that I had any choice, but you're welcome. Anyhow, to answer your question, from what I gathered, the storm's winds haven't changed. I know that much."

Linda then took a deep breath in appreciation of the stronger winds.

"Doesn't this feel great? You know we're lucky that the kids don't get seasick. It's great being able to share this with them."

"Outside of this tropical storm riding our asses, I might agree." Dave then turned to the companionway. "Be back to relieve you."

"Take your time, dear. This is heaven."

Both Dave and Linda were thrilled at the prospect of being able to manage the new aggressive winds. Later that afternoon with their sails being stretched to full capacity, Linda entered the cockpit to witness seeing Dave standing between the mainsail and jib relishing their full occupancy.

"I hashed the numbers and this is it. I can't figure out what's been holding us up the last four days. Maybe Randy was right, but it doesn't matter now, because I'll make damn sure we head further north this time. Fool me once, you know. Either way, we're back in business. Hey Gloria!" Dave yelled, facing east while doing so. "Catch us now you stupid bitch!"

"Honey, easy on the bravado, please! Watch what you're asking for!"

The winds never let up. The onset of their strengthening also came with the need of more diligent seamanship. Extra care needed to be taken for safely harnessing the generous forces that were now being exerted onto Gloria's sails. While such a task might stand to pose trivial for any seasoned yachtspersons in keeping with their demands, Dave and Linda being no exception, doing so effectively twenty-four seven and possibly for a fortnight or two without succumbing to mental fatigue was a challenge they both were not only thrilled to embrace, it was one they needed to realize as well.

Revisit of their shortwave in a routine check revealed that Tropical Storm Gloria was downgraded back down to a tropical depression. Just as significant, it also slowed its rate of advance towards them. Based on new calculations, Dave concluded they could now expect to be able to reach the Caribbean region before the ensuing storm would be able to swat the effects of her protracted claws at them. There, they'd likely be able to view Storm Gloria in the morning eastern skies as nothing more than a reddish sunrise. Although still sounding warnings to discourage any sense of complacency, it would at least pose as no imminent threat. Any hope for rescue could then be considered a foregone conclusion.

Recognizing that they still weren't out of the woods yet didn't prevent a wary Costa duo from averting back to their previous activities of a playful nature again. Doing so worked as a conduit for passing the time away by mentally shielding them from the threat still lying to their east.

Linda appeared on deck modeling the lack of attire beneath her prized turquoise tee shirt. She did so, rubbing up against the mast as if it was some oversized dancer's pole. Her next move of then embracing it concurrent to performing a one legged curl and wiggling her toes like some glamorous 1950s bikini starlet arouse a genuine snicker in Dave. Viewing his wife's actions in the same light as some cheesy low budget B-film, he simple sat in contentedness, the meanwhile paying mind to the sails and enjoying his wife's exhibition. He also preferred keeping such an observation private.

Subsequent to a derriere shot and facing Dave again, Linda just grinned with an air of seduction. Then in propping the small of her back against Gloria's horizontal boom, its rigging gave way, thereby destabilizing her only means of balance before subsequently sending her tumbling backwards over Gloria's outer rails in a full somersault. Linda soon found herself disorientated, struggling just to keep her head above Gloria's churning wake. In brief glimpses above the surface and surrounded by seven foot swells, she could only helplessly watch her boat distanced itself further away, veering off erratically without full sail control.

Prompted into fight mode, Dave jetted to the swinging boom with an understanding that if he too was to go overboard, then the branch he solely represented in the continuation of his family's lineage would cease as an entity altogether. With minutes seeming an eternity, he helplessly witnessed his wife lag further behind until unable to decipher any evidence of her at all. He understood waters even as mild as those in the tropics were still capable of eventually succumbing someone in her position to hyperthermia.

This left him no choice but to summon his children from below. Expediting their extra set of eyes as lookouts, Dave could see that his wife's hourglass window of time was already revealing a small heap of sand accumulated at its lower half. Unaware of her whereabouts, he refused to power his engine in fear that doing so might either endanger her if she happened to be nearby or at best mask any cries for help.

While his mannerisms may have appeared businesslike in mien in conducting his search, Dave was no less sick to his stomach. Remembering his wife playfully flirting with him one moment and then the next fearing he just lost her forever overboard, there was complete shock at how quickly the tides of fortune could change at sea. The fragility of life never became more apparent to him than at that moment. Understanding Linda still might be conscious and even able to resist hyperthermia for an extended period of time, it still didn't guarantee she would be able to sustain treading water in the surrounding active sea, especially without a flotation device.

The kids were afforded full latitude near the outer deck railing, leaving it Heather's responsibility for watching over her brother. In panning the horizon with her keen eyes, tears the meanwhile were fighting for dominance in their openings. Her brother, who seemed to be doing the same as her, was simply numb with dread, his mind blanked.

Dave privately wagered giving up their life earnings just to be able to go back in time so he could once again enforce his wife's employment of a safety vest when outside of the cockpit. He instead had just traded such a preventive measure simply for a cheap thrill.

Giving credence to his desperate frame of mind, fifteen minutes of grueling searching led him to climbing his mast. Being no friends of heights, Dave was left no choice but to do so, even in the face of Gloria's erratic heeling.

A few minutes of frantic searching perched eventually led to the spotting of Linda. Seeing her struggling just to keep afloat and fearing any of her next submersions might be a last, Dave wasted no time in employing his engine to exact a rescue. Soon in being able to clasp her cold slippery hand from their transom, as far as he was concerned, there wasn't any force that was going to prohibit him from maintaining his unyielding grip.

Thereafter pulling his terrified wife back into the safe confines of Gloria's cockpit, all four family members were soon locked in an inseparable embrace. It was one laden with intense emotion. With Linda still in shock, she was unable to process her relative safety and thereby still unable to count her blessings. Upon Heather and David having fetched blankets from below at their dad's request, the four Costas were once again all huddled together in the cockpit. In spite of Linda still shivering uncontrollably, everyone was simply relieved to be together again in whole as a family.

In eventually relinquished her part of the group hug in focus of her kids, Linda did so with the acknowledgement that she not only almost left her kids without a mother, but she nearly also left them with only a dad to potentially face a dangerous storm by himself. Tapping into an untouched reserve of strength, she held both her children tightly, meanwhile reaffirming her love repeatedly and promising never to leave them again.

To soften the hard reality that he almost lost his wife at sea, Dave chalked the experience up as a sober reminder to once again comply with his safety measures as were outlined before. It had just become clear to him that the Mid-Atlantic wasn't some kind of erotic playground to be careless toyed with. He could envision Randy staring down at him in total disillusionment, disappointed in not having taking his warnings serious enough.

The shock of recent events dissipating led Dave on the track of Gloria's failed boom. With the jib not cutting it alone, he needed to effect a quick repair to the failed assembly in any hopes of keeping out of harm's way of the ensuing storm. Doing so led to a smoking gun. It was a shackle pin whose inferior replacement of a standard bolt was sheared into two sections. Upon visiting his parts box and discovering no replacement for his swivel pulley, disbelief left Dave seated idle in a squatted position. He now understood that such a discrepancy overlooked beforehand likely just condemned him and his family to facing a monster advancing from the east.

As a last ditch effort to keep Gloria sails in a run position, nylon line was employed to tie them off at several points to his boat. While confident rigging his sails in such a crude manner would work, Dave was also aware such jury-rigging would render his sails less effective than any pulley system. It equating to both a loss of a few precious knots and less flexibility in making sail adjustments at a moment's notice.

Making matters worse, a midnight forecast revealed that the once downgraded tropical depression was again intensified back into a tropical storm. It could best be likened to a promising rookie boxer having falling to the canvass on their first professional bout. In their comeback, a much hungrier and more disciplined fighter is unstoppable in their quest. Similar to the reemerging boxer, Gloria too was now stronger, more mature, and seemed to carry with it a far more determined attitude than that of before.

A reddish glow to the east revealed by the next day's sunrise substantiated that Tropical Storm Gloria was no longer just some abstract data being transmitted. It in turn warranted the need for the Costas to get a lot more acquainted with their hand radio.

Later that Friday morning, Dave was below following only a couple hours of sleep. He was there with the others preparing to man the helm when their boat suddenly heeled 90 degrees. Along with a deafening roar sounding throughout their cabin, Gloria's heeling also caused everyone to first tumble to its portside before then cascading back to the floor in its recovery. Upon verifying no injuries, Dave quickly ascended the companionway. Peering out a small window atop it, he could see water spilling out of Gloria's cockpit.

"What is it that you see out there, sweetie?" Linda asked, the meanwhile attempting to comfort her children.

"Water draining—looks clear besides that. I guess we must have just gotten hit by one of those freakish waves I heard come out of nowhere. As soon as the water clears, I'll go outside and check that everything's okay." In panning the interior, he added, "at least it seems okay in here, thank God. The kids aren't hurt."

Linda observed Dave in commence of his exit to outside. "Be

careful, honey. There could be more of those."

"You don't have to tell me twice. I've got a soiled pair of skivvies to attest to that."

Outside and with nothing in the seascape indicating the source of any anomalies of a threatening nature, Dave knew better than taking any comfort in such an observation. An ominous spectacle also paying little comfort was an alarming display of their mast fully severed. Its unattached section steeped in the water was only being held to Gloria by an inextricable entanglement of twisted lines and sails.

Punctuating the reality that the family would now need to face a storm increasingly strengthening by the hour, Dave just stared at the mess. It was as if his will too had just lost all of its wind. In viewing their previous ticket to safety now in shambles, he just bowed his head in defeat.

"Dammit! Can't we just once catch a freaking break? God, what do I tell others now?"

The only thing Dave was certain of was a desire to wrap his hands around the neck of the individual responsible for their substandard pin replacement. Outside of the wave, he was also astounded at how the difference between life and death in the open ocean could boil down to a same size piece of metal, but of a lesser grade.

The Costas were now sitting relatively idle, approximately one day ahead of Storm Gloria's advancing center. Unless it was to suddenly veer either north or south, their sailboat stood to soon find itself rendezvousing with her leading northwestern edge by the following morning. Their predicament could best be likened to that of a quarterback standing in the pocket of his own end zone with no available receivers, the meanwhile witnessing uncontested defensemen all bigger and faster than him quickly approaching.

Dave slowly made his way below to break the news of the mast to Linda. Witnessing his demeanor, she commented. "Oh my God, this can't be good."

The news thereafter fell hard on her. It left her feeling as if she would need Gloria's bilge pump to force the cold blood in her veins to resume flowing again. Never before did Linda ever see the rich tanned complexion of her husband appear so grey.

The family's future now hinged on how well Dave would be able to ride out an already dangerous and strengthening storm by virtue of diesel power. A condition that no mechanical failure would further exasperate their predicament was no less of a factor either. Negotiation of a fine line such as battening down and signaling for assistance without alerting their kids something was amiss required vigilance. Doing so would require keeping them below and out of sight of their broken mast, of which its severed section still needed to be expelled into the ocean.

Even in the face of such bleak circumstances, both parents still refused to accept something appearing as an impasse to the future actually spelled any foregone conclusion. They also didn't neglect to overlook that by having indulged in less than wholesome activities on Sao Vincente a few weeks earlier, they had essentially violated their Christian upbringing in doing so. Like those in extreme peril sometimes submitting to a future of piety, for Dave and Linda, consideration of doing the same was a likewise self-serving vehicle.

The two believed relinquishing their fate to God would then allow the burden of what could be done to make any difference to be realigned. While neither parent believed they deserved any mercy due to their own stray from the flock, they did take some solace in believing their two innocent children didn't deserve the same fate as them. In rationalizing they could then survive the storm by riding on the moral coattails of their children, both Dave and Linda also understood the fragility of such reasoning stood no chance of holding up against the powerful winds that a storm such as Gloria was poised to deliver.

Later on that Friday afternoon, most recent available updated storm data revealed that although its wind velocity didn't increase, its pressure did decrease; good news only for hurricane enthusiast watching from afar. The storm's center was headed just south of the Costas at a clip of 16 knots, placing Dave least where he wanted to be in proximity to it. Use of valuable diesel fuel to evade its advancing center by heading either north or south was still too much of a gamble he was willing consider. For Dave, consideration of any such desperate move wasn't going to be contemplated until first hearing of the next weather report slated for that midnight.

Upon expelling everything but the intact portion of their mast,

Dave duct taped their antenna to its remaining section with the hopes that its limited elevation might still afford some capacity of transmission. In returning below to see how his children were faring, he did so just to find his son sitting on the floor fiddling with his Transformer. In taking notice of him singing unmelodic tunes in an undecipherable language, he squatted next to his boy.

"When you see Mr. and Mrs. Woodson, are you going to thank them for that? They gave it to you."

David continued murmuring more tunes before eerily mumbling in a monotone. "Thank you Mr. Woodsin."

No longer playing his son's behavior off as just normal child preoccupation, Dave gently guided his little boy's head upward. "Hi David, are you in there?"

"He's scared Dad," Heather chimed in. "He thinks were gonna die."

Dave laughed at the ludicrousness of his daughter's comment in not imagining that his son possessed the capacity of entertaining such a notion as death. It in turn prompted both him and Linda to focus their attention onto her instead. They were mindful their boy's fears likely stemmed from something that she may have said. Linda approached her daughter, also mindful her and Dave's own actions were directly responsible for having placed their children in such a precarious position in the first place.

"Did you say something bad to David?"

"Heather said we're gonna die," David interjected.

This prompted Linda to sit on the floor next to her son. "David, do you know what die means?"

To his parent's dismay, he responded, "Yep, my hamsters Denny died. He was still and never woke. I don't wanna die, Mommy."

Their boy then began tinkering with his toy again, once again vocalizing tunes of an indiscernible nature.

Linda gently placed her hand over her son's. "Sweetie, Denny was old for a hamster, and it was his time to go to heaven. You're young. You and Heather don't have to worry about that."

"Are you and Dad gonna die? You're old, like Denny."

Struggling to contain her tears, Linda turned to Dave, who picked up on her distress.

"We'll go to heaven when were good and ready, which means you're stuck with us for a long time there buddy, okay?"

The father's little pep talk was also a self-therapeutic one as well. "David, Daddy's going outside now to keep you guys safe. That's what I do every night when you're asleep. Grab a life vest and come upstairs with me, okay buddy?"

Soon seated with his son outside, Dave explained the conditions that were likely to confront them. In doing so, a short but violent thunderstorm they experienced en route was mentioned.

"Do you remember the thunderstorm?"

"Yep, it was noisy. The boat moved round a lot. I was willy skeiwd."

"Why were you scared?"

David grew fidgety, "I donno, I was juth skaired, Daddy."

"I wasn't scared. I was outside having fun."

His statement was a half-truth. Dave was an adrenaline junkie, which is where his enjoyment of helming during the storm went no further. At the height of the storm, he would have entered the cabin for cover in fear for his life, but was instead too afraid of leaving the relative safety of his seat to do so. It caused him to come clean, sitting his son on his lap and grabbing his shoulders in a reassuring manner.

"David, hear me out. There's a storm heading our way and will be like that thunderstorm the other day. The only difference is this one will last longer, and don't worry, this boat's made for that type of weather. Do you follow me, buddy?" Upon his son nodding, he continued. "This boat likes storms, and Mommy will be with you and your sister below, keeping you safe. Do you still follow me?"

While the little boy was normally incapable of accommodating so many consecutive statements, the nature of the subject matter being conveyed was evoking enough for him to barely be able to do so. With his son's acknowledgement, Dave continued. "Santa will be watching you as well. He'll give you anything you ask for if you make Daddy proud, okay?"

"Anything Dad?"

"I swear, anything." Before escorting his son below, he kissed him atop his head. "Mommy and Daddy love you very much and would never let anything bad happen to you. You'll even have Santa keeping an eye on you as well, okay slugger?"

At that point, the lump in Dave's throat felt as prominent as the storm closing in on them. He needed to clear it again when David spotted the snapped mast in returning below.

"Daddy, why is the stick broken?"

With his wheels spinning, Dave responded, "They do that all the time, big guy. Right now we're on the way to getting a new one." The thought then crossed his mind. "Yeah, but unfortunately we'll likely have to weather the freaking apocalypse first."

Linda also engaged her daughter in a heart-to-heart talk about the events to follow. Although Heather questioned the validity of any man's ability to pop in on billions of households within a span of twenty-four plus hours of darkness, she still held on to a belief in his spirit. It wasn't enough though to fall for the likes of the same negotiations, as did her brother. Linda's tactics were more direct, and to her surprise Heather calmly accepted them. That in turn left her somewhat wondering afterwards if she had really actually gotten through to her bright daughter.

While guessing some may have been nothing more than the product of folklore, both Dave and Linda still believed in the existence of rogue waves. They mostly received accounts of them through the veneer of a few testimonies. Such a lack of concrete proof was likely a result of most mariners' unwillingness to summit to the notion that any entity delivered by the sea could render their abilities, ineffective—or they were dead.

Dave believed some disproportionately size wave approximating twenty-feet was likely responsible for their present predicament. While such anomalies were dangerous in their unexpected debuts, they didn't fit into the same deadly category as the much larger crushing rogue waves. Like many others who saw the original *Poseidon Adventure* back in the early seventies, the two also found themselves holding their breaths throughout most of the movie. For many, it was the movie that introduced them to the idea of the existence of such monstrous waves.

In spite of how badly the elements stood to hammer him outside, Dave still believed Storm Gloria could be weathered with the full supply of diesel fuel they had. Radioing for help and if unsuccessful eventually needing to buckle down outside and stay aboard was now the only viable option he concluded was left. The haunted faces of his distressed children were a sober reminder of that.

With Saturday, September 21 just lurking around the corner, Linda was tending to the radio while Dave was outside checking the horizon for any signs of maritime activity—including waves. In viewing the setting moon to his west, an eerie sight of Earth's celestial partner emanating a rich ruby crescent glow held his attention in its soon convergence with the horizon. Mesmerized, Dave understood the unique setting moon was a likely result of some unknown weather anomaly located opposite of Storm Gloria's approach far beyond the horizon. Its location west afforded him the luxury of being able to just sit back and enjoy its splendor.

It was then in panning east that prompted him to believed luck was finally within their grasp when the debut of a distant light caught his attention. Linda soon joined him, but instead looked west to Gloria's port side.

"Holy shit, look at that moon!"

Relinquishing his binoculars, Dave directed her to view their aft starboard side. "Never mind that. Check out the light?"

With Linda soon embracing him in feeling on the cusp of rescue, Dave was again fixated on the distant object.

"Linda—stupid me, would you please get me the flare gun? The moon distracted me here for a moment."

Having just entered their full line of vision to the east, a distance midsize freighter could be seen heading southwest. Meanwhile being situated directly between it and the unique moon, Dave believed his flares stood to be easily visible to anyone aboard the vessel in question. In assuming there was a possibility that the captivating moon might be beckoning the attention of those aboard it, he therefore concluded the prospect of their flares being spotted was likely at its peak.

The freighter of interest was a French vessel racing towards the Island of Guadeloupe, a far-reaching eastern Caribbean island Dave previously believed his best chances of reaching lay. Also capturing the attention of those aboard the French vessel, the reddish moon left them discussing among themselves of how lucky they were to be making such good time west and the contrary for anyone less fortunate. Dave fired his several flares when believing their chances of being spotted was at its optimal.

A thousand miles north of their present position and some forty plus years earlier, German U-boats were having a heyday on merchant vessels supplying Allied forces in Europe. In the war's early stages, American torpedo planes were unable to engage their targets without first being spotted. Whatever color their skins were painted made no difference.

Such an equation changed when the Allied torpedo planes began mounting lights along their approaching wings. Doing so adjusted the degree of light being emitted from the aircrafts, allowing their profile to then blend in with the rest of the day's surroundings. Such an adjustment decreased their detection time several fold, in turn helping to tilt the tide of the Second World War deadly U-Boat campaign to the side of the Allies.

Similarly, the same effect also caused the red discharges of Dave's flares to be obscured by the likewise moon. Consequently, those aboard the French freighter never saw them. Instead their ship eventually slipped behind the southwest horizon leaving both Dave and Linda only able to guess if their signal were ever spotted. A strong inclination left Dave in doubt.

"I don't get it. Anytime there seems to be some glimmer of hope it just seems to flicker away. Sometimes I swear this boat must be the *S.S. Minnow.*"

Understanding her husband's fascination with World War Two history, Linda asked, "the *S.S. Minnow*—what was that, some unlucky Nazi U-boat?"

Conceding, Dave just snickered in despondency.

"Yes it was dear, and I'm freaking O'Kapitan *Gilligan.*" He then grabbed her travel hat lying nearby and hit himself over the head with it.

"*Gilligan!*"

Never having seen the sitcom before growing up, Linda was bewildered at her husband's actions.

Soon appearing as some doomed vessel succumbing to the depths, the couple just watched downheartedly as the large reddish crescent moon slipped peacefully behind the horizon. While their chances of rescue may seemed to have waned with the last vestige of it's setting, it was the moon itself that prohibited their chances of rescue from ever having taken hold in the first place. Dave felt as if he was facing some overpowering pitcher and with two strikes on him, he just barely fouled tipped the only hittable ball he believed was likely to be thrown to him.

There was nothing more to do other than call for help and wait for the sure arrival of an already dangerous tropical storm, still growing evermore powerful. Both parents couldn't help but feel deep regret in having taken their children along. Meanwhile with the storm still shifting in slight erratic patterns, Dave was still unable to settle on any direction in which to evade it. This left Linda understanding that she would soon need to be dealing with two frightened children below while her husband, who elected to stay isolated outside, would hopefully be able to make some difference by keeping their boat both pointed downwind and in sync with an upheaving ocean.

Fatigued from a culmination of stresses dealt over the past week, Linda eventually succumbed to shuteye. Dave instead returned to the helm and treated an empty stomach to a beer. Although less stressed than Linda, he still hadn't received any full night of sleep since Santiago. His first beverage therefore raced to his head uncontested while the next one carried him onto the doorstep of sedation. Dave needed such a reprieve from reality to feel for a moment that he still held some control over one facet of his present predicament being his sanity.

Fading there at the helm, his mind began wandering with random thoughts prompted by a clouded sense of clarity. His most profound notion grew out of a muddled perception in support of a claim that if he had just allowed Storm Gloria to overtake them while still in its infancy, then it would have presently been nothing more than a footnote to their past. Their path would have at least then been clear to the Caribbean. While likely correct in such a assessment, any purposeful subjection to succumbing to long hours of uncertain sea conditions, especially in a relatively small vessel, and with children aboard, might not be considered the wisest of strategies. Such surmising was the same brilliance often displayed by Monday morning quarterbacks.

Dave's onset of musing soon led him ever deeper into a dynamic flood of mental images brought on by a REM state. A vision began taking form in a familiar cemetery located in his childhood town of Fairfield, Connecticut. Although the cemetery seemed somewhat familiar to him in spite of many other inconsistencies surrounding its realm, it shouldn't have been in his parent's back yard as it was laid out in his dream.

A late summer air was reverberating with the sounds of a local New England carnival playing out in full swing. It consisted of people celebrating in promenades to an assorted array of festival music ranging from one-person bands to carnival music sounding from rides. While the unsettling commotion of festivities seemed to be surrounding him, there was the likes of no carnival activity visible to account for its existence other than a ghostly translucency barely giving credence to its mostly disembodied representations.

Dave then noticed Pamela skinny-dipping with others in a green algae laden pond. This concerned him. He feared his good friend might get sick if she happened to ingest any of the still water. He was then relieved in remembering that his mother worried about such a thing and that she would have likely already mentioned something from her back window to the naked group in believing there might be some threat to their health. Buffers brought on by his dream elected to ignore the fact that in reality a Fairfield police dispatcher would have already received a complaint by her.

Before Dave appeared three newly set granite stones bearing the names of his wife and kids. In front of them stood Jim dressed in drag. Behaving like a concession attendant, his old friend was able to recognize him while on the other hand unable to place his face. On the other side of the stones were seated Linda, Heather, and David picnicking on a red-white plaid, linen tablecloth. With his wife motioning Dave to join them, Jim wouldn't have it, claiming he versus some prominent biblical figure was the gatekeeper to the afterlife. In Linda's voice referring to Pamela, he pointed towards the skinny-dippers. "Are you going to fuck her?" Repeating it continually, Jim struck Dave in the arm each time as he often did back in high school. With his mannerisms soon taking on that of a lifeless automated nature, his voice began racing like a speeding record.

Dave then shifted his attention away from the bazaar spectacle of his friend to his picnicking family. With a soft quality to her voice, Linda again asked him to join them. In response to her request, he reached his hand across the back of the three stones just to find that it had vanished. Puzzled yet not alarmed, he stared at his missing hand, the meanwhile attempting to make sense of it.

"Please don't be frightened, honey," she reassured him. "The kids forgive you and so do I. Come join us."

Dave then looked to Pamela, who was donned in a white sassy sundress. With tears spilling down from her eyes, she nodded affirmatively for him to join his family across the stone's threshold. Hesitant for a moment, he became void of all emotion before then leaping forward. In landing, there was only dead silence. Any indication of the carnival was gone including Jim dressed in drag and Pamela in white. Dave's family was gone. All that was left were three stones bearing their names, this time on old weathered, white marble. Beneath them was sequentially scribed: "Bye Dad", "Bye Dave", "Bye Dad", and on each: "SEPTEMBER 21, 1985".

Left feeling emotionally destitute, Dave could only hear the wind rustling through surrounding trees. Having been flourishing beforehand with the rich hue of summer's greens, their colors were instead transformed into the lifeless earth tones of post-foliage brown. A lively breeze that was interacting with their brittle leaves gradually changed to that of the trade winds and unsettled sea interacting with Gloria. From a lying position on his side and feeling sluggish, Dave sat up from the bench shaking his head in dismay.

"Holy shit! That was messed up."

In as much of a relief that the bizarre dream was only that of a dream, a stone-cold reality of an uncertain future left Dave filled with a loathing contempt. It was born out of extreme frustration. Those few precious minutes of sleep, seeming an eternity in their invoked imagery, was also the only shut-eye he would come to know in preparing for the upcoming day.

By 5:00 am, clouds began blanking the eastern sky with their cover, encroaching on the Costa's usual picturesque mornings of brilliant sunrises and soothing blue skies. The playful mornings of breakfast with a smile as his flirtatious wife would greet him outside seemed as distant as did the day the family descended onto Sao Vicente.

Two hours later, Storm Gloria's actual center was located 175 miles east of Dave's position and was heading 55 miles to his south. His previous idea of employing engine power to evade its full onslaught was falling apart with the rapidly deteriorating seas surrounding him. The prospect of being able to make any run either north or south seemed as plausible as walking a straight line in a sobriety test amidst a powerful earthquake.

Active winds of the storm's leading edge began making their presence known. Although still relatively benign in voracity considering their boat's durability, Dave was nonetheless aware that the seascape spanning his east was anything but.

Final preparations for the storm meant either securing anything that might come loose during the anticipated foul weather or jettisoning nonessentials overboard posing as potential threats. It included their remaining mast, which Dave viewed the greatest threat to him outside. He also believed the same reigned true for the erection of their cockpit's protective canvas dodger.

In wishing Gloria to be as streamlined as fighter jet while as hermetically sealed as a ping-pong ball, he wanted nothing less than a wave of ridiculous proportions to be able to write their last chapter. While mindful a storm like the one confronting them was quite capable of delivering such threats, Dave still believed that by staying aboard and keeping his air passages clear in the process, there stood to be no reason to believe he and his family couldn't survive the next several hours, intact.

Before affixing himself in place at the helm wetsuit and all, he went below to spend some last moments with his family. In doing so, his demeanor was likened to more of a confident skipper. Even though both his children understood a rough ride was ahead, Dave still felt compelled to reassure them regardless.

"See you guys in a few hours, and don't give your mother any lip either, okay? Daddy's going to be busy outside, and you know Mommy's going to tell me about it later if you do, so be good."

Dave believed a threat of which his kids knew held validity based on the past was the best way of instilling the illusion that the future was a certainty. With Linda then joining him outside before deteriorating conditions would prohibit it, he pulled her into an embrace.

"Honey, do you have any sleeping pills or tranquilizers for the kids—even alcohol?"

"What? You think I keep a stash of drugs tucked away like that? And do you actually mean doping your eight and five-year-old up?"

"I don't imagine Doctor Spock has ever written any journals on freaking hurricanes, do you? And if he did, this would be a fine time to enlighten me."

An elicited response was the first time in days Dave was able to see his wife laugh, although it wasn't one laden with any feel-good endorphins.

With tears spilling from her eyes, she held him ever tighter.

"I'll see what I can do, but you be careful out there—you crazy bastard."

"Not crazy enough to let my family down. Now get inside. You've got the hard job. Me? All I need to do is keep the straight and narrow—that's all."

The two then held each other's faces in an emotionally charged bid, Linda's warm tears mixing with a pre-deluge of cooler rain being driven by strengthening winds.

"Just remember, honey," Dave explained, "block the air hose once, 'yes', twice, 'no'." The two had set up a makeshift breathing tube leading to inside just in case. It was believed any standard communication equipment would be rendered worthless in the conditions expected to follow.

"I'll check the hose sometimes just to feel you with me," Linda added, dreading leaving her husband alone.

"Well just don't hook it up to the bilge pump and I'll be okay,"

"I think I can manage that—see you soon, dear."

Upon kissing him, Linda exited the cockpit braving a smile. Not only was she deeply concerned for her husband's safety outside, she was also saddened that it might be the last time she would ever have the opportunity of being able to hold him again. Their parting also came with the understanding that his inability of being able to survive the ensuing elements would likely translate to their boat becoming a $150,000 coffin, assuming it was to stay intact at all.

By 8:00 in the am, the Costas could finally realistically consider themselves caught in the storm's grip. Dave sat like a daredevil in wait with his safety harness attached to a lanyard. It in turn led to a jackline that ran the span of Gloria, fore and aft. In addition to having applied duct tape for goggle reinforcement, the all-purpose gray tape was also key in securing his makeshift breathing line into a sealed hole leading into the cabin. A day prior, Dave had joked with Linda about how they wouldn't have any chance of surviving the upcoming tropical storm without the use of the common household product. He recognized that *Force-12* conditions (The Beaufort Wind Scale most extreme state) might prohibit breathing for long periods, so it was guessed the use of such a line stood to pose lifesaving.

An hour later, 65 mph plus sustained winds at the storm's center were producing treacherous conditions to which Dick, Gloria's previous owner, could have never imagined their likes. Dave guessed if he had done so, then he likely would have boasted about having weathered such conditions with pride. Meanwhile lesser winds of thirty-five mph stirring 125 miles west of the storms approaching center were causing him to be dealing with active swells heaping in access of twenty feet.

Below, the situation there took a turn for the worse. With no pills available to calm the children and Heather refusing to drink tequila, even in the form of a pleasantly sweet turbo, the problem arose with David, who didn't have any issue with the consumption of the sweet drink. Trashed as a result, the words, "Mommy, I don't feel..." no sooner exited his mouth whereupon subsequence, a gruesome stream of projectile vomit followed afterwards, spraying the entire area—including Heather.

The young girl screamed, freaked out by the disturbing spectacle that her brother just summoned for all to see and for her to be showered by. Linda quickly grabbed her son and directing his next wave downward while her daughter stood, frozen in shock.

"Mommy, it stinks! What should I do?"

"Rinse yourself in the shower and get into your jamis. You'll feel better afterwards. Just make sure you're holding onto something so you don't fall, okay sweetie?"

Matters thereafter didn't improve for David where unlike most excessive drinkers who are unable keep their stomach contents in check upon having one too many, throwing up offered no relief in his case. Thanks to a triggering effect set off by the tequila, his normally sea-friendly system was no longer, friendly.

While engrossed in the brutality of Mother Nature's fury outside, Dave eventually received a lungful of a foul smell from inside in testing his air tube. Concerned, he undid his restraints to check below.

"Is everything okay, honey?" he shouted, yelling from atop the companionway with the storm's turbulence spilling through.

Linda was still huddled over her son. "Apparently, tequila isn't his thing." she answered. "I see that thing works by the way. That's a good sign."

"Need help?"

"No thanks. This isn't my first rodeo with the kids, believe it or not. Go back and keep us safe. Thanks for checking up on us. I love you, honey!"

Linda eventually cleaned the mess and settled her daughter to the point of feeling obliged to baby-sit her very sick brother. Meanwhile the boy continued dry heaving into an empty pale in spite of having nothing else to evacuate from his stomach.

By 10:00 am, events were becoming evermore precarious for Dave outside. Located 105 miles northwest of Storm Gloria's approaching center, increased gales of a sustained 40 mph began generating more defined swells. Off their surfaces, blinding sheets of sea foam were being discharged into the air. Concurrent, there were two events that were taking place to which Dave was unaware. Sustaining winds circulating near the storm's center were reaching speeds exceeding 70 mph while the other event was taken place less than a thousand feet above him. An Air Force WC-130 Hercules of the 53rd Weather Reconnaissance Squadron was en route to its home base. Neither its busy crew above nor Dave dealing with the harsh conditions below was ever aware of the other's presence.

Dave's job outside was becoming evermore taxing in the hour following and Linda's less so. After positioning her children in plain sight for the sake of affording them some sense of comfort, she returned to a radio that had already lost most of its transmission capability. Adding to the racket of the sea pounding their hull and making for unsettling acoustics, an agitation of Gloria's jackline running her span was also joining in an unrelenting mishmash of an increasing decibel level. A constant reminder of its increasing volume was a distinct indicator signifying the intensification of Storm Gloria. Anyone seated as the Costas were knew they were in serious trouble.

At one moment little David was feeling as if he weighed 30 pounds, and the next, tenfold. It caused his afflicted stomach to feel as if it were some short length of rope being manipulated by a power lifter attempting every knot craft configuration possible. With both his throat burning and the storm outside frightening him, Santa bringing anything he wished for on Christmas was the last thing on the boy's mind.

Heather the meanwhile was managing better compared to her brother. She was too worried about him to be feeling any anxiety herself. Prior to each dry heaving occurrence, she noticed that he would first turn flush and would then sweat. In the inception of each onset, she placed a cool damp cloth over his forehead and held him assuredly through it. Such a display of compassion brought tears to their heartfelt mother. It also freed her up to be able to police the cabin for leaks, of which up until then none were visible.

Eighty-five miles northwest of the storm's approaching center, Dave was left with no choice but to finally employ his engine. Doing so provided the extra inertia necessary for negotiating increasing swells rising from beneath. Meanwhile in shielding his face to allow for easier breathing, the only sleep he received in a twenty-four hour span took place in a cemetery with its imagery still haunting him. As unsettling as its memory may have still been seared into his consciousness, its eerie recollection was evermore exaggerated by a darkened bluish-grey surrounding rendering visibility for the most part, negligible.

Noontime in Miami, an hour ahead of the Costas' present time zone, Racine, a young female photo interpreter employed by the National Weather Center, was studying some newly decrypted photos when something caught her eye. She called her boss over, a seasoned geophysicist specialized in ocean-atmospheric studies.

"Dan, check this out. This just sent shivers through my spine."

The young lady's tone struck a nerve with her boss, a chain-smoking, middle-aged man who employed a comb-over to cover the evidence of his male pattern baldness. He approached her, grabbing the images taken by the WC-130 on its return flight to Keesler AFB.

"Thank you, dear. What do you got?"

Directing his attention to a faint appearing white spec, her boss's expression changed from that of curiosity to one of deep concern. He then proceeded to remove his loop magnifying glass from its cracked leather case. Leaning over and examining the point of interest under a bright retractable light, he spoke. "You know I use to have keen vision just like yours, but of course not your bedroom eyes."

In response, Racine cringed inside in having little recourse at the time to take issue with her bosses comment, except maybe fighting off a yacking feeling the likes of his similar comments never failed to bring about.

He soon stood straight again. "Great catch Racine, especially with all that sea foam distortion. That thing just sent chills down my spine as well. We need to contact someone immediately. Please come with me." With the two exiting the room, he added, "I just pray its not too late to rescue those poor souls."

Soon, Rear Admiral Richardson, attached to the Atlantic Second Navy Fleet and assigned to patrol the region northeast of the Caribbean Islands, stood yelling into his bulky headsets.

"Are you telling me neither the Coast Guard nor we have anything capable of reaching the occupants of that boat closer than a two hour ETA? Time's not a luxury of theirs, and the cat's out of the bag on this one. I don't need this coming back and biting me in the ass if it turns out we could have rescued those people— whoever they are. You only have to deal with the logistics of the situation. I need to deal with the PR aftermath if we fail here. Call me back when you have better news, got it?"

Richardson followed with a few deep breaths, then grinning at a seasoned Petty Officer First Class, present. "The man's a lieutenant. He doesn't have to put up with that shit. A lieutenant." The rear admiral then shook his head in disbelief. "Don't get it. Must have been a pencil pusher before coming here. Now he's in my strike group—damn!" Ensuing a brief pause, he asked, "So Petty Officer, was I too nice to him?"

"Glad I wasn't on the other end of the phone sir, though I do think you let him off a little too easy."

"Yeah, maybe so," Richardson smirked. "He'll get use to me, but I'm disappointed with him nonetheless. By the way Petty officer, that's some smooth brown-nosing you've perfected over the years. I must say that I'm quite impressed with it," he concluded

The Petty officer stood red faced with embarrassment. "I don't know how to respond to that, sir."

"It is what it is. I'll tell you one thing though. If we do end up relocating that boat, leaving me no choice but to risk the lives of talented rescue personnel just to then discover that that damn sailboat or whatever the hell it is out there is empty, I'll send some Tomcats in there afterwards for some target practice."

Soon afterwards, straws needed to be drawn of many pilots who volunteered for selection of the dangerous mission of relocating the Costas. By 1:00 pm (Eastern Time), the US Navy Second Fleet was scrambling to locate a rescue squad close enough for rescuing them. A spot of their whereabouts first needed to be reestablished for narrowing any search.

50 miles directly west of the storm's approaching center, Dave was dealing with near unbearable atmospheric conditions there. Producing swells reaching 30 feet, their increasing steeps of rapidly forming rising heaps of water were becoming ever more difficult to negotiate. At moments Dave was finding himself entrenched in the grips of some darkened watery valleys before seconds later being suspending atop their crests, thereafter plunged back into the blackened crevasses of their shadowy ravines again—never-ending.

Playing mind games of convincing himself his body could still function effectively for the next several hours, Dave did so, envisioning better times at home when everyone would be safely seated about their dinner table discussing daily matters. There he lay absorbed, imagining the fantasy of normal life. Included was the wonder of what ripple effect the success of overcoming his present bout might tender him later, guessing then it would likely resonate throughout the rest of his life as well. Projecting into an uncertain future, such conceptualizing was aimed to pertain to his family as well.

Hunched forward in an effort of economizing energy against the constant weight of wind and precipitation being driving from behind, a painful thirst came into play in haunting Dave; his wetsuit was working better than expected. He dared not take it off or even unzip the suit partially despite of its onset. Small amounts of water collected from his surroundings mostly led to disappointment by consequence of its enriched saline character. Dave was finding himself at one moment in apprehension about his chances, there fighting for his life with everything he had, and the next there was nothing more consuming to his psyche than a craving for the chill of a refreshing beer.

By mid-afternoon, he was becoming evermore concerned about his embattled Gloria's midsection. With both her bow and stern periodically riding opposing walls of crested swells, it was feared that the exposure of its amidships stood to become victim to a destructive amount of seawater suddenly descending onto it when most vulnerable. An expanding number of troughs continuing to increase in both depth and frequency thereby rendered the use of diesel propulsion evermore vital for steerageway purposes. Such impetus was vital for the purpose of preventing Gloria from dangerously floundering against the strengthening horizontal winds of Storm Gloria.

With their predicament worsening by the minute, Dave knew he was in serious trouble there lost amidst a mountainous range of 40-foot swells. While still able to traverse such rising mountains of water, he correctly assumed his surroundings were destined to deteriorate evermore. Although engaged in the fight of his life outside, comparatively, he guessed the conditions for those below were likely evermore harrowing than even his own. Dave was correct. For his family below, the unknown there was the greatest contributor to their already heightened state of trepidation.

With hope all but waned in the chaos of his surroundings, an F14 Tomcat streaking hundreds of feet above and then disappearing into the tumultuous murkiness instilled a new sense of buoyancy into Dave. Such short-lived euphoria was quickly tempered by the notion that the aircraft jetting above may not have spotted his boat through the obscurity of their surroundings. His doubt was laid to rest when after what seemed be an eternity, three Tomcats individually streaming a few hundred feet ahead moments later let it be known to anyone below that they needn't feel alone anymore. Upon their flyby, the quick moving F14 rocketing into the thick soupy canopy above gave him little time to react.

A lead sortie pilot spoke to his first wingman, following. "Spotted a black something in aft of the vessel. Couldn't make it out—too much foam, and this rain."

Next in line, his wingman pilot spoke. "Something or someone's moving. Cant' make out anymore—too dark. You, Jim?"

"Think somebody waved," the third pilot responded. "Tough to tell with this rain. I didn't give them much chance to react either. Don't envy the poor soul. That's for sure."

"Well if we don't bug out of here now," the lead pilot charged, "that might change. Great job men. Let's get above this thing. Not sure if the engineers had this much rain in mind when designing these bad boys. Never seen so much of it in my life—holy crap!"

Dave's celebration of newfound hope if heard through his breathing tube might have instead caused those below to mistake the Tomcats' deafening roar as the precursor to their surroundings possibly imploding at any moment. Meanwhile, the flyover with its best of intentions only contributed to the anxiety already being experienced there. From below, the blast of the F14's deafening roar was interpreted as something far worse to ensue at any moment.

Even with the planes having giving cause for hope, the Costas were essentially still in the same predicament as before. Still isolated and surrounded by lethal seas, nothing was changed. The only consolation upon which they might be able to perch in any optimism was in not needing to feel alone anymore. Although offering little in the way of hopes for any viable rescue, from Dave's standpoint, it was still more than he had been able to attested to prior to the debut of the three Tomcats.

<< CHAPTER 8 >>

REAR ADMIRAL RICHARDSON achieved his first objective of at least giving some impetus to the occupants of a boat in question. Surrounded by others in the command center of his group carrier, uproar momentarily filled its area upon the third pilot announcing Dave waving in real time. It included Richardson pumping his fist.

"Yes!"

It gave credence to intelligence gathered, sparked by a seaman's premonition. The hunch was arisen in the reading of an article from her hometown Newport, RI newspaper. Referring to the Costa's September departure from Cape Verde, its origin stemmed from Jim having relayed the information to Linda's parents, who in turn notified a local Newport paper. Linda's father had clout.

The ripple effect of the alert seaman's premonition eventually reached Richardson upon having been substantiated by a phone call placed to Linda's parents. It verified the timing of their last known fix point. A collective body of circumstantial evidence giving credence to the Costa' plight meant that the rear admiral plausibly had an American family with two kids in duress on his hands. Well aware of how hungry the American press could be, especially when children were involved, he guessed it was only a matter of time before the whole country would be affixed to the story and would in turn expect him to expedite some kind of successful rescue.

The upbeat mood of the room soon changed from celebration to that of query when the carrier's commanding officer, Captain Peterson, addressed Richardson. "Sir, what can this vessel do for you?"

Heading towards the exit, he motioned for the captain to join him. "We'll stay course at normal speed to the coordinates that the pilots' last transmitted. Meanwhile we'll take route through the storm's southern fringes. When she passes, we'll employ all the available salvage teams we can muster to search and retrieve whatever lingering objects might still be afloat."

The two senior officers continued en route towards the exit when Richardson suddenly erupted in rage. In doing so, he struck the steel surrounding its hatchway.

"Shit!"

The rear admiral wasn't one to mix words, but his men loved him nevertheless. Sometimes poking fun amongst each other at his often over-the-top mannerisms, they would do so mostly with an air of affection. In having taken everyone by surprise, not excluding Captain Peterson, the decibel level of the room became deadened in response. Outside of the normal ambiance of ship's operation, mostly coughs and shuffling of feet accounted for any remaining noise.

In grabbing his hand to make certain no bones were broken, Richardson continued. "I'm sitting here on tens of billions worth of sea equipment and thousands of highly trained personnel under my command, and yet I can't do a damn thing to save those people out there. Give me three—two hours even, and I guarantee those people would safely be established aboard the US sovereignty of one of our vessels within the next couple hours. And if they did end up being that American family, the first thing I'd do is approach that numb-nuts father who took his children along with him. I'd grin, shake his hand, and then knee him in the nuts with everything I have—that asshole."

Having assumed beforehand the powers to be had matters in hand equating to rescue being a forgone conclusion, the general mood of the room mellowed to more of a sobered somber state.

Escorted by his immediate non-commissioned officer (NCO), a seaman just fresh of basic training broke the thick silence. "Sir?"

A few select new recruits carried with them a mistaken sense of entitlement of which everyone present knew hadn't been attained in boot camp.

Taken aback at the young man's audaciousness, not excluding several stunned specialists who were manning their stations, Richardson approached him. Noticing the seaman recruit's eyes watering, he spoke softly. "Son, what is it?"

In awe, the seaman stepped back and saluted to a few snickers in the room to which the rear admiral gently guiding his right hand down again. "At ease, seaman. You did that already when I entered the room. Now that you've got the undivided attention of the whole Second Fleet—state your mind, son."

While the seething rear admiral wanted nothing more than to scold the boy into tears before then laying him to rest at sea, his restraint did have an agenda. It was to encourage those who were actually qualified to voice their suggestions to do so instead.

"What about our sub forces—" the seaman recruit uttered in a shaky voice, continuing, "or the Coast Guard? Even the Royal Navy, sir? Maybe they're in the area of those people."

Laugher erupted until Richardson muffled it, bellowing in his trained command voice. "Hey, quiet!"

Once the other's calmed, he continued, thereafter directing his next statement at a few officers present. "Why didn't any of you suggest anything? You know I'm open to suggestions. This young man may have just grossly overstepped his protocol and knows shit about the complexities of what we do out here. And yes, he has also just loss his security clearance as well, but I didn't hear any of you speak up."

Richardson turned to the young man, speaking softly still. "Don't worry, kid. You can at least stay until I'm finished with you. And to answer your question, *recruit*, most of the submarine force is commissioned elsewhere outside of our theatre-level, and it's the Coast Guard who contacted us. There are also no Royal Naval vessels near those people either and if there were, I wouldn't tell you. I imagine everyone involved including those not under my command must be doing all they can, as we are. But I give you credit, son. You showed some balls here. For now on though, you need to show a little more sensitivity to military etiquette, okay? You did familiar yourself with the Bluejacket's Manual, no son? Or have you been spending too much of your free time holding a magazine in one hand and your little willy in the other?"

The young seaman was too flustered to respond with the rare admiral responding. "Looks like you just answered my question. My advice is you get reacquainted with that thing and remember you're no longer a *sillyvilian*, okay? I would like to think the Great Lakes [Naval Boot Camp Training Center] would have already made that quite clear to you. I just need to ask you this last question. I hope you can answer it."

"Yes, sir! I will answer it to the best of my abilities, sir!"

"One *sir* will do, kid. That said, are you good at cleaning vomit?"

The seaman stood stunned for a moment while those present snickered briefly.

"I don't know, sir. I've never done so before."

Richardson grinned, patting his shoulder. "Don't worry, son. I'm sure you'll do just fine." Patting his shoulder again before turning to exit, he concluded. "Let's hope that those people will be okay. Now make me proud."

Richardson then turned to the seaman recruit's NCO, who was shooting bullets from his eyes at his subordinate. He squeezed the shoulder of the veteran sailor while grinning. "Senior Chief, take it easy on the kid. The *UCMJ* [Uniform Code of Military Justice] has strict parameters outlining what is considered cruel and inhumane punishment towards subordinates. I trust that you'll abide by them. Unfortunately, I didn't write the book."

The NCO returned a grin. "Yes sir, I'll review the perimeters and go from there. I'm sorry for the interruption, sir."

Making matter worse for the young seaman, Richardson patted his NCO on the shoulder before exiting. "I trust you will. Such the likes of anymore reoccurrence will reflect on you next time. This one was free. I'm authorizing the kid's transfer by the way. Relay that to your CO for me about this. Let him also know that I requested you hang on to him an extra day or so if you feel you can use his services for whatever reasons, okay? Your CO will take it from there, I'm sure."

Although in not as much imminent danger as the Costas were with the four of them stranded in the heart of Gloria, the naïve seaman recruit was correct in making mention of the Navy's submarine force. Rear Admiral Richardson wasn't about to divulge to the green seaman that his strike group did have its own submarine shadowing. Usually joined by another, it was doing so while submerged vessels elsewhere were also engaged in the daily maneuvers of operating under stealth of water, stalking their Soviet counterparts.

As to the likelihood of any of the other vessels being redirected for a civilian rescue, the Commander in Chief was a man of vision, and redirecting such resources no matter how critical their role just for the sake of one American family might project his vision to the world that the United States with its formidable military machine would stop at nothing in protecting either its citizens or friends at whatever cost. Such a statement would have especially been aimed at the Soviets. Deployment of his forces to Grenada two years earlier could have been considered an example of that same vision, although the circumstances leading to the raid differed significantly.

The Costa's were now alone to determine their outcome—luck pending. With the seascape pulsating as if breathing and appearing ready to swallow them at any moment, in spite of the ridiculous odds stacked against him, Dave's disturbing surroundings only caused him to be battling them evermore diligently. Having been contending with progressively deteriorating conditions for a taxing stretch of five plus hours, he was still oblivious to both the storm's true magnitude and his exact proximity there within it.

Meanwhile seated at his favorite café late on that Saturday afternoon, Jim sat quietly, nervously tapping his empty glass still smelling of gin and tonic. Accompanied by Pamela, he did so atop a colorful mosaic tabletop.

"I'm hoping the Navy or whoever has made it to those guys. I had us come here in learning that the storm I told you about before is a hurricane now. My understanding is that our friends are still trying to outrun the thing—or something. Pam, I really don't know."

Jim stared down at his glass, pausing for a moment. "The only information I was able to get on them was sketchy. Can you imagine that? The freaking thing's a hurricane now. Man, if I could go back in time with this knowledge, I would have cut every line and slash both of Gloria's sails. Yep, hindsight's everything, isn't it?"

"Honey, don't blame yourself. Those two had their minds set. You even fought Dave about it. I know that had to be difficult."

Jim slipped his hand into Pamela's. "Sweetheart, this isn't guilt. And obviously I couldn't have sabotage his boat like that—too sloppy. Sinking her in the harbor instead would have been a more tactful choice. It's just that the worse thing is, is not knowing—you know?"

While the basis of Jim's frustration was in his ignorance to the Costa plight, it was unlikely observing Dave through some crystal ball just to witness him battling deadly seas at that same moment would have provided him any peace of mind.

With Richardson's strike group poised in the Caribbean for their next mission of Soviet submarine detection, the rear admiral just received the latest news of Storm Gloria's status to that of a Hurricane. He sat quiet with Captain Peterson in the flag-mess while other officers were engaged in a heated discussion. Using their battle skills, they were in the midst of arguing amongst each other their own predictions of the next day's professional football matchups. Half listening, the plight occurring further east was never far from the rear admiral's mind.

He took it personally whether his ability of being able to carryout a mission involved the thousand of men and women under his command or instead just a few stranded civilians of whom he was directed to effect a rescue. Not minimizing his concerns for the Costa's wellbeing, Richardson was more obsessed in the perception that the ocean was getting the upper hand on him. In calmly wiping his mouth with a lining napkin and slowly rising, he excused himself.

"Are you okay, sir?" Peterson asked, believing the rear admiral's distress might be linked to two of three Tomcats that almost failed in their return back to their carrier.

"Is it the two flameouts, sir?"

"That's part of it. I'm sure you can understand. I should have never ordered those planes in there, especially for a non-combat sortie. I wavered to the political pressures to resolve this thing. From here on they can just kiss my ass."

"Well at least our boys made it back, thank God."

"'Thank God' is right. I'll be back at my guest quarters if anyone asks. After that, I'll probably head back to my cruiser to hit the rain locker and catch some rack-time. I was up all last night being briefed about our new mission."

The carrier's guest quarter was actually the official cabin of the rear admiral. Because he had a love affair with the strike group's new guided missile cruiser, he preferred conducting most of his duties from there.

By mid-noon, an hour following the F-14 flyover, Dave found himself fighting for survival in close to world's most violent waters stirring just then. Unfortunately for him and his family, what did lie ahead were the world's most violent seas stirring anywhere in the world at that particular moment.

Dave found himself aloft yet another upheaving 40-foot steep of water. This time something rang differently for him. Through the blinding havoc of heavy precipitation and sea spray, transfixed, he suddenly witnessed a horrific spectacle of a mountain of water still some thirty feet higher than him approaching. Its heart-stopping spectacle became plainly visible through the natural strobe effect of the surrounding lightning. No more than a ten count later and in barely being missed by the heinous 70-foot wall of water, it was only a roll of the dice that prevented the Costas from being in its direct path. Even then the huge billow of death's eerie palpability seemed as real to him as did its haunting display.

In having just looked death in the face, the Costas were granted yet another few seconds of reprieve before another such wave might make an appearance—maybe just beyond the next swell. Added to his frightening surroundings was a darkened ghoulish hue of olive green casting its shadowy gloom. Only interruptions of lightening preceding their thunderous explosions would briefly mask any of its murky gloom with its ultraviolet emission.

Prior to the storm including earlier in it, Dave held onto the flawed belief that such cataclysmic conditions stood to augment his general confidence. In believing so, he grossly underestimated the true power of nature's fury at sea. His present experience wasn't as much as some adrenaline induced macho thrill ride as he once believed could be played upon afterwards, but was instead something that was delivering far more negative stimulus to his senses than his mind was able to process; no longer the windfall he had once imagined. Numb with fear, it wasn't only concern for his family that was contributing to his state of apprehension either.

If conditions weren't crippling enough for someone who already expended most of their available energy surviving to that point, the conditions to follow stood to provide little reprieve. 75 mph plus winds closing in stood to create an unimaginable state of mayhem for both Dave outside and his family below. If those same sustaining winds were occurring in some suburban setting, then non-boarded windows would be filling interiors with the shards of their remnants. Such a quick turn of events could be expected to leave most dwellings susceptible to irreversible water damage. A few fleeing roof shingles would likely lead to an all-out exodus of the rest. Weaker trees would be getting uprooted and tossed about while stronger were releasing the deadly projectiles of weakened branches from their grips. No less subject to those extreme conditions would be the nerves of anyone seeking shelter inside their vulnerable surroundings. Meanwhile anyone caught at sea could only wish to be finding themselves in such a far more stable environment as those on land.

For Dave, any successful negotiation of the hostile sea wasn't enough in itself to guarantee a promise of survival. He also needed to deal with an endless myriad of lightening, of which there was nothing protecting him from any direct strike. In addition to its constant flashes inundating his surroundings with deafening rumbles of continuous thunder, an unwelcomed appearance of some freakish twister wasn't beyond any realm of possibility either. There enveloped in danger, the surreal sense of Dave's surroundings left him feeling as if he was existing in some fabled tempest, wishing at any moment he could just blink and in there doing, imagine it all away.

Below, in addition to David's acute seasickness, the collective level of emotional strain there was near intolerable for both his sister and mother. The two had become prostrated by their version of battle fatigue. The only life seeming to remain in David were his dry heaves, at most causing his body to be convulsing like a lifeless corpse receiving jolts from a defibrillator. In rubbing his knotted stomach while visualizing transferring her own life force into his, Heather's doing so had become more of a reflexive response of shielding herself from her own fears.

In a desperate move compelled by hopelessness, Linda retrieved the empty bottle once containing the homemade wine she and Dave drank from days earlier. Having gathered a pen and paper while stumbling about the cabin like an impaired drunk, she planned on composing what was hoped wouldn't become some last will and testament. Entering the bathroom to do so, an unexpected wave slamming into Gloria's portside sent her tumbling to an opposite wall. Disorientated, the boat's quick recovery then sent her lurching backwards where she then struck her head against their stainless steel toilet. There she lay prone next to it for a moment, dazed but still conscious.

Concerned about her children and struggling to make her way towards them, Linda was faced with a disturbing sight of Heather in tears, lying just outside the owner's cabin. Inside the room and having been spared some of the jolt as the result of lying down at the time, David instead fell off his parent's bed in an agonizing tumble to the floor. In his case, the sudden jostling of his body produced the same effect as an explosive blasting the life out of a fire. His involuntary bouts of dry heaves were replaced with the sounds of him crying. Regardless of viewing it an opportunity of wetting his pallet, Linda omitted doing so in fear of reigniting them. For the time being, she was simply relieved that her son was no longer seasick. A sweet turbo therefore wasn't on her list of possible antipodes slated to reinvigorate him back to health again.

With Linda taking a moment to compose a still unharmed Heather, the young girl in turn was alarmed at the sight of her mother's normally rich blond hair on its right side drenched with blood. With no time to address her wound, she ignored her daughter's concern. Instead Linda found it more pressing to situate her and David together at the base of her bed in a makeshift cranny of a mattress and blankets. Satisfied they'd be safest there, she then exited to resume her letter again. Linda did so oblivious to the need of her head requiring immediate medical attention.

As the result of his attention being diverted elsewhere at the time, the same wave also blindsided Dave outside. Although not different in size compared with other waves battering them, it was its angle of approached that wreaked so much extra havoc. Having undone his seat restraints beforehand due to discomfort didn't help his cause either. Caught unprepared, he was unable to take extra measures in bracing for it. In viewing the chaos on his starboard side, Dave suddenly found himself being carried away as if his lanyard was being stretched beyond its failing point. Seconds later, he lay dangling off the side his boat, helpless, struggling there just to gain both his senses and breathing back again.

Grasping for air any moment he could, he recognized the need of getting aboard quickly before another such wave might make an appearance. Exhausted, doing so posed a daunting task. In being dragged along for what seemed forever with his body being tossed about like an old rag doll, whatever amount of energy he may have possessed prior to his latest predicament was all by then tapped.

Although not as severe as the previous one, another violent clash of Gloria's bow against a wall of water eventually changed Dave's status. A sudden rise and fall sent his body catapulting once again to being deposited in a jackknifed position, lying prone on Gloria's cockpit barrier. Its abrupt yet extremely fortunate outcome was an unexpected finale to having previously been yanked about in the water mercilessly for an exhaustive few minutes with no hope of any recovery. There he lay still for a moment, both disorientated and with the wind knocked out of him as well.

Upon slithering down to the cockpit deck to take refuge, Dave assumed a fetal position there. With his knees and chest tucked and embracing Gloria's compass's base, he lay still, both grasping for air and attempting to regain his breathing back. Processing what just took place, he did so as his 43-foot cutter was being thrashed about uncontrollably, meanwhile, its only means of helming lying there helpless on the deck, frozen in shock.

With water still spilling out Gloria's cockpit, a soon revitalized Dave was able to return to the helm and this time affix himself in place. His first priority was getting his bow pointed downwind again as quickly as he could. This time feeling rejuvenated while still processing the last few minutes, he kept a vigilant eye on his panorama in recognition that it was only a stroke of luck that just preserved his life in such a improbable return back aboard Gloria. Being it a stroke of bad luck that placed him in such a perilous predicament just minutes prior, Dave understood the nature of his present environment stood to leave him far more predisposed to the probability of misfortune than the likelihood of any good luck.

Dave understood such a repeat occurrence would likely result less fortunate for him. He was further sobered by how effortlessly an unexpected wave had just ripped him from his position without the aid of his restraints and persuaded him overboard. It couldn't have become clearer to him than at that moment that the fragility of life amidst the churning seas where he and his family were presently fighting for their survival could at best be measured in seconds.

With Linda below and resuming her letter again, there she took an emotionally charged moment for summing up the significance of their lives in what limited span of time she believed still remained. When satisfied the cohesiveness of both her words and thoughts were in sync, a sudden throbbing pain prompted her to press the area just adjacent to her fresh wound. Then in rolling up the letter and seeing blood smeared on it in the process, a few expletives were expressed before she employed a cork for securing the note into its bottle. After stumbling about the main living area in search of a safe place to tuck it away, Linda ended up doing so into a nearest cubbyhole.

She then made quick work of checking up on her kids before climbing the companionway to do the same for her husband. The accumulative effects of all that had been taken place over the previous several hours and punctuated by an injury led to her feeling woozy. Once atop the companionway, Linda observed Dave through a small window there before recognizing the need to descend its stairs in avoidance of making an involuntarily dismount first.

Feeling concern for her husband outside, she installed a cassette tape that was geared specifically towards his taste. In doing so, Linda isolated the music to play outside so not to blast her and her kids out of the cabin in the process. The interaction of both the rough seas pounding Gloria's hull and her noisy jackline rapping the deck above was already accomplishing such an effect.

In turning the music up full volume in hopes of permeating the elements outside, its base seemed to shake their boat in chorus with the assaulting sea. Below, its general effect was likened to that of white noise, masking some of the storm's havoc by its familiarity.

As if displaced in a different reality, Linda first gripped the chart table for balance before then breaking into a gyrated dance. Her distant puckered grin spooked Heather with its dark and detached nature. Having been monitoring her mother's behavior from just out of sight, the troubled girl became alarmed at the sight Linda taking her strange dance back towards the companionway again.

"Hey, Mom, where are you going?" she cried.

In slowly turning to respond, Linda's face turned pale just prior to collapsing to the teak floor below.

"Mom!" Heather cried again in her young healthy lungs.

Dave the meanwhile was feeling some sense of relief outside. He believed the music meant that his wife's sense of humor was still intact, translating it to the events below still being somewhat manageable there. Believing death had just been cheated coupled with being uplifted by the music, he refused to let go of the idea that something was eventually likely to break, and his only job outside was to make certain it wasn't going to be their boat.

Soon with the conditions outside becoming evermore hostile, Dave could have never unimagined beforehand that such mayhem could be stirred up by nature. With the ambient noise virtually drowning out Gloria's stereo and visibility hovering near zero, the rain relentlessly battering him from behind made him feel as if some world-class wrestler was unrelenting in their effort of forcing him down into submission.

Intensifying winds in his proximity were also befuddling for in the face of the storm's apparent escalation, off his portside and through the thick but translucent air, a much lighter hue of gray illuminating his immediate region deemed inconsistent with the tumultuous backdrop surrounding him. For Dave, its somewhat opaqueness was still evermore welcoming than the dreary green backdrop of before. Despite still riding a rollercoaster of crushing waves tossing his boat about and being battered by the elements in the process, he was still able to hang on to some trace of hope.

Down below, Heather grabbed a roll of gauze from Gloria's first aid kit and poured rubbing alcohol over Linda's wound before then wrapping it. What should have sent her reeling through the ceiling in excruciating pain, instead elicited nothing more than a faint groan resonating from her.

As for her father, adrenaline generated prior to miraculously finding himself aboard Gloria again presented him the luxury of being able to ignore four broken ribs. Any wrong move on his part posed potentially fatal. His injury left Heather the only non-casualty aboard Gloria—health wise. In hearing what she believed was a drippy faucet, the frightened yet thirsty girl stumbled through Gloria's quaking interior in quest of a quick drink. In doing so, paralysis gripped her at the sight of water trickling down several places on its port wall. Evidence it was occurring for awhile could be witnessed in any of Gloria's descents, whereby water seeping from beneath the teak floor was doing so before then shifting about its surface and then trickling back below again.

Sensing the surroundings collapsing in on her, the panicked girl still possessed the whereabouts of being able to remember hearing her parents discuss a pump located beneath the floor. An ensuing check of several compartments including one beneath the floor revealed an alarming amount of water already pooled there. It prompted Heather to race about Gloria's rocking interior in precipitation of a solution. The frantic girl eventually struck what she believed was gold inside a compartment adjacent to the companionway. It was a switch labeled "bypass pump-switch".

In engaging it, nothing happened: no humming, no gurgling of water, nothing. Remembering hearing it operate before when her father bumped it just prior to purchasing the boat, in frustration like a rat ending up in the same dead-end of a maze, the troubled girl continued hitting the switch repeatedly with no results. She did so until the effects of her accumulative stresses finally took their toll. Now subjugated to hopelessness, Heather leaned against a nearest wall until the violent churning sea knocked her limp body off balance and onto the floor.

Lying there on her side both numb with fear and whimpering in despondency, the dispirited girl was eventually able to spot her dad's breathing tube. Soon climbing the companionway and praying that he was still there, she blew into it for all she was worth. Following a brief spongy sensation, her breath was quickly met with firm resistance; it wasn't any code of her father's either. It instead resulted from his inability of being able to absorb his daughter's unexpected influx of frantically delivered exhalation at the peak of his own inhale. She tried again, the second time receiving no resistance. In continuing, her ears eventually popped from pressure generated by Dave plugging the end of the tube with his palm. It on the other hand was a code that he and Linda had established beforehand. From outside, his daughter's attempt to contact him led Dave to initially believe it was his wife attempting to do so instead.

Having been contending with severe conditions and assuming the meanwhile his family below was still faring relatively well, if conditions outside weren't dreadful enough for an already battle fatigued Dave, chills consequentially ran down his spine when upon bellowing, 'Linda!' through the rubbery plastic tube, his call was met with complete hysteria.

Regardless of his critical role outside, Dave wasted no time in combating unforgiving conditions to enter below. There he was no more prepared for what struck him next than the punishment nature had been dealing him over the previous several hours. Panning the interior with Hurricane Gloria's chaos still blasting through the open companionway made it feel as if he had just come home from an exhausting day of work just to find his household victim to a home invasion.

A wooden floor below bearing witness to scarlet strokes of Linda's bloody hair led to layers of gauze dressing her wound. The sight of blood still oozing through her bandages troubled Dave. In crouching next to Heather to comfort her, he was then able to receive the full scope of his remaining family's condition in seeing his ailing son appearing so pale. Upon scooting over and holding him tenderly, the concerned father was there able to identify his son's cold and clamminess, nonetheless limpness of body. Also noticing his faint breathing, Dave spoke softly. "Hey champ, I'm sorry things are so bad, but Daddy's getting us out of here. This should all be over in about an hour, so hang in there, okay buddy?"

Upon kissing his boy's forehead prior to repositioning him in his makeshift cranny, he summoned Linda's attention next. His attempt in doing so elicited nothing more than an indiscernible mumble. Despite everything, Dave still recognized the need of returning outside. The resourcefulness his daughter had exhibited in caring for her mother paid dividend in the confidence of being able to return there again. Mentally bracing for the chaos awaiting him outside, he first chose to take on the issue of the bilge pump. Before doing so, Heather's assistance was employed for carrying Linda into the owner's cabin to be with her son. Her role was to guide her mother's feet as Dave led the way. Soon with only Heather outside the room, a huge wave approaching outside was on the verge of reminding everyone that the cozy comforts of inside were at best a fragile existence.

As Gloria dropped, a massive cresting 60-foot wall of water lifted her bow fully upright before then collapsing atop it, temporarily submerging its remaining structure beneath its turbulence. With the cascading wave's remaining weight dispersing outward in an impressive display of nature's power, a buoyant Gloria was able to spearhead upward out of the destructive forces of its crushing chaos. Had it been positioned in any other manner, the Costas would have likely become victim to the ocean's devastating forces. Instead with no major structural damage sustained to her, their boat could once again go about dealing with all of the previous punishment of the near hurricane conditions of before.

While the massive weight of the waves might have come short of destroying the Costa's only sanctuary due to an eggshell effect, it did further aggravate already existing stress fractures that were plaguing its hull beforehand. The incident also added new ones to the mix as well.

In Gloria's recovery, everyone but Heather ended up on the owner's cabin floor subsequent to tumbling back from its aft wall. The parents did all they could in the process to avoid their frail son. Meanwhile Dave's failure to have shut the outside hatch in entering below led to a substantial amount of newly introduced water now vacillating throughout Gloria's interior. For him, the sight of many items freed from their locations and sloshing about in shifting currents may have seemed alarming to him, but nothing in comparison to the absence of his daughter. It triggered him to start yelling her name repeatedly, and he did so in contest with the howling wind spilling in from outside, the ocean and jackline battering his hull, and their stereo's music resonating throughout Gloria's structure. From his place there standing ankle deep in swaying water, the surreal feel of muffled music spilling in from a darkened companionway entrance and coalesced with everything else made him believe he was dwelling in purgatory, and hell was just outside poised to extradite everyone at any moment.

With no time wasting, Dave raced up the companionway still yelling Heather's name. Only pausing briefly before doing so repeatedly, his many attempts only bore witness to nature's indiscriminate fury outside. It was a fury he understood would soon need to be faced again, this time deeply grief-stricken about his daughter.

Inside again and heart pounding, staggering through the interior in access of the bilge pump led to joy and no less relief when the distraught father found Heather next to the bilge pump switch crouched in its confined space. Just beforehand, he feared his daughter had become the first victim of Hurricane Gloria. It was something she was able to avoid by taking refuge in the avoidance of falling objects that were spilling down from Gloria's quickly rising bow.

"Daddy!" she screamed, to which Dave pulled her into a forceful embrace, eyes laced with tears as if his daughter was Lazarus resurrected.

Upon a heartfelt but short-lived celebration, a failed pump engagement prompted Dave to carry Heather to the owner's cabin. Without mixing words, he flew over to the electric panel praying the meanwhile that the breaker in question was only off versus tripped. His blood ran cold beforehand with the understanding that a tripped breaker, versus one just in the off position, would likely seal everyone's fate. Paying little mind to contemplation, he swung the panel door open and in seeing the bilge breaker off, he engaged it. Just then, a faint drone added as a new sound to the ambient clamor sounded more gratifying to him than any of the music that Jim provided in their care package.

Racing through the water in collection of all available ice from their freezer, Dave entered the owner's cabin, instructing Heather.

"Take this and wrap as much of it as you can over your mother's wound. I Love you sweetie and I'm so proud of you, but I need to get outside, and now."

During his ice retrieval, quick note was taken to the lack its melting. Meanwhile with Gloria being flung about the way it was, the need of entering outside seemed far too pressing of an issue to pay any tray of ice any mind.

Dave successfully reclaimed his place at the helm, which took some treacherous lumbering about in arriving there. He gave little thought to any of the dangers of doing so, because a greater need of manning his post caused complacency to be feared more than anything else. Having somewhat stabilized the debacle stumbled upon minutes earlier, both the bilge pump working effectively and Heather tending to the others below left Dave freed up again to take his place outside.

Cataclysmic like convulsing seas greeting him outside seemed bewildering in its ultra-violent behavior, moreover, overwhelming hurricane winds that could only be construed as such. A wetsuit previously affording some shield from the harsh elements was the only reason Dave hadn't become overwhelmed by Gloria's fury beforehand. Meanwhile the newer extreme state of the storm wasn't consistent with any of the conditions he had been dealing with earlier. Despite its ruthless character seeming to be worsening evermore, a translucency appearing to the portside of Gloria and glowing disproportionately bright in contrast to the blackness elsewhere seemed incompatible with Dave's present surroundings. Regardless of its hopeful spectacle, he still needed to negotiate rapidly forming mountains of water expelling vast amounts of foam off their surfaces. No longer able to dissipate out of Gloria's cockpit below like the seawater surging in from everywhere, an overflow of a more buoyant froth collecting around him was instead being jettisoned away at near hurricane speeds from above its confines.

Taking note of a brightening region portside, Dave had difficulty identify with its heavenly-like domain seeming a short distance away. It wasn't consistent with an apocalyptic like environment both battering his person without relent and unmercifully tossing his boat about. Nothing added up to him. The still opaque yet promising spectacle portside at best instilled him with a guarded sense of hope that maybe the worse of the storm might soon be behind him. Meanwhile, in spite intuition telling him otherwise, a blinding deception of hope was influencing any sense of common reasoning for Dave.

Ultimately, nothing more needed to be carried out as far as helming was concerned to eventually discover the answer to the meteorological enigma brightening the eastern sky of Gloria's portside. Like a freight train at full momentum and forging ahead, its mesmerizing spender soon overtook the Costas, there seeming to illuminate their surroundings with the intensity of countless floodlights raining down at night.

Dave might have been able to admire such a stark polarization of worlds if the ferocity of his already raging surroundings didn't climax so violently just then. Any hope of helming was rendered negated—including his senses. Overwhelmed by elements to an extent even his wetsuit could no longer shield him, a fearful Dave took immediate cover. Quickly taking refuge on the cockpit floor, there he laid once again in a fetal position bear hugging the compass base as before. It was an odd environment. There was no sensation of actually being submerged underwater or the like, yet Dave still needed his breathing tube in an environment where the distinguishability of breathable air and the liquid surrounding him was at best, ambiguous.

His latest round there on the deck left him no choice but to yield all domain as steersman to chance alone. Helpless, Dave just laid there praying that neither some giant wave might come crashing down at any moment nor that Heather would suddenly blow into his breathing tube summoning his immediate attention.

With a white towel of submission tossed to the sea, he spent that helpless moment preparing for nothingness: no reflection of the past—no awareness of the present. With both of his mental and physical receptors fully engaged, fear could be best likened to that of water rolling over the glass surface of a windshield with its skin effect prohibiting the permeation of any of its destructive influence.

Numb—beyond any effects of emotion—almost at peace—there submerged in the soup of semi-fluid, Dave found a new sense of spirituality in hearing a highly distorted version of *Mr. Roboto* by Styx. Despite both his devout love and likewise commitment to his family's welfare, such a defining moment forced recognition of any inability of being able to protect them for any longer. It meant committing their fate to the hands of chance alone.

Lying on the cockpit floor for a grueling span of time while helpless to his cause, Dave was the eventual recipient of a sudden blast of air rifling down from above. It quickly cleared a thick soup of froth that was previously pooled around him. While his new surroundings did endow an ability of being able to see and breathe independently again, its onset was still met with a wince. Dave held his position lying on the soul of deck until it became clear to him that the climate surrounding him was fully changed in character.

With the previous horizontal winds now gone and instead replaced with an unrelenting slew of potent airbursts rocking their boat from above, the Costas were now dwelling in a new reality. It was one Dave found difficult wrapping his mind around. The new environment that was no less dangerous than before was instead dramatically different. New vertical forces were producing somewhat the same effect on the sea as were the more severe hurricane winds of before. Meanwhile their disruptive surges of kinetic energy were instead being infused into the surface in disrupting clashes from above. Its effects only further agitated an already treacherous sea being stirred up from within the hurricane winded region, from there spilling over to the Costas proximity. Forty-foot plus churning seas just don't dissipate beyond a line drawn in the sand, especially when the sand being spoken of is located two miles below. It is not uncommon for their effects to stray hundreds of miles away from their points of origin, although somewhat dissipated by then.

While the present swells were slightly less extreme in size versus the predominately monstrous ones of before, their random character lacked any patterns to which Dave could devise any practical means of attack. The new seascape could best be likened to that of a wash machine the size of a city block, and the waves being stirred there were being generated in a heavy load cycle.

Similar to discharges ejected from volcanoes, masses of sea foam were being expelled from waves in clashes with an endless slew of powerful down bursts. The scene seemed fitting to some science fiction horror film, not conforming to any sense of oceanographic description Dave ever heard or read about before. With the constant howling winds and assaulting rain now gone, he still needed to keep a diligent heads up for thick masses of sea foam filling the air, some often substantial enough to briefly envelope a vessel the size of Gloria in one dousing. Although the bizarre discharges generally lacked the density of causing any serious damage to their boat, they still posed a danger for Dave outside.

Weighing the risk of leaving the helm unmanned against the benefits of the moral support he believed could be instilled into his family by checking up on them, he entered below. Outside in an environment where the stratum bordering the sea and air was still undistinguishable, its queer environment led him to believe its unpredictability was mostly rendering his piloting skills ineffective.

Below again just prior to securing the hatch behind him as he failed to do earlier, Dave expressed his deep gratitude for Heather's show of courage. He reasoned that her layperson's efforts could likely be credited in their contribution to her mother's new state of awareness. Linda's new grasp of her senses also came with the price of excruciating waves of pain emanating at the site of her wound. Dave touched her chin gently.

"Honey, can you hear me?"

"Heather's unbelievable," Linda responded, adding in a weak and strained voice, "by the way—you're one hell of a navigator, sweetie. Don't quit your day job."

"That's what you get when you hire cheap labor like me," Dave responded, accompanied by a heavyhearted laugh. "Honey, is there anything I can get you?"

"Got a gun?" she laughed before wincing in pain from doing so.

"We won't have any of that now. We're out of the storm, but the waves spilling over from it are still pounding us. They probably will be for a while. Thanks for the music by the way. Quite the morale booster."

Unable to remember turning their stereo on, Linda glazed over his statement. Instead being able to hear its reverberation resonate throughout the structure of their boat, she simply expressed her approval.

"I like it, keep it on. Shouldn't you be on the deck by the way, Mr. Captain? Still feels pretty rough outside."

"Going there, ASAP. Just came to check in on things. This should all be over soon, so just hang in there, okay?"

"By the way, I feel weird, and David's quieter too. I'm not sure if there's any connection. And speaking of which, his skin's cold and clammy. I'm worried about our little boy. Heather's done a nice job at covering him, but it doesn't seem to be enough to be keeping my little pumpkin warm."

Feeling somewhat light lightheaded himself, Dave had already shrugged it off as a side effect of the most mentally, physically, and emotionally grueling several hours he had ever experienced. Upon checking David's forehead and heartbeat, he repositioned his son next to Linda, draping the little boys body against that of hers.

On the way out and in visiting the radio for Mayday purposes, doing so seemed futile with no viable antenna at their disposal. It was therefore evermore astonishing when contact was made with the US Coast Guard. Its aircraft was located fifty miles northwest Hurricane Gloria's most outer bands, a distance that should have prohibited any such contact. Whatever kind of atmospheric bounce was permitting such a link to be taking place might have seemed short of a miracle to Dave, but considering the horrific waters still stirring outside, 'miracle' could have been considered a subjective term to him at that point.

"This is the US Coast Guard, Mayday," a Guard serviceman in a C130 responded. "Do you copy me?"

In excitement, Heather jumped in to join her father.

"I copy you loud and clear. It is so nice to hear from someone. Tropical Storm Gloria has just overrun us down here, and now I'm waiting for its last remnants to clear. I also have injured family members aboard with me here."

Three perplexed enlisted Coast Guard personnel who were all eagerly huddled around the radio traded looks of perplexity at each other.

"Sir, I'm sorry to hear about your family, and we'll get you assistance as soon as possible. If you can give us your coordinates, we'll bring you home before you know it—over."

"I have no references to go by yet, but when I'm in the clearing, I'm hoping I can give you some kind of accurate latitude reading and then a rough longitude one as well. The seas are still pretty nasty right now."

The three exchanged bewildered looks again before the highest-ranking NCO guardsman grabbed the mouthpiece.

"Sir, define rough seas, please—over."

A brief synopsis of the outside conditions was giving when the Coast Guard senior rank enlisted serviceman came back. "Sir, this is Petty Officer First Class Henderson. Do you have any access to a barometer, and if so, what is its reading?"

Dave instructed Heather to go back to the owner's cabin and join the others. In avoidance of being overheard, he then lowered his radio to the point of only being decipherable by him. His hand quivering in having absorbed all the setbacks his disciplined will could muster, he relayed his readings, to which the Guardsman verified.

"That's a 1000 millibar reading if I did hear you correctly. Can you confirm that, sir? Over."

Dave did, and upon the data being called back to the base of the serviceman, the commander there in turn relayed both it and the nature of their communication to their naval contact. This meant it eventually reaching the ears of a stunned Richardson.

Becoming increasingly antsy about his need of returning outside again, Dave relayed such urgency to his petty officer contact. Understanding the Costa's plight, the guardsman pleaded for his patience. His effort in doing so was unnecessary since Dave wasn't about to hang up on him as if he was some soliciting telemarketer interrupting dinner. Instead he patiently waited out a few more minutes for further information, the meanwhile feeling a strong sense of optimism in the process.

The petty officer soon summoned his attention.

"Sir, this message comes straight from Rear Admiral Richardson, the US Naval Battle Strike Group commander in your region. It states that you're presently in the eye of Hurricane Gloria. Repeat— you're presently in the eye of Hurricane Gloria. He states no rescue will be available until the storm's eye passes over you due to the logistics of incompatible proximities—time constraints if I may clarify. Once outside the eye, rescue aircraft will be near enough to canvass your region in an effort of locating you. At that point rescue will be imminent. He asks that you do what is required to survive and states that both his and the prayers of those of his strike group are with you. He ended, 'Rear Admiral Richardson'."

Now joined by the commanding officer of the C130, Petty Officer Henderson and two other Guard members sat quietly afterwards, all in a somber state. In standing, the plane's CO patted the petty officer first class on the back.

"Nice job men. When you finally turn in tonight, just remember you've done all you could for these people. I just need to get back to the cockpit and fly this thing. Ensign Byron's probably shitting his flight suit at the moment, going it alone. If you believe you have any comforting words to share with this man and his family, feel free to express them. They've already been through hell, and now they just found out they're only half way home." The plane's CO paused for a moment. "How the hell they managed to make into the eye of this storm baffles me," he commented, adding, "The conditions inside there are scary enough, especially with that converging surf."

Upon their CO leaving, Henderson held the radio mike against his chin.

"Sir, are you with us still?"

"Yeah—yes I am," Dave replied, still digesting the news.

"Sir, although we can't imagine what your family's actually been through, we do know enough about these storms to understand that you guys have been through hell. Just get through this, and the crew and I will track you down afterwards for a beer. Not on our base though. They only serve the 3.2 percent alcohol shit there."

The guardsman could have later been reprimanded for his usage of an expletive over a civilian channel when representing the Coast Guard, but in their unique circumstance Henderson believed he was merited some level of latitude by anyone listening; especially any serviceperson who had ever consumed the former mentioned beverage.

"I appreciate that, and my answer is, yes. What's your name by the way, and the radioman who spoke to me first?"

"Sir, that would Seaman Apprentice LaPlante who spoke to you first. And I'm Petty Officer First Class Henderson, as I mentioned."

"No, your real name, guys. First names will do."

Every eye was glazed as Henderson responded. "Sir, my name is William, or call me Bill. The gentleman who you spoke with first is Dennis, and we also have a quiet third party here, Dave."

Dave grinned at mention of his own name. "Thanks Bill, Dennis, and Dave. Don't underestimate what you guys have done for us, though I did detect a little crack in your voice. Since I only drink beer with real men, I'm hoping that was only a throat tickle—or whatever."

Henderson cleared his throat, his need to do so made necessary by Dave's show of bravado. "Please excuse me, sir. The air in here's pretty dry." The first class petty office then sat quietly for moment, recomposing. He was finally able to speak again, though barely so. "I'll see you soon, Dave."

"Right back at you, but there's going to be hell to pay before I can make good on any beer. So please wish us luck. I know we're going to need it." Dave then bowed his head. "Thanks guys."

His response was never received. The transmission had become terminated just prior.

On the verge of tears, Henderson concluded to the sound of static. "Good luck to you and your family, brother (Softly) out." Upon bowing his head in understanding the full scope of the Costa's plight, the troubled guardsman then broke down into tears.

Unwilling to throw the towel in just yet, Dave was eager to revisit the deck again. He trusted through the distant hell being an approaching eye wall, there still might be some singularity of light flickering there—an imaginary pinpoint of light difficult to detect through low lying, swirling clouds disintegrating and reforming in the chaos of an endless barrage of potent airbursts.

The ocean's surface eventually lessening in severity meant that the western progression of the storm was now becoming an ally of the Costas. Dave viewed such a reprieve as a window to take inventory of their faculties and to prepare for yet another round of what he and his family had just endured. He also didn't neglect to recognize that although resilient, his war-ridden daughter had already endured far more than any person should ever need to, notwithstanding an eight-year-old. Even in the face of some hull damage only detectable though some water seepage, he was still confident in entering a lesser extreme half of Hurricane Gloria with both a still structurally sound vessel and two-thirds tank of fuel. For the time being, Dave chose to keep their whereabouts a secret until figuring out a way of breaking it to his wife.

The still upheaving sea calming as the unforgiving parting eye wall distanced itself further away came with the understanding its other side's arrival was just as imminent. The storm's 13 mph rate of advance meant that the Costa's were destined to face its meteorological wrath within the next hour. No less a factor was prior to doing so, conditions preceding the eye wall could be expected to be just as treacherous as those within the storm itself.

Dave maintained his place at the helm with a slight swagger of feeling emboldened. He understood nothing else needed to be carried out except maintaining his boat's stability by thrusting and easing up on its engine. Well aware the storm would do the rest in its passing, he seized the opportunity of their lull by entering below again and grabbing a quick snack. Quickly making work of it, he then returned back to the helm again.

Any hope of rescue wasn't just some fragile based confidence of which three F14's instilled with their flyovers to boast his morale as before. Instead it was the reality that many of the uncertain variables that were plaguing him and his family beforehand were replaced with a valid cause for hope. It was a reality punctuated by the promise of a rear admiral, one in which he refused to just write off.

Meanwhile neither Richardson's carrier strike group, nor Dave's unwavering will, nor the absence of any killer waves, nor the still structural soundness of Gloria could prevent a final blow from occurring to it, a boat that had so brilliantly braved the wrath of nature's indiscriminating fury up until to then. Instead it was an infinitesimal size crack in Gloria's refrigerator copper propane line that had ruptured in kinking during their boat's vertical dance with the huge wave earlier.

Failure to shut the refrigerator door properly by slamming it in his haste caused it to bounce back open again at the same time a concurrent movement of Gloria prevented the engagement of its latch. An undetectable amount of gas then ignited when the fridge's thermostat demanded cooling air, thereby creating just enough of a minuscule flash to ignite a sheet of paper crumbled behind it. The small ball of flames ignited other flammables adjacent to it, soon leading to a small, unattended fire. By the time its smoke got noticed by either Heather or her mother, its fire had already spread to the point where an extinguisher was required. Frantic, Heather climbed the companionway, opening the outside hatch.

"Dad—Fire! There's a fire!"

Wasting no time in reentering below, Dave was met by a couple feet of smoke already blanketing the top interior. After choking the gas at its source, which both he and Linda failed to do earlier in their battening down for the storm, he entered the owner's cabin.

"Linda, where's the fire extinguishers? They're not where they're suppose to be!"

Linda did her best to answer him, rubbing her forehead in pain. "Honey, check around the cabin area. This boat's been all over the place. They must have come loose."

With two of their larger fire extinguishers having exited through the companionway along with several other items during their run-in with the large wave earlier, the last remaining one, a smaller extinguisher, resulted in being too little too late. Bellowing smoke that was soon rendering visibility virtually nonexistent fought for dominance against the sheer panic it was generating below. Despite her sluggish state, Linda still possessed the faculties of being able to assist in a hurried evacuation of everyone. It included grabbing a few necessities on the way out to their small newly deployed self-inflatable life raft secured to Gloria's transom.

Even in its less active state, the still upheaving ocean didn't create an ideal setting for a family of four to pile into such a raft. But the term life raft implies the use of one will likely indicate a less than desirable environment for ones deployment. After severing it from Gloria's umbilical cord, a nylon line, Dave used his mariner's knife to cut more of the line for the purpose of loosely securing everyone together.

The family was soon adrift separated from their boat, it now engulfed in flames. The events had developed so quickly, it was difficult to imagine that only a few minutes earlier everyone was all secure and nestled within its somewhat protective confines.

Increasing swells began dwarfing the Costa's raft, leaving their four bodies huddled together in what appeared at a distance as some desolate orange cylinder tube meagerly inhabiting four souls drifting about aimlessly, sharing common memories. The stark appearance of the small orange point as seen from afar against the vast turbulent colorless seascape represented everything that made up their family, the four of them now adrift and at the mercy of an indiscriminate, unforgiving vortex of monstrous proportions called Gloria. Unfortunately for the Costas, their predicament wasn't any haunting nightmare of Jim's playing out this time.

"Where we goin? I'm skeird," little David cried.

In embarking Sao Vicente, this was the boy who once believed he was only going for some short sailing excursion, the meanwhile him being unable to understand the true magnitude of what dangers might lie ahead. Heather latched onto her bother weeping while Linda followed her lead in the shedding of tears. She did so while watching in horror as engulfing flames began causing their boat to start listing in the worsening sea. There she lay, still uneducated to the true whereabouts of their family.

"Dave, where are we?"

He gave her no response, instead wasted no time in silently interweaving nylon rope through both the eyelets encircling their raft and each other's lifejackets.

In a manic evacuation of a doomed Gloria, each family member had grabbed what he or she believed might either be practical or comforting aboard the life raft. Linda carried along two jars of peanut butter and several bottles of seltzer waters for both nourishment and hydration. Meanwhile thanks to his dad, little David didn't need to surrender his stuffed tiger while his more pragmatic sister salvaged both a blanket and a canvass tarp to protect everyone from the weather, and then later, the sun.

Dave in turn grabbed nylon line for mainly one purpose and it generally contradicted the reason his wife had instead retrieved potentially day's worth of vital nourishments. He took the rope along in knowing that in less than a half hour the four of them would all fall victims to the sea. It was his wish that at least their bodies might be found together post the meteorological slaughter to ensue and their remains might then stand as a testament to who they were and how they had perished together.

Sea spray increasing in intensity began raining down on the family where they lay adrift. Dave held back his tears of which only Linda was able to detect. Everyone the meanwhile was draped with the canvas tarp Heather had brought along. In beginning to address her husband again, Linda instead faded into unconsciousness. Her doing so left Dave alone as the head of household to make a decision that beforehand he could have never fathomed would ever needed to be considered, either as a parent or husband. An inability of imagining allowing his kids to face the deteriorating seas ahead in turn compelled the tormented father to question the virtue of doing so. It forced him to consider the need of preempting their grim fate by committing an inconceivable act of mercy such as taking everyone's lives beforehand. In doing so, he would then face the storm alone and there afterwards pay a repentance by suffering through his own ending like some anonymous martyr.

As difficult of a concept euthanasia was to consider, Dave also needed to contemplate yet one more allusive query. No less demoralizing than the act itself, it was, if so, then when? It was a litmus test whose time for any solution was running thin.

Sick to his stomach and brooding over only grim options, he chose instead to delay taking any action until conditions would pose too prohibiting for the likelihood of any rescue. At such a juncture, his plan would be carried out by first inducing sleep to each of his beloved victims before then taking it a step further. His method in doing so, which was perceived to be the most merciful option available, had also been contemplated under extreme duress. Its subtle means the meanwhile made the heart wrenching need of carrying out such an act no less sickening or unthinkable. What propelled any such consideration, nonetheless carrying it out, was Dave's familiarity with the likes of the conditions awaiting them. An available breathing tube then was the only reason he was still alive.

For Dave, his state of crisis bore to mind a time in history his martial arts instructor once depicted in grisly detail. Simplifying the complexities of a highly chaotic ancient battle, he did so in a lesson of never giving up no matter how unfavorably the odds may seem to be stacked. It occurred near the end of the fourth century several miles outside of Adrianople, a place now located in modern Turkey. Refusing to wait for reinforcements, an impatient Roman Emperor Valens hastily sought out his barbarian foe with over ten thousand of his outnumbered foot soldiers (legions). Unprotected by their cavalry, they found themselves baking for hours beneath a searing sun. Their drawn out subjection to its unrelenting rays rendered the large fighting force both parched and famished.

The exhausted infantrymen also found themselves surrounded by a much larger merciless fighting force of Goth infantrymen, cavalry, and archers ready to seek retribution. Crowding as a result generated mass-confusion throughout the organized professional army. It in turn caused a systemic breakdown throughout its ranks to take place, thereby rendering a normally triumphant Roman war machine ineffective. Their Achilles was once again exposed, as was the case many times when faced by Hannibal, pre-empire.

Like the Costas packed together adrift and surrounded by a deadly eye perimeter, the helpless Roman forces trapped inside also had no place where to escape. An outside perimeter of legions being void of necessary mobility were being subsequently cut down systematically, layer by layer, ruthlessly slaughtered by a vicious angry opponent that when one of their own fell, another was there to take their place. Attrition didn't favor the Romans, who were falling at a far greater rate than that of their enemy. Their infantry engaged on the battlefront was also in constant subject to waves of highly chaotic attacks, as the Goth cavalry would make random strikes there without abandonment.

As bleak of a prospect it may have seemed for those engaged in battle on the killing perimeter, a place where thousands of others would also come to meet the same fate, the ill-fated throng of those within could only wait their turn either to be viciously cut up, impaled, or bludgeoned. Unable to assist their brothers falling in great numbers to the crimson ground below, the men inside could only listen helplessly to the cries of their friends and comrades filling the dusty air with their chilling shrieks of agony. It was a horrific chorus mixed with the anguished bellows of their foe systematically slaughtering their way towards them.

In panning their surroundings while packed together against fellow combatants, those terrified men would have only been able witness the gaunt faces of their doomed peers for seeking any comfort. Such would be the case while sometimes bearing witness of entire groups of brothers in arms falling to the ground all at once. There they lay seconds later, victims to a barrage of javelins and arrows appearing out of nowhere through a blinding cloud of dust. It was both a repeated event and a dreadful reminder to those not engaged in battle yet that no one was safe, not even for a moment.

Such grim expressions calcified on the faces of the Roman foot soldiers is what Heather observed in peering into face of her father, the meanwhile unable to understand the true significance behind his lifeless expression.

Upon thousands awaiting and eventually meeting their brutal demise back in the late fourth century, only the fall of darkness prompted the enemy to finally relent. It brought some reprieve to a few mentally, physically, and emotionally exhausted men who were accustomed beforehand to being the victors. They were but a few men who were able to find cover beneath the carnage of their fallen peers and through the stealth of darkness were able to eventually escape into the night, counting their blessings. Success in doing so was hinged on being fortunate enough not to get chased down by some rouge zealous barbarian who happened to spot their escape beforehand.

Such a depiction was an extreme lesson of survival where the odds were highly stacked against any Roman infantrymen who dare hold onto any notion of survival in the face of such a monumental slaughter, yet some still did survive. As for the Costas, anybody seated as they were would have had just cause to argue their predicament wasn't any more survivable than that of any of Valens's doomed men. Unlike them, Dave was well aware the only darkness awaiting him and his family offered no sanctuary where to seek any cover.

Increasing slews of airbursts propelling heavier amounts of spray onto the family began strengthening in ferocity. Just to keep afloat, both Dave and Heather needed to scoop water from their small raft via cupped hands. The family was soaked, cold, Linda unconscious with her health still deteriorating, and her son only moaning in a semiconscious state.

Scooping along with her dad, Heather did so while whimpering. She recognized that although he hadn't expressed it, she knew their situation was grave. There was no bliss in the ignorance of hurricane conditions lurking just beyond. Nor was there any in the reality that conditions approaching the ensuing eye wall would prohibit any likely rendezvous with the high-velocity winds that were succeeding them.

"Daddy, when are those people supposed to come? You spoke with them, didn't you? I'm scared."

"Soon sweetie, soon."

Then grasping her little hand, Dave sat eerily silent. His look was that of a thousand-yard stare in noting the increasing volume of the winded region still miles away sounding similar to countless freight trains advancing through the murky eastern skies. It included increasing rumbles of thunder echoing a distance away as well. They gave a general reference that the approaching eye wall was preparing to soon spell their end. Dave was feeling the same helplessness any Roman infantryman trapped in the center of the killing fields might have felt in hearing the clamor of battle creep closer. In knowing the storm would soon come fast and furious, he wanted to make sure nature wouldn't decide everyone's outcome before him. It was his belief taking such a passive role would be a selfish one on his part. Even understanding his intent was to spare his family a certain bout of terror made such the daunting task as committing euthanasia no less painful. It was Dave's in-your-face Masada.

Possessing an old soul in such a young body, Heather began weakening from all the accumulative stresses experienced over the previous several hours, the present being no less an exception. With her being the most coherent of everyone beside him, Dave was swayed to relieve her from her senses first; he wished for no witnesses. Freeing enough slack of the nylon rope tethering everyone together, he snuggle his daughter's small frame against his. This was his smart and well-behaved daughter who always made him so proud. It was the young girl he witnessed entering the world from her mother's womb even before Linda ever laid an eye on her. This was the same girl who once constructed indiscernible objects pasted together from separate cuts of colored Manila paper, spelling "Happy Birthday to the GREATEST Daddy. I Luv You"

The small frame in his arms was the same young girl he figured he'd someday need to protect from other boys, knowing all too well the need of eventually giving her away some day to a husband, like him or not. In understanding how gifted she was, this was the daughter he relished saving money for, for paying her way though college someday. Only able to see the eventuality, the tormented dad just held her tightly, still refusing to follow through with the unthinkable.

It could have never beforehand become more apparent to him than at that moment that whatever level of strength does stem from ones love and sense of devolution, warrants that one needn't ever consider their own wellbeing in a circumstance requiring the sacrifice of their own life in exchange for the preservation of another dare to them. It was also reigning true for him that such an unwavering love in turn was tendering nothing in will for taking such a life as a means of sparing them a worse fate.

Whether the question could be posed in the development of

human emotion where such a trait might go against everything love was intended to perpetuate, life not death, procreation versus extinction—a certainty existing there in the Costa's small orange cylinder was that its answer wasn't written into the genetic code of Dave. Consequently, Jim's words were ringing through his head like a fire siren amidst a hangover. While he had argued so adamantly to prevent Dave from taking the course which essentially led to his present peril, the Costa's present situation would have never been the "I told you so" Jim would have ever wished to have conveyed to him.

With his throat burning, skin clammy, and tears being displaced by sea spray soaking his face, Dave sat both weak from emotion and sick to his stomach, contemplating. Still holding Heather tightly, procrastinating, silently saying goodbye to his daughter, he heard her faint voice.

"Is that them?"

Dave needed to clear his throat while also believing she might be slipping into delirium. "What is it, sweetie?"

"Daddy, are those the people who you talked to before?"

Dave turned only to witness a large swell lifting them. "I see nothing, honey. There's nothing there," he ended in frustration.

"Yes there is Dad. Keep looking!"

Void of all hope and therefore believing there was nothing to lose with just a limited time left, Dave gave his daughter the benefit of the doubt. Completely resigned, he just waited for another swell to lift them in better view of the seascape. The last thing he needed was having come to terms with what needed to be done in the face of no hope, just to then be ensnared in the trap of yet another elusive cause for hope. Any hint his daughter might be slipping into delusion was supported by the knowledge that the US Navy was presently incapable of exacting any kind of rescue at such a juncture. It was quite clear to him that any further procrastination on his part was soon destined to lead to a very bad moment for everyone. Nature would then have a final say.

Witness of several ensuing swells only substantiated what Dave already suspected. It wasn't until a particularly higher rise of water lifted the family that left him believing maybe it was he who was hallucinating after all. A submarine lurking a distance away could accomplish one of two courses that Dave would soon come to consider humane. It could either rescue him and his family from a certain meteorological wall of death approaching or instead blow them out of the water. Contemplation of the latter was only being considered, because after a few long minutes of frantically waving at the darkened subsurface vessel with Heather, there wasn't any response from its conning tower. Instead there was only the movement of a quad loop and that which he recognized as a periscope peering in their direction. Aware the US Navy knew of their peril, he therefore assumed such curious spectators would have already established some form of contact if their intent were that of any rescue.

In viewing the submarine's periscope, Dave assumed the eyes there within the vessel were carefully examining them—probably wondering what four people all crowded into a small life raft were doing meandering about in the unlikely confines of a hurricane eye surrounded by deadly Force-12 conditions.

While being unfamiliar to him, the 265-foot submarine was mesmerizing in its sleek lines despite its projection of intimidation. He found it astonishing something so malevolent in intent could also be so captivating to the eye and no less give hope to the faint-hearted, as was he and his family. There was also amazement that something so spectacular to behold might also possess the capacity of committing genocide of biblical proportions with either a scripted push of a few buttons or the turning of a couple keys.

While his absorption in the vessel almost rivaled the necessity of rescue, the reality still stood for the family that if the submarine was to suddenly to slip beneath the waves and never reappear again, then it would only have prolonged the inevitability to which Dave already prepared himself the best he could. The introduction of the submarine into the theater if not friendly only stood to complicate matters furthermore. It would make justifying any inconceivable act such of committing euthanasia so much more difficult in the face of a possible rescue at any moment.

Although not evident in any activity other than appendages stirring atop the submarine's conning tower, there still seemed to be an air of something stirring within its darkened hull. It at worse gave Dave an array of hope that at least he and his family weren't going to perish in their life raft without any recognition. While it seemed his fascination may have been mutual as with his onlookers only a short distance away—unlike with those dwelling within the impressive feat of engineering, the lives of him and his family hinged on the certainty of any such an assessment.

<< CHAPTER 9 >>

CONCURRENT TO THE COSTA'S DEALINGS with a wave's crushing forces just prior to Heather being feared lost an hour earlier, 27-year-old submarine sonar officer, Lieutenant Styopa Malitzka, was caught between his headsets by an irregularity capturing his full attention. The young officer grew up in a small state apartment in Leningrad (Now St. Petersburg), a large city whose location east of the Gulf of Finland was a focal point of both Russian naval and maritime activity. Its region, home to both a prominent naval school and several shipyards, also held the distinction of being the birthplace of the Russian Navy. Both its history and origin dated back to Peter the Great.

Ultra-sensitive instrumentation located aboard Styopa's *Alfa Class* submarine (NATO designation for reference purposes. *Lira Class* and *Project 705* were but a few of the Soviets designations of the same class of submarine) had no difficulty picking up the Costa's stereo blasting less than ten miles away through a thunder ridden, muddled turbulence. The likes of Hurricane Gloria's chaos presented an ideal environment, so it had been suggested by his superiors, for the 49-year-old Captain Second Rank Polivanova (Styopa's commander) to test the detection boundaries of his vessel, one that had been commissioned into active duty five years earlier. Born in the town of Lomonosov, a smaller municipality located just west of Leningrad, the commander was carrying out orders handed down to him by the commander in chief of the Soviet Navy. The second rank's mission was a risky one due to his counterpart's ability of being able to decipher the signature of the likes of his vessel even through extreme weather conditions. He knew that. Meanwhile served up by nature, Hurricane Gloria's noisy environment was to pose as an ideal setting for him to conduct his mission regardless of its futility.

In a quest of testing the stealth boundaries of his Alfa Class submarine within the new hurricane, many members of his small crew also needed to pay a price for flirting with such *ideal* conditions. They did so while manning their stations and puking everything their seasoned chief starshina (Their cook) had served up to them into a nearest container. To Captain Second Rank Polivanova, such a stifling repugnancy overwhelming his ships cramped inner workings represented a badge of courage he was proud his resilient crew of less than forty wore. It pleased the commander that many were still able to conduct their long drawn-out mission effectively in spite of their debilitating state, especially the starshina. By comparison, his crew's present surroundings still paled in contrast to the more treacherous ones he once needed to endure upon entering into submarine duty years earlier.

Like most submarines, Polivanova's could also roam about the vast underworld at low speeds, undetected. Even in the face of sensitive tracking instrumentation equipped aboard most NATO vessels and an American detection networks laid about on the ocean floor, lower patrol speeds could still be maintained for evading the attention of such systems. Furthermore, an Alfa Class submarine's high-speed capability was likely to cause other submarines giving chase the need to at best keep tabs on it by use of their tracking methods. While no vessel was ever safe from any enemy's weapon systems once their whereabouts was known, Polivanova's quick acceleration and impressive maneuverability rendered his vessel the most capable of evading such threats.

While the talented commander had been briefed his mission to roam about a stirring surface at borderline detection speed was to buy a few extra knots for the books, he suspected there was more the picture than that he was informed. His vessel was normally stationed in Zapadnaya Litsa Naval Base, located south of the Barents Sea. Typically moored there in wait as an interceptor for the Soviet Northern Fleet, the captain second rank was uninformed to the reasons the higher command suddenly assigned him to such risky a mission, especially just out of the blue and a thousand of miles south of his normal prowling grounds. It didn't mean he didn't embrace the challenge of silently waiting about for a storm of opportunity in the active waters a thousand miles west of the Cape Verde Islands. While assuming his mission may have been one of trivial experimentation there without backup and pushing the envelope of detection deep in US dominated waters, its sudden timing mostly elicited a sight curiosity that he found noteworthy. There were other Soviets subs in their arsenal capable of achieving the same objective with longer sea endurances, there placing his submarine in jeopardy of exceeding its own limits.

Polivanova guessed there were other factors related to his new orders. Apart from other Project 705 vessels commissioned before his, it was his understanding his vessel carried with it many new technologies making it unique from its predecessors. Unlike other attack submarines of the same class, his was fitted with two nuclear warheads. The second rank was uninformed to the scope of their use. He was instructed their uses would later be revealed. He was also aware his submarine, the most current Project 705 vessel in the fleet, had also been suited with the newest generation of electronics whose function was also to be divulged only on a need to know basis at some unspecified time later on.

The sagacious Polivanova for the most part had already reached his pinnacle in the Soviet's naval chain of command. Any inability of climbing higher reflected nothing in the way of any shortcomings over a long and distinguished career by him. There were two reasons an elevation to captain first rank was the best Polivanova could expect to achieve. Despite an unquestioned level of respect he had gained from all who knew him, his brusque mannerism caused him to lack a political savoir-faire necessary for dealing fittingly in the realm of subtleties often required in the higher echelon of military command. The same course personality could also be credited for tagging him with a reputation of that of a shark beneath the waves, a quality his superiors felt was most conducive for commanding a fast-attack submarine with limited endurance, especially deep in American friendly waters, and no less solo.

Such a lack of refinement also caused Polivanova to peeve off many in both the navy and politburo; thereby many in a position to grant him any higher status of rank could still feel the fractures of their toes from when he had once stepped on them.

While the steadfastness of his loyalty was never questioned, the commander's sometimes crude and often unorthodox approach to attaining results did concern those who only a few months earlier felt such practices stood to cause a hiccup in a highly secret and sensitive mission conducted by his fleet. When it came to their general consensus about him, Polivanova's superiors felt one pit bull penetrating noisily into US waters was risky enough, especially giving their previous mission's success of territorial infiltration.

The full scope of second rank's new orders was to follow a powerful storm of opportunity and then keep pace with it up the U.S. East Coast if it happened to veer that way. While doing so near a rough surface posed as a challenge to many of the stomachs aboard his Alpha Class Submarine, versus indefinitely masking its acoustical signature at slower speeds and in less turbulent waters many meters below the sea surface, the commander's orders was to test the boundaries of American detection abilities. Therefore, any conservative approach would have been considered pointless.

Second Rank Polivanova took a keen interest in the signature of the music being detected. Its obvious irregularity of proximity in which it was sounding so prominently caused its queer occurrence to spark his curiosity. Having ordered his submarine to the origin of the noise, the soviet submarine eventually caught up with it in Gloria's eye. An eventual calming sea presented the opportunity for Polivanova to canvas the surface in stealth with his vessel still at periscope depth. Steadying himself against his large periscope in compensation of the sea still exerting its will on his vessel, the intrigued commander turned towards his senior executive officer, Captain Third Rank Yegor Golovkin. Speaking in Russian, which was the only language spoken aboard their vessel, he summoned his second-in-command's attention for viewing.

"Captain, look outside. Be patient. The waves will reveal it."

Golovkin then gazed into the eyepieces as Polivanova waited patiently with the understanding that the Costa's sailboat would take some effort in the spotting of it. His senior officer eventually locked onto them.

"Captain, is that what Lieutenant Malitzka [Styopa] picked up?"

"Unless this is some NATO social spot, I would conclude yes. I see light through the boat's portholes and might have also spotted movement of some kind, astern. I'm not certain."

"Commander, we have a mission to follow this storm up the American coast if it warrants. Should we really be detouring like this for some stray civilian, recreational boat?"

Polivanova turned away from Golovkin aimlessly canvassing his well-lit command center, one reflecting an air of pale yellow. Other officers seated at their consoles took notice of the dialogue being spoken, including one who was sick. The curious men masked their interest while still continuing their tasks.

Polivanova turned to face Golovkin again. "Comrade, I am well aware of our mission. But in case you haven't noticed, we are dead in the middle of this damn storm. I'm therefore confident we're not digressing from any kind of objective, do you?" He then pointed to his sick officer. "I'm certain Lieutenant Komarovski would concur with me, and I'd wager that he'd also give up his first born just to be able to spend a few minutes outside on the sail [conning tower] to regain his equilibrium back. Are you going to be okay, Lieutenant? You're stinking up this cabin." Grinning, he added, "but I commend you on your dedication to the motherland."

Affirming with a quick response, his navigator nodded before responding. "Yes, Commander."

"You're replacement is also sick, so unfortunately relieving you isn't an option. If you feel you can run to the head and rinse your pale quickly, everyone here would appreciate it. Do so, please."

Upon a quick acknowledgement of his navigator's labored nod, Polivanova continued. "If we were fifty meters below, much of my crew would be able to hold their breakfast down. But the spirit of my orders requires we stay here near the surface. We don't need either the American surveillance grid or one of their Los Angeles

Class Submarine (US fast-attack submarine) detecting us this close to their back yard where we have no support. So comrade, within any mission you must never overlook the potential significance of any anomaly, even if they do appear to be insignificant. I need more information here."

"Captain, what if it's some American decoy?"

Polivanova patted his second on his shoulder. "In this line of work, suspicion is everything. It'll serve you quite well when commanding your own vessel. With that stated, common sense is just as important. Do you really believe NATO would subject any personnel to such suicidal conditions with only the remotest of a long shot for some successful surveillance? That boat is about to get ripped to pieces in the next half hour. I'm amazed they even made it this far."

"I can see someone as yourself being bold enough to volunteer for such a mission, Commander."

"Flattery has no place in my crew, but pertaining to my younger days, your statement would be actuate—speaking of which, many a young brave sailor has selflessly volunteered for suicide missions before like the brave ill-fated comrades aboard the K-19 [USSR Submarine involved in a deadly reactor incident]. I just don't expect any men under my command to ever to die in vein. They'll good men and will volunteer for any task I ask of them. It's therefore our responsibility as those in command to make certain that a mission is never smaller than the lives we ask to risk, even if some brave comrade is willing to do so. There's also something else I need to discuss with you in private just outside. Please follow me."

Upon the two men exiting the area, the commander continued. "You have been with me for nearly five months now, but Captain Lieutenant Komarovski's replacement [The other sick navigation officer] as you well know is also new aboard. I don't trust him. He's quiet—seems to pay too much mind to what others are saying. Keep an eye on him for me as, well as for yourself. I've seen these no-names come and go before. So for the sake of any successful future, you therefore need a lesson of this type of crew activity."

"Commander, I'm not clear."

"Look captain, this ship is carrying the latest most sophisticated detection equipment leading me to believe there might be either some KGB officer or low ranking party official nearby aiming to kiss as many asses as possible with his eyes set on the Politburo. I'm only asking you be an extra set of eyes and ears for me—that's all."

"Understandable Commander, I know the type. But our nuclear warheads—wouldn't such weaponry be of more interest to such an opportunist? This ship's classification isn't normally configured for such armament."

"I have weapons officers of clearance to oversee them, so I don't see why. It might seem odd that nuclear armament would be of less importance to any electronics to say the least. Why we're carrying such armament, I don't know. Your guess is as good as mine. Then again, nothing about any decision originating out of the Kremlin ever surprises me." He grinned. "You'll learn that lesson in time."

"Then what should I do then as far as interacting with the officer in question?"

"Nothing. You see we have a very cohesive crew, as you should very well know by now. I'm only asking that you'll assist me in protecting them from the likes of some undercover agent, being it that some of our comrades may sometimes choose to engage in illegal recreation to break up the monotony. I just don't want some overzealous KGB officer or party member tainting their promising careers just because some of my men are simply trying to maintain some degree of morale."

"Illegal activity?"

"Easy Captain, and don't be naïve—gambling, the sort, that's all. I don't condone such activities, and God help the men I find doing so. Giving my crew should carry with it a little more professionalism because of their higher ranks than those of other vessels, you never know, especially with a couple of our warrant officers we have aboard. They're talented men and I don't wish to lose them, but sometimes I do need to keep an eye on them as well—that's all. I was once in their position and understand the game. I will admit the ambiances of the submarines I once dwelled in were so much more cruder than this one, but you know men will be men, and where there are men, then you can often expect some kind of inappropriate activity to be taking place." Polivanova lay still for a moment reflecting on his past. "Sometimes the conditions that we were forced to contend with were borderline inhumane, Captain— deplorable to say the least."

"Sir, I can't even imagine, and with that stated, how long are we going to trail the people out there, whoever they might be?"

"Honestly Yegor, right now I'm not certain. As long as we're able to mask our presence here out of sight, I need to know how some small goddamn fiberglass boat could have made its way into this eye in pieces. What I need to do now is make my rounds and raise the morale around here if that's at all possible. I mean it's tough cheering up a man who can't hear you over their own dry heaving."

"Well then commander, I'll go back in there [command center] and take my post while you do so."

"Yes I would appreciate that. Please keep an eye on the boat out there and let me know if anything changes. Eventually the other side of the storm will overtake them, and we can go on from there. Maintain our position back some and raise the antennas to listen for any communications traffic. I don't need the Americans joining us here as spectator of the same show."

As much as the commander was itching to share his feelings pertaining to the Costa matter, he instead let his concerns play out as mere trivial curiosity. Contrary to anything he may have already hinted, the captain second rank was feeling strong concern for any possible survivors who he believed might still be dwelling aboard the Costa boat, and he did so to the degree of feeling a compelling desire to initiate a rescue. Furthermore, Polivanova recognized that any likely occupants still aboard Gloria had conceivably already experienced their share of horror. In tandem with checking up on his crew's wellbeing, he also intended to use his time away from the command center for brainstorming. There he hoped of finding some way of justifying some rationale for rescue.

Pending a miracle for the Costa's, it was highly unlikely any hard sell on the part of Polivanova to his command stood to render any positive response. The Soviet government didn't spend such a large chunk of money for the likes of his submarine just to play the rescue card unless there stood to be a propagandist benefit from doing so. The commander knew that.

During his rounds of a lower deck, the commander walked in on two unsuspecting warrant officers playing cards in the galley. At the sight of rubles laid before the men, he chastised them harshly, especially not appreciating them conducting such activities in a business area. Afterwards, en route to checking up on more of his crew, a still fuming Polivanova suddenly faced a bulkhead in rage.

Gripping a couple conduits there and taking a few deep breathes to calm, he did so in avoidance of taking his anger out on anyone else without cause.

In envisioning the stupidity of his crewman exchanging money in front of a suspected KGB agent with both an old deck of Mayan cards and rubles lied before them, a revelation then cooled the commander's seething temper. It did so like the feel of a cold beer soothing the stomach on a sweltering day. While Polivanova's brainchild stood to offer little reprieve to the ears he had just scolded, it did give him a glimmer of hope. He figured that his new idea stood to have a better than zero chance of falling on the receptive ears of his superiors versus the zero to which he had already subscribed. The commander just wasn't one who was willing to give up without a fight.

In additional to being married and co-parenting three teenagers from afar, Polivanova was also a traditional man of strong spiritual beliefs. He gathered if a worst-case scenario led to the Costa family needing to fend for themselves through the next half of the storm in what appeared to be a still viable sea vessel, it would then mean being able to take some solace in at least having lobbied his best case for their cause. Those were the types of feelings he preferred keeping private, lay hidden beneath a thick-skinned, brash exterior.

During making a general inquiry of his ship's reactor, Polivanova was summoned back to the command center. In entering there to find Captain Third Rank Golovkin steadying the periscope for his immediate viewing, he hurriedly pressed his eyes up against the rotating column's eyepiece. There he witnessed smoke bellowing out of Gloria's companionway while also watching in shock as the Costa family evacuated into their small life raft. In doing so, he didn't miss the image of the American flag affixed to the hull of Gloria. It caused him to slowly peel his eyes away from the large scope. Polivanova now understood sitting back and taking a laissez-faire attitude was no longer an afforded luxury. Beforehand, a lack of urgency provided him an ability of being able to detach him from the events that had been unfolding outside.

Due to Dave's failure to have shut off Gloria's propane tank in its battening down, such a frail reality could be seen disintegrating with the sight of a spiraling plume of smoke bellowing up in front of his eyes. Disheartened, Polivanova handed the periscope back to Golovkin before bracing himself against one of his communication's officer's seat. In grabbing its thin backrest, he bowed his head and spoke in a low defeated manner "It looks like they're Americans— and they had to have two small children aboard with them as well. What were the odds?"

The Captain Second Rank Polivanova wore with his uniform over thirty years of decorated naval service, two thirds of it related to submarine duty. Upon graduating from the prestigious Frunze Naval College in Leningrad, he later received a crash course in the dangers of submarine warfare. It began in the cruder, unreliable, cramped, and smelly diesel-driven Whisky-Class submarines of the sixties and the early seventies. Having paid his dues in them, he eventually graduated to the full command of his present Lira Class titanium submarine.

Arrived in the navy as both a quiet and hard working academy student, it was his later treacherous sub missions aboard vessels prematurely squeezed off their production lines that ended up hardening him into the loyal, but cynical officer he was. Aside the frustration of his country's way of doing business, often leaving its scar on military personnel as was the case with him, the navy did at least secure his family back home with relatively comfortable living. While their living arrangements may have been considered meager by western standards, most soviets by comparison would have instead considered such living conditions privileged. As a result, the captain second rank was well aware of the stakes in his position.

With his expertise in both anti-submarine and missile warfare, Polivanova's primary mission if the Cold War was to become hot was to naturalize any NATO fast attack-submarines of opportunity or instead defend his nations' doomsday submarines if needed. The latter such vessels in small quantity possessed the capacity of blanketing hundreds of millions of souls with mushrooms rivaling temperatures found beneath the surface of the sun. Within just a half hour's notice, they could transform any country from that of a vibrant entity thriving with the hopes and dreams of tomorrow to a wasteland of suffering and death devoid of any hopes of tomorrow.

In the simulated warfare that took place during the Cold War, passive meant hunting each other and in there doing provoke whatever response possible to expose the defensive tactics of a counterpart. Years of dangerous cat and mouse games; hazards posed by the sea itself; dangerous subsurface obstructions that sometimes included other submarines friend or foe; and poor workmanship never prepared the captain second rate for the Costa equation. Introduced with his new arena of moral conflict to the likes he was never prepared, its introduction made him feel as if his slate had just been wiped clean of all his dues paid over a long and distinguished career. Polivanova also understood a prospect of improved relations between the Soviet and American governments were being hinted to from above. Such a factor by itself was contributing to his softening ideals.

Unprepared for the queerness of the events unfolding outside, he contemplated the justification of how his own children should being giving a fear chance to a bright future while the like of his own could just be left to perish in a violent hurricane awaiting them, and moreover reasons related to his past. The likelihood that such occupants had already experienced many hours of extreme trepidation just prior was also being taken into account as well. Polivanova searched for some meaning to the coincident now placing him face to face with the Costa family including a twist of irony causing him to ask privately, "why did they have to be Americans?"

His demeanor then changed in remembering the crewmen he scolded earlier. Upon hypothesizing what was to be gained by the execution of a rescue, the commander then broke his silences to a communications officer seated before him.

"Lieutenant Shkarov, channel this message to the fleet admiral."

To the astonishment of the other officers also present in the commander center, the commander began his dictation.

"This is Captain Second Rank Vladimir N. Polivanova requesting authorization for extraction of suspected American civilian family trapped within the confines of a hurricane eye. Stranded there in small life raft—two young children involved. Witnessed sailboat succumb to fire. See strong propaganda potential in rescue and will compromise neither position nor secrecy in keeping occupants in question contained under secured confinement. Here in a noisy vessel tiptoeing past a wolf's den, the meanwhile rustling through some dry leaves in doing so. Stranded occupants might serve as bargaining chip [Idea hatched from card game] in case of detection. If Americans presently knows of occupants' plight, who to their knowledge would have already been presumed perished at sea by now, I would then relish the opportunity of being able to savor their expressions in a handover. If the storm instead heads west, thereby terminating our mission up the American Seaboard, will pick up some fresh Cubans upon returning [kidding]. Situation urgent, therefore requesting an immediate response. Transmission complete."

While intrigued by their commander's reasoning, those present were no less shocked at the boldness of his request. In spite of an attempt made of masking his concerns, there trivializing such a rescue as a three-tier objective, Polivanova's crew was nevertheless able to read further into it, Golovkin no less. Meanwhile with their senior superior shouldering the burden of risking losing face at such a request, he in turn afforded those in watch the luxury of being able to privately feel relieved in not needing to witness the Costa family fall victim to an approaching eye boundary. Third Rank Golovkin on the other hand took strong exception.

"Commander, we're not really going to risk good men for the sake of some goodwill gesture towards our enemy, are we?"

Polivanova was taken aback by his second's tone. "Next time be more careful the way you phrase your remarks, comrade. I do what I do because I'm the commander. But if you wish to question my actions—did you notice all I did just now was merely a request for authorization? If fleet command grants my request, I will carry out the rescue. If not, then the people out there will perish in a few minutes, which in that case I hope them doing so might allow you to sleep better at night in knowing we haven't given up any vital Republic secrets to what appears to be some distressed American family who may have just endured more in the last few hours than you have your entire career."

The commander then moved about his control room, bracing in compensation of his sub's increasing undulation.

"You may not see it yet, but we have an opportunity thrust upon us here with little risk of detection in seizing it. I see it as a foregone conclusion—a win-win situation for us. A propagandist marvel discrediting the *evil empire that was* tattooed to our motherland by an American President—and a little payback the meanwhile. Do you understand what I'm insinuating, Golovkin? And as far as any 'enemy' is concerned, I didn't see any 406-millimeter [16 inch] cannons mounted on their *fiberglass* deck, did you?"

Still seething in having felt the piercing bite of his commander's contemptuous remarks, Golovkin objected. "Captain, with all due respect, I'm not sure you're aware of the specifics of my career to make such a notion of its past. And no—I didn't see any cannons."

In approaching his second-in-command and then patting his shoulder, Polivanova did so in believing he had made his point to who was boss while still maintaining some sense of fairness.

"You're correct, Captain. I was out of line for insinuating such a notion. It looks like you have something else to add. What is it?"

"Your plan does have merit, but what if it backfires?"

"Any decision that I make as a commander can backfire at any moment. A terrible consequence could mean the destruction to a crew that I admire and value. Any orders I give can even have repercussions that might endanger those at home to whom I've been commissioned to protect. That's a heavy burden to carry, but in doing so it assists in keeping ones priorities straight. You need to be willing to put your neck on the line by any command presented. If I receive appropriate authorization, then I will personally assist in the rescue of these people you see out there. And if I die doing so—" grinning, Polivanova continued, "—then you'll assume full command. Do you wish such a command, comrade?"

"I would secure and conduct such a command with impunity, but I don't desire it through attrition. I just see the men of this vessel and the sacrifices they've made to belong here, which conclude me to judge. I don't feel the people out there are worthy and therefore haven't earned any right to be side by side with our men here in our prized submarine."

"Maybe you're right Captain, and I will scrub this whole idea of rescue if you can look out at that family right now in the raft facing such a terrible death and convince me you'd rather be unworthy like them versus secured in the safe confines of our world-class vessel, as you are right now."

There was no response. Meanwhile a few of the officers, most of whom didn't like Golovkin, grinned privately in appreciation of their commander's savvy knack of persuasion.

Polivanova then approached Golovkin, once again patting his shoulder. "If I'm wrong comrade, everything will play out as it will, and then I'll need to face the fire. In commanding, the heavy-handed words you're sometimes forced to carry can fall back and crush you in return."

Polivanova's submarine continued to tail the Costas from an obscured distance before eventually giving into making itself visible for the sake of instilling hope. The commander was first hesitant in doing so in fearing such an action might give a false sense of hope to those who it was presumed might have already accepted their fate. His submarine trailed them as long as possible, the meanwhile him pondering the irresponsibleness of having done so. Compelled to such an action, he was tormented in witnessing Dave and Heather both frantically waving in a desperate plea for their lives.

Upon viewing Polivanova's encoded message at headquarters in Moscow, in disbelief, the Admiral of the Fleet dropped the printed request on his desk. He then took a deep breath and sighed. "Oh my Vladimir, Vladimir, Vladimir. What the hell are you doing over there with the prized gem of the People's Navy?" He then grinned in disbelief, slowly shaking his head. "The guys at the top are going to love this one. The part that worries me most is they might actually go for it."

With both facing the submarine, Dave grabbed Heather and held her tightly, his forehead rested on her shoulder in frustration. The seemingly endless routine of waiting with the submarine in full view continued as he began taking notice of both cracks of thunder beginning to increase in volume and the sea's uneasiness doing the same in voracity. As their surroundings became turbulent to the point where rescue seemed prohibiting, Polivanova's vessel began a slow approach towards them. This new development filled Dave with a newfound hope that maybe the tides of misfortunes were finally beginning to recede. He sat in observance of what appeared to be a windshield erecting atop Polivanova's sail bridge. A hatch then opened just prior to a thick pressurized circular door doing so next. A warrant officer in storm gear emerged from it, and as much as the commander did insist on partaking in the rescue beforehand, his crew refused to subject him to such hazards before themselves, convincing him otherwise. Polivanova took no issue to submitting to the wishes of his men in believing his younger and more able subordinates were better suited for conducting such a rescue.

As the submarine inched closer, Dave reached deep into the water to hasten their movement towards it. Prior to doing so, he didn't believe he still harbored such a reserve of strength. It took several attempts for the Soviet serviceman to overcome worsening weather before finally being able to manipulate a rescue line in the Costa's direction. In doing so, Dave was able to get a hold of it and secure it to his raft. Another officer dressed only in blues and galoshes joined in the rescue as the two highly charged servicemen began pulling the Costa's raft towards them with extreme urgency. In Dave's attempt to assist by pulling also, his action was meant by a repeated "no!" shouted in Russian. The Soviet servicemen didn't need him complicating what was already a treacherous rescue.

Although unable to understand them, he got the message. He also recognized the language being spoken as well. There spawned the wonderment of whether his family was being the fortunate recipient of some good-willed gesture pre-arranged between two giant foes or instead were some floundering fish getting caught up in some political net. Either way, Dave believed that the latter still beat the alternative he and his family stood to face within the next half of an hour.

As the Costas made contact with Polivanova's submarine, the Soviet warrant officer quickly dismounted the sail bridge, repelling next to their raft now butted up against its base. Just then a hatch opened there with the commander still inside yelling in Russian to his warrant officer. "Quickly! Hand them to us! We'll concern ourselves with any injuries later!"

Both the urgency and professionalism displayed by the seamen impressed Dave. He first grabbed Heather, knowing she was most able of speeding the rescue process up by rendering the raft more spacious in her absence. The warrant officer then held little David, speaking softly in Russian as he handed his limp body to waiting arms. "Hang in there, son. Don't quit now."

Dave assisted in handling Linda, whose dead weight made her transfer awkward, but still manageable. In assisting Dave last, the sailor following confiscated his mariner knife from its sheathing before entering the submarine. Inside last, the warrant officer then secured the outer hatch behind him, instantly shutting out the sound of the turbulence behind and there leaving only its echo momentarily sounding until the inner workings of the ship entered back into focus.

The Costa's rescue still wasn't complete as far as the commander was concerned. A few on looking crewmen were in shock at the sight of the family's deplorable condition. Even Dave appeared a different man from the one who entered the storm hours earlier. The commander approached him, the meanwhile ordering some nearby crewmen to bring the others to their infirmary.

"Have Lieutenant Tretskii [a medic] see to the woman and boy first. I don't need these people dying."

It was at that moment when Dave collapsed onto the hard floor, uncharacteristically breaking down into an emotional meltdown. It was a reaction the commander could recognize in having witnessed even the most steadfast of individuals react in the same manner throughout his career. Polivanova then broke his cover when he squatted next to him, speaking fluent English. The captain doing so in turn halted Dave's emotional meltdown in its tracks.

"I assume that is your family with you. They are now being escorted for immediate medical attention. If you have not figured it out already, you are aboard a submarine representing the people of the Soviet Socialist Republic, and I will need to confine you and your family to security containment until we can give you up, that for the sake of everyone's wellbeing—including yours."

In an attempt to express his gratitude, Dave first needed to expel more emotional baggage that he had been unknowingly harboring over the course of the previous several hours. Seeing into his eyes, the commander understood both the toll and humbling influence the likes of the experiences he presumed Dave underwent could do to change or even break a person, especially in a case when such loved ones lives had also been held in the balance.

"I will let you get this out of your system first before your family sees you like this."

Eventually mustering enough composure to be able to stand independently, Dave then discovered he could no longer fool his body of the pain being generated by his broken rips. In keeling over, he was prevented from hitting the hard deck again by an alert Polivanova, who hadn't bought into his guise of good health. In response, the captain just shook his head.

"Your stubborn American attitude will be your undoing. My men will assist you to the infirmary before you injure yourself any further. I prefer to hand you back to your own people in one piece."

In realizing his position as that of an American civilian aboard Polivanova's vessel, the thought crossed Dave's mind of the irony that while an enemy might callously kill or commit torture without hesitation when it's in their best interest to do so, the same enemy might instead bend over backwards and assure of ones sustenance, sometimes even more so than their own, when doing so serves them better. In the Costas case, their place aboard the highly secret Lira Class submarine was Polivanova's ploy, masking them as playing chips to cover his concerns for the family's wellbeing.

"I need to emphasize the sensitivity of your position here and the privilege we have extended you aboard my vessel. To assure you that do not attempt or even contemplate overstepping your welcome, I will keep two armed officers at watch over you and your family at all times. I am confident you will maintain order with the others in preventing any unfortunate incidents. We mean no harm and wish your safe arrival home, and I personally as commander of this vessel will assure that promise. In turn, any foolish actions will regretfully leave my men no choice but to use deadly force in response. Know and respect my position, and you'll be fine. Any questions?"

"I'm overwhelmed and can't begin to express my gratitude for saving us. Why are you doing this?"

"No time to answer that. I meant questions pertaining to your immediate needs. Otherwise, there is much to talk about, and we will do so later. As for now, I need to tend to my ship, and you obviously need medical attention like the rest of your family. There is a hurricane out there if you haven't noticed."

Dave's slight amusement shown at the cynical nature of the commander's last remark was meant with excruciating pain originating at the location of his broken ribs and then shooting out throughout the rest of his upper torso as well.

"Easy Comrade. I will also make sure someone there speaks English, so no more questions, please. Our medical facilities are limited, so I don't need you damaging yourself any further by speaking. One more thing—the officers I will send for translation will be there for official business only, such as tending to your needs—no conversation."

The following three days were touch and go for Linda. While her head wound was cleaned and carefully redressed, limited medical facilities aboard Polivanova's submarine left only time to determine any outcome. Unable to verify the extent of her injury, the medic was therefore concerned about the likelihood of possible internal bleeding, brains swelling, and infection no less.

Little David was administered fluid for hydration and nutrients via intravenous halting his deterioration to the point where he became coherent by his second full day of care. Meanwhile upon being sedated and treated with painkillers in prevention of every breath feeling as if he was being lanced in the ribcage by a bayonet, Dave instead took a turn for the worse. An ensuing infection resulted from *broken ribs versus protective lung sack* became both the medic's and Polivanova's greatest concern. Like his wife, his next three days of unconsciousness prompted a highly concerned commander to take periodical inventory of both their conditions.

Post her rescue, a healthy but exhausted Heather was able to sleep soundly until the following morning by way of a mild sedative. Its numbing effect temporarily buffered the young girl from the ill effects of her new memories. In coming to, a visit by the commander later led him to guess that allowing his crew to do the same might boost the general morale aboard his vessel. With many of them having children of the same age, he saw the possible mutual benefit some limited conversation with such a young girl might tender as a result. Polivanova went as far as taking Heather for a limited tour in non-military areas before then realizing the young girl possessed short of a photographic memory. It prompted him to quickly escort her back the same route they took. In her case, deadly force wasn't believed to be an appropriate response.

By the end of the 23rd, the Costa' s second full day aboard the submarine, David was up talking and playing with his sister Heather. The commander was meanwhile able to retire to his quarters pleased at the news of their parents' stabilized conditions. Outside of both his fascination for what the family experienced and a desire to speak with either Dave or Linda, the last complication Polivanova wished for was the presence of two dead American civilians aboard his vessel. He emphasized those same concerns to his stressed out medic. "Such an unfortunate event would be problematic for all of us. I'm counting on you."

Later on the commander also expressed those same concerns to Captain Third Rank Golovkin, still in training. The second-in-command simply responded with a grin underlined with malice. "Commander, wouldn't it be easier just discarding any deceased into the ocean instead of letting the problem become greater than it needs to be?"

"If you're implying we should just bury whatever evidence we feel fit and it'll all go away, I couldn't disagree with you more. While it may seem sterilization is a simple solution on the surface, I need to remind you. The misdeeds of history can sometimes come back and bite one on the ass in due time. I'm not just referencing those directly responsible for whatever deeds either. Such underhanded actions could also stand to leave our nation prone to political damage down the line should such an action become known. You can never keep anything a secret forever. The world is in a constant state of influx, meaning the truth is likely to surface eventually. You know very well Beria and several of his comrades found that out the hard way in a cold dark basement when they no longer had the protection of a deceased Stalin. They ended up receiving a taste of their own medicine dealt over the years."

"But Commander, that was an internal Soviet affair. In contrast, many of the bastard Nazis who committed such heinous atrocities have managed to slip through the cracks of a worldwide manhunt throughout the years, haven't they?"

"And you choose to reference yourself in the same light as them, comrade?"

"No, of course not, sir."

"I'm glad to hear that, Captain. And let me remind you. These people are American citizens. You can't take a nation lightly when they have thousands of nuclear warheads aimed at every populous square kilometer of your homeland. Remember? That's why we're down here?"

Just prior to the Costa's rescue, Polivanova was pleased at the news of Gloria's new status to that of hurricane. His satisfaction came with the understanding it was still too soon to conclude that it was destined to head north up the US East Coast as he was hoping. Considering the capriciousness of such storms, he was at best cautiously optimistic about the news. Meanwhile that which stood to please his Soviet brass back home could in turn be construed as an ominous threat to the hundreds of millions of Americans, nonetheless the Free World if the true intent of his whereabouts was to be discovered.

Another event also taking place the meanwhile to which the commander was unaware was that Rear Admiral Richardson was once again being interrupted from the consumption of a juicy cut of semi-rare filet mignon, this time aboard his own vessel.

"Yes Lieutenant, may I help you?"

"If I may sir, your immediately presence is required in the communications room."

Richardson stood, fully committed to the potential seriousness of what might lie ahead. He was also disappointed in having looked forward all day to sinking his teeth into the premium slab of steak lied before him. Upon wiping his mouth, he tossed down his napkin.

"Sutton, this better be worth it. It took some doing getting this masterpiece to my plate."

His right-hand man lieutenant briefed him of the goings on en route to the communication room.

"I think you might want to speak with Captain Lindquist [The commander of one of Richardson's two submarines, presently separated but commissioned to his battle group] for further detail. He just picked up the signature of an Alpha Classer treading the surface in Gloria's eye, but it doesn't match anything we have in our acoustic library."

Making reference to his peers of the 2nd Fleet, the rear admiral responded like a predator smelling blood. "Ah, they slipped one past us before, but we've got those bastards this time." He then took on a more sober tone. "But it seems this guy still slipped past us when it comes down to it. I have to give this guy credit, though. He's got some brass ones. The last thing we need is him surfacing and waving his damn red flags for our boys at Norfolk to show off his new toy. Did Lindquist indicate the Russian's position, or ETI?"

"Well sir, he can give you better details than I on the vessel's uncertainty zone. The captain mentioned there being no consistent fix on the vessel in question—just a general location. He stated it's more of a flicker which might be the storm's turbulence playing with the Russian's varying speed. Captain Lindquist explained it's like trying to follow a firebug, and with that stated, based on his rough estimates he does figures over a day's reach, sir."

Richardson shook his head. "That goddamn *Domitrovich* [an alias given for commander in chief of the Soviet Northern Fleet]. This has his filthy fingerprints smudged all over it. Have they detected any more ships, or should I say, *any flickers?* The ambient sound of the turbulence stirring up its surface layer shouldn't be making any difference except maybe to some of the stomachs aboard that vessel. They know that. I know that. Hell Sutton, even you know that. This guy's just fucking with us—probably testing out his new boat—maybe accelerating to keep pace with the storm and then easing up to lose his emission. Who knows?"

"Could be, and thanks for the vote of confidence, sir. That aside, let's just hope he keeps generating noise as well as anyone else possibly lingering about."

"Well I don't know what's up with this guy. He thinks just because his shell's makeup is titanium, our MAD sensors [Devices often located aboard aircraft, capable of detecting magnetic anomalies in the Earth's magnetic field likely indicating steel or iron structures below the surface] wont pick up his damn vessel. Actually, as long as he's in the storm he might be right. Gloria's giving him some decent air cover. Doesn't matter now, and once that storm starts picking up speed if it heads north, anyone else presently crawling along at patrol speed will eventually be flushed out, or left behind. This guy just doesn't seem to care. I'll discuss this with Captain Lindquist first to make sure he hasn't contacted Fleet headquarters [Norfolk Virginia] already. At least he better not have. I'll tell you this though. One day I'm tracking American tourist," in pausing briefly in solemn hesitation, Richardson added, "and then we lost them. Now I'm chasing the Soviets sneaking up our asses. I should retire before this shit kills me. And the worse part in having just stated that is this shit turns me on like no tomorrow."

The lieutenant grinned. "You and me both, sir."

"Well in spite of their charade of having snuck up our coast a few months ago, I think it's about time we teach these guys who the true owners of the oceans really are, especially with this guy playing outside of his normal sandbox. I'll say this though. They [The Soviets] sure took all the fun of my job when they began quieting their damn vessels."

While Polivanova's vessel was capable of diving several folds deeper and outrunning a Los Angeles Class submarine such as Lindquist's, it could essentially run but not hide from Americans tracking methods. NATO's high-speed torpedoes were also capable of wreaking havoc on the likes of it, not to mention several other means of weapon deployment initiated by either surface or air. The Cold War though wasn't a seek and destroy setting unless one side overstepping established boundaries and getting caught doing so refused to comply with the demands of their counterparts.

Such a subsurface clandestine arena was more a tug of war of posturing for advantages over ones adversary where running for friendlier waters or taking cover beneath the surface at low undetectable speeds would have most likely warranted no more than a chase versus any actual engagement of weaponry. In each instance when such incidences did occur, as with any wartime arena, there stood to be some degree of either intentional or unintentional exchanges of valuable tactical and/or strategic data that both sides would receive as a result of the other's actions, reactions, and inactions no less. Win or lose, a final outcome usually carried with it the likes of a double-edged sword.

Such posturing for advantages wasn't just any friendly game of tag either, but was instead dangerous to all submarines involved, let alone the world. Both the Soviets and Americans felt compelled to maintain an upper hand in their clandestine posturing in believing doing so was detrimental for maintaining the integrity of a MAD (mutually assured destruction) doctrine. Its concept was similar to two foes facing off within a tightly confined space, both trying to counter the threat of the other by means of clenched hand grenades held tightly, arming pins drawn and arms cocked. It was a Mexican standoff of global proportions.

Dangerous occurrences, both planned and unplanned, were an ongoing reality during those years of cat and mouse maneuvers, as each side would nervously be clutching their respective armed hand grenades in their jittery sweaty palms—muscles twitching. Post the Cuban Missile Crisis of 1962, a direct line was established between the two top leaders of the US and Soviet Union. Its purpose was to be put through to each other in times when matters might become too intractable for the opposing forces at the lower levels to quell on their own. At the height 1962 missile crisis, a lack of direct communication between the two top leaders almost caused the baby boomer generation to become the last. Most people are presently still unaware of how close the world actually came to experiencing a catastrophic nuclear war back then, which mostly became known following the 1991 Soviet breakup.

While the hot line did pose as a last ditch insurance policy for averting the unthinkable, it wasn't any sure bet either. Due to the nature of some complexities often having already evolved to such a degree, the need of two such top leaders to heed each other's attention stood to pose futile if any tipping point was already compromised. The core of any such escalation always stood the risk of an underlined momentum where at some point even the most levelheaded might have been incapable of prevailing, as with the case of attempting to regain control of a runaway locomotive. 1983 was another example of how an unexpected world population came frighteningly close to either experiencing a very bad September or November day. The *"Red Phone"* hot line as with the case in the latter offered no way out when the so-called voices of reason were responsible for the close call in the first place. September was simply a malfunction of the Soviet detection system where the cool head of a Soviet duty officer at a command center likely prevented a deadly retaliatory strike in the face of several ensuing false readings. It is believed by many that his heroic act of inaction may have been responsible for having saved the world as a whole. It was a malfunction that couldn't have developed at a worse time, unless maybe some illness had rendered the duty officer absent for that particular shift.

Two years later and almost to the date, it was Captain Lindquist, a talented American submarine commander, who was at present in the spotlight of a subsurface pursuit of his enemy. There he held the element of surprise over his counterpart. It meant that unless

Polivanova was to about-face and engage his turbines, then the near future was likely to place him and Lindquist, face-to-face. Further exasperating such a scenario would be the second rank captain's unwillingness to just throw his hands up and submit if it was believed there was still another recourse at his disposal. He always did.

In additional to all the drama the family experienced leading to the juncture, the Costas now found themselves amidst possibly the only active Cold War pursuit stirring on the globe at that giving moment. Jim observing such unlikely events unfolding in a crystal ball would have likely led him to another Emmanuel's visit. Whether it could be stated the Costas were either victims of an unrelenting string bad luck or were instead the recipients of many perfectly timed breaks, two questions could then be posed. The first is when does ones streak of luck either good or bad finally run its course, and the second, if and when the law of averages does come into play, is it more a matter of perspective as to whether it ever did or not? Pending Captain Lindquist next actions, such a riddle stood to be answered in the next twenty-four plus hours.

With Polivanova treading a region where neither any decisive aerial nor surface support by the US Navy would be at Lindquist's disposal in aiding and cornering the Soviet quick and deep diving submarine, such an instance would in turn mean that the American commander's failure to have showed up with any more than that of overwhelming force would equate to his soviet counterpart's unwillingness just to shy away from any anticipated confrontation. Although Lindquist's Los Angeles Class submarine with all of its highly sophisticated equipment and weapon systems was well up to such a challenge, having a few buddies nearby to stack the odds in his favor would have stood to pose as an appreciated advantage.

In entering consciousness the morning of September 24, Linda's mother-child reunion couldn't help but touch the members of Polivanova's crew present. In visiting her in the infirmary, the commander expected nothing short of complete disorientation on Linda's part. He therefore wasn't surprised in viewing her seated on a medic rack wearing a look of total perplexity.

"How are you feeling, Madam? Please don't be alarmed. You're presently aboard a submarine representing the Soviet People's

Navy. We rescued you and your family after finding you stranded in the eye of the storm still above us. Pardon my manners. I am Captain Second Rank Vladimir Polivanova, the commander of this vessel. If you have any questions, I will answer them to the best of my abilities, or limits."

In spite of having been somewhat briefed by her daughter Heather beforehand, Linda was still both stunned and out of sorts in examining her surroundings.

The commander continued. "Your recovering husband did suffer some broken ribs, but he's faring better now. His injury caused an infection, so we needed to address that complication, as we also needed to do with you as well. This is a lot to take in, so if you choose not to speak, I will understand."

In Linda's asking Polivanova to repeat his name, Heather jumped in and pronounced it perfectly to his amusement. Linda smiled, politely reprimanding her for the interruption.

"Madam, that's okay. Your daughter has brought life to a crew that is more homesick than they realized—or willing to admit."

Linda strained in attempting to pronounce the commander's name correctly while still attempting to play catch-up. "Mr. Capitan Vladimir Po-li-va-nova. Why is your English so good? Am I really aboard a Russian sub or is this just some elaborate joke—like *Candid Camera* or something?"

Unable to grasp the meaning behind her last comment, the commander glazed over it. "Madam Costa, I trained many years in English at Frunze Naval College in Leningrad, and this is no joke. I would also prefer that you refer to my vessel as a submarine representing the Soviet People's Navy. That stated, I cannot divulge much else for security reasons, and please excuse my officers with side arms. For the safety of your family and the assurance of my ships security, I have confined you here in secured containment. Leaving this area without escort will get you killed, so I made sure such a tragic incident does not occur. Eventually we will release you to your people, but for the time being we prefer to keep you in one piece."

He then pointed towards his two appointed guards. "You see Madam, this is the best plan I could devise to keep you safe from us and likewise us from you as well, so please excuse my methods. The Socialist Republic of the People's Navy has established no protocol pertaining to American tourist residing aboard one of its world-class submarines. While I pay apology for the food, it is the same stuff we eat, so don't believe I am singling you Americans out for mistreatment because of it. I know how testy your people can get, but changing the subject. If you need to use a head, my men will stand close by while at the same time affording you a respectable sense of modesty. If someone is sick in there, we will get them a container so they can be so elsewhere. There is not much prospect for modesty around here, especially for a woman, but I assure you, it will be no issue for either you or your young girl. If any of my crew does disrespect you, let me know and I will address it."

Linda was still dressed in her Pamela inspired tight shorts and likewise snug fitting braless tank top. The latter was adhered to her upper body with both of the items collectively leaving little to the imagination. It was also cool in the area. With her tank top still bearing some traces of blood stains post cleaning, she had difficulty absorbing everything, especially with her last recollection dating back prior to her injury.

"Madam, your husband's sedation will commence wearing off soon, and hopefully then he can answer many of your questions. I assure you."

Following a few finishing words of formality, Polivanova turned to his two officers upon leaving and addressed them in Russian. "I know it's hard to ignore, but would you stop staring at her tits. You're embarrassing me and the People's Navy."

Knowing enough afterwards to keep full inventory of their eyes, the two guards eventually snickered, in turn causing Linda to laugh as well. Having no idea what just transpired in front of her, the captain second ranks voice echoed again in Russian, still a short distance away.

"I hear you laughing and I'm not joking either. The poor woman doesn't even know what's she's laughing at. And if you do continue by the way, I will enlighten her, and you will pay afterwards for it as well. I assure you."

Upon Polivanova's threat, the two guards found it in their best interests to exercise more professionalism from then on.

Once snapped out of his grogginess, Dave felt revitalized in awakening. His upper torso was wrapped to prevent any careless movement proving potentially harmful. While attempting to grasp his surroundings, the commander made a brief visit in hearing of his return to consciousness. In doing so, he wore a guise of indifference. With Dave being the same age as many of his men, he believed such a factor stood to stir up an unhealthy level of animosity in them, even with Dave being a civilian. For the time being, Polivanova was concerned their lack of goodwill towards any American male might create a rift in how they viewed him as commander should he appear being too chummy with him. Despite his unquestioned supremacy aboard his vessel, the commander still preferred not pushing the limits of their devout loyalty, and he did so only for the sake of maintaining his crew's cohesiveness.

With Dave having been subjected to an underlying threat of nuclear inhalation throughout his life coupled with the knowledge of tensions still plaguing the US and the Soviet Union, both he and Linda were well aware of the magnitude of their position aboard a Soviet vessel, no less in the heart of the Cold War. Even in the face of their surroundings, both still found difficulty swallowing any of it as real.

With Dave aware a civilian's presence aboard any military vessel is generally frowned upon, nonetheless an American aboard a Soviet submarine and no less in the midst of ongoing clandestine maneuvers, it was therefore difficult and equally unnerving for both him and Linda to grasp. They also speculated only a handful of Soviet officials knew of their presence there. In spite of both viewing Polivanova in the light of an honorable man by way of his demeanor, Dave imagined any judgment handed down by his superiors at any moment linking their position to that of a threat to national security might in turn lead them to conclude that he and his family may have already been subjected to an unacceptable measure of sensitive information. It led to a supposition that the same level of commitment that had already been forwarded to assure their good health, safety, and comfort even, could instead in a blink of an eye be catapulted against them at any moment.

Dave had seen the likes of movies before whereby individuals being treated well by an adversary were suddenly revisited with guns pressed to the chest or head for no assuming reason. There they would then be executed in cold blood with neither thought nor delay. He was also aware that such obsessing likely lacked any substance for validity. But with so much time to ponder, both the fear and awe that was sewn into his psyche throughout his life linked to the Soviet Union translated to never being sure what to expect next.

Due to the humbling effects of Hurricane Gloria, Dave's previous persona of fearlessness was all but eradicated. He was rendered a different person. His cerebral rambling was abruptly cut short by the commander reappearing, this time handling a blindfold and accompanied by a guard. While unsettling him by way of its eerie coincidence, Polivanova explained. "I and my armed guard will escort you to my quarters where we will hold a discussion. You must be blindfolded until arriving there."

Dave approached Linda before exiting, kissing her. "I love you."

Approaching Heather to do the same, Polivanova caught wind of it, breaking into laughter. "My American tourist! Either you believe you're not coming back or you Americans have very loving families. Keep this blindfold on and no harm will come to you."

While reassuring, such a guarantee was no less sobering. Dave understood he was resided aboard a minefield of security hazards whereby even a slightest misstep wasn't an option.

En route, he asked the commander while trailing slightly behind, "Captain Polivanova, can I ask a question?"

"There is much to talk about, but go ahead."

"While I would first ask for mercy on behalf of my family, if for whatever reason you're going to take any of our lives, can you at least spare theirs and just take mine? They've been through so much."

"That is quite an admirable request, but we have no intentions of taking anyone's lives." Annoyed, Polivanova then stopped. "Please don't make us out to be a bunch of barbarians. We have a job to do, but we also have families back home. If for some reason you left us no choice but to harm you, then the men doing so would likely regret their actions later, as would I. When you're eventually taken into the custody of your own people, your American comrades will likely grill you for information as if you were the enemy." He then chuckled, adding, "we may be treating you better than your own people will be later on. The matters I need to speak about have nothing to do with military issues, so let your mind rest. We didn't go through so much to rescue you just to in turn harm you."

In ducking a few head bangers as well as maneuvering around tight areas, the commander noticed Dave wincing.

"Comrade, I am a big believer that pain can be instrumental in enhancing a man's character, but we didn't extract you from the ocean and make great efforts of assuring your health just so you can re-injure your ribcage. I take my accessibility around this vessel for granted, but didn't consider the obstacle it would pose for you. We will slow down, so just be careful."

Polivanova was less concerned for Dave's discomfort and more so for his continued improving health. Dave in turn responded as if his wind was just knocked out of him. "I'll be fine. I don't want to slow you down."

"I respect toughness, but this is not a race. You are blindfolded, so just be careful. If you were one of my men, then that would have been an order."

Upon the two entering into his sanctum, Polivanova removed Dave's blindfold. He then gestured towards a coffee table and two chairs positioned next to it for him to make himself comfortable. The room was both his designated office and private quarters of which he entrusted it hallowed grounds to but only a few trusted officers.

"Comrade, take a seat and make yourself comfortable. What would you like to drink? It will help you forget about your side for awhile." Upon a guffaw, he continued. "So instead later, you can dwell about a throbbing head, or what you Americans call, a hangover."

Favoring his right side, Dave took a seat. "Do you have tequila?"

"You Westerners and your tequila. No wonder your ribs are so fragile. That stuff has been rotting them out. I have scotch, gin, and vodka. What will it be?"

"Vodka please. But with all due respect sir, in defense of tequila, it's a most misunderstood drink."

Listening to but ignoring Dave's tailing comment, Polivanova grinned with pride. "Vodka it will be then." Raising its bottle, he added, "*Luksusow*, my favorite. Made by my Polish comrades, but the tastes buds are non-discriminating when choosing the means of satisfying their thirst."

He then poured both drinks with his armed guard keeping watch from outside his quarter's hatch, it positioned slightly ajar. This provided both men some level of privacy while also granting the commander adequate security. He carried both drinks over, placing Dave's in front of him.

"You have two beautiful kids and a beautiful wife, now that she is not covered with blood. Most of my men have children and miss them, so they therefore appreciate your kids being here."

A detail that Polivanova omitted to mention was the eye candy of which Linda's presence had been serving up to his crew in their women starved state, even rendering him no less immune.

"I have three teenagers and a wife who I love and miss, but my life down here assures their comfort back home. I do have some questions, but I must first pose. Unlike with your wife and children, my men aboard this vessel are trained to be suspicious, so they will at best be cordial with you only because I have ordered them to do so. Unlike my typical countryman back home who might gladly invite you into their state dwelling for a drink, most in here may disapprove of you simply because you are an American male. Therefore, don't mistake their cordialness for friendliness. I am forty-nine years of age and less idealistic than them. But I was once like them and therefore respect how they feel. Please know your place and I can then guarantee your safety." Polivanova then lifted his glass.

"Join me."

Dave did so on cue while thinking: "Both of are nations have thousands of thermonuclear warheads aimed at each other ready to turn the other's land into a sheet of glass, and I'm presently sharing a toast with a Soviet commander poised to carry out the unthinkable—damn."

With the armed officer positioned outside rendered oblivious to any conversation due to a constant subtle drone of ambient noise surrounding him, Polivanova proposed his toast with it in mind. The inner workings of his vessel were relatively quite subdued by means of pneumatic cushioning devices, whose purpose was to limit any unnecessary noise made by their submarine that could in turn give away its acrostic signature, thereby compromising its position as well.

"Both our countries are spending so much of their money trying to prove they can annihilate each other while we are all trained down here to fight a war that neither side can really afford to engage in. Yet somehow our two nations loathing and distrusting each other gives both of them some degree of purpose and identity. Just like your people somewhere out there who are assigned to destroy us if necessary and us them, we're only doing our jobs, and doing so to protect those back home as many before me have. I hold none of this against you, a civilian, or even your American comrades somewhere out there assigned to exact harm on us due to the same reason. Therefore, based on the terrible repercussions of any kind of actual confrontation between our two powerful nations and the fear of mutual annihilation that neither side wants to experience nor commence, I would like to propose a toast to a status quo."

Polivanova had gone as far as rehearsing his satirical toast upon hearing of Dave's improved health, to which he just grinned in agreement in appreciation of its spirit.

The two then toasted, slugging their respective drinks with only Dave's glass being subsequently refilled. Polivanova was anxious beforehand about their meeting, especially giving he had never spoken with, nonetheless ever spent time with any American in any casual setting. His nearest occasion was a brief encounter with both American and British military personnel in a neutral setting. It took place at an international sporting event whereby both sides were instructed to treat each other with respect for diplomatic reasons. There upon having applied their mastery of the art of passive aggression in both cases, both sides were able to fulfill their own agendas throughout the event of silently posturing against and exasperated their counterparts the best they knew how. It would have required the trained eye of an expert in body language to catch wind of any of their passive exchange.

In preferring to allow the commander to speak first, Dave was responded to by the inquiry of his own silence.

"Comrade, I will allow you to shave later. You look like a man out on his luck, and on my ship I can't allow such an abject look. Speak up anytime if you wish. My intention is for this to be a two-way conversation, and although it is both wise and natural we be a little circumspect in conversation with each other, I don't consider you and I enemies."

"Thank you, Captain." Dave then thought for a moment before

finally asking, "why did you end up rescuing us?"

"I will eventually answer that, but you can do better, comrade. You're sitting with the commanding officer of a Soviet naval vessel in his quarters and sharing Vodka with him, and that is the best you can do? And by the way, you have watched too many American propaganda films making us out to be a bunch of monsters while your president publicly referred to us as an *evil empire.*"

Dave felt a brief discomfort while listening further.

"In addition, you believed I was taking you somewhere to be executed after all we did to rescue you and your family. This was after I have gone as far as endowing you with many of the same amenities as my crew. In growing up, they must have taught you that we are nothing but butchers in my country."

While not meaning to throw is country under the bus by his silence, Dave also didn't believe it was appropriate to engage in any heated discussion about the matter either. He was well-schooled to the fact that many Soviet past actions didn't always reflect any sense of best of intentions to the outside world, at the same time understanding his own nation's actions didn't always coincide with its own ideology when its best interests took precedents instead. In his opinion, such an argument was better left for others. His only battlefront was the assurance of the wellbeing of his family. Instead he just bowed his head in having been subjected to the likes of such beliefs growing up. Dave also understood that the commander was seeing matters from his own perspective, and respected it. He also believed the commander was provoking him to be more assertive and responded accordingly.

"Captain, are you a Stalinist or a freethinker?"

Taken aback, even slightly angered, Polivanova grinned briefly. "You really know how to quickly jump to the extreme, no? You see Dave, that is both a provocative and inflammatory subject in my country. But I do respect your knowledge of its struggles in spite your naive approach, which lacked any finesse in its boldness and ignorance. That stated, I entered the navy during very prominent Stalin times; although he died a few years earlier. The man had great visions for the navy, and yet he killed many fine officers who earned their grade prior to the Great Patriotic War [Soviet term for World War Two) For that, I don't look improvingly at him. It is probably safer for me to share this with you than any of my crew, although most officers probably don't admire any leader who murdered the likes of their peers for no valid reason. Yes the man did some great things for our Republic to bring it to the forefront of world prominence, but he did so at such a tragic cost to millions. My feeling is outside his paranoia, his motivation for making our nation so great was his intent of personifying himself in it. But that is just my opinion. There are millions in my country who still admire the man, although I can state with confidence that a few of my Ukrainian crewmembers aren't among that number. Look comrade Dave. I am proud of what I have accomplished, but I personally have no desire of erecting some 50 meter statue of myself in promotion of my own self-glorification."

Dave's question struck a nerve, bringing up deeply harbored anger towards the commander's former leader. Soon regaining his composure, Polivanova continued speaking again.

"Because of Nakita Khrushchev's later condemnation of him, it might be okay though not always wise for me to speak about my formal leader like that. So please, no questions about our political past. Whatever you might have read about and trivialized related to our history or even our present is sensitive context for me. The Great Patriotic War still bears its scar on the collective mindset of my people, even four decades later. Losing over twenty-six million of your fellow citizens—men, woman, and child at the hand of one foul vermin [Hitler], whose name I will not acknowledge, weighs forever on those who needed to endure it. Its terrible legacy even bears its mark on my small crew, of which one was raised without a natural father and another by the state as an orphan. A decade or more prior, such numbers would have been far greater. Leningrad [now St. Petersburg] itself lost over a million and a half souls over three years—my neighboring town not spared the same scourge of starvation or harassment either."

Polivanova sat silent for a moment before speaking again. "I will let you in on one of the darkest moments of my life. It was the winter of Forty-two, and the Germen's had already turned the greater Leningrad region into a living hell of death and suffering. It was nothing that any human who wasn't there could ever imagine the scope of its suffering. It is still very painful for me to recollect, but if I may, I will share this one experience with you. You have earned it. Comrade, I was no more than four, but I had learnt to grow up real fast. Too young to understand world events or at least that which we were allowed to know about, I didn't know why the events were happening around me the way they were. I only knew all too well what was happening. I can still feel the pain of hunger in my stomach as if it were yesterday again. Its agony spanned to the beginning of my memories. Being intelligent beyond my age served me no solace in that hellish wasteland. Death was as prevalent around me as was the sound of artillery fire and bombing raids—sometimes gunfire. Starvation was the greatest evil and disease its shadow, not discounting the sadistic harassment by the German military. The cold was also a reminder that maybe the fires of hell might be that of ice instead."

"Dave, there weren't any rats to eat the deceased, because the hungry were in wait, ready to consume the rodents. No part was ever wasted. That's what I was told by my mother, who hid nothing of the truth from me—or mostly nothing that is. One night Dave, my sister and I lie alone at night—cold, starving, numb with no sense of any hope. I thought hell was a norm and knew no differently. At night when the Nazi guns were sometimes quiet, you could literally hear the screams of those who were breathing their last ghastly breaths of agony, and thereafter, the wailing of the loved ones they just left behind. One night my dad came home and woke us up. I could see the stone face of my mother watching us in the dark as my dad fed us some fresh meat. It was too dark for us to see except the best our eyes allowed on a moonless night. My father was a wretched man, who during the darkness did his best to find food for us. Both my sister and I grabbed the mostly raw meat with our filthy hands and ate it like animals ready to fight over it."

Polivanova sat silent, chewing the insides of his mouth as he attempted to continue. He finally did in a solemn tone.

"Comrade Dave, the meat was not that of a cat or dog, because they had all been eaten by then. I knew what both animals tasted like. By then, any pet had become someone's meal two years prior. I knew the meat wasn't that of any fowl—pigeon or seagull even. It didn't taste like either of those. There was just none of that around. It wasn't rat or any other wild animal either. I knew what all that shit fucking tasted like—there was simply none of it around. I only remember asking my father what it was and then my mother approaching and backhanded me in the face. She shouted, 'Just eat what we give you and never ask what it is!' Eventually the bite of the bitter cold subdued some of the stinging effect of her punishing blow. That moment was so poignant, I never dare ask my parents what it was, even as an adult. I lost my last surviving parent three years ago, so that will always hold true. All I knew from experience years later was that it tasted like raw veal, but I can tell you this Dave with confidence—it wasn't veal. What I ate that night and a few others was not of any animal. It was too fresh—too available. All I can attest to is that we ate it without question—and we lived."

"Let me end by mentioning it was day when we were rescued by members of the Red Army. Both my sister and I were left alone each time my parents disappeared. We never knew if we would ever see them again. Eventually we always did, but in the case of our rescue, we thought it might be Germans breaking into the ruins of our small dwelling. My father had destroyed it so the Germens or Finns wouldn't target it. That in itself was a desperate act since the state did not take very well to anyone defacing its property, even considering the circumstances. Stalin wasn't big on that. So Dave, this is what I remember most. I remember the voices coming closer and closer. Soon I see the blinding glare of daylight, and there stood before us were six members of the Red Army. At first they stood stunned—just staring. Then what must have been the highest in command shouted for assistance. I have never seen the likes of six battle hardened men shed tears like I did with those soldiers that day. Two then came over and gently picked up each of us. I knew then that we would be okay. It was a new feeling for me. The effects of the three-year siege spanned the limits of any memory I held beforehand. I was but few of the lucky ones. Fortunately I have no recollection of the winter two years prior. It was worse than the next and the one I just spoke of. Forty-two and forty three offered some relief because of the Red Army's presence across Lake Ladoga to the east. Some were rescued. Meanwhile their presence there also gave some relief by way of supplies that were able to make it into the area including some food—though it wasn't enough. It was still a dismal existence for most trapped between Ladoga and the Baltic Sea, but their presence there did lend some reason for hope. All I understood as a child was that there was good people who were trying to get to us. Such hope didn't exist for the poor souls who needed to bear the winter of Forty-one. I was too young to remember that period or I have blocked it from my memory. A terrible realty for those who were not so lucky was that they couldn't even be guaranteed that they would even have a nation to call their own once the Nazis and Finns were finished with them. I had learned this years later through hearsay versus the ruling Party, because our leaders didn't wish for us to believe a possible defeat at the hands of an invader was once a viable truth."

Polivanova was quiet for a moment, his eyes distant, almost teary.

"Comrade, mankind's greatest affliction will always be its brief recollection of tragedy's misgivings. There's a lot of pain I have experienced growing up and I've witnessed my share of tragedy of innocent people that I've known and loved as a result of what is being discussed—tragic, I say. But comrade, since I encouraged your questioning, I will be fair and state where I stand before leaving the subject. I'm here in the navy, because here you just conduct your mission. Sure there is politics involved in the military as with any organization, but here you get rewarded for carrying out your duties and conversely reprimanded accordingly. Although not always the case, it seems to be the general rule. So to answer your question Dave, I am neither a Stalinist nor am I a freethinker. Instead I am a career military man who simply wishes to provide for his family and keep his nation safe the meanwhile. I also do this to honor the millions of comrades who have fallen for my great country, and that alone was enough reason for me to have made the military my life.

As I was saying before about my beloved Leningrad—a city so devastated yet never defeated. When I saw the six members of our Red Army through the openings of my malnourished, light sensitive eyes—so war ridden were those brave men, yet appearing so majestic there standing before the well lighted entrance of our hiding place, their bodies somewhat silhouetted by the sunlight in the brilliance of its corona, they appeared to me as emissaries of God. Since then I always wished to be like those men—angels of a greater cause."

Dave was quiet for a moment, unable to muster any fitting words worthy of a response. After a brief period of silence, he finally spoke. "Wow, I'm totally speechless. If I may change the subject, you speak great English. Where did you learn it?"

"Excuse me for boasting, but I can also speak German, French, Spanish, Portuguese and to some extent, Mandarin Chinese. Down here that seems to be a wasted talent, but you never know when being able to do so could someday become indispensible."

Dave spoke Portuguese. "Do you prefer Portuguese or English?"

"I would prefer Russian if you spoke it," Polivanova responded in Portuguese, continuing, "but let us speak English instead. If my men overhear us speaking in Portuguese, then they may distrust us—meaning me." He then continued in English. "They know you are an American and therefore expect to hear me speaking English with you. And trust is a vital component a commander must maintain with his subordinates in maintaining optimal effectiveness. You can always count on them having your back."

A knock then came on the hatchway with a voice ringing out. It was his second-in-command Golovkin summoning him to speak in private. Believing the interruption was related to business of the ship, the commander obliged.

In private, Golovkin spoke. "Commander, you know I respect your judgment, but I see two glasses of vodka on the table. Is it wise to be getting cozy with the American? That's what the other crew members might think."

"My crew trust me Captain, and this is an opportunity of being able to peer into the mind of a full-blooded American male without the impedance of military suspicion. There is something to be learned here, and applying our custom of sharing a glass of vodka has seemed to place this man at ease. You see Captain, if you know both the strengths and weaknesses of your enemy as well as the likes of your own, then you'll never need know the foul taste of defeat. I mean no disrespect to the spirit of Sun Tzu in having paraphrased his quote in such a way, but if Gangues Khan's victims for instance had submitted to his wishes beforehand to be assimilated into his society, they could have avoided being butchered by his forces the way they were. The ruthless conqueror actually believed his wishes would emancipate the willing into a better lifestyle, with full trade. The man just didn't take 'no' very well for an answer."

"Are you insinuating the protectors of their lands should have just laid down and blindly surrendered to Khan, just to have then ended up becoming vassals of their former land?"

"Apparently yes Golovkin, because they didn't know the strength of their enemy, and everyone was therefore slaughtered as a result—men, women, children. What good is ones land if their only claim to it is their collective blood soaked into its soil—and one spared witness to authenticate its slaughter may I add? You see, sometimes patience can be a most effective strategy, someday allowing you to fight on a better day." Polivanova then grinned, elaborating. "Look Captain, it all had a happy ending when our great nation eventually formed from the ashes of his assimilation—unless you would have preferred a different outcome."

Golovkin tendered a rare grin. "Commander, you so elegantly sanction a rationale for butchery with such convincing practicality."

"Well thank you, Captain. So as I was about to state before pertaining to our American detainee—this may be but a small piece of a puzzle we may someday add to a collective pool of knowledge in the way of our adversary's mindset. People are the same by nature, but it's their cultures that distinguish them from others. You don't always get the chance to pluck such an opportunity like that out from the ocean—" Polivanova grinned, adding, "never mind from inside the eye of a hurricane. As I mentioned before, I also need to know how this man made it into the center of this goddamn hurricane—mariner to mariner."

"Yes, I'm curious myself. And I do see the value of probing to learn what makes this man tick, but what if he's doing the same?"

"We didn't rescue this man from some American submarine. And did you notice a family in a crisis—three of them badly injured? If this is all some American version of a Trojan horse, then we've probably been grossly underestimating our adversary's capacity when it comes to their level of ruthlessness."

"I agree there too, Commander. But you know when we hand him over, his people will grill him about us."

"Mutual exchanges are always a risk. I'm getting mine firsthand, seeing into this man's eyes."

"But he's seen the inside of our vessel. You took him this far through it."

"The spirit of your suspicions is always noted in light of the positive, but some of your concerns spawned as a result often lack any substance in reasoning. We must keep working on that. The American was blindfolded the whole time, so let this discussion be ended. I do appreciate your concerns, but please return to the control center after making your rounds. I need you up there. And whatever rumors you may hear, you will quell, okay Captain? Do that for me." Golovkin then saluted Polivanova and exited.

The commander was soon with Dave again. "I can't determine whether it was a stroke of brilliance or pathetic sailing, but how did you fucking end up in the eye of this goddamn hurricane still above us?"

Dave shook his head in disbelief. "Luck Captain. Pure luck, and may I also add, a lot of bad luck as well."

"Sorry comrade, I want more. Have I not earned the right?"

As Dave reached down for more details, Polivanova noticed him struggling to relive the horrors of three days prior.

"Yes this is hard. Believe me, I know. I have plenty of vodka if that may help. Take your time. You will be sharing this with someone who has experienced his own share of anxiety at sea. And along with serving my curiosity, you will also be serving your own healing as well. Do it for yourself and for your family. They will need you later on."

Polivanova filled Dave's glass for a third time, the meanwhile revealing a humbling tidbit of information pertaining to him. "Comrade, my medic nearly vomited in taking your wetsuit off. Apparently whatever you had experienced out there was severe enough to have caused you to defecate yourself. So unless that was either a case of your inability of being able to contain yourself or was instead just something you normally do and it is an American custom I am not aware of, then there are still some serious issues you have stirring inside. The sooner you confront them my friend the better you will feel."

In viewing Dave's humiliation, he aided him. "I have been there myself comrade Dave, although in my case I reacted in a way you Americans would refer to as number one. Either case, such bouts of incontinence are not something that you can brag about to your comrades later. Having stated that, heed this opportunity and get this shit out of your system now." He then concluded with a straight face. "Just don't stink this cabin up while doing so. This is where I sleep."

Humiliated, Dave finally spoke. "I'm sorry about the wetsuit. And what do you have to gain from this commander, if I may ask? Knowing what I do about our nation's relationship with each other, what you've done with us is unprecedented to say the least."

"Good point, though not always the case. While it is rare, there have been cases where personnel of both of our militaries have shown respect by averting the personal tragedy of the other in the case of mishaps. But as far as apologizing is concerned, it is my medic you need to apologize to, and thank. Look, I told you this is an equal footing conversation, so in continuing, I want to know how you made it into the eye of this hurricane. As a mariner, the plight of your family has captured my intrigue."

To ease his way into the more disturbing memories that were still haunting him, Dave made brief mention of his Cape Verde experience, then establishing a starting point from there. Upon consuming a forth vodka refill, a mistaken mention of the Tomcat flyover didn't go unnoticed. Then in realizing his slipup, Dave omitted the mention of Rear Admiral Richardson's promise of canvassing their projected proximity upon entering the tailing half of Gloria. Foregoing the mention of communicating with the Coast Guard and there stemming the Navy, he backpedaled. "Apparently they never saw us. The proof I'm seated here right now bears witness to that."

In running a gauntlet of US detection systems approaching the Americas, Polivanova had already ordered his submarine to be on its highest alert. He therefore believed any information Dave might have, especially as that of a civilian, would at best be unreliable. Being near American dominated waters, he assumed that US Naval vessels were likely in the shadows anyhow, leaving him no choice but to place his confidence in his crew's ability of acquiring such intelligence on their own. While Dave's mention of the flyovers did catch his attention, it didn't warrant enough suspicion for the commander to fish for anymore likely dead-ends.

Dave went on to explain everything in vivid detail from his dream the night before the hurricane to the contemplation of committing euthanasia on his family. To the shock of Polivanova, his mention of how close he actually came to following through with his plan, beginning with Heather, unsettled him greatly. An explanation of those accounts expressed with extreme emotional touched the core of Polivanova's father-side. There he listened in total shock, wondering how his own conscience might have been affected had such a tragedy occurred within the lapse of their inaction before the rescue, assuming Dave somehow survived afterwards to tell his story.

Sick to his stomach and unable to fathom considering such a heart wrenching option, especially now that he had already met the other three Costas, Polivanova envied nothing about the moments Dave just finished recounting in such concise detail. It in turn solidified his belief of not considering his American acquaintances unworthy of being within the safe confines of his prized Soviet vessel.

Quiet for a moment afterwards and in reflection, Polivanova sat, stunned. He eventually resorted to a subject to which everyone universally holds a common interest.

"Did you know the storm outside is now a strong Category-Three hurricane, pushing four? Until I hear from my fleet command for further instructions, unfortunately we need to stay in this storm, so it may be an unsettling ride for a while." In realizing he just made major slipup, the commander continued with it in mind. "I wish they would just let us go around these things instead of through them. A non-military vessel wouldn't have to put up with such ridicules conditions as we are right now."

"Wow, almost a Category-Four hurricane?" Dave responded to Polivanova's relief. "Holy shit!"

"Holy shit is correct, my friend. Not belittling what you have just been through, but your sailboat would have lasted no more than minutes out there now, and the storm is still strengthening as we speak."

Rewarding his forthcoming accounts, Russian style, Polivanova continued his generosity of keeping Dave's drinks topped off. As for his curiosity of how the Costa family was able to make it into eye of Gloria' intact was concerned, the accounts that Dave depicted not only satisfied his curiosity, but they also moved him deeply as well, something which came as a total surprise to him.

Shortly following less prying dialogue, Polivanova was then able to determine that his conversation was approaching its diminishing return. It was substantiated in the mention of a chilling moment he once experienced aboard a naval trawler in the Chukchi Sea. In following, an indication their dialogue had already lost most of its remaining momentum soon became clear when a predominantly impaired Dave commented. "I remember that. Your boat was sitting in Boston Harbor when I was in Fenway with a friend watching Milwaukee play the Sox. Yeah, it was just after college. I remember it clearly."

The Commander appeared bewildered at the randomness of Dave's statement, the meanwhile still wondering if he unwittingly forfeited any intelligence of the soviet use of fishing vessels for naval purposes. Dave's next comment dispelled any such notion.

"Before the game, my friend and I were at *No Names* [A popular restaurant on the pier] and we could see two Coast Guard vessels next to yours like I saw on TV. Fucking blow-sox won the first game—should have gone to the twilighter instead. Was that you?"

The commander was disappointed in having lost the ability of being able to discuss anything further with Dave, witnessed by the character of his induced dementia. Regardless, satisfied that his vodka had served its purpose, he eventually pinpointed what his guest had just mentioned. It was in remembering hearing of the Boston incident through the grapevine, years earlier.

"Yes, I think I did hear about that. It was spring in 1977. I believe I was on sub duty when that happened. That was just some eager countryman of mine venturing into your fertile fishing grounds. Believe me, our navy would have never attempted anything as foolish as that."

As Dave continued, Polivanova made provisions for having him escorted back to his family.

"Yeah, that harbor's a shit-hole thanks to Deer Island. It always smelled like everyone in Boston crapped in the damn thing—which in a sense, they did. What about those 1980 Winter Olympics, huh? Our college boys kicked your seasoned veteran sorry asses. Go USA, brother!" Dave shouted, clenching his hand above his head in a battle cry. "Is that why you sorry Ruskies boycotted the Olympics last year?"

It took some effort for Polivanova to be able to ignore Dave's off-the-cuff latter comments. In not appreciating the spirit behind his behavior, he refused to validate his question with any response. Dave's ranting only solidified his belief to be joined by two other crewmembers in assisting him back to his family. Concerned a lack of buffers might lead to a foolish move on his part in returning, they also fitted him with restraining cuffs for the trip back. Dave never resisted. He mostly just slurred his way though the process, ranting about how much he loved everyone within his visual range and how the American and Soviet leaders should just sit in a large room and learn to talk out all their differences.

Back at sickbay, the commander went straight to Heather and hugged her upon requesting permission from a curious Linda, who felt inclined to oblige Polivanova's request.

"Your Dad told me you are a very brave girl." Upon releasing her, he looked to Linda. "Your precocious daughter is an old soul. You are both lucky parents. I will miss her after we release you. Your husband by the way got sick on the way here. Apparently his system isn't ready for vodka yet—at least not the Polish type. I am certain this vessel's undulation isn't helping his cause either. He didn't wish for you to see him like that."

While his comment did raise some concern in Linda, she trusted Polivanova enough to gather there was no malice attached to her husband's absence. She also understood that she was powerless in taking any recourse should there exist any such intent.

"That sounds like something my Dave would have said," Linda commented, braving a forced smile.

Polivanova made arrangements for the Costa's new quarters to be set up elsewhere. With the family's new location freeing up space in his small infirmary for his own men, he later explained.

"You will have more privacy here as a family, and my guards can keep better tabs on you as well. Let them know when you need to use the head or need our medic if necessary."

"This is still better than being crowded up to each other in the life raft," a more sobered Dave commented in making the best of their position. "That's for sure."

Polivanova grinned. "I am glad you feel that way, because this will be your home for the duration of your tenure with us." Rubbing little David's atop his head, he concluded. "I will see you in the morning."

Prior to exiting the area, he turned back to Dave. "In answering your earlier question comrade—my best guess would have been had the competence of your American athletes stood to rival your ability of being able to hold down your vodka, then the event of our nation showing up in Los Angeles would have only been a cruel example of competitive exclusion."

He then grinned with an air of satisfaction and exited.

"What was that about?" Linda asked, bewildered.

Dave just shook his head in embarrassment. "Nothing, honey. I just need to watch my mouth a little better when I'm drinking, that's all. In other words, I think I might have struck a nerve of his when I was lit a little earlier—maybe twice that is."

Linda replied, almost appearing sick in doing so, "Oh no Dave, please spare me. I don't want to know. Oh God, I just don't want to know."

Grinning with a new sense of enlightenment, Dave just added with a whisper, "Touché, comrade—touché my Soviet friend."

<< CHAPTER 10 >>

WITH THE COSTAS STILL recovering, licking their wounds, and now a deck below from before, it was an odd arrangement for them all crowded and pent up together in a location adjacent the ship's galley. The family had been rescued just to end up being confined as prisoners, although Dave and Linda understood their means of captivity was in everyone's best interests.

2:00 AM, September 25, third-in-command Captain Lieutenant Talkovskaia was leading the nighttime crew. Unlike Polivanova, he played the conservative card by lying course at less than that of Hurricane Gloria's rate of advance. Although not his approach, Polivanova was okay with it, knowing at least then he could count on a full night of sleep. Consequently, a strategy of moving about silently in Hurricane Gloria's churning waters caused Lindquist to lose fix of their vessel again. Meanwhile, Polivanova never knew he had been tagged in the first place.

With the routines aboard the Soviet submarine maintaining the status quo in its heightened state, Captain Lindquist in contrast didn't relish the prospect of needing to explain to a presently sleeping Richardson that he had just lost detection of Polivanova's submarine. In an attempt to defer such an action, he continued a same course of before, but did so at a slower pace nearing patrol speed. His hope was to reestablish a new fix on his target without reversing his role of hunter to that of the quarry, especially with his counterpart being local to his proximity.

With two additional attack-submarines already dispatched from Norfolk and on the chase, Lindquist didn't relish the embarrassing prospect of them entering into the arena just to discover him unknowingly being shadowed by Polivanova's vessel. Hurricane Gloria pushing Category-five and raising havoc above provided the Soviets ideal natural cover from any threats possibly stemming from there. It wasn't the same storm in stature of which the Costas found themselves limping half way through, but was instead a monster, whose DNA had interacted with a farmer in its genesis eleven days earlier. It was presently stirring up conditions to the likes that Dave could have never previously imagined.

Limited only to passives means in the searching of Polivanova's whereabouts, doing so was difficult for Lindquist, who was feeling the urgency of relocating his adversary before his boss might make some inquiry into his progress. Suspecting his target was local to their region, like a true predator, he could smell the blood of his prey nearby while daring not turn the tides of advantage away from him due to impatience. In his pursuit, he was confident his margin of error was keeping him safe from any possible collision due to maintaining a course 35 meters below the depth where he had been tracking Polivanova. Had he instead considered the common principle that no military strategy ever goes as planned, the American commander might have served everyone aboard both vessels best interests. Seconds from colliding with each other, a chorus of yells and frantic commands in both control centers reached fever pitch as each ship picked up the other's approach.

By design of the circumstances, frantic yells of countermeasures sounding aboard both vessels mutually attempted to achieve the same goal. When both crews' desperate efforts fell short of averting an ensuing collision, final commands resulted in the initiation of alarms for impact. The only action personnel aboard either vessel could take next was to brace for impact. As for the Costa family, their guards failed to relay the same message to them in time.

Whether lying asleep or conducting their business, everyone aboard both vessels were simultaneously jolted out of place as the sub's ear piercing sirens made grasping the instantaneity of the proceedings nearly impossible. Nobody aboard either vessel was immune to a hair-raising calamity that was being infused directly into their cores. It didn't make any difference whether they were as seasoned and knowledgeable as any of the senior servicemen aboard either vessel or were instead unsuspecting like the Costas, who literally found their four bodies layered atop each other as a result of the ensuing collision.

An unprecedented blow of both vessels colliding with each other and echoing throughout both structures left no ear any reprieve from its thunder. Neither was any soul spared from a bedlam that followed. Its eruption was only a quick overture to a bone-chilling shriek emanated from below that lingered afterwards. It was one so intense, anyone yelling at the tops of their voices would have only been able to feel the vibrations of their bellow through the bones beneath their faces. Such an effect was evident when Dave was unable to hear the blood curling scream of Heather being generated right next to him, as he did so while also taking notice of their two guards sharing looks of shock at each other. Their expressions indicating to him a likeliness that the significance of the collision occurring was possibly beyond any magnitude that their vessel was designed to absorb.

By reflex of his training, the commander was able to spring from the deck where he was abruptly deposited from a sound sleep. He then listened to the shriek play out, scrutinizing its characteristics through the tenure of its episode.

Several leaks in Lindquist's vessel in which shut off valves were able to choke is where matters got no worse for the American submarine. Meanwhile matters took a path towards the ominous for Polivanova and company. In waiting for the tenure of his and Lindquist's vessels grinding against the other to play out, the meanwhile noting the characteristics of all variances in inertias during the occurrence, an ensuing brief silence then became the most grueling moment for him. The commander just stood helpless, praying the meanwhile not to hear a secondary collision that he was dreading would ensue.

It did. A subdued clunk sound and then a likewise jar seeming inconsequential in comparison to the previous clamor caused him to shutter. Worse, the secondary tremor Polivanova first hoped was a collision of a portside rudder was instead that of his main prop assembly.

Similar to the jousting a of knight, the slender bow Lindquist's Los Angeles Class submarine severed the Achilles of its robust Lira Class rival: its legs. Meanwhile its own bow only sustained minimal damage during its contact with Polivanova's vessel. While the main structure of the Soviet submarine was well up to the task of handling such brute forces as the ones just exerted on it, its prop assembly wasn't.

Three of the top officers were soon together in the command center, Polivanova the meanwhile attempting to assess the crisis. Upon having been briefed that the collision was with that of an American vessel now maintaining a posture of neutral buoyancy meters above them—and counting—he addressed his third in command, Captain Lieutenant Talkovskaia.

"Why are we still pitching? It's a giving we've lost all hope of any propulsion."

The captain lieutenant explained. "Sir, that is the main issue giving the status of our ports. In avoidance of the serious yawing we were experiencing from the storm, I was descending to calmer waters when we were suddenly clipped from beneath. I deemed it too dangerous near the surface to stay there any longer."

"Understandable, the storm above us is beyond anything that I could have ever imagined. Looks like we may have inadvertently stepped in the way of those damn cocky Americans attempting one of their notorious shadowing maneuvers from below. Sorry guys [referring to Lindquist], this is no Yersy or Som Class you're playing with now."

Polivanova panned around the control center for a moment before turning back to Talkovskaia.

"Has any diagnostic been conducted on the status of the ballasts ports?"

A diving officer then stepped in. "Sir, I was able to secure the Kingston, but the main upper vent is still frozen. I've tried both hydraulics and manual, but it won't close."

"Great! The Americans must be enjoying this shit show that we have going on down here. That's what I love so much about our automated marvel of the People's Navy—nothing's accessible for field repair. Well your job there is to get that damn thing closed Lieutenant, and mine is to find some recourse if you can't. How about the trims, can they stabilize us?"

"No sir," another officer replied, "They're functioning just as normal—just not enough to make any difference."

"Right. What difference does our pitch make anyways when our main nemesis is our descent. Well looks like I need to earn my money. Lieutenant Zhilin [senior lieutenant], stay atop those trims regardless. At least attempt to give us some impression that we're not descending."

Through the means of attempting to stabilize the descent of their ship, no one dare dwell on or even mention the nature of their plight. As for Polivanova, his crew, and the Costa's, together they were all were sinking into the pitch-blackness below.

There wasn't any other way of countering such a development except to plane upward and then purge their ballast once their submarine broke the surface. With their main props damaged beyond any chance of repair, less than fifteen minutes remained before even the robust structure of Polivanova's vessel would succumb to the crushing forces of the ocean.

While a lingering threat of drowning plaguing the Costa's over the previous several days was one they were able to evade over such a span, the same outlook was a prospect they couldn't shake over the same period.

With all vital systems sound and functioning on the Los Angeles Class submarine, whereas business being conducted aboard the Soviet submarine was solely being carried out for the purpose of survival, Lindquist's own non-threatened position afforded him the luxury of being able to analyze the incident as a whole. It also gave him a more fitting reason to notify a concerned Rear Admiral Richardson onto that of their status, unlike before when he had lost tabs on his counterpart's vessel. His main focus was now the fate of its sinking. It might be said that sub dwellers in general are unable to relish the witness of another submariner, friend or foe, of becoming victim to an implosion at the hands of the massive pressure required to cause such a failure, in part because such an occurrence is an always present threat that stands make the unfortunate demise of such victims highly personal to them as well.

With such looming for Polivanova in the case of his vessel, Lindquist still needed to keep a cautious eye open. He was aware its queer behavior could be some ploy, especially giving its speed and no less ability of being able to dive far deeper than his own submarine. In maintaining a 70-meter static posture just below the harsh turbulence of Hurricane Gloria, the American commander intended on keeping airing on the side of caution.

Another reason Lindquist chose not descending any further was because of the uncertainty of his own hull. He understood the unrelenting characteristics of water in its ability of being able to infiltrate anywhere, especially with the added variable of pressure figured into the equation. By the time Polivanova's vessel reached a depth of a thousand feet, there sinking further into the blackness of the abyss at the rate of three feet per second, it was at that moment Lindquist began intermittently bouncing his active sonar off of it.

A fretting Captain Golovkin, who was still accompanied in the control center by both Polivanova and Talkovskaia, grumbled. "Were sinking to our deaths, and the fucking Americans have nothing better to do then to ping us!"

Eyebrow raised, the commander took exception. "Godammit Golovkin! First of all, no one's going to die! And what do you expect them to do? They don't know what's going on with us. Jesus Christ! It's not Mother Theresa commanding that damn vessel out there, you know!"

While Polivanova feared the goings as much as anyone else, his main focus was on resolving the predicament of his ship. Golovkin's demeanor therefore didn't go unnoticed. This was the man he had entrusted, taking him under his wing to groom for command of his own submarine someday. In containing his anger the best knew how, the irate commander instead relieved Golovkin back to his quarters. Such an action in turn humiliated the captain third rank in front of the others. Meanwhile present circumstances prohibited Polivanova from being able to celebrate the field promotion of Captain Lieutenant Talkovskaia's to that of second-in-command over any toast. The nature of Golovkin's action had also caused the commander to lose full confidence in any leadership ability in him.

Both numb and sickened by the feel of their descent, Golovkin hiked his way up an angled lower deck leading to the Costa's two guards. Like many others aboard their vessel, the two were quiet in reflection. When the disgruntled senior officer interrupted their meditative state, he explained it was on behalf of Polivanova, who wished to extend them some private time.

"But Captain, we have strict orders that only the commander himself can relieve us," one of the guards stated.

Leaving the Costas unattended made no sense to either guard. It wasn't Polivanova's style either. He wasn't the type to either relieve anyone during their assigned shifts or foolish enough to subject his crew and vessel to such a security breach. Such a fact should have been obvious to Golovkin, but both his normally deliberate and calculated mindset was clouded by fear and no less blinding rage.

"He's busy containing the problem and sent me around to relieve all non-essential personnel," he insisted.

The guards bending to Golovkin's non-sanctioned orders would in turn undermine Polivanova's intentions for the Costa's. It would condemn them to a precarious standing in spite of their innocence where their guilt in such a highly classified area would need to be alleged simply because of a lapse of supervision. In the case of such an unfortunate turn of events, Polivanova would be in no position to grant them any kind of pardon even in believing the Costas may have never ventured anywhere during such a period.

"With all due respect sir, I need to receive orders directly from Captain Polivanova, himself," the first guard explained, still holding fast to his directives.

Golovkin began growing concerned in have nothing to show for having just crossed such a very strong-willed man, as was his commander. From his standpoint, his own actions were a one-way ticket and he intended they not have been acted out in vein. As for the Costas, the last thing they needed added to their resume of bad luck was to end up having dodged yet another bullet from outside just to then be arrested afterwards and possibly never allowed to return home again. Polivanova's threat of deadly force was mostly a deterrent tactic, but an unmentioned threat of a criminal trespass wasn't.

Understanding that he had just crossed a line that couldn't be backtracked, a desperate Golovkin therefore believed the only way of avoiding the certain wrath of his commander would be the crushing forces threatening from outside. Turning belligerent, he focused his anger on the other guard, and in intuitively picking up on the discord in spite of it being spoken in Russian, Linda pleaded.

"Please don't leave us alone!"

"Shut up you American bitch!" Golovkin responded in broken English. "This not your matter!"

Taking notice of the captain's invective language, Dave knew he still needed to hold his cool. Doing so quickly paid off when a voice rang from the shadows, instantly changing the demeanor of the unruly captain.

"(Russian) No, it's my matter! And the only bitch I see here is you, Golovkin!" Approaching a guard and borrowing his pistol in spite of carrying his own, the commander did so, placing no less emphasis on the blatant disregards of Golovkin's transgression than the lethal pressures that were building from outside his ship. In approaching the third rank captain, he shouted in Russian before attempting to pistol-slap him. "You follow my orders as I say, *matros!* [Insult of lowest rank]"

Unbeknown to Polivanova, Golovkin, a highly skilled combatant, grabbed his pistol and subsequently sent him plummeting to the floor with a swift kick to the abdomen. The ensuing sound of the commander's 49-year-old frame hitting the hard slanted steel deck echoed, causing the others present to feel his pain.

In response, his other guard quickly drew his pistol, aiming it at Golovkin's back. "(Russian) Stay as you are, Captain! Don't move!"

Golovkin froze for a moment before then spinning in a sideway motion. There, he discharged his weapon before the unexpected guard was able to react. What wasn't heard due to its discharge being masked by Golovkin's pistol was Polivanova's own weapon being fired simultaneous. Golovkin ended up missing his target because Polivanova didn't.

Upon regaining his composure and joined by the other, the stunned guard subdued Golovkin, who in turn was spun by the force of Polivanova's weapon. There he lied prone on the angled deck, his shooting shoulder obliterated. Other's soon joined in, bringing the incident under wraps including escorting a profusely bleeding former second-in-command away to the infirmary.

A highly skilled martial arts enthusiast such as Dave, who prided himself on quickness, was shocked at both Golovkin's swiftness and instinctive reaction. He was also no less impressed by both the commander's quick recovery upon having been prostrated to the steel floor and his split-second response to a grossly insubordinate senior officer, and furthermore his accuracy.

Witness of the whole incident gave credence to an undaunted level of dedication towards Polivanova by his crew and no less an undeniable level of fear the omnipresent commander was able to instill into Golovkin by his mere voice. It reflected his ascendancy aboard their vessel. To the further astonishment of Dave, upon the commander commending his guard's actions of staying fast to his orders, he also approached him and Linda in notice of their shaken children.

"I'm sorry your little girl and boy needed to see that, but you're safe now. That son of a bitch isn't fit to wear any navy uniform."

While finding the commander's specialized attention in the face his ship's extreme peril admirable, surviving their present course and thereafter facing the American Second Fleet, no less alone and in a crippled vessel, placed an insurmountable measure of added value to the stock of the Costa's wellbeing. Polivanova addressed Linda before exiting the area.

"Madam Costa. I am sorry for the foul mouth my former officer exhibited to you. Sometimes being down here for too long can cause a man's mind to slip in judgment, and display unfortunate behavior. Again, please except my apologies."

Meanwhile nobody residing aboard his vessel was safe from the increasing water pressure mounting from outside. The ship was mostly quiet while a few qualified crewmembers were engaged in the hopeful release of a frozen ballast vent valve in question. In the interim, nothing else could be contributed by anyone else except to just sit back and to listen to the creaks of their submarine as it was being squeezed increasingly tighter every square inch throughout its entire structure. A pitch gradually ringing higher in tone was a constant reminder to those listening that they were slowly sinking into the pitch-blackness below. Its resonance heard throughout the submarine bore a semblance to a ticking time bomb, a possible overture to an eventual implosion.

Any premature evacuation to an escape pod was prohibitive for reasons Polivanova didn't wish to throw the towel in just yet and in there doing condemn his vessel to the depths, especially given his nuclear armament aboard. His vessel's class normally didn't carry such weaponry, presently leaving him feeling no sense of honor for having been selected to do so. With such armament aboard, their present predicament therefore qualified as an instance where the preservation of their vessel would be worthy of the sacrifice of him and his crew. Thereby adding further wound for the Costa family was the notion they stood to become part of that same sacrifice for the sake of the Soviet motherland without the same recognition of heroism everyone else aboard it would be honored with.

Polivanova held out as long as possible before finally giving the orders for evacuation. His vessel just surpassed a depth in excess of a half-mile and was on the fringes of approaching uncharted limits of pressure. Lindquist was meanwhile listening, both in disbelief his adversary was approaching such depths without imploding, and disheartened in understanding they were soon destined to do so.

Having ordered the immediate evacuation of all nonessential personnel to his vessel's emergency escape module, Polivanova headed to command center to relay coordinates of their doomed vessel to his superiors. The same could have been carried out from the safe confines of his escape pod en route to the surface, but he was attempting to buy yet another few seconds of inaction. In addition, with his diving specialists still working on the problem, he wasn't about to leave them behind while seeking his own safety. Meanwhile the evacuation of the rest of the crew commenced with calm efficiency. It included the Costas, who were being escorted to the pod as well, their heads draped.

Nobody relished the idea of being ejected to the surface in the escape module, all crowded up in its cramped confines and facing horrendous sea conditions above. The prospect of being cooped within its tight quarters while being tossed about by an ultra-violent sea made it a forgone conclusion that doing so would be the case as everyone would be getting sick and falling all over each other. It was a price they would need to pay for realizing any hope of safety. With survival at that point being at best a shaky prospect, any such dealings with Hurricane Gloria, especially in its more fiercer state, was a full circle in which the Costas could have never beforehand fathomed would ever likely play out even in their wildest imaginations.

In the midst of the organized evacuation, a different feel to their sub was met with both celebration and sighs of relief. In addition to monitoring the depth sounder for keeping abreast their upward progress, Polivanova also kept a keen ear tuned for the subsidence of his vessel's contraction; it was a much sweeter sound to his ears. He wished to make certain any exit of his crew from their escape pod wouldn't be that of a premature one.

Meanwhile the feel to his ship could be likened to that of an elevator that is is slowly ascending. Beforehand, he had also taken the interim of the crew's evacuation as a means of delaying any transmission of their peril to his superiors.

While Captain Lindquist pumped his fist in viewing the Soviet submarine's uncharacteristic reemergence as an indication it was likely damaged beyond any reasonable field repair, he was also relieved the success of his mission didn't need to coincide with the loss of his adversary's lives. Being a Cold War versus that of a hot one (actual confrontation) allowed the American commander to own such a sense of benevolence.

Lied in wait while perched in a static buoyant state two hundred feet below his adversary, Polivanova held his position there. Now at the mercy of his foe, he believed there was no reason not to give reprieve to many of the stomach aboard his ship, those that had been retching violently over the past several days. Polivanova was a believer in tough love, not a sadist.

Apparent to him that his adversary wasn't going anywhere soon coupled with also feeling no urgency of forcing his foe up to an inhospitable surface, especially with help on the way, for Lindquist it meant that a waiting game was to ensue.

Word of the incident including the status of both vessels climbed its way up the American chain of command with the swiftness of one frantically climbing out of a bear's den in seeing its cubs unintended. It made its way vertically to the Secretary of the Navy and halted there for time being until further verification of the status of Polivanova's submarines could be ascertained.

The commander placed his confidence in Captain Lieutenant Talkovskaia to hold fort for the remaining early morning hours.

"Apparently they're either too damaged or too chicken to come down here, so for the time being I'm not conceding to any wishes. I believe with the storm above us, no one's going to be taking any action, anytime soon. But wake me if anything does change. This bog has ruined a well-deserved sleep, and I want to be fully rested when it comes time for playing cards with the Americans. Speaking of which, I must first visit our tourist to make sure they're alright."

"What about Captain Golovkin, sir?" Talkovskaia asked.

Polivanova shook his head. "That man makes my blood boil—coercing my two guards to disregard their orders because of a hissy fit. Then taking aim at a Chirkoff. I should have shot his balls off, but he turned too quickly on him. With the episode behind us, it's now unfortunate I'm responsible for keeping the bastard from bleeding out. Keep three men on him and have them maintain their distance. Even with his shoulder blown off, I can't afford underestimating the man again. It's ironic we have four Americans aboard our highly classified vessel, yet its one of my own men I feel most threatened by—not withstanding my once trusted first officer. I pray this is only an isolated case for the sake of our navy."

In exiting the control center before turning back to his men again, the commander thanked them. "Keep an eye out for any leaks," he added, "and don't wake me up with anymore sirens either, okay Talkovskaia? I prefer getting out of bed under my own volition next time."

Post sunrise, Hurricane Gloria, which was still sucking up energy from the warm sea further northeast, was long since passed. The sun revealed in its wake complimented by a blue sky brought to light a picturesque aqua stage for Lindquist's vessel's resurfacing. Its emergence was met with cheers emanating from an array of naval vessels amassed in the surrounding area. While the assembly of Naval vessels and hovering aircraft was nothing less than what Polivanova had expected, the fervor of their aggressive persuasion following wasn't. The commander understood resurfacing was an eventuality, but in his usual defiance chose to milk the moment to annoy those of the strike group above.

First ignoring the warning of a less intense depth charge summoning him to the surface, Polivanova waited for the Second Fleet's next move. He believed that any following warnings would sequentially come closer. His defiance was quickly swayed with the urgency to surface when a helicopter omitted the use of any further such warnings. Use of the outdated weaponry was in fulfillment of Richardson wishes, and its general obsoleteness in modern warfare didn't undermine any shortcomings of sway.

What ensued next was the powerful detonation of another depth charge exacting its will at near lethal proximity to the Soviet sub. Its intense percussion reverberated through every living cell aboard Polivanova's vessel including two terrified children and no less their parents. Having lost his commanders cap from the discharge, Polivanova quickly retrieved it, placing it atop his head again. He then let out a pronounced sigh-of-relief, ordering his men.

"Okay, let's bring it up. I think we've overstayed our welcome here." Still startled and shaking his head in relief, Polivanova sighed again. "Whew! That was close. I don't think that was their signal for us joining them later over trepaks and vodka. I guess those *things* [depth charges] still have a use. I'm convinced."

Polivanova viewed the long faces of his crew.

"Comrades, don't look so bleak. This mission has been a partial success considering what the Kremlin asked of us carried with it the strong likelihood of failure. I explained that from the onset." He then grinned. "Besides, I still have a ace I my hand, and playing it would have been difficult if we were all blown to pieces, no? I'm heading to the sail, so prepare me a raft. Upon speaking with the Americans, I have a feeling headquarters will be contacting us with some more favorable news afterwards."

Still lagging several miles behind and on his phone, Rear Admiral Richardson responded to Canptain Peterson, his carrier's CO. "The man's sitting crippled in the damn water, and yet he's demanding to speak to me—a rear admiral?"

"Sir, he states that he wants to offer you something, but wouldn't specify. He only hinted that it might benefit whoever heeds its advantage."

Richardson smiled in vexation. "Advantage my ass. This guy's got more tricks up his sleeve then I have hemorrhoids. Get the picture? I'd really hate to validate this guy's false sense of entitlement by capitulating, but this has to be good. Benefit my ass. And thanks Captain by the way. I'll be joining you at your birdfarm in about a half hour. Ah, make it an hour. I'm not rushing for this guy. I think I'll change into some clean ironed for the occasion."

Later on a small gunboat, the rear admiral, two of his trusted officers, and a petty officer were waiting further than standard practice as Polivanova approached. Aboard the Russian raft, the commander grinned at Talkovskaia. "Captain Lieutenant, watch this closely. The American officer there is posturing from a position of supremacy, as would I. I'm confident I can push this guy's buttons. Learn something here."

From the rear admiral's standpoint, he was relishing such an opportunity of being able to go head-to-head with a Soviet officer. He turned to Captain Peterson.

"Captain, no matter how badly I'll want to reach across to his raft and squeeze that Slovik throat of his, I'll be cordial with this guy just to piss him off."

Like the logic of sports commentators withered in the first few minutes of play, Richardson was caught off guard by a Polivanova salute, which he subsequently returned, then retracting his hand in a deliberate manner, almost grinning while doing so.

Not appreciating the spirit of his return, Polivanova addressed him in Russian. "I can't believe that beige uniform is still a required issue."

Appearing bewildered, Richardson panned to the two officers adjacent to Polivanova's in believing one was an interpreter.

"What did he say?"

"I said it is a pleasure finally meeting an American admiral in person," Polivanova responded in English, smirking the meanwhile.

To the shock of everyone present and Captain Peterson no less, Richardson responded in fluent Russian. "I like it better when you speak in English. You don't sound so ignorant."

Caught aback, Polivanova tittered in response to a stern-faced rear admiral, who was savoring having just taken the younger Soviet commander to school.

"What is it you want to offer? I have ships willing to escort your crippled submarine back to your waters. My men will enjoy taking pictures that they can send back to their families to frame. And by the way, who died and left you military fashion critic? They're khakis. This uniform has a proud history that I needn't remind you of. Look at your own damn position for crying-out-load."

Polivanova turned to Talkovskaia. "The man is sensitive about his clothing." Facing back to an annoyed Richardson again, he took on a more serious tone.

"(English) Mr. Admiral. I would prefer being towed back home by my own people, thank you."

"If you look back and assess your own position, you'll notice you haven't a leg to stand on—" Gesturing to Polivanova' submarine, he added, "or let me rephrase, a boat to sail in either. In fact, if I had a couple canvas ones in inventory, I might lend you a couple sails to hang on your conning tower appendages. Maybe then your navy might finally have itself a reliable vessel."

Polivanova nodded for Talkovskaia to hand him photos taken of the Costa family. In them, they appeared both comfortable and well provided for. Taking the pictures from his newly appointed second-in-command, he purposely orchestrated the whole proceedings before then handed them over to a reaching third officer aboard Richardson's small gunboat.

"Speaking of sails, I believe some of your F14s were searching for these people in a hurricane. We found them in a life raft about to get swallowed by its approaching eye wall. They just evacuated their burning boat. Mr. Admiral. If you knew you were incapable of rescuing your own people, then you should have called for a more capable navy to do so." Grinning, he added, "We would have been happy to have assisted you."

Richardson studied the photos uttering aloud the meanwhile. "Take a look back at your own vessel and we'll talk capable." He then faced back up again. "First of all, what do you expect me to do, kiss your ass after you just tried sneaking into our waters? And second of all, are they okay?"

"First let me state—since when have these international waters become yours. Second, no thanks to you, they are okay. In fact, I have treated them better than my own crew, although I am not giving them up until my fleet orders me to do so—not you. We will see then who's kissing whose ass by the end of the day." Polivanova grinned. "But of course I have not notified my people yet. All I want is a dignified escort home by my own navy. I do not care if yours follows from a distance, as I expect it would anyhow."

The rear admiral grunted in frustration as Polivanova continued. "Think about it all you want, my American admiral. I believe you understand the matter is no longer ours. Look deeper than your own pride and do what is right for everyone. I imagine you do not want this turning into some high profile event, no?"

Richardson understood that Polivanova had just cleverly turned the nature of the events from that of a military issue to a political one. He did so to assure the safety of his crew, as well provide them a dignified retreat home.

"Take those photo for verification if you please. There is plenty more where they came from."

"You're holding these American hostages here!" the rear admiral lashed back in frustration. "I don't know what else to call it!"

"Easy, my American Admiral. I will not harm these people no matter what. In fact, I would happily give them up right now, but if I do, I assure you a large force of our People's Navy will be here before you know it to aid in my return home, and you know that could get very messy. I'm only asking for one of our small salvage teams and no harassment in turn. Admiral, this isn't your call."

Richardson sighed in frustration before replying in Russian in a more businesslike tone. "Such an escalation won't be necessary. I'll notify you what my command instructs me to do next."

"You are not hearing me, you stubborn admiral. I will not make any move until my headquarters notifies me of my next course of action. I'm haven't contacting them either. This means you have a full chain of command to climb. And I know how my fleet operates too, so don't attempt anything foolish. Eventually I will receive my next instructions from them—not you."

With Richardson's boat soon storming away to Polivanova's pleasure, the rear admiral vented.

"That bastard just trumped my ace high with a duce. These photos need verification, but my guess is they're probably valid— F14s and all. Circumstantial evidence points to that. I'm just surprised he didn't have their heads [the Costas] dressed in sables. And with that said, I just want you to look at me and explain two things. First, what the hell was that boy thinking by taking his kids along, especially this time of the year? And second, what were the odds that some small fiberglass boat would have made it through hurricane conditions intact just to then be picked up by some joyriding Soviet submarine in its violent eye—even worse, trying to sneak into our backyard? What were the freaking odds of any of this playing out, now making my life miserable?"

Lieutenant Sutton, the officer who notified the rear admiral of Polivanova's detection two days earlier, responded to Richardson's rhetorical question. "Sir, if I may. One would likely expect stepping outside an aircraft at 5000 feet without a parachute would mean certain death, but there's been documented cases supporting otherwise."

Appearing impressed, Richardson turned to him. "Interesting Lieutenant. Then you must know of documented cases supporting the likelihood of your own survival in stepping outside of this moving vessel. What would the odds of your survival be then?"

Sutton's good report with Richardson tendered the lieutenant some latitude in engaging in such banter, although the rear admiral didn't appreciate his interruption being made in the presence of Captain Peterson.

"I would guess my likelihood of survival would be close to a hundred percent, sir. The likelihood you'd return for me—maybe zero."

"Yeah right, Sutton. Try omitting the 'maybe'. And by the way, just minutes ago when the Russian commander and I were going at it, where were you anyhow? With that Mensa aptitude of yours, I'm certain you could have gotten under his skin. God knows you do mine."

"Maybe so sir, but you know in my doing so, I would have been overstepping protocol. Besides, I could see experience in that man's face, putting him more in yours or the Captain's league, sir. With that said, would you like my opinion of how I felt you handled yourself with him?"

"Not really, but go ahead. This boat's still moving."

"Frankly, I was impressed with your Russian. In fact at that moment I was never so proud to be serving under anyone, as I was with you then, sir. With that being said, the rest of the proceedings were just too painful to bear witness."

Frustrated in only listening, the captain intervened. "I know he's your subordinate, but may I step in?"

Resigned and just shaking his head, Richardson attempted to appease him. "I appreciate your back Captain, but this time the lieutenant's right; although you have to admit I got a pretty good licking in on the Russian beforehand, agreed?" He then looked over to his smirking Lieutenant. "You're a real prick, Sutton. You know that, don't you? Someday when you make admiral, as I have no doubt someone like you will, then some brain-fuck like yourself will come along and torment you like you do me. In fact, maybe we should about-face and revisit the Russian commander now. Maybe that prick might consider taking you as a tradeoff for the family, and then this whole damn thing could just be done with. Hell Lieutenant, I'm all for that."

The captain then stepped in. "And when the Russians demand we take him back, just transfer him to me, sir. Our ship has plenty of demeaning tasks to keep the boy busy."

Savoring his captain playing the bad cop, Richardson concluded. "Hear that Sutton? How's it feel being loved? I'll make certain the captain gets first dibs on you. Meanwhile there's more important matters pressing here, agreed? By the way Captain, in speaking of demeaning tasks, how is that new seaman working out in barf detail anyhow?"

Peterson just stood, partially distracted by the events that were taking place. "The boys a pro, sir. I was told his replacement has bit more on the ball though."

"Yeah, like that useless waste of skin sleeve was a tough act to follow. Just keep an eye on him for me, okay? Make sure the kid's not a jumper. In fact, foreseeing the future, I might be the one the choppers will be searching for in the drain when the dust settles. I just had my ass handed to me by that shithead Russian captain."

"I didn't say it was that bad, sir," Sutton insisted.

"Too late for any backpedaling, Sutton. I just had my ass handed to me—giftwrapped, thank you, and I can also see it'll be a gift that'll keep on giving—brilliantly played. Damn, I hate that man."

In its second round, word of the incident climbed to the US President, who in turn directed a State official to resolve the matter. He did so to keep news of the potentially damaging developments under wraps. The appointed official in turn was given no choice but to notify a surprised but pleased Soviet Ambassador about the incident. The diplomat was both pleased in believing he had new ammo in which to taunt his American counterparts and relieved his country's expensive submarine and the personnel manning it didn't perish in the process. He was also bewildered as to why word of the incident hadn't been relayed to him by his own people yet. It was in the unawareness that he was yet the next chain's link leading from the Americans to his Soviet countrymen—Polivanova's wish.

In wishing to elicit a propagandist headache for the US, it was Polivanova's design to spread the broadcast of the Costa equation to as many government officials of both nations as possible. The commander was confident his means of communicating its relay would likely force the news of the incident to eventually reach him by route of direct command. For a man who disliked politics so much, Polivanova was displaying a masterful demonstration of playing its players simply by the employment of the command structure as a convenient medium for his agenda.

An unmentioned detail of intentionally forcing the knowledge of the submarine incident to travel bilaterally through both ranks of command was omitted by the Americans, simply because the US officials refused to forfeit any information that might somehow give their Soviet counterparts an upper hand, satisfaction-wise. They preferred leaving it where the Soviets could only speculate as to why they hadn't heard anything from their navy first, claiming the reason was likely due to some systemic breakdown typical of their order. The Americans played the ignorant card, the meanwhile understanding the flawed translucency of such reasoning would eventually be revealed in its full relay back to Polivanova when the full spectrum of his master plan would eventually become common knowledge.

Several high-level emergency meetings of bitter polemics played out before a final agreement was negotiated. The main issue where the Americans refused to waver was denying the Soviets their own escort home. It stemmed mostly from them having taking exception to Polivanova's attempt of masking his ride up the US seaboard, even in spite its uninspired approach. His doing so was the second such known attempt accomplished by different means made by the Soviets in recent months, although neither side was innocent of such covert activities. The truth underlining all the rhetoric being tossed about was that such activity was the basis of the whole Cold War's subsurface strategy. It's just that this time the Soviets were caught and the Americans couldn't capitalize on it because of the semblance of goodwill Polivanova inserted into the equation via the Costas.

The Soviets insisted that only they were to escort their crippled vessel back home, whereby the Americans instead demanded the release of the Costas without any conditions. A final consensus made in the face of stark differences stood to fulfill Polivanova's wishes. It flowed like water down both the American and Soviet chains of command and eventually settled onto the ears of both Richardson and the commander. The orders left the rear admiral no choice but to greet the Costa family for immediate airlift back to the States and to wait for a Soviet naval salvage team to toll their crippled submarine back to neutral water harassment free.

Beforehand, a stipulation that the Soviet rescue fleet wasn't to be accompanied by any submarines per agreement was a weak but crucial element the American's had demanded. It was just enough of a bone agreed upon which prevented dangerous exchanges of political posturing from leading to a catastrophic breakdown of negotiations altogether. The grease in which the Costa equation added to the wheels of the talks essentially led to a sought-after way-out that may have otherwise led to that of an Armageddon-like scenario. It was almost a repeat of a 1962 Cuban Crises or 1983-blindside playing out again.

In believing they were at least equals, the Soviets were tired of always appearing in the shadows of the might of the US Navy. The Americans in turn were fed up with what they interpreted as Soviet expansion, whereby each occurrence never failed to provoke what the US believed was a needed response. With the likes of such a pressure cooker having been building tension for over forty years and consequently quieting the voices of common reasoning to the point of dangerous silence, the Costa component could be credited for working as a relief valve that eventually led to the whole situation being defused.

Such political bickering in turn caused everyone en masse some 300 miles north of the Dominican Republic the need to wait. It was a hiatus that lasted until the following morning when both the Americans and Soviets would be able to cash out the decisions rendered from their respective governments. It would in turn allow all the players to be able to go about to their business-as-usual, meaning they could all return back to stalking each other again.

The following day's sunrise was as stunning as the previous, except the sea lay calmer. With Hurricane Gloria distanced a few hundred miles further northwest from where it had trailed the day before, any traces of her wake had long since dissipated. Meanwhile her eye was heading north and would eventually make landfall only three towns east of Dave's childhood town of Fairfield, Connecticut. Landed there as a weakened Category Two Hurricane, it stood to become a final punctuation mark to what he once mentioned of the storm's symmetry.

Both he and his remaining family members were blindfolded in their escort while an observing crew cheered their parade through the submarine. Polivanova had no qualms in reminding his men beforehand of how the Costa's presence aboard their vessel was about to afford them all a dignified retreat home.

Adding a punctuated jab at Richardson, the commander used the leverage of a little guilt on Dave and Linda for having ensconced them aboard his vessel. He did so by requesting they be fitted with non-insignia Soviet Navy apparel in fulfillment of his wish. Still experiencing a tinge of Stockholm syndrome, they gladly obliged.

Back in the conning tower where the Costas had boarded the submarine days earlier, they were there once again, but this time in better health and spirits. With both Lieutenant Tretskii [medic] and Polivanova standing near an open side hatch ready to see the family off in their disembarkation, removal of all blindfolds bore witness to three American naval frogmen await and only a short distance away. With them poised in an inflatable motor craft ready to chauffer the family to an awaiting carrier, hugs of gratitude laden with tears were exchanged from Linda and her kids to the small crew in attendance.

Upon their exit, Polivanova recommended his men present place their farewells to Dave as well. While doing so would have posed highly awkward for them days earlier, an air of changed attitudes mitigated any such action. Wanting to speak to Dave alone before he too would need to disembark, the commander then ordered all those present to fall back to their post. Everyone there afterwards within the local aqua theater would finally be able to get back to their normal duties of before, meaning the Costas would also finally become freed up to go about their lives again as well.

Once alone, the commander spoke. "Both of our governments

have spent so much of their money preparing for a war of which neither side can afford its consequences, not withstanding the world. It is ludicrous I know, but aside a few proxy conflicts, it's kept our two powerful nations at bay by preventing any actual direct conflict with each other. You might be feeling some mixed emotions now, because your comrades waiting for you up there (pointing) would give their lives on command to protect you as an American—that while my men who have rendered you sanctuary would in turn exact harm on those same men, or they us if some tragic breakdown between our two powerful nations ever took place—which almost did."

Dave was shocked by the commander's tailing comment, shaking his head. "'Mixed emotions' is an understatement."

Polivanova grabbed his shoulder. "Comrade, don't let it get to you. You have no control over it, or even I. I have a wife and children back home who I love, so believe me, I have no desire for war between our nations. Tens of millions of my countrymen perished during the Great Patriotic War (WWII), and to this day its horrible memory still lingers in the core of our people. You see your children reminded me of how insane this whole underwater posturing really is. But our nations are like two men with guns drawn, ready to fire. No one really wants to pull the trigger, yet nobody is willing to lay down their weapon first either. My suggestion then is for you to get on with your life and enjoy the peace that we down here provide you from both sides. Although my men aren't doing it for the sake of any American and likewise, consequently they are. I have been hearing recently that high-ranking members of our Politburo are leaning to a more open society and your leaders are taking notice. So who knows? Maybe both our governments will finally be able to point their guns downward and even someday normalize their relationships. My guess is some residual mistrust may take several generations to dissipate among the power players and those younger that may have served as their loyal subordinates. And I am not asking that you go back home and praise us as a righteous people either. We are just people in this world trying to seek security the best we know how, like yourselves. Yes I am not naïve to the notion that both power and greed drives the world, but both of those elements in their many forms is mostly the result of ones perverse means of establishing a safe perch in this world, quite often at the cost of others—a collective means of Darwinism in one of its many complex forms."

"I never viewed it that way. And in reference to my wife, even if I don't make any such praise of your people, she certainly will."

"Ah yes, women aren't plagued by the same stubborn macho reserve as we men often are. But I do want to leave you with this bit of knowledge, and..." grinning, he added, "from all I am about to state, you might conclude that I have too much time down here for pondering." Following a guffaw, he added, "and comrade, there are times when that is not a stretch to admit either. What I do believe because it is fact versus that which is sometimes misinterpreted as 'what was meant to be', is everything that we have both seen and experienced in our past carries us to our present juncture. What I mean is all of our actions, intentional or not, and no matter how insignificant they may seem, stand to change the tide of the future to move in whatever random direction its compounded ripple effects may lead it to. I am not speaking just for ourselves either, but for others as well. It works both ways. Know what I am saying?"

"Sure. If you drop a pebble in the water, it eventually affects the whole pool—but both ways? I'm not following you."

"There is a lot on your mind I know, but you know the answer. And let me add. The effects I speak of are not always as fluent or predictable as you just stated. So to answer your question, it is simple. While our actions represent the epicenter of the ripples that expand outward from us, and both the actions of others and events in general represent the ripples that eventually affect us, of which by the way, those effects I speak of may not manifest for years or even eons later. Lay dormant for any indefinite amount of time, they might suddenly make a profound difference at any point in the future; hence, there stands the lack of fluency that just I mentioned. Think about that and relate it to everything that has just transpired in the past few days, especially in your case."

Polivanova Pointing below. "By the way, the same applies for us too, and what these past few days have meant for all of us as well. Think of how the slightest single action or thought on your part may have led to these events that have reached the top levels of both of our governments. This might be a lot for you to swallow. Do you follow me, comrade?"

In spite of finding it odd that the commander was referencing his take of the butterfly effect, especially giving the circumstances, out of both respect and curiosity, Dave played along.

"You mean like if I hadn't been the lucky recipient of the wave I told you about that essentially tossed me back onto my boat again, none of this would be happening?"

Polivanova grinned slightly. "Good start comrade, but think of it with a more random approach, and subtle it may be at times too. I will give you one quick example, and although extreme or a stretch it might sound, its approach could still be considered trite in representation of my point. You see—you walk beneath a gentle snowfall of which in spite the countless snowflakes that make landing within your visual range over the span of one dropping, upon entering inside for shelter you find yourself covered with no more than a slight dusting. This may reoccur throughout your life whereby such dustings will be the most you will ever need to contend with. Now take those same harmless snowfalls as they occur over the same span of time and let them accumulate. At some juncture, all it may take is but one sight shift of even one single snowflake to trigger the rest into that of a deadly avalanche. What I am saying is that if even the most negligible occurrences can have short-term and possibly long-term effects in secular terms, then imagine what effect any choice you make or action you take might have as well—of which by the way, it already has. While you have paid with great suffering to obtain it, you and your family have been presented with a unique opportunity. Think of how you can shape the course of your own life and consequently that of others, simply resulted from an evolutionary series of events that have transpired. I will even add history itself to the list as well. So don't waste that, comrade. Exploit its momentum."

Still attempting to absorb the magnitude of what Polivanova was implying, Dave acknowledged him. "Interesting, and quite thought provoking too. I'll do that."

"Good. And one more thing before you leave, my friend"

"What's that, sir?"

"Stay the fuck away from hurricanes. It is highly unlikely that I will be there the next time to save your American ass again."

A highly moved Polivanova then approached Dave, grabbed both sides of his head, and kissed him three times on the cheeks as was customary with high-ranking Russian officials amongst each other. He then handed Dave back his sheath still containing both his mariner's knife and marlin spike before then backing up in a military like manner as if to salute, but not doing so. In an emotionally strained voice and slightly quivering lower lip, he concluded. "You have allowed my men to go home with dignity. Now please leave my vessel. Both your family and country are awaiting you."

Moved by such an unexpected show of respect, Dave turned to the commander with his body partially exited outside the sail bridge. "Thank you, Commander." He then disembarked.

While being escorted by three of Polivanova's men, cheers from nearby vessels greeted the Costas as they approached the American frogmen awaiting them. There was no posturing taking place between the opposing servicemen handling the family as a result of neither side wanted anything to do with allowing harm to come upon such a politically charged family.

Feeling both the fresh sea air and warm sun grace their faces again together with finally being able to realize their safety, both Linda and Heather broke down into tears. Preferring to contain his emotions for the time being, Dave just sat quietly with a pondering grin. Along with the exhilaration of absorbing his family's new lease on life, he was still deeply moved by his last encounter with the captain second rank.

Meanwhile when it came to matters pertaining to their so son, nobody was aware of the magnitude the last several days played in messing with his developing mind. The disorientated boy just sat quietly, sometimes smiling, clinging to his mother for security. Deeply festering within the young impressionable boy was a toxic salad of deep confusion and fear. He wore it like a cancer taking root, attempting to digest all that took place over the pervious several days. Unable to understand his position of safety, he was still fearful that something terrible was destined to take place any time soon. Little did the small boy know was that for him, his sister, and parents, the pendulum of fortune was finally swinging their way and none of them had any reason to be apprehensive any longer.

A select group of Naval personnel aboard Peterson's carrier

crowded the Costas with orders handed down by the Secretary of the Navy to warmly receive them. They had no objection about doing so, for in viewing the crippled prized Soviet possession to their port side, they subconsciously connected it to the Costa's presence. Meanwhile all personnel were fitted with strict orders to neither gawk nor even sneak a peek in the direction of Polivanova's crippled submarine once the Costa's were aboard. Such an order was in accordance with carrying out the wishes of those who had negotiated the terms of the family's release. It stated any personnel wishing to do so, nonetheless take a picture, would face the stiff repercussions of a court-martial.

For the Costa's reception, the Secretary of the Navy ordered the halt to all sortie activities aboard the aircraft including rendering the flight deck hazard-free of all associated equipment. While still unimpressed with Dave for having endangered the lives of his children, Richardson was generally pleased that both he and his family were finally safely aboard US sovereignty. In approaching Dave, he relayed his congratulations, which wasn't followed by a swift knee to the jewels.

"Sir, was that you who sent those three planes to find us?"

Upon an affirmation by Richardson, he commented. "Thanks for doing that. Did the pilots make it back okay?"

Pleased at his concern for the pilots, Richardson spared him any detail of two of his aircrafts' flameouts, ones that almost prevented both fighter jets from returning safely back to their carrier.

"They were fine, and thanks by the way for your concern. I just need to know one thing though. Why did you tell the Russians about the Tomcat flyover? Did they torture or coerce you in any way? I know I really shouldn't be asking you this with you getting debriefed later, but I'm just curious. And of course you don't have to answer."

Dave needed to think for a moment before being able to make any connection. "I was drunk and it was a slipup. The Russian commander was obsessed as to how we had made it into the eye of the hurricane and he understood it was probably too much of an emotionally charged subject for me to face sober. We were actually treated quite well."

"I imagine he wanted to take good care of his currency."

Still in a hyper-digestive mode, Dave glossed over his comment.

"What was that, sir?"

Richardson realized he had just overstepped his boundaries. "Vodka? Did he give you vodka? That would be my first guess."

"Yes vodka, Admiral—*Luksusow*, to be more specific. And damn, I'm not afraid to admit this either, Admiral, but boy did I need it."

"I bet you did, and the Polish shit, huh? Not bad. Sorry I can't extend the same level of hospitality as your Russian friend did when it comes to alcohol."

"No problem there sir, I puked it back up again. I'm good for awhile."

Richardson laughed, genuinely amused. "Good. I hope that damn commander had to clean it himself. Now would you mind if we get you out of those damn Russian costumes and instead fit you with some unmarked GI issue before you go stateside? Those clothes are like sandpaper on my eyes."

Later in having conformed to Richardson's wishes, everyone was allowed to keep their Soviet issue for sentimental reasons. Dave had applied the term, "souvenirs" for getting his wish. Not yet understanding the full magnitude of what had transpired over the previous couple days, little objection would have been given had he asked that any prominent street or highway in the United States be renamed after his family.

Post a medical checkup; an engrossing hot shower afterwards; a clean change of clothes; and first, a hardy hot meal of which little David barely touched his, the Costa family was boarded on a small transport plane slated to arrive at Fleet headquarters in Norfolk, Virginia. Everyone slept soundly during their flight with the events of the previous several days having finally caught up with them. From Norfolk they continued more shuteye on the second leg of their trip to Arlington, Virginia. There the family was to meet with some high-ranking FBI officials.

Upon receipt of an official congratulation and a "welcome home" expressed by an agent slated to debrief him, Dave just sat quietly for a moment. He did so, panning his surroundings while tapping his fingers atop a table seated before him.

"Believe me, I'm quite humbled by the lengths my country has gone to receive us and not to undermine my appreciation of that, we're all just so exhausted to say the least. I'll give you the soup to nuts of what you need to hear, but please just leave the others out of this, okay?"

"We'll still need to talk to them, but I'll keep it brief in their case."

To the astonishment of both the FBI agent questioning Dave and those observing remotely, he was eventually able to provide a detailed account of the previous two weeks. All those present included other agents watching from behind a two-way mirror were stunned at the emotionally charged details he so vividly described. In painfully reliving his bout with Hurricane Gloria, Dave chose to do so without actually mentioning his contemplation of committing euthanasia. He was unable to do so.

Soon in having gained a newfound respect for what he and his family had endured including the wonder that the man seated before him was even alive, the agent spoke.

"Listen, I know that you're a reporter. In fact our analysts have worked feverishly in compiling a file that profiles you and your family, by which it's been concluded that you're a good law-abiding citizen."

"Sounds like there's a big *but* about to be stated here. And why are you questioning me instead of the CIA. This is Arlington, isn't it—you know, the Pentagon?" Dave ended, growing a bit defiant.

"True, and I am well aware of the building *believe it or not*. But besides the fact you're on American soil right now, do you not believe that we're qualified?"

"I didn't say that. And tell me. What kind of information have you guys acquired about us anyhow?"

"I'd prefer not to reveal our methods through their results, but since you've been through so much, I give you a slight nibble of a very large carrot. Your fourth grade teacher's maiden name was Nancy Phelps and you had a crush on her."

Dave was taken aback slightly. "Not bad, though I bet you the CIA would also know my wife's favorite color," he commented, busting chops.

"I doubt that—it's alabaster by the way."

"Holy shit! That's messed up."

The agent got a charge by Dave's reaction, adding, "though it's not really an official color. Imperfections don't constitute an actual color."

"Yeah, try explaining that to my wife."

"I'll pass on that, thank you." the agent responded, grinning slightly. "Besides, that's a domestic issue. Listen though. The stuff we need to discuss right now is serious, and having stated that, here's the *big but* you were inquiring about. You being a reporter is going to pose extra challenging for you, but hear me, and hear me out. You see Dave, this whole submarine incident was a major embarrassment to both us the United States and the Soviets—especially the Soviets. Through bickering and infighting amongst us and them, a systemic breakdown in negotiations almost took place altogether." Shaking his head, he ranted slightly. "It wasn't good. Oh believe me when I tell you this, it wasn't good at all. And that's whitewashing it if I may add. Anyhow, amazingly a consensus was eventually agreed upon in good faith, which by the way is especially amazing since there's about as much good faith between us and the Soviets as two drunks arguing over a woman in a bar. Do I still have you?"

"Oh yeah, you've got me. And I think I can guess where this is going too."

"Good, then I know I have your full attention. You see changing politics in the Soviet Union is favoring better relations between us and them, but the aftermath of this incident almost threw a wrench in it, which could have and still could kill the tender shoot of a seed just breaking through the dark soil of both of our pasts."

"Quite profound. Did you rehearse that?"

"Actually, yes I did. Like it?"

Dave just sat annoyed and quiet.

"Okay then. You still need to hear this, and I can see that you're getting short with me. I'll give you an idea of the degree of this whole incident's gravity, events you may not be aware of. You see, the Soviets spoke of sending both warships and submarines in addition to a smaller salvage team to take back their vessel. Of course we weren't going to have any of that. Consequently, it took a lot of top-level finagling to bring you about to where you are now and avoid worsening relationships before our two leaders are to meet in November. So in taking into account that you and your family have experienced some extraordinary events including a lot of suffering, this phenomenon is much larger than your duty as a reporter is to tell all. This is also about the best interests of two hundred and forty million of your fellow Americans countrymen, and possibly the world as a whole. Bear with me Dave and see the larger picture here."

"Oh don't worry. I haven't wavered."

"Just making sure. You see while the Soviets respect power, they don't relish the idea of feeling cornered either. Nobody does. That almost led to grave consequences two years ago. The frightening part is we knew nothing about it until afterwards. Hundreds of millions of Americans including myself would have awoken to a thunderous boom and seconds later every inch of our bodies, eyes, and lungs included, being cooked as if we had just all been dropped in some deep fryer. Every soul inflicted would have experienced a total sense of isolation within the searing shell of their soon to be corpse. The lucky ones at ground zero would have felt nothing."

"Hey, you don't need to sell me on that. And I do remember hearing something about that Eighty-three incident too."

"Well then Dave, my point should be taking as that much more poignant. You see, we've been able to convince them through some complex negotiations and reassurances that in this case, both our interests and theirs coincide. It was that common thread that defused the whole incident with the promise of us prohibiting you and your family from ever making any mention to any Soviet connection to what happened. And yes may I add, we'll enforce the compliance of that promise even on you, a private citizen. It was a quid pro quo our two nations could live with, and I meant that literally. The issue for all practical purposes is dead. You lost your boat and we rescued you early in the storm. That trail has been fabricated and there are people who will testify to it, rendering you a liar otherwise. This includes any Navy personnel you saw earlier. I can't emphasize this enough to you, and I myself also have no control over this matter either. Understand?"

Dave was physically shaken. "How can you stand there telling me that I can be deprived of divulging my own personal experience, that which my family and I have so dearly paid for? You're denying me my rights under the First Amendment. Moreover, you said it yourself. I'm a private citizen, meaning not bound by the UCMJ. You can't do that. And by the way, eventually someone who witnessed this earlier will break their silence. They always do."

"I don't think so, and I'm going no further than that."

"Even the rear admiral?"

"And face court-martial? I don't think so, and you didn't hear that from me either. Though believe me in his case—he has no interest of this going any further. That's for sure."

The agent felt bad for Dave, but he himself had no latitude for concessions on the matter.

"And as far as us denying your right of speaking out on the subject is concerned, the hard reality Dave is, yes we can and we will. I know this is a hard pill for you to swallow, but please don't let those wheels in your head keep spinning. I can see them. But you need to see the much larger picture here. The stakes are just too high, and you'll pay more than you can imagine for doing so. As an educated man of good sense, I'm sure you can read further into that, and I'd rather stop there."

"You mean a threat?"

"Okay, call it what you wish—a threat, warning, whatever. Let me mention too that the public will gain nothing by this scoop you feel the right to expose from all this. Therefore I'll ask you this bluntly. Is it really worth fucking up an opportunity of cooling decades of tension between two giant nations that are aiming thousands of thermonuclear warheads at each other just so you can write some provocative story that the public might briefly choose as the topic of some water cooler talk, but soon forget? Look. Isn't one of your most critical roles as a reporter the best interests of the public—and I mean all two-hundred and forty million of them?"

Dave became silent in reluctant acknowledgement of the agent's reasoning. Later, a Costa collective agreement of complying with the FBI wishes, including signing their rights away, was rewarded with extra amenities for their remaining stay. The family was also left with an underlining sense of solace in knowing they would soon be home again. Higher-ranking government officials also pulled the necessary strings required for cleaning the family financial mess left by the incident's wake. It included a generous grant of hush money for further assurance of everyone's silence.

Rather than going for any future sailing excursions, Dave instead received no resistance in convincing Linda to head inland for any future odysseys. The incident had rewired his previous notion about superstition and the like. In the ensuing years, they and the Woodsons each visited the other once, resulting in more standard social behavior on everyone's part. In conjunction with Dave and Linda both still carrying the burden of the trauma resulted from Hurricane Gloria, Pamela becoming pregnant post their final Sao Vicente visit also congealed the unlikelihood of the group ever meddling in such conduct again. It also marked the end of her wildflower days.

Decades elapsed caused the Woodsons to interpret their friend's aloofness over those years as a manifestation of their trauma, an unshakable hangover caused by their dealings with Hurricane Gloria. While partially true, Dave's itch to divulge its truth led to believing that spending too much time with his friend might someday lead to him opening up about their ordeal. The two couples consequently drifted apart post their mutual visits, mostly limiting their contact thereafter to exchanges of Christmas cards and congratulations for Pamela's three offspring, including the first to whom they anointed the name, Gloria.

The fully documented account of the Costa story became labeled "top-secret" and was tucked away for fifty years, its title labeled for reference purposes: "*Inside Gloria*".

Once the Soviet towing team found themselves in friendlier waters, a high-ranking KGB official arrested Polivanova upon him boarding a newly joined battle cruiser. Rather then being arrested for both crossing and then striking his commanding officer, Captain Third Rank Golovkin was instead relieved from his naval duty and refitted back into his appropriate uniform as a KGB officer. It was a position he held prior to boarding Polivanova's vessel, several months earlier. There were many in the higher naval ranks who didn't like Polivanova, which in turn led to them to planting a high-ranking KGB officer to keep watch over his tactics. The nuclear armament his vessel was carrying were inert warheads, nothing more than extra weight. The latest most sophisticated electronics—more weight.

Successive to the Golovkin shooting incident, the acting captain third rank could have authorized a Polivanova arrest back then, but didn't due to concerns of retaliation that might have ensued at the hands of his loyal men. It was a tactful move of self-preservation on Golovkin's part even for a man who was by far the most combatant adept individual present aboard their vessel, wounded aside.

In the following weeks, Polivanova was seated like a sitting duck at his military tribunal as Golovkin pasted him with accusations. His charges not only ended the commander's career in disgrace, but they also landed him in prison as well. Consequently, his family was stripped of their secured privileges, those that beforehand had allowed them to be able to live with extra comforts, ones deprived to most others who were living throughout the Soviet Union.

A latest General Secretary of the Soviet Communist Party, a charismatic figure relatively new to his title, eventually caught wind of the tribunals that led to Polivanova being incarcerated for over two harsh years. Pleas sent by his wife Natalya's over that same span eventually met the eyes of leader and went as far as proclaiming her husband as a 'Hero of the People'.

In response to her plea, the General Secretary appointed a small committee to check into the commander's actions. Its findings eventually led to him being exonerated from his alleged crimes. As a result, his previous stature of captain second rank was elevated to that of first rank for the purpose of retirement when the General Secretary learned what Polivanova did to keep his adversaries hands off of his submarine. In recognition, the former commander was both exonerated and then granted an honorable discharge from the navy. The new status then allowed his family to be able to live comfortably once again in a state apartment while no longer needing to slavishly work for meager state benefits as a so-called common proletariat.

In his retirement, the former commander used both his free time and adequate money supply to repress his previous shame with a constant panacea of vodka. A consequential deterioration of his marriage and likewise family breakdown led to further abuse of alcohol, accelerating the former commander into a downward spiral until 1991 when the Soviet Communist Party ceased as a governing system.

It was then a plea from his oldest son that moved Vladimir Polivanova to take responsibility in the face of his loss pension by taking on work in a factory. He did so in partnership with his wife to keep a roof over their heads, never touching alcohol again. The two eventually took up resident in a lesser affluent section of St Petersburg, which had just been renamed from Leningrad.

While the freedom afforded by the new state brought hope and new life for many in Russia, countless others previously sheltered by the large umbrella of the Soviet bureaucracy found difficulty coping within the new capitalistic way of life. The Polivanovas were no exception. Resultantly, a common cause for mere survival and the codependency that it engendered eventually led to the former commander and his wife Natalya reconciling through its necessity.

<< CHAPTER 11 >>

IN THE SMALL TOWN of Genoa, Illinois, Christmas Day 2004, two brothers and a sister visiting their aging parents all stood with heightened curiosity staring at an old bottle with a curled up letter contained within. Upon inquiring about its origin, their mother explained about how they purchased it earlier that year from some native Chamorro vender in Guam. As much as the three siblings lobbied to extract the note from the bottle, they instead needed to rely on their imaginations, their mother making light of it. "When we die, then you can open it, okay? How's that? Doesn't it look so charming next to your high school trophies?"

Four years later upon the last surviving parent passing away, the three siblings all stood once again fixated on the mystery bottle. It was one that so many times intrigued them since its introduction into their psyche. Realizing its antique potential and therefore contemplating some way of processing it, a visit to a local antique dealer squashed any prior notion of its antiquity when learnt that bottle was no more than thirty-years-old. In reaction, the three siblings all exchanged looks before the oldest of them, Pete, glanced to the dealer. His words reflected the thoughts of the others.

"If this is for real, then this might be some message some poor soul has been trying to communicate from their grave. We might as well open it up in front of a witness and see what that massage is." Looking towards the curious dealer, he added, "if you don't mind."

Finding it inappropriate to take any stance in the matter, an eager dealer took no issue with the idea. A lack of objection on her part prompted Pete to hand the bottle over to his sister, Haley.

"You have the honors."

Youngest of the three, Haley nervously uncorked the bottle with deliberation. In doing so, she released the same molecules of air that once echoed the peril that was taking place while Linda was weeping uncontrollably in note's desperate composition and Dave was hanging off Gloria's side struggling just to keep his head above water.

It took several minutes of creative thinking before the letter could be extracted without either shattering the bottle or damaging the note itself. In gently laying it flat to read, no one was prepared for the invoking emotions that sprang from its faded words. Their poignant effect quickly became evident in Haley's cracking voice and tearing eyes as she began reading it. The words scribed were a plea for remembrance, praying ones family's identity making up all that she was as a mother wouldn't need to perish into the void of obscurity. To everyone surprise, the spirit of the letter lacked any appeal for any help. It instead only reflecting the extreme state of hopelessness by which its words were presumed to been written.

Triggering Haley's spilling of emotions was the sight of faded bloodstains still embedded in the note's fibers. Anyone possessing even the remotest of compassion couldn't help but to be watery-eyed in hearing the plea for validation of four desperate souls, especially from a mother who it was presumed her words were likely written with the knowledge that they would never be read. Atop the letter were listed everyone's names and ages including the Costa's Narragansett address and phone number. Incase a lack of time prohibited the note's completion at the hands of tragedy, Linda figured at least then the information would stand as a record of both their lives and disappearance versus some general mention of four souls lost at sea scribed on some slanted granite memorial.

While overseeing her parent's house during a Toronto visit, a trip requiring no sea travel, a thirty-two-year-old mother of two and lawyer, Heather, was carrying out the tasks of both securing their mail and checking their answering machine. In hearing its messages late that particular morning in June 2009, the significance of a massage left by the soft-spoken Haley didn't register with her at first. It gave a vague explanation of a note that she and her brothers had come across, almost causing her to skip over to the next message until a mention of September 21, 1985 was made.

While the events of twenty-four years prior may have seemed like yesterday to both her parents, for Heather, it seemed displaced a lifetime away in reality. Being late for work, she jotted down the information, choosing instead to follow up on the letter from there. The note hinted to seemed eerily coincidental to one that her mother once made a slight reference of. Because so many years had elapsed, it took some recollection before she was able to make any connection, partly because it took so many years to outlast the painful legacy of the terrible dreams her traumatizing moments aboard Gloria had seared into her memory. Seeing her mother soaked with blood while everyone else's lives were in the balance was a recollection she hoped never to have to revisit again.

In the hopes of sparing her parents the need to relive that period of their lives again, the introduction of the letter prompted Heather to take the helm and to run with it herself. She was also concerned that if the message did hold any legitimacy, then her parents in their more settled and complacent lifestyle might just instead choose to ignore it, thereby leaving an opportunity of potential significant unheeded.

In responding to the number left on her parent's answering machine, one that was made with extreme apprehension, Haley in turn had difficulty containing her own excitement in responding from work. She realized her call responded to further substantiated the validity that an intriguing story was likely encrypted in the DNA of the bottled letter.

In recalling some of the fragmented clips of her dealings with the FBI whereby she and her family were swayed to comply with a high-level gag order years earlier, Heather was still reluctant as a result to divulge anything about the past. Brainwashing by a very convincing group of Bureau couching specialist still bore its scar on her even as a mature and wiser adult, notwithstanding a lawyer. The same held true with her parents, who from time to time still questioned the need of keeping quiet about an incident whose sensitivity related to national security had long since become irrelevant following 1991. The same even held true with her introverted brother, who had strayed from the family years prior. While Heather was still able to maintain a fragile relationship with him and to lesser extent his mother, in referencing Dave, there wasn't any such father and son relationship to speak of.

Upon a Friday night flight to Chicago-Rockford Airport and from there, a taxi to Genoa, Heather joined forces with the three siblings at Haley's house. There she was introduced to her mother's letter. Delicately handling the curled piece of paper in her shaky hands and feeling an array of unsettling emotions stirring inside in the process, she began gazing over it. Doing so caused her to be bombarded by an influx of unwelcome flashbacks as she stood quiet and still, remembering handling the same bottle seated before her years prior when it still contained wine.

From the start, the sight of her mother's blood causing her to break down left no doubt to the others that the young girl whose name was listed on the letter was the same person present before them.

Drudging her way though the note, Heather couldn't help but to imagine both the terrible degree of sadness and hopelessness her mother likely bore at the time, now being echoed in her words two and a half decades later. Its sobering message was highly unsettling to her. It was the first time she was ever able to conceptualize her own thought processes at time, and in doing so as a then young child, she could presently see where her parents, her heroes, how they must carried with them a far deeper notion of the dire gravity of their grave predicament, and they were able to do so back then without projecting any inkling of it to either her or David.

Upon completion of the letter, a heavy silence overtook the room. In recognition of an opportunity believed to have arisen out of the great coincident that brought everyone together, Heather eventually broke it. She guessed tucked away in some forgotten filing cabinet containing secret archives and doing nothing more than collecting dust, an entire record of the 1985 events was likely located there. She surmised her journalist father must have also been heavily burdened in keeping silence about the incident for over two decades. It was with the understanding about how the cumbersome nature of large government bureaucracies could be at causing information to become buried forever. She gathered if not dead, then those who once likely tucked such information it into their secret classifications years prior were either retired and didn't wish to lose their pensions by making any waves, or instead whatever they tucked away years prior may have simply slipped their minds altogether. This led to the supposition that her family's unique story stood to meet such the same fate.

In reasoning that the needs of the country had long been served through everyone's silence while also confident no harm would be exacted through any disclosure, Heather believed the bottle's appearance was a sign signifying the moment was at hand to make a move. Including a vague suggestion of the submarine incident, she also leaked a few other hints as well. Her hope was that her new acquaintances would be able to seek out the full-blown truth without any assistance on her part.

"While the sensitivity of what I'm suggesting for all practical purposes is no longer a factor, be careful. You have a priceless diamond in the rough at your disposal. Getting sloppy in your methods of seeking the truth could shatter that which you have no idea of its gravity. In other words, you'll be left with nothing to show for your great stroke of fortune here, and I state that with all due respect to your late parents. Also, being it my parents were granted a generous amount of hush money years back in keeping quiet on the matter as I explained, which by the way essentially paid my way through college and my brother's technical school, that's why I prefer not being any part of this either—understand?"

The three siblings acknowledged her by nodding their heads.

"Good. You see, spoiling this could result in the government somehow placing some of the same kind of constraints on you as they have with us—discount any hush money unfortunately." she concluded in jest.

Pete grinned with confidence. "I know a research journalist with connections and a good one at that. I see no problem here."

His statement was a tipping point. From then on, Heather was able to keep herself out of the research process including avoiding the use of social networking to keep abreast the matter. Success was eventually achieved when a former seaman spoke openly about witnessing a crippled Soviet submarine and cheering on some family who were fitted in unmarked Soviet attire. From there the researchers were able to establish a benchmark for furthering their investigation, no longer needing to be motivated or guided by any hearsay.

With the new tangible evidence of the seaman's testimony giving credence to Heather's hints and coupled with the date's timing contained in the bottled note, a distinct puzzle began taking shape. The researchers were now confident in being able to pave their own way to the truth by means of trusted connections, and to be able to do so without actually viewing the suspected secret archive that outside of its numerical categorization was labeled: *"Inside Gloria"*. The group was both certain of its existence and confident of what lied within its contents.

An impressive portfolio eventually took form. It gave a well-rounded scope of the magnitude of that which transpired over 24 years earlier less the most fascinating detail that would have boggled even their minds, being it was that the Costa's improbable appearance aboard the Soviet Lira Class submarine that likely averted a dangerous escalation between the two superpowers thanks to the keen foresight of Captain Second Rank Vladimir Polivanova. In spite such a detail still unearthed, the researchers still believed the story relating the Costa family aboard a Soviet submarine was highly intriguing in itself. Satisfied with the substance of their portfolio, the head researcher confided with a high-level politician who informally owed him a favor for several favorable public relation spots winning him a close election. Believing his story was well worth spending the capital that he had earned with the politician previously, he also figured it stood add more of the same in the future. This was vital since the whole presentation bidding for the truth and spanning the Costas desire to cross the Atlantic to their rescue by a Soviet submarine was designed to intrigue the one man who they understood could release it from its classified restraints.

"Mr. President, some friends of mine have stumbled upon some remarkable information we believe relates to an event that we also feel has been documented and tagged 'classified' years back. In consideration, we also believe that a political climate changed with the 1991 fall of the Soviet Union renders the need for such a classification, pointless—that is, if there is such a file. Finally sir, we also believe in these tough times it's a feel-good story that an American public might be able to embrace."

Approaching his trusted friend, the President smiled, reaching for the envelope.

"You've got my ear, Thomas."

In carefully opening the envelope, his curious eyes gazed onto a high-resolution reproduction of Linda's tear-jerking letter. The President's look soon changed from that of casual intrigue to one of stern seriousness when upon spending a moment reading the note, he gazed back up to his friend.

"Is this blood imbrued into this note?"

"Yes it is, sir," his old friend stated, nodding slowly.

In reflection, the President glanced downward for a moment before speaking again.

"Thomas, please leave me to canvass this document that your people have so brilliantly compiled. I'll reach you with a response before day's end. Thank you for bringing this to my attention."

In being summoned back to the oval office later that evening, the legislator did so just to find the President handling the actual classified document that everyone suspected did exist. He signed an executive release order for his friend to witness, speaking the meanwhile.

"A few knowledgeable colleagues to whom I've spoken with feel the spirit in which this document has been labeled classified no longer holds any significance. I'm authorizing the good folks who have assembled the material you've presented me to contact the players they feel are relevant to attend a ceremony that the State Department will sponsor. This includes any of the former Soviet state personnel who were aboard that Alfa Class submarine. Such an assembly I'm certain will be an ideal way of commemorating this unprecedented fusion of clandestine and historical significances centered on the nucleus of a humble American family. I'll have a copy of this file made up for you ASAP, and your office will be notified as soon as one is ready for your viewing."

In handing the previously classified envelope to his legislative friend, the President grinned. Pointing to its new label, he scribed in pen prior to adding his initials. "Its new name is *'Inside Gloria Declassified'*. Assume I will respond 'yes' to any RSVP." He then chuckled, adding, "I hope I'm not being too presumptuous in the notion I might be invited."

"Sir, the organizers may feel inviting you may be too imposing on a man of your stature, but I'll make sure that doesn't happen if that's your wish."

"To this day I've learned not to assume anything," the President came back in jest, adding, "and for the record Thomas, I wouldn't miss it for the world, thank you."

On a late sunny, mild Saturday morning of the following May, a fifty-five-year-old Linda received a certified letter she needed to sigh for. Unnerved, she called Dave over.

"Honey, I've got this letter from the US State Department that I needed to sign for."

Dave raced over from another room as if in his twenties again. The two were apprehensive, their minds racing in believing they may have slipped up somewhere in compliance of their sworn silence. If correct, their greatest concern was the Government possibly demanding their money back—with interest.

Dave ended up never going big-time with his career, having preferred instead to stay in Narragansett, RI to be near his friends and family. The once go-getter journalist was therefore intimidated by the significance of the correspondence's origin until learning of its contents. Receipt of theirs prompted Linda to call Heather, who had been expecting hers, but hadn't received it yet. By request of the research journalist, her services were employed by the State Department for consultation, which she in turn graciously accepted upon learning of the lifted constraint authorized by the President.

Linda waited a couple days before contacting her alienated son, who never forgave Dave for taking him across the Atlantic at such a young age. The whole episode traumatized him in his youth and the years following manifested into rage. He later came to resent his father, leading to the abuse of drugs and alcohol beginning in his early teen years. It was a woman he met at the age of twenty-one who swayed him to reverse his downward spiral. Before then, David had dropped out of high school to his parent's horror, deepened further when he ran away soon afterwards. It was a few years later that his then future wife swayed him to earn a GED that he later capitalized on by entering into a plumbing apprenticeship. While the lucrative trade did eventually reform him into that of a productive citizen, it never quelled any of the loathing contempt he still harbored towards his father.

Post the 1985 incident, it took Dave some convincing in swaying Linda that he should take the full blame for having taking their kids on such a risky voyage. She gave into the idea and only reluctantly, because both her and Dave believed their children would be better served over time by at least having one parent that they wouldn't feel the need to blame. Their hope was in preventing either of them from becoming emotional orphans.

Their plan was a partial success even though David never fully subscribed to the idea that a woman with such strong convictions as his mother would have easily caved, especially when it came to any matter pertaining to the well being of her children. Regardless, their strategy did work out to be a partial success mainly because David chose to overlook such reasoning. He saw the need instead to at least have one accessible parent of whom he could both love unconditionally and confide in when necessary while also being able to passively torment as well—and borrow money from.

Eventual contact with him led to Linda's disappointed in her son's response.

"Yeah Mom, I received it. I signed for it, and then I trashed the fucking thing. Is there anything else you need?"

Linda always walked on eggshells when it came to dealing with her son. Her hope was that he would someday soften his rage's edge. Meanwhile both she and Dave were still able to take some consolation in the knowledge that he was at least alive, healthy, and married to a woman to whom they had both formed a bond. David knew better than denying his parents the latter.

Back at Sao Vicente, the saga's origins, Jim, who was enjoying a successful chartering/hotel business with Pamela, just took a seat in his hotel office. Following an exhausted day of trying to appease a group of uncooperative guests, he was ready just to sit back and decompress via a couple beers. There, an envelope seated on his desk with the return address: "The US State Department", squashed any such hope. With the correspondence's debut denying him any chance of relaxation, Jim catapulted from his seat with urgency and sprinted home to show Pamela the package. While the information contained in the parcel was vague, its intrigue was still evoking enough to prompt the two to grab a bottle of champagne and watch a movie. Perplexed as to why they would be invited to such a State event, it was because Dave had made it a prerequisite to himself of mentioning nothing about their own connection to the event when giving his input into his friend's invitation. The best Jim could guess was that such an improbable invitation might somehow be related to his own service with the Navy, several years prior to 1985.

A mild autumn Sunday afternoon, September 26, 2010 and the 25th anniversary of the Costa's release from their Soviet rescuers, an impressive array of guest filled the seats awaiting the President to make his appearance. Many of Polivanova's crew were present, whereas he wasn't. The former commander lay bedridden in his small rundown St. Petersburg apartment ailed by a failing liver. Its diseased state was diagnosed as the indirect consequence of his excessive alcohol consumption that he had engaged in following his prison release. At the age of seventy-five, he was finally faced with the repercussions of his earlier indiscretions of gluttony.

Yegor Golovkin's omission as an invitee was unanimously agreed upon by his former crewmates for reasons not yet understood by anyone outside their circle. As for Rear Admiral Richardson, his passing over a decade prior to then rendered his seat empty at the ceremony, whereas the former Captain Lindquist, now a retired admiral, was present along with many of his crew who also served under him during the 1985 incident. Although Dave never made good on his beer, the Coast Guard crew that he was able to speak with upon entering Gloria's eye were also present in the crowd.

Seating was prearranged in such a manner as to minimize any residual tension possibly still lingering between former enemies. With that in mind, Dave, who teamed with Linda in taking a roll in some of the seating arrangements, found brilliance in her idea of having Jim situated among Polivanova's former crew.

"Maybe later he can enlighten you about any 'Ruskie' sightings," she explained to his amusement.

It was a detail that Dave had familiarized her with during their

Atlantic crossing when she asked what the two had discussed on their first night in Sao Vicente. For Dave, the conversation had long since slipped his mind until Linda brought it up again.

Puzzled by the degree of the high-level proceedings surrounding them, the Woodsons were in the dark as to what to expect. Because most of the specifics related to the ceremony were kept shrouded in secrecy thereby leaving only a small group of attendees to be informed as to the events to come, Jim was therefore beside himself when the President approached a podium. Up until then, he had only heard the buzz of roamers.

The Nation's Chief Executive kicked off the event by stating his intentions of just sitting back and to just let the body of the formal proceedings speak for the past instead. He introduced the keynote speaker, the same research journalist who had spearheaded the entire process.

"Thank you Mr. President. It's an honor to have you present and share in the enormity of what took place 25 years ago today—as well as one day prior (agreement ratification). I also wish to thank you on behalf of all those who have so graciously choose to be with us here today, those who once as former enemies experienced events of an unprecedented nature. Mr. President, I'll also wager history itself thanks you for having declassified the details of a pivotal incident, one that took place so many years back finally bringing to light its truth."

"I am also both overwhelmed and humbled by the display of bravery seated before me, exhibited by the evidence of their past dedication in carrying out duties for their respective nations. A quarter century ago, these servicemen of opposing sides wore their courage through their commitment to what they believed in, but sadly needed to do so unrecognized in a world where the distrust between two powerful nations caused men of the same level of valor the need to hunt each other from opposite sides of an Iron Curtain. They did so to assure the security of their respective nations, translated to ensuring the safety of their loved ones back home. Men of both nations—you bravely carried out your duties in the stealth of the silent service, warranting the need to distrust each other and thereupon act upon your suspicions in stressful moments so that no non-submariner ever need imagine nor care to put themselves into such the same position as you have."

Upon his statement, the keynote speaker grinned, pointing out Dave, Linda, and Heather, the three seated together.

"—except those three over there who happened to hitch a ride inside the eye of Hurricane Gloria aboard a Soviet Alpha Class submarine."

Everyone broke out into laughter and then applause except for a dumbfounded Jim, who expressed his dismay in a soft drawn-out tone. "Holy shit Pamela." He did so, also slowly shaking his head in complete disbelief. "I know I didn't hear what I think I just heard. Damn, guys." Pamela in turn just sat smiling with goose pimples covering her body.

The speaker continued. "Sadly, two men admired by both their respective subordinates and bosses alike aren't with us today. Captain First Rank Vladimir Polivanova, as he was promoted from second rank before retirement, is seriously ill. He's presently at home quietly resting with his wife Natalya in the great city of St. Petersburg, Russia. Also a hard-nosed man of the old school, Rear Admiral Richardson, as most who knew him, passed away in 2004. His passing was surely a loss to his family, friends, and servicemen alike. Had both men been able to be with us here today, I feel most who knew them would agree that the two would have needed to been confined to opposite ends of these grounds to enable these proceedings to continue without the constant disruptions of their outbursts."

His comment mostly elicited a rise of polite laughter from the crowd that soon settled upon the speaker making an addendum to his previous statement.

"Hearing your reaction, I'm assuming then it'll probably surprise to know that in 1998 the retired Rear Admiral tracked down the former commander Vladimir Polivanova and visited him in Saint Petersburg, whereas their next and final rendezvous took place in Tallahassee, Florida. Apparently, the retired Rear Admiral needed to understand why the Second Rank felt compelled to pick up a distressed American family in his prized nuclear submarine, not withstanding having done so while conducting a secret mission. Apparently, the two had mellowed in their later years, and their collective wisdom eventually overcame their previous feelings of hostilities." The speaker's last statement eventually raised a stir in the audience and then shortly afterwards, a gradual applause.

"Thought that would catch your attention. So, on behalf of all of us who have arranged this including the President, and with the necessary added cooperation extended by several of the nations once comprising the Soviets Union, we wish for the comfort of your former commander and solemnly send our prayers his way."

Next came a surprise for the Costas, and Heather no less.

"If it is okay with you men who served under him, both the United States and Russian government have both agreed to co-sponsor a Costa family trip to St. Petersburg in visit of your beloved former commander."

Polivanova's former crew, including several who were not of Russian descent, shrugged their shoulders in an okay manner. They did so while exchanging looks of puzzlement at each other. Their bewildered reactions were in believing they didn't have any say in such a matter. Linda the meanwhile became filled with joy upon hearing the news, expressing it with tears and hugs to Dave and Heather, the two seated next to her.

Finding the keynote speaker banal at times in his approach, Dave whispered loudly before getting elbowed in the ribs by Linda. "Unless you have a vomit bag, I hope this guy's not going to turn this formal proceeding into some freaking high-level love fest."

The speaker continued. "Okay. We all didn't come this far just to hear me speak all day. But before I hand the mike over to the former Captain Lieutenant Talkovskaia, I want to emphasize that the purpose of this event is to bring to light a fascinating story of both brave servicemen conducting their duties and the difference a family about to succumb to utter hopelessness were able to make in history thanks to a card playing soviet submarine commander. This is meant in everyway to be a feel-good moment, so if you all instead end up fist fighting outside in the parking lot to settle some old scores upon the gavel being sounded, then at least for now can we all hold onto these more civilized proceedings—*here now?*"

The crowd laughed again but this time less so, and mostly out of politeness. Dave in turn just placed his fingertips on his forehead, looking downward and shaking his head in disbelief. He did so softly muttering as the speaker continued. "'Here now?' Hear ye? Ozey, ozey, ozey? This guy's freaking killing me," he commented.

"While part of history is built on many feel good moments—the more trying times, whether it be our early Patriots having suffered starvation in a bitter winter at Valley Forge or our dedicated men and women presently serving in both Iraq and Afghanistan—or in the case of the former Soviet state, both its brave and resilient citizens of both St. Petersburg and Stalingrad (Volgograd) and the Red Army alike who endured so much suffering during the Great Patriotic War (WWII) in defiance of an evil Third Reich—the collective misery of those deplorable times was far more of a painful burden to those who needed to endure them than ever the joy spawned from the freedom granted by their sacrifice to their beneficiaries. Therefore when the world can function somewhere between the bliss and tragedy as an ongoing continuum, then under those best conditions can we all expect and hope to be able to live our lives and raise our children within a general peace that can be afforded somewhere in the median. Your bravery in a hostile environment beneath the waves has assured us of that. So let's both savor and embrace this feel-good moment and kick things off with our first witness to the past."

Dave whispered in Linda's ear. "For someone who did such a brilliant job at bringing this whole thing together, man this guy sucks at speech writing."

Linda hushed him, to which he brushed it off, adding, "if he said St. Petersburg, then he should have said Volgograd, not Stalingrad. The man's facts are not time consistent. I'll only give the guy kudos on mentioning our guys in the Middle East."

Suffering from a stifling case of a bout of pre-stage jitters, Linda responded with a familiar look of displeasure. Getting the hint, Dave slipped in one more comment. "Hey, its not my fault this guy sucks."

To the audience's undivided attention, everyone slated to speak gave their rendition of what took place in 1985. As a result of stage fright, a nervous Linda spoke briefly while Dave in turn didn't have any difficulty giving his angle of the whole experience. In doing so, he omitted the consideration of carrying out euthanasia prior to being rescued. Such a dark, gnawing dead zone that had been eating him away like a cancer since the incident was one he had every intention of taking to his grave. Therefore, divulging such personal feelings for the whole world to learn concurrent to his family was the last thing on his agenda. Although he did do so to the shock of Polivanova in his quarters, it was only while under the influence of alcohol and still in a state of shock.

In ending, Dave did his part of warming the crowd up to his daughter. He did so, spending a few extra minutes conducting an impromptu piece, giving witness to both her quick thinking and nurturing acts of bravery as a young eight-year-old.

"So as you know by now, when it came to stepping up to bat, she was the Babe Ruth of our family—and apparently still is, which is why we're all here. In reading a remarkable piece of literature written by a remarkable individual, my daughter Heather, who I couldn't be anymore proud of, will conclude our witness to the watershed event being celebrated today—one which took place two and a half decades ago. I'll let you take it from here, honey."

Approaching the podium, a vibrant and polished 33-year-old Heather hugged her dad as he surrendered the floor to her. She did so to an uproar that rang out from the group of aging former Soviet Russian officers as if they were twenty-five years younger. These were the men she had charmed for the short duration aboard their submarine. Her presences there gave them a little taste of home during their isolation at sea.

In spite of Heather's notable presence, Polivanova's former men still viewed her as the same eight-year-old girl they remembered from years back. Appreciating their enthusiasm, she was no less humbled by their reception, and almost to the point of tears. In response to their expression, she couldn't help but to laugh out loud, thanking the men along with everyone else for their warm reception. Heather did so repeatedly until able to lower the volume of their praise by repeatedly attempting to speak out loud, the crowd eventually allowing her to do so.

Felt excluded, Jim stood and shouted. "Heather, I love you!"

Quickly realizing doing so was grossly inappropriate in such a formal and prestigious State affair, he turned a shade of red before cowering back into his seat next to Pamela, who was covering her own face with her hands in avoidance of recognition.

Again Heather laughed, responding affectionately. "Thank you Mr. Woodson, I love you too." As a young adult, Dave had explained to her the firm stance Jim took prior to leaving the Verde Islands back in 1985. From then on she always held a special place in her heart for his selfless act.

Keeping her massage brief like her dad, any axiom suggesting a last speaker's message has any less of impact on listeners due to attention fatigue was about to be dispelled. She proved it in her conclusion.

"I'll end by introducing a piece of hand scribed text written by an extraordinary individual of whom we're all familiar."

Heather then gave a brief synopsis of how the writing fell into her hands, pointed out the three siblings in recognition of it. She was also able to prepare the crowd without raising any suspicions in her mother, especially giving twenty-five years later Linda could have never fathomed the idea that some bottle she tucked away back in 1985, mid-ocean, would suddenly make its appearance as the focal point of some State sponsored event.

Invoking anticipation throughout an eager audience in wait, she disappointed no one. "I dedicate this message to the woman who composed it—Dad?"

In orchestration of the scene, it was Dave's cue to retrieve the original wine bottle secured beneath Heather's vacant seat, the note slightly protruding.

"Mom, remember this? This bottle either became freed up when I imagine Gloria's propane tank eventually exploded or maybe the fire beforehand—or maybe it fell out the companionway when that wave lifted us vertically. Remember that—when Dad couldn't find me afterwards?"

Still able to remember his disturbing nightmare from years back, Jim uttered softly. "Holy shit guys, this is creepy on so many levels." As a whole, the entire process was coming across as surreal to him.

Reaching to embrace Dave, Linda immediately began shaking with a chorus of emotions stirring inside.

"Mom, this is the same letter you said you wrote when I was with David and while Dad was hanging off the side of the boat. I hope you don't mind, but I feel there's no words that our more purer in emotion than the ones written here." She then beamed for a moment in continuing. "You should have never encouraged me to attend law school if you didn't wish to be blindsided like this in front of the world. I'll let your letter do the rest of the speaking."

Several days leading to the ceremony, Heather was able to make use of the time to canvass the note endlessly in an attempt to build some degree of immunity to the poignant effect of its raw message. Doing so initially helped her cause until the contagiousness of the crowd's reactions eventually overwhelmed her as well. Along with the notes chillingly dark and brutal realism, its candid message was both passionate and deep in soul in its appeal for the substantiation of ones family's subsistence as a desperate mother. Heather ended her part of the limelight, there laboring to slip the words past the emotional strain of her voice.

"I would imagine had Shakespeare been given an opportunity to canvass such a letter, doing so might have inspired yet another play added to the anthology of his works. Thank you everyone. This has been an honor."

Heather couldn't have chosen any more of a fitting means of punctuating the ceremony. The quiet left in the wake of her reading was eventually broken when a solemn President interceded.

"Heather, the honor was ours. And thank you Linda for having presenting all us present here a view into the window of your soul. Unfortunately my executive powers aren't substantial enough for securing a spot for your heartfelt letter in the National Achieves next to our beloved Declaration of Independence. But I have a feeling its distinction of Shakespearean influence has likely already earned it a place ingrained in Americana, and who knows, maybe someday the Smithsonian."

The President then gave his parting words before inviting all those present to remain for an impressive State cuisine.

With everyone generally conglomerated around an impressive array of food and grouped in small cliques, the President the meanwhile made his rounds. He did so, shaking hands with anyone connected to the workings of twenty-five years earlier. It would include the Woodsons, who Dave made sure were next to him and Linda as he worked his way towards their old friends.

For many directly connected with the incident relabeled: "*Inside Gloria Declassified*", the collective body of facts that was presented the previous hour was still lodged in the throats of many like peanut butter in a dry mouth. It therefore made a bowl of a mildly spiked punch the beverage of choice for washing away whatever anxieties of which might have resurfaced during that time. Only a few select individuals had been privileged beforehand to the body of information that was presented at the ceremony, and even then it was only revealed to them on a need to know basis. It was therefore only through the process by which everything was presented as a collective piece that everyone was able to become aware of their place in a puzzle of extraordinary events that almost led to a third world war a quarter century earlier.

Still in shock, Jim joined Pamela in a beeline to their old friends. The four of them hadn't been together in any capacity for over two decades. Virtually speechless, he squared off to Dave, there taken a moment to find some fitting words.

"You communist sympathizer, you. I would have never pegged you as one, bro."

"Sorry buddy." Dave laughed in response, explaining. "This was the main reason we drifted from you guys. I was afraid of a slipup. This whole thing was just way so much larger than any of us."

"Understatement to the max. And to think I was worried sick about you guys during the hurricane when the whole time you were joyriding with the *Red October*."

After hugging both the Costas, Pamela continued holding both Linda's hands. "Are you okay, sweetie? I missed you so much." The two were in tears.

"Pam it's been years, and speaking of which, if you have any vacant rooms at your hotel, we might need a vacation after all this. That's of course after we cater to an American public that I imagine will expect us to do so. I guess this is our fifteen minutes of fame, and it still hasn't even sunk in yet."

"In that case, we better book you for January," Jim interrupted. "The Paparazzis will be all over you guys like flies all over shit."

Dave grinned. "See you haven't loss your touch with words, buddy. But now that we're on the subject, since the State's flipping the tab for St Petersburg, would you mind joining us? For years now I've been itching for any opportunity of being able to speak to the Second Rank Captain Polivanova again, and damn, this just fell on our laps. I want you to meet the guy. I know that's a bit of a financial nut to ask of you, but since our tab's covered, there's no reason we can't cover yours."

Jim communicated with Pamela through a nod before turning back to his old friend.

"Our answer is yes to the trip, but no to you paying our way. But thanks for the gesture though. We just need to keep Pam and Linda separated on the trip. I mean look, they're holding hands already."

Linda backhanded her old friend's abdomen which wasn't as conditioned to absorb such a strike as it was years back.

The President then came over and greeted everybody. Upon him engaging in a little small talk with the group and continuing on, a dazed husband of Heather approached the four friends afterwards, shaking his head in disbelief.

"When Heather had told me we were coming to Washington, I thought it just was for some sightseeing. Now she's over there speaking with a bunch of former Soviet submariners, and I just shook hands with the President. This is awesome."

Linda jumped in. "You mean it didn't raise an eyebrow when she made that sudden trip to Illinois?"

"No, I swear. She just told me her trip was related to some case. Man, my wife can sure keep a secret."

"Then you better check her PC to make sure she's not keeping any more," Jim asserted.

While Heather's husband, Lenny, laughed at his comment and agreed in jest, Linda instead took exception.

"It's shit like that that makes me just want to wrap my fingers around your neck. You just met the man."

"It's okay, Mom."

"Don't try playing mediator with those two," Dave jumped in. "Even I still haven't figured them out after thirty-five years—and counting, apparently."

"Yeah, and I've known Dave even longer, and today I just find out that he was some kind of communist sympathizer—or maybe still is. Go figure." Jim then took notice of Lenny grappling with the significance of what he was implying. "It was Cold War thing. You had to be there."

Dave grinned. "Buddy, just give it a break. That's some old school humor. And besides, if I am some kind of a communist sympathizer as you claim, then I guess I'm one who just got you introduced to the President—so bada bing!" he interjected in ending.

"Oh by the way, that was pretty awesome. Thanks, bro"

"Yeah, don't get use to it."

Dave then placed his arm over Jim's shoulder with the intent of visiting some of Polivanova's former men.

"Excuse me ladies. Brother, if you're going to be visiting St Petersburg with us, then you need to meet some friends of mine I've been dying to introduce you to."

"Bro—no you're not"

"I don't get it. You must have had guests at your hotel from some of the former states of the Soviet Union. What's the problem?"

"And you're right—I have. The problem is I know these guys in particular might have had me in their crosshair at one time or another. I can only guess."

"And you them. So let me understand this. Three decades hasn't changed anything for you?"

"I never really gave it much thought until I found out who those guys next to me were, and then heard them whispering amongst each other. It gave me the freaking creeps. I mean I spent two years underwater afraid even to fart too loud, and next thing you know I'm surrounded by the guys."

"Oh," Dave reacted, choosing then to keep his part of his seating arrangements under wraps. "When all said and done though, all of us back home were also in their crosshairs all those years with the threat of nuclear annihilation, you know?"

"Not the same, bro. I'm sure you didn't dwell on it every freaking moment while submerged—underwater—twenty-four seven."

"Granted, so are you still okay with St. Petersburg then? I would understand otherwise."

"Ah don't worry, I'll suck up whatever I need to suck up. I mean I feel like I'm amidst some sort of crazy epic right now. I'd be nuts to pass up such an opportunity of a lifetime."

"Are you still willing then to join me over there with some of Polivanova's former men? I owe them my life."

"In that case—sure. But this isn't going to be easy for me, so understand that."

"Just don't fart and I'll be okay," Dave grinned, then thanking his friend.

"Don't worry, brother—not even an SBD. I suppose when all said and done, I guess I owe those guys a debt of gratitude as well. I mean I would have been devastated had I never heard from you guys again." The two began walking towards Polivanova's former subordinates when Jim added, softly speaking. "Missed you, man."

<< CHAPTER 12 >>

BOTH THE COSTAS and Woodsons were once again relishing being together like old times. Filled with anticipation, they all stood waiting in a hotel lobby that was located in a historical section of St. Petersburg, Russia. Spoiled by a milder Cape Verde climate back home, the Woodsons needed to prepare themselves for some bone chilling rain accompanied by raw forty-five degree air blowing in off the wings of Finsky bay.

"Bro," Jim jested in his discontent. "You've picked a fine time for visiting this city. St. Pete, Florida would have been more like it."

"Pussy." Linda interjected.

Jim then added, "By the way you two, I can't believe you guys were in cahoots with each other on the seating arrangements at the ceremony. That was messed up, thank you."

Linda gave Dave a leer of disapproval to which he was briefly caught off guard. "Oh, you told him, huh?" she asserted.

"No, you just did, honey." Dave came back, adding, "Sorry about that bro. It seemed funny at the time. I really am sorry."

It was silent for a moment as an air of awkwardness filled the room.

Jim let it play out before finally admitting with a slight grin, "Heather told me about it after the ceremony. I was hoping to bust your chops about it, but that was awesome."

Dave came back, "Touché, brother. That was good."

Linda was less impressed. "Bitch."

To disappointment of everyone, Heather's absence from the group was the result of her involvement with a trial while David's nonappearance was a conscious effort of defiance on his part. While both parents had let the likes of their son's elusive behavior go unchecked in the past, they finally confronted him on the matter with Linda expressing her disapproval. She did so as a quiet Dave lent his support through an unwavering stare.

"If you want to go on for the rest of your life hating your dad and torturing me in the process with your freaking indifference for what happened twenty-five years ago, then go ahead. But refusing to see the man who saved your life, maybe even at the cost of his career, and jail time as well—then you're on your own there, you asshole! I've had enough of this self-centered, infantile attitude of yours. I'm over it! So grow up already and start acting like a real adult for a change!" David just stood stunned, unable to conjure any response. He also knew better than making any attempt.

"Oh, by the way David, as your mother I've always loved you unconditionally and still wouldn't think twice before jumping in front of a speeding truck for you. It's just that at the moment I really don't like you very much, and you can only blame yourself for that—not us!"

While it pained the parents to be taking such a firm stance, it was also the first time they had ever shook the fence to such an excessive degree regarding their son. It left the next step of any rectification of their parent/son relationship in David's hands. It was also the last time they heard from him since then, leading to the juncture.

With the exception of Dave, whose nerves were overshadowed by anticipation, the other three adults waited anxiously for their expected Russian guide to show up. He was assigned to escort them in their visit to the former commander's communal apartment.

A kommunalki as it was called in Russia, Polivanova's dwelling was one of countless such places that were constructed throughout the tenure of the Soviet several decade reign as the result of the regime's prohibition of private ownership. His was constructed under Nikita Khrushchev's seat atop the Communist party. Their cramped living space like so many others were ones where whole families occupying a single room also needed to share the same kitchen, laundry room, and a cramped bathroom with others. Such restroom facilities that were typically crude at best, seldom exuded any sense of cleanliness. As a whole, a kommunalki posed little reprieve to anyone wishing just to be able to retreat back and seek seclusion. Prior the 1991 collapse of the Soviet Union, conditions in such dwellings would have been evermore unpleasant, as multiple families would have likely needed to coexist in the same already cramped living spaces. In such common settings, privacy was a luxury difficult to come by.

The guide ushered everyone to his small vehicle upon arriving at the hotel lobby. Dealing with the outside elements meant coping with an uninviting, raw climate awaiting them. Soon all five adults were tightly squeezed into the cramped interior of their guide's boxy sedan.

"Jim, being squashed in here together feels familiar [Reference to his old Volvo], except we've all gained a little weight since Eighty-five."

"Thanks for reminding me of that," Linda came back. "Women love being reminded of their weight."

"I'm sorry I don't have big car like you in America," the guide added, having also taken exception.

Hoping to meet them again someday, Dave had learned Russian out of respect for his rescuers. It finally paid off in being able to speak with some of Polivanova's former officers in attendance at the ceremony. Unlike with their first encounter, the same men later embraced him at the State event while also appreciating being spoken to in their native language—as broken as his Russian was. Such dialogue played out while Jim just stood in shock, having only learned about it then.

"I mean not disrespect, Sergei you," Dave responded in defense, attempting Russian. "Your car like my American friend Volvo we all crowded in years before." He then grinned, adding, "Later, we go out and have four-way on ocean."

"[English] Ah, a four-way! [Russian] You guys sound like fun Americans."

"Not so many anytime, Sergei," Dave laughed, still attempting Russian, "I think you'd need lot of vodka before stomaching see our fat bare derriere."

"Dave, I hope you didn't say what I think you just did," Linda objected, having only caught onto Sergei's spoken English.

"Sergei meant a four person sedan, honey. It all gets screwed up in the translation, right Sergei?"

"Your equivocation sucks by the way. Like 'four person' and 'four-way' mean the same thing in Russian. You're so full of shit. How do you say, 'you're so full of shit' in Russian?"

The guide enjoyed the infighting that was taking place, siding with Linda.

"I sorry comrade, it don't matter what language you speak—bullshit is bullshit."

"(English) Thank you for having my back there, Sergei," Dave responded in a defeated manner.

The escort just grinned, responding with his a strong Russian accent. "Anything for my American guest—anything, my comrade."

In preparing the four friends for what might shock them inside, the guide took on a more serious tone in approaching Polivanova's communal complex. There were strict rules that were formulated by design of necessity giving the presence of so many tenants crowded together in such a confined living area. It was to avoid any intentional or unintentional incident of someone overstepping the boundaries of another occupant's assumed rights or privacy, to what little there was of the latter. Such an occurrence stood to pose unpleasant to any perpetrator, especially in a case where the guilty party might be unaware of any such misstep.

Approaching Polivanova's rundown building, bland at best, almost institution like, both Dave and Jim's minds began racing with similar thoughts. The two were strongly acquainted with twentieth century Soviet history and the many plights its people needed to endure throughout its long tenure. In approaching the unkempt structure, a lingering vestige of a nation that invoked so much fear to much of the Western World for over four decades of the Cold War, images the meanwhile stemmed from accounts learnt throughout their lives began flooding the minds of the two history buffs. The two friends had grown up in an environment where the Soviet Union filled the general population of the Free World with an underlining sense of doom at less than a half hour's notice, especially those living in the United States. Soon standing in place and waiting at the entrance of the building, the two friends also understood most the fear the US and USSR brought about to the remaining world was a result of their own paranoia towards each other. Those that lived outside of both countries stood to become collateral damage if any unfortunate all-out nuclear exchange ever did take place between the two powerful enemies. It was a madness that only seemed to have made sense to both the United States and the Soviet Union. Though risky, it did prevent a third conventional world war from ever taken place between the two nations.

Dave and Jim were in meditation at the sight of the old building, one in which it and so many others akin to it were shrouded from the likes of them in secrecy behind the Iron Curtain for so many years. While any local might just view the structure, the meanwhile thinking nothing extraordinary about it, the two history junkies were instead awestruck. Projecting back, they each visualized how many times during Stalin's rule and thereafter Nikita Khrushchev's reign, that some poor hardworking and unsuspecting citizens might have heard an unexpected assertive knock at night just to then be abruptly arrested by some KGB agents. Such an event in which the assumed individuals might have then found themselves either subjected to an indefinite sentence of harsh incarceration in some inhumane gulag or instead the victim of the wrong end of an executioner's pistol—either case might have been an instance where the unfortunate citizen was either victim to some fabricated story concocted by someone aiming to gain favor with a local ruling party, or instead their punishment may have been a preemption to an assured compliance of civil-obedience with the consideration of ones state of innocence weighed as a non-factor.

Such reflection of an old building that stuck the two friends as time forgotten couldn't help but evoke them into hearing echoes of frightened family members in a state of extreme anxiety—them screaming while someone who only minutes earlier was asleep and nestled in their arms was suddenly being dragged away, possibly never to be seen again. Such type of activity was behind some of the pain Polivanova once expressed to Dave in speaking of his feelings about his former leader. The building standing before them was mostly spared of such activity due to its time of construction, but it still didn't prevent the imaginations of either of the two friends from wandering to such thoughts.

In entering Polivanova's building, the four friends walked with deliberation. They mimicked their escort's cue in an effort of not offending anyone going about their daily business. En route, a young man in his late twenties recognized Dave from a short clip he had seen on TV. It prompted him to get Sergie's verification of it. Grinning, the guide glanced to Dave, who got the hint.

"(Russian) Yes that me. What your name?"

The surprised co-occupant approached Dave, greeting him in Russian. "Ivan. Ivan Talesnik." Shaking his hand with enthusiasm, he continued. "I never meet an American, and finally when I do, they're a fucking American celebrity."

"(Russian) Thank you, but not me, Ivan. I was in bad place at bad time. Besides, back house, someone like me got forgotten pretty fast." Grinning, he added, "In fact, they already been." Meanwhile in witnessing the dialogue playing out, the guide just stood quietly as a bystander, amused by Dave's attempt of speaking his language.

As the result of the young man's interaction, the group's nerves were somewhat put at ease. In making their way to Vladimir's door, his wife Natalya came out to meet them in the hallway in hearing their approach. In her mid-sixties, the distant look in her eyes seemed the only sign of life peering through the hardened exterior of her face. Their windows bore the scars of time's misgivings, forever harbored. Inept to speaking English, she joined forces with Sergei, as the two ventured away from the others to speak in private.

Meanwhile, some of the thoughts previously reflected by the two friends of a historical nature were being replaced by a more human sense of realism. It hit home to them that the place where they were now standing wasn't so much some historical relic of the past, but was instead simply a place its present occupants called 'home'.

A slight clamminess intensified by the rain exacerbated many smells of which anyone non-acclimated to them couldn't help but to notice. It affected Jim the most. For years after leaving the Navy, he still carried some degree of animosity towards his former Soviet counterparts as an osmotic effect of time spent below the ocean surface learning to distrust faces he never saw. Those longtime rooted feelings were beginning to erode under the stark realism of his present surroundings.

In returning with Sergei, Natalya first entered her apartment alone to make certain it was okay for the others to do so. There, the former commander could be heard responding to his wife with a distinctly potent but of late, a somewhat raspier voice than that of years back. Still so familiar to both Dave and Linda, it sent shivers through the two of them, briefly taking them both back.

"Yes Natalya, please let them in. If I died before they entered, then that would be tragic, no?"

Heavyhearted, she castigated the former commander with an air of affection in understanding it was only a matter of a short time before his ailment was destined to render her a widow.

"Vladimir! Don't talk such nonsense. Someone like you lives forever." She then pulled back before exiting, surrendering the door for her four guests to enter their stifling, single room. They all did, the four slowly filing forward tender footed towards the former commander. Pointing out four prearranged borrowed chairs, a somewhat irritable yet still warm Vladimir encouraged the group in. He was in frame but a shell of a man in comparison to the one they remembered from years back.

The former commander spoke, this time in English. "You do not have to walk as if you're in some minefield. I have cirrhosis of the liver, not some high explosive strapped to my old hairy ass. Please be seated and make yourselves comfortable. At least someone in this room will be." Upon everyone taking their places, he continued. "My American friends. You sure look better than you did years back when you came aboard my vessel. Please introduce me to these friends of yours."

Seated uncomfortably in their respective seats post making their acquaintances, everyone settled into their rickety chairs. Dave was positioned closest to Vladimir's head with Linda seated next to him. The former commander then took over.

"That was a hell of a ride we went on back in the day. Sorry my captain lieutenant was not watching where he was going." Upon a labored laugh, he continued. "Look who I am talking to. You didn't even see a hurricane the size of Europe coming your way. Anyways, when I suddenly awoke airborne, hearing the siren and that ghastly screaming sound of our two hulls scraping up against each other, I nearly shit my blues."

Vladimir's comments about his fearful reaction surprised his four guests. Lying in an inclined position of pillows and blankets, he took notice of their expressions, especially the Costas'. Projecting back to the encounter of Golovkin's shooting incident, both Linda and Dave were still able to remember how relatively composed the former commander appeared, both in the midst of his vessel's extreme peril and during the shooting event itself.

"What is it? Just because I was a commander meant I should not have experienced fear in the face of such calamity? Fear doesn't label a man a coward. It's a natural instinct to danger, and a sinking submarine is every sub-dweller's worse nightmare. I am confident even after a quarter century you two still shutter in remembering the sensation of my vessel sinking. I will also wager you that still remember the frightening sound of the increasing pressures that were being exerted onto our hull from outside. That shit could be heard throughout my vessel."

Dave had introduced Jim as a former submarine dweller, causing Polivanova to conclude, "Right James—one of a submariner's worst nightmare?"

Jim nodded in agreement. "Your men had told us about it at the ceremony. How far below were you submerged before your vessel began its recovery? I missed the amount at the ceremony."

"Over 800 meters, my friend. That translates to over a half-mile for you Americans, if that makes it any clearer."

Jim was quiet for a moment before responding. "Holy shit! I guess I heard right then."

"Don't fault yourself. Such an unnerving depth is still difficult for me to fathom even to this day, especially considering the damaged sustained to the aft of my vessel. Please excuse me for being quick on the matter, but I would rather we change the subject."

"I hear you there. I prefer not thinking about it myself."

In spite of the improbability of such a get-together, Dave had always wished for the likes of such a meeting with Polivanova ever since speaking with him last in existing his submarine. He imagined doing so with a man he viewed larger than life might pan out as some enlightening experience. However, as far as a drugged-up Vladimir was concerned, his primary agenda for their get-together was to see how the couple he saved years earlier was doing and to bid them a general farewell.

Dave quickly ascertained the former commander's less than spiritual state in bringing up the subject of fate. Before releasing him to the US Navy years earlier, he had so adamantly conveyed his views on the subject. Giving the circumstances at the time, Dave still believed the former commander might have been holding out on some deeper wisdom related to his speech about destiny back then. He did so in believing there were so many other profound subjects of actual relevance that Polivanova could have elaborated on in their parting.

"Commander, remember pulling me aside and explaining how you don't believe in a predetermined fate, but instead you live by the truth that everything that has occurred beforehand whether it be our own actions or the random progression of existence itself brings us all up to the moment where we now exist? Have you giving that anymore thought?"

"Dude, that's heavy," a serious Jim added.

The former commander belted a cynical laugh. "Yes, comrade. You drink vodka non-stop for over four years and almost lose your family. Then later in life you find out your liver has the consistency of rancid beef. Is that what you meant?"

Believing this unique man who he always held in such iconic esteem might shed some new light on the subject, those weren't any of the words of wisdom Dave had been hungering for, for so many years. Nearly speechless, he yielded to Vladimir's blunt sense of reality in responding to his cynical comment.

"Yes Commander—I see."

"Dave, please call me Vladimir. You see my own country doesn't recognize me as a commander, so there's no reason you should. But thanks for your gesture anyhow. That is what I always liked about you and your family. You were always respectable. Before that, it was my belief that arrogance was endemic of most Americans."

Dave grinned. "Oh, we have our share back home, but you know very well Commander—sorry—I meant Vladimir, that when one props themselves with arrogance, their eventual fall's so much harder to absorb. An over sense of entitlement seems to be more the case with some of my American folk back home, not so much arrogance—and it's too bad. I mean it's those people specifically that taint what is generally a population of good hardworking folk back home. It's the obnoxious ones unfortunately who get their share of attention because of their foul behavior. And besides, giving our position aboard your ship, we weren't about to boast any demands of any entitled nature. That's for sure." He then grinned. "Although in our position back then, I presently know losers back home who would have been ungrateful and foolish enough to have done so back then."

"Losers—I like that. And those people you speak of—those are the types I would have enjoyed being able to attach to the outside my submarine just to see how much of a descent it would take for their fucking heads to finally implode. But then again, stones don't implode, do they?" The former commander then shook his head in disgust. "Unmerited entitlement is so contemptuous to those who have earned their grade. I loath those type of people."

The former commander eventually focused his attention to the others, inquiring about their lives. The discussion of David Jr. came up as a result of questioning his and Heather's whereabouts. It was after having changed the painful subject away from the mention of his own late son. The four friends then noticed the ailing former commander appearing nauseous by his increased fidgeting, so in believing he needed rest, Dave made mention of it. He was also concerned about overstaying their welcome.

In spite his discomfort, Vladimir viewed it differently. In feeling their get-together was likely the final chapter of his life, he was wishing just to hang on to the moment for a little while longer. Feeling the dark curtains of mortality being closed on him, he was therefore becoming increasingly uneasy about it. It went along with being saddened about what his death would mean to his wife afterwards.

"What ever happened to that undercover KGB officer after you shot him?" Dave asked. "Did that asshole have you arrested for that?"

The former commander contemplated for a moment, eventually giving into a long time conviction held fast to in keeping silent about the event of his arrest. He had only done so with the retired Richardson upon their first visit with him, and out of respect the rear admiral graciously carried his secret to his grave.

"My American friend. Golovkin was out of line, and I hated that he was so in spite of being KGB. KGB or not, I was the commander of that submarine, and no one presides over my orders aboard my vessel. That asshole thought he could assume such authority, yet when we were sinking and needed his services most, he cowered in posture like some fleeing cockroach. For that I say you can speak disapprovingly of the man. But there is something I need to tell you which I have nothing to lose in doing so here in my deathbed."

Troubled by his tailing statement, Dave asked, "What's that, Vladimir?"

Contrary to a general belief, the State event that had brought so many players of the 1985 events together wasn't in entirety the divulgement that it was intended to be.

"Golovkin did not have me arrested for that incident, but instead only testified against me for something his duties required him to. I cannot blame him for that. Remember when I explained to you in my quarters that I needed confirmation from my headquarters for authorization of your rescue, which by the way is why we waited so long before actually coming for you? That was a half-truth."

Giving the length of time that was lapsed, Dave needed to think for a moment before finally answering. "Yes sir, now I remember you saying that. But I'm confused. I don't understand what that has to do with Golovkin."

"That is because I have not finished. You see Dave, Golovkin was nothing more than a high-ranking witness to my crime against the state. I left him and anyone else in his position no recourse. You see, I asked for clearance from headquarters to rescue you, but never actually received any. Because the storm was approaching and time was of the essence, I felt I had no choice but to order the rescue of you and your family, prior clearance or not." Vladimir continued as the stunned listeners clung to his every word.

"The state later denied my plea which I initially attempted to pawn off as some propaganda that my country might be able to exploit in the world of public opinion. You see, glasnost was finally materializing out of the ashes of Stalin's death. It took a few decades for it to finally become embodied into the movement you Americans came to know in the late Eighties. Even though I was never big on politics, I always did enjoy a good strategy of cards." Noticing the wheels spinning in Dave's head, he commented, "looks like you need to say something, comrade. What is it?"

The four friends were still stunned by the former commander's admission, and in addition Jim was still laboring to absorb that the events being discussed actually ever took place at all. Vladimir's new detail only further deepened a saga that already had it share of both depth and drama. Meanwhile Dave and Linda were greatly humbled in not feeling worthy of such a demonstration of self-sacrifice.

"Vladimir, I just don't know what to say. I thank God for every moment we were spared of the hurricane, but why did you rescue us without authorization if you knew doing so would ruin your career—never mind bring hardship on your family?"

"Two reasons, and the first was for my country. You see my friend, at the time I did not know why, but there seemed to be a heightened sense of tension within your American fleet. The core of my military instincts was the only evidence I needed. As a result, I felt getting caught by your people stood to cause further strain between our two nations, that verses the normal apprehension and humiliation which gets attached to getting cornered with your pants down in someone else's dominated waters."

The former commander spent a moment readjusting his pillows before continuing. "With the Cold War now being nothing more than something the newer generations can read about, I rescued you for my country. I figured your family stood to be a catalyst for averting any escalation that might ensue between our two nations. You see Dave, one thing us Soviets understood that you Americans just did not get was that the most effective medium of proliferating our propagandist agenda was the exploitation of the paranoia of your own people. With that stated, the core of my motivation was mostly just based on a hunch."

Dave grinned. "One hell of a hunch, Vladimir. Thanks on behalf of us—and the world as a whole."

"Ah, it was just a lucky hand. It could have backfired. With my leadership, it often did. What I'm saying is that your people seemed to be quite resourceful at responding to the many empty threats that our many propaganda campaigns use to paint, thereby, we often underestimated the creativity and resolve of your engineers, hence your F15 Eagle, Abrams tank—and yes that brutal beast of an aircraft you call the Warthog (A-10)."

Dave sat absorbed for a moment before responding. "Interesting to say the least. What was your other reason for rescuing us?"

"If a may be candid—had it been just you alone in that raft Dave, I might have just left you there in spite of later regrets. It was your two children that compelled me to question my own place in this world. I mean how could I leave a mother and two children to meet such a terrible death after all they had been through and then eventually go home to my own wife and children with any sense of justification? It was the first time in almost thirty years of service I was ever faced with such a personal and moral dilemma. I was not trained for the queerness of such an event. One more thing Dave that I hope you can remember me speaking of years back in my quarters. Seeing your son and daughter in such crisis took me back 1944. It was my opportunity to fulfill a destiny. I had no choice."

Dave appeared perplexed at first until the meaning of what Polivanova just mentioned sank in. It was a deep poignant feeling that gripped him with its profound relevance.

Linda the meanwhile was in tears and to no surprise, a still lachrymose Pamela as well. Dave reflected their feeling by stating his own. "I've always felt indebted for what you've done for us sir, and now if I could live yet another thousand years, I'd carry that same level of gratitude through every one of them."

Vladimir took notice of the girl's display of emotion.

"Ah my sweet ladies, there is no reason for weeping. To put it into perspective, I remember telling you Dave, I was never too fond of my former leader, Joseph Stalin. But he once did state something that had a cynically dark though true connotation to it in speaking of our incapacity of viewing human loss."

The former commander then waited out another sudden wave of nausea before continuing. This was after assuring the others he was okay.

"As I was about to say, our once former Party leader once stated that a single death is a tragedy—"

Without his objection, Dave joined in the latter half of Stalin's quote: "a million deaths is a statistic."

The former commander was impressed. "I am pleased to see that your scope of the world isn't just limited to the subcultures of Americana."

Both Dave and Jim were amused by his comment, whereas Linda, who was less educated to the former leader's dark history, wasn't.

"Sounded like a charming man," she stated with sarcasm.

"Interesting enough, I heard he could be quite charming at times. But one thing I learned early in life about charm is it is more often a self-serving trait rather than one of any virtue." Vladimir then moved his fingers as if feeling for his next thought.

"What I am trying to say is, while I understood all to well the scope of my duties and the terrible repercussions of carrying them out if necessary, in some ways the concept of the deadly force we were capable of carrying out at times seem only an abstract to me—too difficult to fathom. While it is difficult for me to imagine Stalin had any kind of honorable or enlightened objective to what he stated, it still seemed quite fitting to the psyche my duties. Then when I saw your family floating adrift, helpless, ready to meet a certain and terrible death, I knew right then that my life had just changed—rescue or no rescue. It just seemed too coincidental for me to accept your position as only some random event. Dave might be able to explain that to you later if he wishes, " Polivanova stated, directing his comment at Linda.

The former commander then focused his attention onto Jim. "I mean you no disrespect in referencing any of your comrades this way, but it would have been more burdensome for me to have felt the solemnity of having neutralized an enemy sub close by once the satisfaction of the kill was gone than it would have been for me to grasp a collective misery instilled into an entire population such as the US continent for instance being blanketing with hundreds of megatons of nuclear fire and radiation. That is mostly based on the understanding that the people who we have just destroyed would have been sub dwellers like ourselves in the case of the former."

"But I thought it was a fast-attack submarine you commanded," Jim commented. "I didn't think you had such a capability."

"But the ships we were commissioned to protect did, as I am

sure was the case with you. It was all a collective effort as with any military operation—" Polivanova then tittered before continuing. "—Please forgive me...your name...help me here."

"It's Jim, Vladimir, and I understand your point."

Dave then jumped in. "What about Golovkin? You were speaking of him."

"Oh, please excuse my tangents. Of him—I just didn't want you condemning the man for the wrong reasons. Had Golovkin lied for me, he too would have been held accountable. I had placed him in that position to testify against me because of my guilt. Because my means of achieving my goals were often of an unorthodox nature added to having made enemies higher up in the ranks over time, I was set up by having Golovkin oversee my methods." The former commander paused a moment, reflecting back.

"Not only did I not pass the test of my superiors, but apparently I failed miserably. I will say this though. Like him or not, I still have to give the man credit. I never suspected Golovkin was KGB. With all my training in body language and so forth, he still had me fooled." Polivanova belted out a quick laugh before continuing. "I thought the man was a wimp when in reality he was a highly skilled, well-seasoned killer. He was just out of his element cooped up in the confines of my ship with it sinking—unable to make any difference. Totally uncharacteristic though I must say—still do not fully understand it. It must have hit raw nerve with him that apparently he wasn't screened to coup with—his Achilles, I guess. Then again, who knows? Ten or five years earlier, maybe even just a year—I might have just left all of you out there to die. I hate to admit that, but that's a stone cold reality." Straining, Vladimir then grinned with pride. "You just happened to catch me on a good day."

Soon unable to mask his increasing discomfort any longer, the former commander finally admitted to needing his rest. He also wished to speak to Dave alone before doing so. Upon giving their thanks and heartfelt bids of farewell in leaving with Linda's in particular being highly charged with emotion, soon she and the Woodsons were all standing just outside of its entrance, there patiently waiting while crowded together in a manner so not to infringe on anyone else's space.

Inside, the former commander spoke. "I know what it's like to have a heavy heart about your son. I loss mine, and only in death I may see him again. That in turn leaves my wife alone to fend for herself. That is harsh, but life's ironies and paradoxes can often seem cruel and unfair. I may not show it in my voice, but my heart is just as sick over this as is my liver, my friend. About your son— you took on the burden of blame for your wife as she mentioned, and I believe you having done so was both wise and self-sacrificing on your part. I mentioned my son because he is gone now, and a part of me died with him on that terrible day I lost him. Your son is still alive. Take care of yourself so you may have more time in this world. And who knows? Maybe someday he might come around. That means easing up on that stomach rot tequila shit. Hell, look at what vodka's done to me."

"Oh, I've already done that, sir—a long time ago."

A labored grin, Vladimir continued. "Good—now you've got a fighting chance. And as far as your son is concerned, he can choose to feel scorned at you forever for what happened twenty-five years ago, but that doesn't mean he should hate you. As long as you've attempted to reach out or at least not repudiated him as I guess you haven't, then he will someday need to come to terms with the fact that his father is only human. That means he can't spend the rest of his life using self-pity to torture you. Do not let him either. If he ever throws it in your face again, stand your ground, comrade."

"Thanks for that advice and your concern. It may interest you to know that Linda seems to have done a pretty effective job of doing that a couple of weeks ago when we both finally confronted him on the matter. Unfortunately we haven't heard anything from our son since we last confronted him that day."

"I regret hearing that, but you can't save your son though enabling his foul behavior. That means you may have already done all you can for now. Just remember, he is an adult just like yourself and needs to man up to his responsibilities, as I am sure you have throughout your adult life. So start living your life again comrade, and let him make the next move. I will end our discussion by saying to you man to man, it has been an honor to get to know you. I am a better person because our paths have crossed, and yes, although our association with each other may have initially been that of a symbiotic one I must admit, that changed even before you ever left my submarine."

Vladimir then rested his hand on Dave's and squeezed it.

"Maybe someday you and I will meet in a better place, but for the time being your purpose in this world requires you be here while mine has seemed to have run its course. Apparently, I sealed that fate many years back. Wish your lovely wife well for me, and send Heather my love too. I hope maybe someday you may also be able to relay the same message to David as well. Meanwhile—goodbye comrade and live well."

Feeling a strong burning in his throat, Dave stood, paused, and then approached Vladimir, kissing him on the cheeks three times. Before exiting, he handed the former commander the same sheath that contained his mariners knife which he in turn had given back to him upon leaving his submarine year's prior.

"Please keep this. It means a lot to me."

In leaving, Dave's exit left Vladimir quiet—grinning. "That overly sentimental, crazy American." In taking a closer look at the knife and examining it for a moment, he then shook his head in disbelief.

"How the hell was that American ever able to slip this past airport security?"

Outside his of room, the four waited quietly for the return of Vladimir's wife. Still somewhat in denial, Jim broke the silence. "That man's got a better grasp of English than me."

"And he can speak more languages than there are us standing here too." Dave stated, performing a slight pee dance. "Man do I need to piss."

Natalya then emerged from around a corner. Before asking the whereabouts of the toilet facilities, Dave thanked her in Russian for having allowed them to visit her ailing husband. The others also bid their farewells with heartfelt embraces.

Soon with both Dave and Jim following directly behind, Natalya led the group to the residence's designated bathroom: a small rundown, unwelcoming place of privacy. Upon opening its door, all five were blasted with an impermeable wall of vomit stench with its contents having just been deposited over a vast portion of the room's lower interior. By reflex, Dave was first repulsed by its repugnancy seconds before the others sequentially succumbed to his same reflexive reaction. The four then filed a short distance away where they were able to inhale again without gagging from the foul smell following them.

Natalya on the other hand braved entering the tainted room to take inventory. Slowly shaking her head in disgust and exiting, she approached the other four, who were all standing like frightened children awaiting an adult's reassurance of no bogyman. Upset that someone would have left the room without having cleaned up after themselves, an infringement of the house rules, Natalya had every intention of getting to the bottom of it.

"(Russian) Thank you for show me toilet, Mrs. Polivanova," Dave stated, "but I think l hold now until return to hotel."

Natalya was able to acknowledge his position while also feeling an urgency of rectifying the infringement.

"(Russian) Thank you for coming this far and visiting my sick husband. Please let your fiends know that. It's just that someone in this building doesn't know how to clean up after themselves, so please see yourselves out. I need to find the filthy bastard before they end up stinking this place some more."

With Natalya leaving the area in search of a suspected heroin addict, the lifestyle there existing within their dwelling often posed challenging to anyone wishing just to live their lives uneventfully.

"I give you credit, Pam," Dave commented as a lingering stench followed them out. "I would have just left Jim's sorry ass lying there in Benny's."

With Linda agreeing, "I'll jump on that bandwagon," Jim just shook his head.

"Yeah, you're right. Man the bad luck and shit—that's vile. Mine couldn't have been that bad though."

"Oh yes it was, honey," Pamela explained, "believe me—it was. This just took me back."

Through the blustery, cold and rainy elements, and led by Dave, the four filed down a narrow walkway to a car where their guide was awaiting them inside. In approaching it, the movement of a woman's umbrella jettisoning airborne via a strong gust of westerly wind caught Dave's attention. What also caught it was her small boy running to fetch it before his mother could react.

In Dave jetting over to push the boy out of harms way of a medium size truck that was driving too fast for the wet conditions, first the vehicle's squeaky brakes and then the cries of everyone witnessing subsequently filled the air. Moments later, the boy was pushed out of harm's way while Dave in turn was thrown several car lengths to an abrupt, hard landing. Motionless on the cold, wet pavement against the street's curb, his body laid still, surrounded by a wet collection of litter accumulated there.

Moments later, Linda, Jim, Pamela, the guide, the small rescued boy, and his concerned mother all approached Dave with the three former soon kneeling by his side. Soon, a small group of bystanders having just vacated the comforts of their warm interiors to brave the raw outside conditions all stood quietly, a deeply remorseful truck driver included.

As the result of a quick reacting guide, both a private ambulance and police were soon only minutes away as the disturbing image of Dave's body being catapulted was still fresh on everyone's minds.

Punctuated by the gruesome sound of what nobody knew at the time was the process of his hip being crushed, everyone's horror was soon forgotten in hearing a slightest sigh of a faint moaning resonating from Dave. It at least gave credence to some degree of responsiveness on his part. While only contusions were visible upon Linda having checked his hip area, what her layperson's eyes were unable to recognize was both an onset of paralyses in his lower extremities and internal bleeding above as well. The same shockwave that caused his vulnerable organs to rattle inside their ribcage, similar to maraca pebbles being shaken within their hardened gourd, paid no dividend to the health of his spine.

Sounds of the accident and then minutes later the sirens of emergency vehicles caught Vladimir's attention. It led him to believe the clamor reigning in from outside was likely related to his previous guests. Upon his wife returning from confronting her suspected culprit, he asked that she check on the mayhem that he heard taking place outside. Beforehand, the former commander was only able to vaguely make out some of it from his window.

Soon outside with the others, Natalya came upon Linda, who was standing by Dave while emergency personnel were mobilizing him. Also noticing the Woodsons nearby mutually bringing comfort to each other, she chose instead to approach the distraught mother of the rescued boy. The distressed woman was eventually able to regain enough composure to recount what had just taken place, emphasizing Dave's bravery.

Upon embracing her previous guests, including giving her best wishes without the need of a translator, Natalya returned to her husband. She came away from the accident partially relieved that her former guest was at least still alive and in the hands of sound medical care.

"Dear, did you see anything? I saw you talking to some lady and could only make out the other couple that was here [Jim and Pamela]."

While saddened, Natalya was more concerned for her husband's reaction.

Answering tentatively, she explained. "It was that nice American man, Dave, who tried his best to speak Russian to me. He pushed a boy out of the way of a truck and was struck himself. He's still alive and they're taking him away. His wife and friends were in such terrible shock."

Mixed emotions filled Vladimir in hearing the news. He was troubled that an uncertain prospect for Dave might bring about an untimely end to a man he felt still had many good years ahead of him. He was therefore saddened that such a tragic loss would also leave the continuing saga between him and his once incorrigible but still estranged son unresolved. Also stirring inside him were feelings of newfound hope. The former commander viewed Dave's selfless actions as an oasis of hope in an environment where daily survival often took on the face of destitute and suspicion. It also pleased him that the man he once saved years back, consequently having resulted in a great cost to him and his family, was someone he could presently confirm as honorable—there worthy of his past sacrifice. For the former commander, life had just come full circle.

Upon letting the news sink in with such thoughts, he signed. "Oh Natalya, that's such tragic news. It looks like you may have just fulfilled your purpose, comrade."

"What was that, Vlad?" his wife asked without having fully understood her husband.

"Nothing Natalya, just thinking out loud. By the way, please go to the hospital later and find out where they brought him. He paid me his respect, so it's only right I return the favor—even if it kills me."

She did, and the next day Vladimir was at the same hospital with her, but not by his own volition. He took a sudden turn for the worse the following morning and needed to be rushed to the hospital where he died soon afterwards. Neither the Costas nor Woodsons knew this at the time with it having transpired only a few rooms over from where Dave was still being treated.

Soon after grieving over the lifeless body of her husband at the hospital, a still grief-stricken Natalya eventually returned to her one room apartment. There she sat on their bedside quietly holding a framed sepia photo of him proudly posing in his dress uniform taken at the beginning of his naval career as an officer. Soon too much for her to bear, she then collapsed onto their formally shared bed taking in the scent of her late husband from its sheets, a last vestige of him she wished to be able to hang onto and refusing to let go. Now alone and never having him to wake up beside again, she continued grieving on his empty bedside, there forever a widow.

It was a cold, inclement, and dreary day, similar to the one in St. Petersburg when Dave received his injury a few months earlier. Now home in Narragansett, he was struggling on a set parallel bars located in his basement gym, working feverishly as on ongoing effort of regaining both strength and coordination back into his legs again. With their feeling having recently returned in full post an onset of atrophy, Dave was complying with a prescribed regiment his physical therapist had laid out for him. Any wish of walking on his new hip again still required several painful and taxing fronts before any such goal would have any chance of being realized.

Alone and contemplating the many events leading to the present such as the hype of his family's new place in history coupled with the publicity of him rescuing the child in St. Petersburg Russia, soon afterwards a fickle public was instead enmeshed in the latest news of a politician's dealings with infidelity. Once again scouted out of the limelight, the Costa's latest fifteen minutes of fame was over and Dave took no issue with it. To Linda's relief, his strong opinion about the news item signified to her the evidence of her husband's improved force of will.

Flooded with an array of wandering thoughts on that gloomy day led to both self-inquiry and no less analysis of his past, Dave's workout room semi-lit. In reflection of the speech Polivanova once gave him to his bewilderment, referencing fate, he now viewed that particular moment in a different light. He did so in understanding the commander recognized at that time his career days were likely numbered and he stood to face being incarcerated as well.

Dave's most present bout of brainstorming was stemmed from a science show he had seen the previous night about both string theory and parallel universes (different simultaneous existences). It caused him to reflect on the subtle differences any deviation of the past might have made, whether it be by either his own actions or ripples occurring elsewhere to which he now found himself in their wake. In relating to it, he wondered how the theory might pertain to his own amazing life, thereby understanding such ripples could have resulted from even the most insignificant of events.

Dave wondered had he given into Pamela during that one spicy celebrated night versus having binged himself into an induced coma which ended up prohibiting a next day's launch, might their string of bad luck been avoided. What punctuated the emphasis of his inference was the knowledge that at one point the US Navy was no more than a few hours from being able to initiate a viable rescue and that a prior day takeoff would have most likely made all the difference to what ensued afterwards.

Dave shook is head in wonder of what unforeseen complications might have later arisen in his marriage had he given into Pamela. It was he after all who enabled Linda's behavior in the water with Jim that night on the beach. He had done so by staging conditions whereby such behavior of the two who collectively had no prior agenda to engage in sex beforehand might have played out anyhow giving their history and setting presented.

Dave then wondered how the previous twenty-five years might have unfolded had he and his son been given the chance to embrace a normal father and son relationship of which any opportunity to do so died with the eventual passing of Hurricane Gloria. This led to him imagining how world events might have evolved had he not been there for Polivanova to pluck from the storm's eye. Would the captain second rank then been able to continue up the US Coast undetected with his career not ending in disgrace? Might it in turn have resulted in both a longer and healthier life for him and his wife, Natalya, and possible their late son as well?

Had he instead not picked them up and left them there to die, then what direction might the fragile negotiations between the two superpowers taken if a similar submarine collision still took place back then? Would the result of Polivanova's inaction possibly led to an Armageddon like scenario without the added variable that the Costas presence aboard his vessel presented both nations? Instead, would such an inaction possibly brought about an impasse to the historical talks that took place two months later between the President of the United States, Ronald Reagan, and the General Secretary of the Soviet Union, Mikhail Gorbachev? While the events themselves weren't enough to have sent either nation off the deep end, it was the last straw of many years of mistrust and raising tensions that had finally materialized into a volatile situation.

Still baffling Dave's were the odds that some bottle containing a note written a quarter century earlier might have ending up on a beach on the small US Territorial island of Guam just to eventually end up in the hands of a retired tourist couple visiting from Genoa, Illinois. It begged the question of how long the native vendor might have held onto the bottle and why they never extracted the letter out of curiosity, thereafter possibly discarding it.

In changing gears, Dave attempted to imagine what his present condition might otherwise be like had he been able to stomach the communal house bathroom, but in doing so, there wouldn't have been anyone nearby to save the child. How would those few extra minutes affected his current state had he not been available to save the child, consequently leaving himself presently healthy, but the boy likely deceased? While having suffered a great deal from the ordeal and still doing so, the rescue event in itself did bring about a strong sense of validation back into his life again. The harrowing experience of Hurricane Gloria devastated his self-esteem by way of its extreme humbling character, whereas it was the boy's rescue that in turn helped him to regain some of his self-worth back again. Dave knew better than crediting himself with any false sense of entitlement to the happenings that averted a possible war, realizing he was but a small piece of Vladimir's puzzle that essentially made all the difference to what ensued afterwards. For that reason, those unprecedented events did little in minimizing Gloria's humbling impact on him. To the present, the idea of even having considered the need of committing euthanasia on his family still caused him to shudder, especially giving how close he actually came to first snuffing out the bright glow of a light that was his daughter.

In remembering what Vladimir stated upon exiting his vessel, he now understood that the former commander was only describing the time continuum, and that which those sometimes misinterpret as "what was meant to be" is simply the apex of all previous events having culminated viewed in retrospect and likely nothing more, nothing predetermined—just the butterfly effect playing out, or in a more intelligible term, 'shit happens'.

It then triggered him to relate the same school of thought to anomalies appearing during major events where upon first glance may seem highly coincidental in relation to the present happenings as if carrying some prophetic significance to them. While Dave understood it was impossible to prove a negative, meaning not totally dismissing the idea of conspiracy or even the paranormal in such cases when such events did arise, he also didn't neglect to consider that in contrast when the seemingly unlikelihood of their manifestations are weighed against the infinite possibilities that never actually materialize, then the likelihood of the onset of such strange occurrences being brought to mind is something that should always come to be expected. In addition to viewing it as simple math, he also guessed it not uncommon for the human mind to seek a deeper meaning in explanation of either the monumental or the random, especially in cases of tragedy—convenient truths to make some sense of it.

Dave grinned momentarily, now glad Polivanova didn't view it in such a way in seeing him and his family cast adrift in the midst of Gloria's eye. His smile was soon replaced by a detectable wince of disappointed. It was in having placed so much emphasis into a deeper meaning of what Polivanova once attempted to convey, as a result rendering his good advice mostly unheeded over the years.

Trivializing in his meditative state, Dave concluded that if the parallel universe theorist were correct in their claims, then every possible and likely scenario was playing out both simultaneously and infinitely times over again, there embedded within the same snapshot of space and time he was presently conscious of—that being his present, painful state of being.

Dave's bout of hypothesizing then subsided, there leaving him void of any further contemplation. Instead the stark realism of his current physical condition, and furthermore dreary surroundings, only descended him ever deeper into his already cheerless state of melancholy. Quiet in his solemn frame of mind while in focus of the wind and rain pounding the glass sliding door leading to outside, there Dave labored in his struggle just to take yet another painful unstable, step forward again.

One reality though couldn't be dismissed and it is, if the multi-universe theorists were correct and there were many other worlds playing out simultaneously while chorusing within the same realm of space and time that he was presently occupying, even then Dave still wouldn't have been willing to trade for any of those scenarios in exchange for six soft-spoken words that suddenly rang out from behind him.

"Dad, would you like a hand?"

And those words uttered with humility weren't any resonated by the voice of his soft-spoken daughter either.